WHO KNOWS FOR SURE WHAT IS REAL . . . AND WHAT IS NOT?

I know I should move on but don't, and the first naked woman of my life runs lightly into the window frame. My heart leaps as though in terror.

Golden, beautiful, her pale hair drawn up in a bun, she shines in the light of the kerosine lamp above her head, her body white in its flare, white as the breakers on the beach . . . She is real and yet not; she may vanish; and her reality is made more unlikely by the fact that she is a stranger . . .

THE DOUBLEMAN

C. J. KOCH

▲ **AVON**
PUBLISHERS OF BARD, CAMELOT, DISCUS AND FLARE BOOKS

AVON BOOKS
A division of
The Hearst Corporation
105 Madison Avenue
New York, New York 10016

The McGraw-Hill edition contains the following Library of Congress Cataloging
in Publication Data:

Koch, C. J. (Christopher J.), 1932–
  The doubleman.

  I. Title.
PR9619.3.K64D6   1986   823   85-19922

First Avon Printing: October 1987

To Cynthia

AUTHOR'S NOTE

I should like to thank Keith Potger, one of the original Seekers, for taking time to reminisce with me about the group in its heyday—a conversation which greatly helped me in depicting a folk group of the 1960s. I hasten to point out, however, that the Rymers are in no way based on the Seekers, and are entirely fictitious, as are all other characters in this book.

My thanks are due also to the television producers Bernie Cannon and Barry Crook, for valuable technical advice.

I am indebted to Les Murray for permission to quote from his poem 'Immigrant Voyage'.

The verses which appear at the beginning of each chapter in Book One are from the traditional Scottish ballads 'Thomas Rymer' and 'Tam Lin'.

Finally, I wish to thank the Literature Board of the Australia Council for its generous support, without which the writing of this book would scarcely have been possible.

CONTENTS

BOOK ONE

THE FALSE KNIGHT
UPON THE ROAD

Some men of that exalted sight (whither by Art
or Nature) have told me they have seen . . . a Doubleman,
or the Shape of some Man in two places . . .
They call this Reflex-man a Co-Walker, every way
like the Man, as a Twin-brother and Companion,
haunting him as his shadow . . . both before and after
the Originall is dead.
    ROBERT KIRK, *The Secret Commonwealth of Elves,
    Fauns and Fairies (1691)*

For she could d'on so manie shapes in sight,
As ever could Cameleon colours new;
So could she forge all colours, save the trew.
    EDMUND SPENSER, *The Faerie Queene, Book IV, Canto I*

I
THE MASK OF PARALYSIS

O see not ye yon narrow road,
So thick beset wi thorns and briers?
That is the path of righteousness,
Tho after it but few enquires.

And see not ye that braid braid road
That lies across yon lillie leven?
That is the path of wickedness,
Tho some call it the road to heaven.

And see not ye that bonny road,
Which winds about the ferny brae?
That is the road to fair Elfland,
Where you and I this night maun gae.

1

The bruise-coloured steeple of St Augustine's was visible
for miles around on the hill of South Hobart: a watch-
tower over a camp of fear. When I go back to my native
town and look up Harrigan Street to that tower, I still feel
the old nausea, the old dread. My case is scarcely unique;
as all too many others have testified, a Christian Brothers'
education in the 1950s had a fine pitch of dread, unlikely
to be matched again.

Fear's height was in the early mornings, when I climbed
towards the steeple and its cross up the asphalt hill of
Harrigan Street, the steepest in hilly Hobart. The cars of
those days would stall on Harrigan Street and then turn
back; but I heaved myself upwards with rhythmic jerks,
helped by my single crutch, my thin left leg aching and
trembling. My thoughts were small and beast-like with

effort, and I was glad of this; it kept my mind from Brother Kinsella. Today was bright and frosty, and I was twelve years old.

Upwards: jerk and heave. I counted the landmarks that brought me nearer to the end of my small ordeal, and so to the beginning of the day's larger one. I knew by heart every mean colonial cottage of ochre brick; every ribbon of weedy garden; every holystoned front step; every picket on every fence. Left below as I climbed was one of the town's few small slums; a place of mean, two-storey tenements, shabby shops and small factories: Hobart's miniature Gorbals. A tall factory chimney there was lettered with a vertical message, repeating itself to my misery as I climbed, winter and summer: UP TO DATE.

The last section of hill brought me to the walls and cypresses of the Archbishop's Palace: the zone of the Church, high above slumdom and the town. Where these walls and Harrigan Street ended Byrne Street would be reached, running across the hill's brow. Here, opposite the Palace, stood St Augustine's; and the reward for my climb was Brother Kinsella, waiting at the top. Just inside the red brick gateposts grew a bare, crooked little thorn tree. I never knew its species; but each morning as I passed it, the notion came to me that this was the tree on which Judas hanged himself.

On some mornings, just before reaching the walls of the Palace, I made a detour. It wasn't a short cut but the reverse—its attraction being that it delayed my arrival. This was a narrow pedestrian footway called Fiddler's Lane, running off Harrigan Street between backyard fences to reach the foot of a flight of concrete steps. These climbed to Byrne Street and the school. Dawdling here was a small, enjoyable act of delinquency; and there was also a sense of trespass, since the lane was usually empty. But sometimes I encountered a man here: always the same man, coming down the steps as I climbed up.

He was seen nowhere else, so that I thought of him as the Man in the Lane. Tall and thin in his long dark overcoat, he studied me for the whole way as he approached, his face absolutely serious. This made me uncomfortable and I began to wish not to have to pass him. To some extent, my caution was reasonable, I suppose: the ancestral readiness for attack when approaching a stranger in a deserted place. But in daylight, it ought not to have had the intensity it did. The man made me uneasy to a degree for which there seemed no explanation.

He was just a man going to work, I told myself—a man who was stupidly interested, like so many people, by the sight of my cripple's crutch and my thin left leg, left bare by my grey school shorts. But I didn't convince myself with this; I was troubled by the notion that he was no ordinary man going to work at all: that he was not like other people, and that his interest couldn't be explained so simply. He was always in the dark, belted overcoat, its collar turned up at the back; and it seemed to me that I only encountered him in winter. His age was hard to tell; he was perhaps in his late thirties. He had a curious walk, slightly bent over to the left, the side on which one hand was usually in his pocket—as though he had a secret wound, which he held to ease the pain.

This morning, seeing the lean, dark-clad figure coming down the steps, my heart gave a little jolt. Today was to be different: I had decided to stare him out.

I covered the whole distance to the steps with his eyes on me all the way; and I told myself, my mouth gone dry, that he had a bloody cheek. But the enigma of his intentions somehow made this bravado feeble. There were men who were over-friendly to boys; they offered sweets, and their voices and smiles were caressing and somewhat sickly. But the Man in the Lane was plainly not one of these: his face and stare were extraordinarily cold, serious and hard, and he never attempted a greeting. We came nearer, and I found my heart thumping in a way that made me giddy. But I kept my eyes on his face; and instead of using my crutch on the slope, something made me decide to carry it, as I did on the flat. The man's straight, short-cut hair was mostly black, streaked with white around the temples and neatly parted on the left. His face was handsome in a cold way, with vertical lines in the cheeks and a long, sad upper lip; and his eyes, instead of being dark like his hair and brows, were of a strong, weird blue that acted like a warning.

As we came level he stopped. I had somehow known he would do this.

'You're not using your crutch today,' he said.

He had a deep, hollow voice, which went with his sad upper lip. It was well-spoken yet ordinary enough, like that of other men.

'No,' I said. 'Not today.'

The man held his head on one side—also to the left. The effect was distinguished; somewhat scholarly. He was neither friendly nor unfriendly; he waited, arched eyebrows raised, apparently expecting an explanation.

But I said nothing; and I found a wave of intense cold crawling up my back, reaching my neck and tingling there like ice. I had experienced this before only rarely, in situations of threat or danger.

'You should use the crutch,' the man said, 'shouldn't you?'

'No I shouldn't,' I said.

This voice had spoken from inside me. It seemed not quite my own. It said the things it now did without thought on my part, as though repeating a lesson: and it flatly contradicted the man, who raised his eyebrows higher at this rudeness.

'You ought to,' he said, 'or you'll strain your leg. It's crippled, isn't it?'

'No. It's not.' I felt myself growing red; the flush crept in a wave above my collar. But I stood my ground. It seemed to me that the man wanted me to be crippled and that it was very important to contradict him. 'It's getting better,' I said, 'and soon I won't need the crutch at all.'

'That's good. Are you sure of it?'

'Yes.'

The man's eyes left mine and looked away down the lane. I felt a surge of triumph; I was winning.

Then he looked back at me. 'Where are you going?'

'To school.'

'To the Brothers?'

'Yes, the Brothers.'

'You should change your school,' he said softly. 'The Brothers are hard men.'

'No they're not,' I said. 'They're men of God.' But then, wanting to be honest, and thinking of Brother Kinsella, I said: 'Most of them are good.'

A little light flared in his weary-lidded eyes; he had seen his advantage. 'Most of them, eh?' he said. 'But not all of them. Not the one who teaches *you.*' He smiled for the first time. His smile too was crooked, travelling up one side of his face; but it seemed confiding and surprisingly attractive. It made me want to grin back, to encourage him to smile more. Why should he be sad? He was handsome as certain saturnine gunmen in the Western films I went to on Saturday afternoons.

'They're *all* good men,' I said.

The man's smile went, and he stared, his eyes cold again. No eyes like them had ever searched mine before: hooded by drooping lids, they were entirely without sympathy yet nevertheless interested, and formidably intelligent. They didn't see me in the normal way; their pupils tiny, they seemed like unnatural lenses, distorting me. 'You're easily satisfied,' he said; and he spoke as though I were an adult. Then with a last, insistent look, he turned and went on down the lane, his sideways tilt somehow elegant, like the affectation of a dandy from another age.

I began to limp up the steps, holding my crutch; and I found myself trembling as though at a narrow escape. As I reached the seventh step I turned to look after him. But the lane was empty.

I still don't know what to make of this, looking back on it. No doubt my imagination played me a trick; but I remember that the lane hummed with unnatural warning, its grey timber fences and sheets of corrugated iron hiding something. What had happened was impossible, I said; the man couldn't have reached the exit into Harrigan Street in such a few moments. Yet it seemed he had; and I would always wonder how he did it.

I wasn't to meet him again for some years; and I concluded that he'd gone away.

2

I had known I would catch Paralysis long before it happened. When it finally struck, I felt almost foolish for having hoped to be spared.

For a long time, even into adolescence, I continued to think of Paralysis as a creature—a being who belonged to childhood like my clockwork train; like chilblains. This entity had come to me in the days before Salk vaccine, when whole populations of children faced it without any talisman. Its full title then was not poliomyelitis but 'infantile paralysis'; and I would never be able to think of it by any other name. It took its time about coming: it waited until I was nine years old. This was at the end of World War Two, in 1946, when the worst of the epidemics were over, and even my mother thought I was safely among the spared. But Paralysis came, after all; it had merely been toying with its lists.

Its most thorough recruiting campaigns on the island of my birth had been carried out in the 1930s, and during the war years. Poor Van Diemen's Land! The leg-irons and the lash of a hundred years before still hung near, like bad dreams; now, suburban and respectable under your new name, you found your children in irons once more, tormented by pains more searching than the lash. Through the streets of Hobart in the 1940s, the children claimed by the epidemic were wheeled by in chairs, or lurched on their crutches. They horrified and fascinated me before I became one of their number, in those years of the War. Shopping in Hobart with my mother, I would study the crippled children with fascination; a fascination that was only rivalled by my interest in the American troops on leave.

The Yanks swaggered and rioted through our staid little city in the world's utmost south, where we knew the War couldn't come; and nothing like them had been seen in Hobart before. Elephant-grey shapes of Liberty ships loomed in the Derwent estuary, dwarfing the wharf sheds below the Post Office; troopships filled with GIs who had fought in New Guinea with the Australians—among whom was my father. The AIF and the Americans were engaging the Imperial Japanese invasion force at Lae; Japan was in retreat, but Australians were still dying in that hot green underworld, from tropical illnesses and exhaustion as well as from Japanese machine-gun fire. All this I understood only vaguely, at five, and when I imagined my father, Eddy Miller, whose censored blue air-letters cut about with scissors were waited for every week, I saw him healthy and heroic among bright palm leaves, yellow hair spilling from under his Digger hat, firing his rifle from the hip and grinning carelessly. I thought that my father would never be killed: only the others.

Meanwhile, GIs in well-cut uniforms and white-capped sailors called gobs passed on the narrow footpath in shoals; laughing strange laughs, shouting, whistling at girls, drinking from beer bottles and vomiting into the gutter in unbelievable fountains. But the Yanks were helping to save us from the Japanese, and there was only a small resentment in the town. My mother's cheerful, fleshy face was blank and disapproving under her brown felt hat and her stare was fixed; she kept close to the windows of familiar department stores, one white-gloved hand firmly gripping mine. And from time to time, we were passed by the crippled children who were no longer ordinary children.

Their parents pushed them in chairs or in crude, specially-constructed prams like huge trays which interested me horribly. Pasty-faced, monstrous babies of nine or ten years old, wrapped in tartan rugs, they stared sadly at me; or sometimes, inexplicably, they smiled, their legs stuck out stiffly in front of them like those of dolls, imprisoned in the paralysis irons.

'Will I get Paralysis?' I asked.

'Of course not,' my mother said. 'Don't talk like that.'

But no use: Paralysis would come for me in three years' time, at six o'clock in the evening, just before dinner.

3

I was playing with my Hornby clockwork train when the intruder arrived. A toy for which I had a special affection, it ran perfectly, and never broke down: British and reliable.

I had been ill yesterday and today: nothing serious, just a sore throat and a temperature which had kept me home from school. I felt weak and somewhat dreamy and there were dull pains in my back and legs—all the symptoms of 'flu, which was what my mother had decided I'd caught. No one was concerned; least of all me.

There was a fire in the dining-room of my grandfather's house, and I had come out here in my dressing-gown to set up my train on the hearth-rug. I had developed a curious restlessness which I couldn't account for. I was unable to read or to fix my attention on anything for long without a feeling of pointless irritability, mixed with drowsiness. My head ached and there was a stiffness in my neck now, as well as in my back. This ominous symptom, which would have been of great interest to my mother, I supposed to be another feature of the 'flu, and I took no notice of it. But my restlessness increased; I wanted something; some reassurance perhaps.

About what? I couldn't really tell. The little red locomotive with its coal truck and two carriages whirred round and round on its silver tracks, recalling happy evenings with my father, before he was killed near Lae. I was safe with my reliable Hornby; and yet I was somehow not reassured. It ran busily through the wooden tunnel my lost father had made for it long ago, and then it began to slow down.

I wanted to reach for the key on the carpet to wind it up again, but I found I was suddenly too heavy and weak to bother doing so. Legs curled under me, I watched the train stupidly as it began another circuit. It laboured down the line towards me, slower and slower, the tension in its clockwork spring almost exhausted. Would it get to me?

This somehow seemed very important, and I told myself I would pick it up when it reached me.

It came almost to a stop, but then gave a lurch which brought it forward a few more inches. I badly wanted it to reach me; then things would be all right. But I couldn't move. It stopped just out of reach, and stood there with a distinctness which was no longer friendly.

It was surrounded by an evil emptiness; a speckled vacuum; and I was seized with terror. The world had become reduced to the static red train, the fireplace with its arch of green ceramic tiles containing leaping flames, and the hearth-rug's pattern of brown autumn leaves. This pattern, which I had always been fond of, now became entirely unpleasant, and of no help. I wanted to call for my mother, but there was nothing to call out for. I made a great effort and leaned forward to reach for the locomotive.

Pain struck me in the back like a great silver club. I knew immediately that this was no ordinary pain: it had a mighty authority which said that my whole life had been changed; that I had been chosen. I tried to get up, pressing the palm of my right hand flat on the floor.

And now I did cry out—an amazed howl, as the silver club fell again with unbelievable violence, with a force which was obviously intended to punish me for daring to move. Terror established itself absolutely; the speckles in the air increased; the pain entered my bones, so that I understood where each one was. Things were turning off inside me one by one, like lightbulbs. A nasty limpness had arrived, and would stay. I heard my mother's feet running in the hall outside; I fell sideways on the hearth-rug, and entered darkness.

In the hospital, where I was delirious, there were banging noises. When I slept, these noises continued, together with echoing clangs and yells of pain from high corridors of torment outside. My face burned, and the aching in my bones from the blows of the club was still there; I woke into semi-darkness with blue lights and called for my mother, whose face appeared in the uncertainty above me; I begged her to save me from what was happening in the

corridors. Then I slept again, and the Mask of Paralysis
appeared, just above my head, looking down on me.

It was without sex, which was part of its horror, and
appeared to be made of crumpled white paper. It had a
parrot nose, like Mr Punch in my puppet box, and nodded
and smiled at me; and the smile wished me nothing but ill.

The next day, the delirium and much of the pain had gone,
but my legs were quite dead, and felt cold, and would not
move when I wanted them to. There were special pillows
under them, and also under my back.

Paralytic polio so resembled influenza in its early stages
that it was sometimes wrongly diagnosed, and no immedi-
ate action was taken. But for me, diagnosis had been
quick. Among those who were visited, the penalties ranged
from a passing weakness of the limbs to death in an iron
lung; or else paralysis of all four limbs that was total and
final, the motor nerve cells in the spinal cord having been
destroyed. In my case, only a few of these cells had been
fatally injured. At first, my arms and legs were tested
constantly, in the hospital. Then for a time I was put into
splints, to prevent the development of deformities through
the pull of gravity, and the drag of the unparalysed muscles. Within two weeks, the first phase of recovery having
begun, I was drilled in the more active exercises which
would become my tedious duty for many years to come.
As it turned out, Paralysis would spare everything but my
left leg.

Here, it would leave its mark; the leg would remain
permanently damaged, and grow thinner than the other,
and for a year I would be forced to go on crutches. Later,
these would be replaced by a single crutch, used only
when I was tired, and finally, by a walking stick.

But there would be other consequences of crippledom:
consequences less obvious than the damaged leg. It was
now that my interest in the Otherworld began.

To make things easier with my wheelchair, they had put
me in a room on the ground floor of my grandfather's

house: a room once occupied by one of my aunts, long gone away and married in Melbourne. The walls were deep pink, and I privately called it the Red Room.

Here at Trent Street, Newtown, I was safe. I took stock of things with a new, secret craftiness, lying in bed. My useless legs lay limp, like tubes of rubber; I tested them and felt nothing, but I wasn't dismayed. Being essentially an optimist, I believed they'd get better; meanwhile, I was prepared to enjoy my status as a bed-bound princeling, whom people approached with anxious smiles. And the shameful pleasure I felt in the situation was one of its compensations, as well as being one of my new secrets. I would grow addicted to secrets from now on, and I saw that for the temporary price of my legs, I had entered a world *without penalties*. In fact, I had re-entered infancy, here in the Red Room, and the price had been a parody of my original birth; but that I didn't see.

Noises came to me from outside, from the day I couldn't join: the shout of an unknown child, across Newtown's big back gardens; someone hammering nails, the good, clean reports carried across a river of air. And I listened for a particular sound to which I became addicted: voices which murmured something about a cook.

Monotonous, stupefying, mysterious, the repeated phrase went on and on beyond filmy, blowing curtains, in the mild, magic heat of late summer. Eventually I would discover that it was the sound of pigeons; but here in the Red Room it was a seductive and maddening code I couldn't decipher, the phrase's last, unctuous *cook* being the confirmation of an extraordinary meaning. It summoned up a slumbrous, sunlit region far as Europe: a country dusted with the pollen of marvel, and of Time.

So began my addiction to a life at one remove.

Symptoms of this were a fanatical devotion to radio sessions, comic strips and books, into which I could escape from the bed and the wheelchair. My affection for the small mantel radio that sat by the bed became profoundly personal: listening to the serials ('Fu Manchu'; 'The Shadow'), and to the children's club on ABS, where the

cultivated voices of Aunt Susan and Uncle Charles assured
me that the world was quite free of harm, I inhaled the
smell of the smooth black Bakelite as though it were a
mystical fragrance; I peered closely into the yellow-glowing
dial, with its cryptic letters and figures, and found a
laneway there whose receding perspectives took me to a
marvellous ether beyond the island: the source of these
voices from the vast, outside world. My love of books,
too, became almost physical. I was soon to explore the
many shelves of books in my grandfather's sitting-room,
inhaling with greedy delight the differing, faded scents of
their pages. And a certain air of the forbidden hovered
about these shelves, giving the sitting-room books extra
savour, since many were considered unsuitable by my
mother. As well as *The Gorilla Hunters, The Jungle Book,
King Solomon's Mines,* and an ancient boy's paper of my
father's called *Chums,* there were big volumes on painting,
with shiny reproductions, and ancient thrillers and romantic novels for adults, lurking beside Dickens and Scott. My
mother suspected such books; she had, in fact, an Irish
Catholic suspicion of most books, since sexual passion and
terrible nudities were liable to be sidling about in them.
When these were discovered, she pushed her lips out as
though she had been personally assaulted, and her far-
sighted eyes sadly accused me, as though I had written
such books myself. The books she approved of were devoted to fairies, and figures of legend. But had she only
known it, these posed a greater threat to my well-being
than any of the romantic novels she feared, or the books
on art with their voluptuous Renaissance nudes.

There was a particular set of Danish fairy tales that I
read again and again. These concerned the Elle-people,
who lived on the Elle-moors. Elle-women were very beautiful, it seemed; they played on stringed instruments, and
danced in high grass. But they were dangerous to young
men; they brought nothing but sorrow, as Sir Olaf found,
who was slain when he refused to dance with them, and as
a certain farmer's boy found, who was enticed away to the
Elle-moors by a beautiful young Elle-maid, who gave him

fairy milk to drink from her breast, and thus enchanted him. The boy stayed in Elfland for three days; when he came home he refused all meat and drink; he pined for the milk of Fairyland. His father grew angry, and forced him to eat; but when the boy woke, he had lost his wits.

As I grew stronger, I became absorbed as well by a toy theatre that my grandfather Miller had brought me from town.

It was made in England, and was called Pollock's Toy Theatre. Constructed of flat cardboard sheets, it had directions for assembly, and my grandfather and I followed these together. Soon, a three-dimensional theatre had been erected. Its characters were also flat, cut from cardboard; but when they were pushed on stage on their wires ('Ben Pollock's special wire slides'), and wobbled about, they came to life. There were texts with the kit *(Blackbeard the Buccaneer; The Sleeping Beauty)*, and my grandfather and I put on these plays for visitors, doing all the voices, with the theatre set up on a low table at the double doors of the sitting-room. I found his acting loud and hammy; but he was all I had.

When he first saw how enchanted I was by this toy, Karl Miller was pleased. But when it became an obsession, resulting in long plays I wrote myself at the cost of the schoolwork that was set for me at home, the old man declared himself sorry that he had ever bought the thing. Too late; much too late.

The artist, the amateur of the arts and the convalescent all pass through the same door. Those, that is, who have been truly broken—but who have afterwards been able to mend. People whose illnesses have only been minor don't understand this birth, which is a birth into the life of dream; nor can they approve a life where dream seeps into things: where things keep shifting, and creatures change their shape. This disapproval, the self-protective instinct of the healthy, is one of which permanent convalescents are aware, and I was aware of it already; it was one of my new secrets.

On the pink walls opposite my bed hung an old sepia photograph of a naked child, holding a bow and arrow behind its head, and smiling roguishly from under its brows, its eyes meeting mine. I would discover one day that this was a popular, sentimental print, found in many houses of the Edwardian era; but in my first bed-bound days back from the hospital, it puzzled me. Was it a relative, or an ancestor? What was its sex? Was it an actual photograph of a fairy? And what did its smiling, intimate gaze convey?

In the second stage of convalescence, I was taken out into the quiet, tree-lined streets of Newtown, pushed in my ugly, gleaming chair by my mother or my grandfather, just as I had once dreaded.

But my strange rebirth made this enjoyable instead of shameful. My servants conveyed me smoothly past high walls and fences and prosperous Edwardian roofs of terra-cotta tiles: scenes I didn't have to join, but need only look at, as though through glass; a passing prince, my good tartan rug over my knees. A cluster of schoolboys of my own age edged around my chair with looks of awed pity; but I smiled on them proudly. They knew nothing of the Red Room, or my marvellous toy theatre: that life which was more important than their crude, ordinary world.

At other times, though, I would fear that I might never join such boys again, or roam free of adult attendants, and that my certainty of doing so was a lie, a fiction. Then a terrible fear would clutch at me and I would sicken of my princely part. But such times quickly passed.

Most of my day now was spent in the sitting-room with Pollock's Theatre, or else in the wheelchair on the front verandah with my books, watching occasional passers-by over the low front fence. A pallid, delicate-looking blonde girl of about twelve, whose name I never knew, passed each day at four on her way home from school; she would look up and smile at me, from under her brown felt hat. Her face was wistful, perhaps tragic, and I waited for her every afternoon, telling myself that I loved her.

My grandfather, arriving home at six every evening to stump along the verandah with his stick, would call in his loud, blustering voice: 'Soon be out of that chair, boy!' In robust health in his late sixties, Karl Miller was a widower, and a successful architect; he had designed this house for himself before World War One, and his brass nameplate flashed on the wall of the verandah where I sat. The walking stick was always in his hand when he went out, his felt hat on his head, a rose from the garden in the buttonhole of his three-piece suit. He was now my surrogate father; my mother and I had moved permanently into his house when my father was killed, occupying the upper storey. My bedroom had its own small balcony overlooking the front garden, level with the top branches of a big blue Himalayan pine that spread above the lawn, its clean, resinous scent coming always into the room.

On Sunday mornings before breakfast, old Karl would unfailingly play military band music or Strauss waltzes on the gramophone, and march about the house downstairs calling incomprehensible commands through his pipe, clad in a cord-trailing dressing-gown and the hat he rarely took off his bald head. He was a big, coarse-grained, ebullient old man with a short-clipped moustache and shovel chin, given to over-loud laughter and obvious jokes. My mother, who found him noisy, would softly moan: 'I do wish he'd stop. How can an important man be such a *fool?*'

Sighting me on these musical Sundays, he would remove his pipe ceremoniously, hold it high, stare through his glasses, and declaim: ' ''Into the valley of death rode the six hundred.'' Eh, boy?' He was fond of such simple poetry; he liked to recite 'The Man from Snowy River', and had hung Kipling's 'If' above my bed.

My mother regarded her father-in-law with a mixture of respect and resentment. Born Nora Brady, she came from a struggling farm on the East Coast, while the Millers were prosperous Protestants—making me a typical case of the Orange and the Green. If there was an establishment in Hobart, Karl Miller belonged to it. He was an alderman, and president of the Institute of Architects; he had designed a number of public buildings, and the town had many rock-solid monuments to his success, his name being carved in some of their foundation stones: *Karl Miller*. He had wanted me brought up a Protestant, but my mother had insisted I should be Catholic. This was the only struggle she had ever won with the old man, so that I now went to the Christian Brothers, instead of to the Anglican school where my father had gone.

My mother's deference towards the man she always called 'your grandfather', and on whom she now depended, was also tinged with dubiousness about his origins. She regarded it as a dark secret—although Karl Miller didn't— that he was not truly an English Miller, but a German Müller, the name having prudently been changed, like so many others, during the first World War. Grandfather Miller's father had been an immigrant to South Australia, one of the Lutheran Germans who had settled the Barossa Valley in the 1840s. Karl Miller was unapologetic about this fact; but my mother, in a low, earnest voice, would tell me to say that the family was English; and I did. But I had lived in dread of being discovered at school.

My grandfather, hearing of this, had come up to my room one evening, and sitting in an armchair had drawn me between his knees, staring at me with the watery, blue-grey eyes whose colour was also mine.

'We're Australian, boy,' he said bluntly, 'and we came here from Germany.' He took the pipe from his mouth. 'Don't ever be ashamed of it. We're not Nazis. We helped to build this country, and we didn't start this bloody war, which your father died in.' He blinked for a moment, and his voice went quiet. 'No real man's ever ashamed of what he is,' he said. 'Remember that.'

But I still resented the old man's being German, behind the solid and inoffensive name of Miller. Why must he be Karl? Why couldn't he at least change that tell-tale K to a C?

Because he was too stiff-necked, my mother said, and sighed.

And so I became divided in myself, and this too, perhaps, made me seek refuge in the Otherworld.

*   *   *

My mother and my grandfather had markedly different attitudes to my crippling.

Since the arrival of my white-faced master, my mother had become subdued and despondent, a condition that no doubt had its origins in the time when my father was killed. Always inclined to feel sorry for herself, she now allowed this tendency to grow; and although I was fond of her, I resented her for sorrowing over me. I wanted to be a prince who was admired, not mourned, and I preferred my grandfather's relentless cheerfulness. It was old Karl who first told me to put aside my crutches, one afternoon on the verandah.

My mother protested that this was too soon; but Grandfather Miller ignored her. Instead, he ordered me to walk the full length of the verandah without the crutches; and he watched me struggle to do it without saying a word, until my legs gave way under me.

While I lay there, sadly inhaling the dusty smell of the summer-hot boards, and the birds called heartlessly in the Himalayan pine, I heard my mother's tragic voice say: 'You see, Mr Miller? He can't *do* it, it's too much!'

The next sound was Karl Miller's big lace-up boots, creaking up to where I lay. They stopped, and I heard him say: 'Get up, boy.' His voice was not sorry, yet not cruel either.

I looked up: my grandfather towered over me like a crooked giant, in his navy-blue suit and waistcoat, watch-chain glinting on his lean belly. His broom-like moustache was twisted to one side, his chin jutted, and his Prussian-blue stare behind the round, gold-rimmed spectacles surprised and half-frightened me; it was not twinkling or indulgent, as it usually was, but absolutely cold. For a moment, I thought he might hit me with his stick.

'If you want to go on being a bloody cripple,' he said, 'you can lie there. If not, you'll walk it, boy, right to the end.'

I struggled to my feet, hating the old man, and staggered, legs trembling and aching, to an old cane chair at the end of the verandah. As I fell into it, I heard Karl

Miller laughing; a laugh that went into wheezy spasms and ended in his pipe-smoke cough. 'Good on you, I knew you'd do it,' he said. 'You'll throw those blasted crutches away, soon.'

And now I forgave him, knowing he was right to despise crippledom, and reject it, and that he loved me in the best way a father could: by ordering me to grow. Yet part of me still clung to these interests of crippledom, which I said that my grandfather was too crude and intolerant to understand.

Once, sucking noisily on his pipe, Karl Miller peered at me from the sitting-room door as I sat on the carpet at work on my toy theatre, its little flat figures spread all around me.

'Still working on that toy? You can't play with those cardboard people for ever, boy.'

He disappeared, and I sat with burning cheeks among my scorned, beloved creatures. The old man had made them into silly pieces of card.

The worst thing was that I knew in my heart that his suspicions were more well-founded than he knew, and that old Karl would have looked with great dubiousness on the theatre's latest evolution: an evolution about which I felt both proud and obscurely guilty.

I had begun to make up plays in which three figures dominated; figures not obtained from Ben Pollock's cards, but which I cut from old fairytale books and mounted on cardboard myself. These were a witch; a beautiful golden-haired Elf-Queen whom I called Titania; and a black-cloaked man of unknowable origins whom I had named the Weird One. As well, there was a handsome, fearless boy: myself. All these figures had appeared in dreams regularly since I was small; they came less often now, but in my theatre, I gave them new life. Like dreams, these figures were not to be shared; and now that I had moved out of the Red Room and back to my own bedroom upstairs, I put on plays simply for myself, watching the magic figures in the dark wardrobe mirror, using a reading lamp for stage lighting, while Tchaikovsky and Grieg played on my small portable gramophone. Once, I staged one of these performances for a boy down the street who was sent to play with me; a boy with quiet, dull eyes and a careful mouth, who seemed not to like or understand the performance; he grew restless, and didn't come again.

I had also taken to escaping into the sewing-room: an enclosed little chamber, dry as cloth, with frosted-glass windows looking on to nothing.

Reached by going down three steps from the sitting-room through a door that was always kept closed, it felt as though it were underground. It was a place where I would seldom be disturbed; where no one even knew where I was. It was absolutely silent, without echo, and its air smelled like paper. Here I read the house's aged books, more of which were in a set of shelves along one wall; and here began my first, innocent explorations of the territories of Faery.

On a rainy afternoon down there, when everyone was out, I took down certain fairytale books dating from early in the century or late in the last one; books that had been my father's and my aunt's. Opening them at certain illustrations, I propped them around the skirting, on the carpet. I was creating another theatre; a theatre I would actually move inside, here in the sewing-room. I would be in Elfland, its creatures all around me. I crawled about the red carpet from book to book; I smelled their pages in a rite of worship; and then I hauled myself on to my crutches and swung to and fro, fairy figures whirling about me, all round the room.

Pointed, feral faces peer through leaves; half-naked, half-childish sprites with butterfly wings fly against the moon. They arch in delight through mauve, Otherworld twilights by Heath Robinson and Arthur Rackham; they soar above the star-soft night-lights of towns by Edmund Dulac. The perfect little faces and tiny, pointed breasts are those of half-grown girls; one looks like the blonde girl who passes at four o'clock, and for whom I yearn. The elves, in their pointed caps, are no older than myself, and certainly boylike—but other naked creatures are without age or gender, their smooth, perturbing groins innocent of sex. Only Titania, the Queen, her face tender as a mother's, has the body of a woman. Watched by elves in a glade of night, she stands shining in her nudity, white as the moon, her adult breasts and thighs awful yet lovely, her long, upraised, dragonfly wings making her more than human, yet less than angel.

And I'm called away by that Otherworld of mauve mists and round, enchanted hills: Elfland! Not to be able to join it, not to be able to fly! Why am I trapped instead in dull Trent Street, Newtown? Where is the actual land of half-lights? Under which hill? Dimly, I know that my yearning to go there is sickly, foolish: and yet I fiercely deny it. Nothing can be wrong with escaping the ordinary world; and nothing's really wrong with these pictures. Fairies are pure, and allowed to be naked; and I tell myself cunningly that my mother would approve, since she likes me to read fairy tales.

Why then do I tremble with exquisite unease, swinging to and fro on my crutches in the dead-quiet sewing-room, walled in by books? Perhaps because I'm made to long for something else; something maddeningly vague: some absolute escape, some icy ecstasy found in far, pure reaches of the air. I want to get outside and run and run; to fly on the icy winter wind. I don't know what else to do with my longing.

Then I hear my mother's voice, calling my name from somewhere in the house. I begin to scrabble about my circle of books, slamming them shut, dropping my crutches, pulling myself about the carpet by the hands. And my haste and thudding heart give me away: Elfland is not entirely innocent.

2
THE GUITAR

But Thomas, ye maun hold your tongue,
Whatever you may hear or see,
For gin ae word you should chance to speak,
You will neer get back to your ain countrie.

1

The whole of dry, Time-flattened Australia lies north of
latitude forty, its climate Mediterranean and then sub-
tropical. But small, mountainous Tasmania, filled with
lakes and rivers, is south of latitude forty; and this makes
it different. Politically, it is part of the Commonwealth of
Australia; physically, it is not.

The island lies in the track of the Roaring Forties, the
westerly winds that blow from Cape Horn. In the upside-
down frame of the Antipodes, it duplicates the Atlantic
coast of Europe; and Brian Brady and I were children of a
green, marine landscape: subjects of the stern winter cold.
Our spirits were conditioned by the blood-thrilling Wester-
lies; snow fell in our mid-winters; we walked to school
through London fogs.

'Seven o'clock,' said the morning radio announcer, 'time
for a Capstan, the Empire's favourite cigarette.' Our seasons were the seasons of English storybooks, and of the
films we saw on Saturday nights, brought from the northern hemisphere. Our great-grandfathers had put together a
lost, unknown home in landscapes that made it all perfectly natural: Georgian houses with classical porticoes;
hop fields and orchards; chimney pots rising on gentle
hillslopes, in the subtle, muted lights of East Anglia.
Banners of cloud hung low across dark blue hills, straight

23

from the Hound of the Baskervilles; Norman and Gothic
churches had appeared; discreet brothels; banks; Salvation
Army hostels. Repertory Societies were run by artistic men
in tweeds; trams ran on wet tramlines; and in the midlands,
the gentry mulled their claret and rode to hounds. Tasmanians, I suppose, were rather like the prisoners in Plato's
cave; to guess what the centre of the world was like—that
centre we knew to be twelve thousand miles away—we
must study shadows on the wall: *Bitter Sweet* at the Hobart
Repertory; *Kind Hearts and Coronets* at the Avalon Cinema; the novels of A. J. Cronin and J. B. Priestley and
Graham Greene; shadows, all shadows, clues to the other
hemisphere we might someday discover. We were living,
when I grew up, in the half-light of that Empire the
ultimate end of whose bridge of boats was Hobart.

And it was all strange. The island was unalterably strange
in the end, hanging like a shield above Antarctica. Who
were we, marooned at forty-two degrees south? Why were
we here, and not there? South of Hobart, south of Port
Davey's last little lights of settlement, there was nothing;
there was the ice. Past that Gothic southern coast, with its
giant basalt needles and pillars of rock, Hebridean seas
rose, grey and frightening as steel engravings, and fishing
boats disappeared without trace. In the cold, virgin rain-
forests of the south-west wilderness, where it rained and
snowed eternally, where rivers ran underground, and where
men had walked in and never walked out, wild flowers and
exquisite little tarns continued unseen, as they had done
throughout time. Settlement was in the island's pastoral
midlands, and the mild, kindly east.

Dean Swift had located Lilliput somewhere near Tasmania—perhaps with poetic foresight. By the time I was
born, the island had become an antipodean Dwarfland: a
place of small, quiet people with quiet smiles, who wanted
to forget that this had once been another island.

The other island's name had been Van Diemen's Land.
It was a name that had rung and chimed in Cockney and
Irish songs of hate; the name of a British penal colony that
had once been synonymous with fear throughout the Anglo

Saxon world. At the place called Hell's Gates, on the savage west coast, a penal settlement so terrible had been created that convicts had murdered each other to secure the release of hanging, or had fled without hope into the icy rain-forest to leave their bones there, and sometimes to turn cannibal. Van Diemen's Land had also removed a whole race: the few aboriginals the colonists had found when they came, and whose last remnants, deported to a smaller island in Bass Strait, had pined away, staring across the water to their lost home.

All this was a hundred years gone; and that century was best forgotten. Gone, the sad aborigines, who had once lurked in the bush like dark, accusing wraiths, threatening lonely farms. Gone, the old convicts from London and Cork, in their mustard suits of shame; ancestors whom nobody wanted to own. When transportation ended, the native-born colonists changed the island's name to obliterate the dread; to make it normal. As clean young Tasmania, it would start anew, the horrors forgotten.

But were they? I would sometimes wonder about this, reading about Hell's Gates and Port Arthur. How long ago was a hundred years?

Sometimes it seemed to me that the fusty odour of fear, the stench of the prison ships, was still in Hobart; and a tragic, heavy air, an air of unbearable sorrow, even in sunshine, hung over the ruined, sandstone penitentiary and the dark blue bay at Port Arthur, south of Hobart, where the tourists went. Was it possible that the spirits of the convicts were silently clustered in that air, weighting it like sacking? Were the floggings and the shackles still invisibly here, hanging above the dark green bush? Still somehow repeated, for eternity?

A certain look of distaste came into Tasmanian faces when you mentioned the convicts; the look of respectability threatened. It was similar to fear, and even the jokes had fear in them. No one wanted to admit having a convict ancestor; because the truth was that long ago was not long ago: not long enough.

Once, I had asked my mother whether the family had a

convict, in that past, and her face took on the look of threatened respectability I'd come to recognise; a prim yet evasive distaste.

No, she said, of course not; how could I ask such a thing?

But she was lying, as so many Tasmanians lied then; I found this out eventually. She was hiding Michael Brady, an Irish political prisoner transported in 1848; not only my ancestor, but Brian Brady's too: our hidden great-great-grandfather.

It was not our blood relationship, however, that was to draw us incongruous first cousins together. It was our penal servitude under Brother Kinsella, in our last year at St Augustine's, on the edge of adulthood.

2

The Christian Brothers were simple men, Irish or Irish-descended, from the old, bare-knuckle, working-class suburbs of Dublin, Melbourne and Sydney: the poor boys of the Church, with little love for scholarship.

They had planted Jansenist discipline in Tasmania's penal soil, and learning was a pill to be forced down the throat with the aid of the eighteen-inch strap they called Doctor Black. They were happiest on the football field or the handball court—red-faced and panting, boys among boys. Many of them were more or less kindly and dedicated in their belief; in Scripture periods, their narrow souls would sometimes open up, and their devotion to Our Lord and Our Lady would engage and utterly convince us. Then, grey-suited and awed in our rows of desks, enclosed in belief as though in a sweet-smelling tent, we knew ourselves part of that Faith which sinners in the town below would never understand.

But no such devotion was manifest in Brother Kinsella. His deepest passion seemed to be hatred; and in the last term of that final year, the main brunt of his hatred was borne by Brian Brady.

It was only when a breaking-point was reached that Brady became my friend. Until then, he had been quite distant with me.

*   *   *

Brother Kinsella faces the Matriculation class, pale, bully-boy's hands joined over his paunch. Down-turned mouth drooping, he hoarsely intones the great litany to Mary, to which we chant our responses, as we've done for years.

With brief respites, we've been taught by Brother Kinsella since Junior School; now, inescapable, he takes Algebra. Pale, bald and massively fat in his ballooning cassock, he is never seen on the handball court or the football field; but because of his violence, his rough Australian accent and his harsh, roaring voice, he is nicknamed Navvy.

'Ark of the covenant.'
'Pray for us.'
'Gate of Heaven.'
'Pray for us.'
'Star of the Morning.'
'Pray for us.'

Star of the Morning! Delight suddenly distracts me from my morning forboding. I'm often ambushed by delight, at seventeen. How has such an atom of beauty flown from these loose, hateful lips?

The walls of Navvy Kinsella's classroom are of cold, glazed brick; the windows frame steel-plated sky and bare trees. The cold numbs our feet; big Mick Paterson has farted, and it isn't funny, no one dares laugh; it's a wretched whiff from the pit, a reminder of the body's foulness and the squalors of the flesh. Meanwhile, an Antarctic wind off the Southern Ocean is blowing straight up the Derwent Estuary below, and into the narrow streets of Hobart. Puddles are frozen over in Harrigan Street. The strap will hurt much more, on a morning like this, and the blokes blow secretly into their praying hands, while a coloured print of St Joseph eyes us with useless sympathy from next to the blackboard. I blow too, but only through fellow-feeling; because of my leg, I'm not strapped; I have the sad immunity of the marred.

With the approach of the external Matriculation exam (administered, we are reminded, by Protestants), the strappings have increased. And this morning, as he reviews our

homework, scribbling the equations violently on the blackboard, the Navvy's bile seems worse than usual. His mighty
rage rises; his shouts can be heard in the Archbishop's
Palace. He hits the blackboard with the side of his hand,
the repeated thumps like the sound of some small animal
being killed; then, his hoarse voice sinking a little lower,
he takes up a litany of his own which we know by heart,
and which I've become expert at imitating: I have often
performed it at lunchtimes, surrounded by an applauding
crowd.

'Blimey, why do I *come* here?' His grey eyes, the
colour of garden slugs, search our faces, the life-weary
lids slanting downwards in disgust, like the coarse, weary
lines of his pallid cheeks. 'I could be having a good *time!* I
could be down at the *pub!* I could be *anywhere*, but
instead I'm here teaching you bloody idiots!'

No one laughs, even though my parody hangs in the air:
even a smile can provoke retribution. The Navvy was
perhaps meant to be a bookmaker or a publican; anything
but a Christian Brother. It's clear that he's secretly rent
with the strain of playing his part, in his cassock and
Roman collar. Longing for the pleasures he sarcastically
dwells on, craving to satisfy his big belly in the pub, and
perhaps to indulge more mysterious appetites, he vents his
rage instead on these rows of respectful, stiff-faced youths
with their Irish names. And the highest pitch of it is
reserved for Brian Brady.

'Mr Brady. Out here, sir, for a little taste of Doctor
Black.'

The summons this morning is over Brady's botched
algebra homework; his homework is usually botched. Although Brother Kinsella is quite tall, Brady at eighteen has
grown taller, and he stands at the front with a slight stoop,
looking down on the Navvy in a way that's comically
enquiring, his full lower lip protruding. As usual, his suit
looks as though he's slept in it, and his brown, loosely
curling hair is an uncombed tangle. He has been strapped
by Kinsella every day for a month, without showing any
sign of pain; and to extract such a sign is plainly the

Navvy's deepest desire. It has become a contest of wills, and has amused us at first. But now it's gone too far; we all know that, and have grown uneasy.

'Why are these equations not finished, Mr Brady?'

'I got bored, sir.'

There is a nervous titter; the Navvy blinks. Then he hits Brady hard across the face, and the class hisses softly. No one hits a bloke of Brady's age on the face: the Navvy has hit a man.

The strapping that follows is agreed to be the worst anyone has seen: a sixer; the maximum. The Navvy says it's for insolence. His black form seems to rise from the floor as he brings the strap down: the reports are like gunshots. Gathering his strength for each cut, wet lower lip agape, his expression is that of a man on the verge of weeping. Brady's arm begins to shudder; and as he comes back down the aisle, bent over, his crossed hands in his armpits, his face is blanched.

The Navvy sinks into his chair, chest heaving. 'Get out your Latin books.'

He pants; his voice is wheezing and small; he no longer looks at us, and we all sit sober and thoughtful.

I decide to search my cousin out at lunchtime, and talk to him.

In furthering the careers of the Rymers, I am one day to accumulate a hoard of photographs of Brian Brady: glossy publicity shots, posters for concerts, newspaper pictures: the bulging archives of success. Put beside these, a picture kept from St Augustine's days makes an odd and touching contrast. This is a football photograph in the school magazine: the St Augustine's Firsts.

Brady squats on the ground, third from the left in the front row in his striped football sweater with its spreading collar. He's already bigger than most of his fellows, and the good looks that will be central to his career are taking form, but not yet complete. His uncontrolled loops of Celtic hair are cut shorter than they will be later, but are defiantly free of the disciplined and oiled side-parting which was the required style of those days, and which all his mates have. His light blue eyes look unnatural in the picture; almost white, like those in pictures of silent screen stars, or nineteenth-century ancestors. His face is both tough and wistful, the broad Irish cheekbones high, the nose already broken from one of his tremendous fights in the gym, refereed by Brother Malone; an epic in which he knocked out Ginger Donnelly. And his face is luminous with expectancy. Not just that expectancy which gives beauty even to the plainest adolescent, but something else, it seems to me: the musing contemplation of a special future, into which he will escape.

There's little pain to be seen, although this was the period when Brady's suffering under Navvy Kinsella was at its worst. Instead there's something more complex: not sorrow, not pleading, but a swift, affronted surprise, which is combined with calculation. It's the ancient expression of the warrior, of all men of spirit under tyranny's attack. And the calculation is directed towards how and when he will strike back.

I was to see this expression on Brady's face many times; but I viewed it from a distance, as though he were a player on a stage, or a gladiator who went day after day into the same arena, against hopeless odds. The truth was that I scarcely knew my cousin, despite all the years of our sporadic acquaintance. This was the first time we'd been in the same form; Brady, who was a year older than I, was repeating Matriculation, having failed last year.

He was unlikely to pass. He seemed not even to try with his work, and was cheerfully disorganised. With the exception of Navvy Kinsella, the Brothers were inclined to tolerate him, since he was good at the two things that made for the utmost popularity at St Augustine's: Australian Rules football, and boxing. He had won every fight he had got into, both in and out of the gym.

For all these things, I secretly idolised and envied him; for these, and for something else, not easy to analyse. It had to do with a remoteness that was always in Brady's cheerful face, no matter how much he laughed and joked;

it made him an unknown quantity at each new meeting: it gave him a mystery. I was too young yet to have grasped that this mystery is the property of very simple and self-contained people, and is often an illusion. In Brady's case, I had partly created it myself; and yet my instinct wasn't entirely wrong. I had sensed the mystery of talent as yet unborn—the sort of raw talent that would never be mine, but which I'd one day nurture and promote. Talent in the strong and inarticulate is always fascinating, since they don't declare it. Not to be pinned down, keeping to themselves the area of their souls where talent is hidden, they tantalise, and then move on; the time they grant us is short.

Our backgrounds were as different as our natures, Brady's and mine. He was a boarder, and came from the East Coast, where his father ran a mixed farm near Swansea. Mick Brady was my mother's brother; the farm called Greystones had been her home, and I had gone there on childhood holidays. Brian had been friendly then, but he had given me little attention: we had eyed each other like dogs, and he'd contemplated my crutches with healthy unease.

When he had first appeared at St Augustine's at the age of fourteen, I had gone up to him in the playground and had introduced myself, reminding him of our kinship.

But my cousin had examined me with only slight interest.

'Yair, I remember you,' he said. 'You had two crutches, then, not one. Are you getting better?'

When I said I was, Brady said: 'That's fine. Good luck to you, kid.' And he had walked away, leaving me flushing. He hadn't really wanted to know me; his friends were blokes a year older; athletes, members of the football team.

I wasn't used to having my friendship rejected; I'd achieved considerable popularity by that time, through the traditional method available to a cripple: I had turned myself into a jester. One of my early juvenile accomplishments had been to perfect the loudest belch in the school. Released at will, it suggested the sound of a gargantuan toad, and I was cunning enough to ration it, so that it never wore out its appeal. There were theories that only a cripple could produce it. I was their mate-on-a-crutch; their lame-boy mascot—the blokes being as sentimental as they were cruel.

Then I found another way to secure approval: I began to make drawings of them. I had a mediocre but facile talent for drawing, and specialised in depicting those who played Australian Rules football: the game I loved but might only watch. The members of the team (including noble Ashton Stuart, the Captain), accepted these portraits of themselves in action with the uneasy pleasure of simple men caught in a dilemma: they despised art, but were seduced by personal immortality. I had learned a form of aggression more subtle than theirs, and I now watched without fear their bloody playground fist-fights, which the Brothers happily refereed; I drew the winners. I knew just how vulgar my portraits of the gladiators were; I was a sort of prostitute really, but after all my options were limited.

My portrait of Brian Brady at football was a little different; I had put great care into it, and he flew into the air like a dark dancer. Presented with this, he had studied it with suspicion as though it were a forgery; then he had thanked me quietly, and once again passed on. Nothing cut any ice with Brian until the day of Brother Kinsella's assault, when St Augustine's and boyhood were almost over.

The weather had cleared, to produce sun and racing white clouds; the ice had melted in the puddles. It was past noon: the day's dreaming summit. We had said the Angelus, and despite my concern at Brady's strapping, a sort of peace had entered me.

'And the word was made flesh.
And dwelt amongst us.'

The words had calmed my spirit as the small, golden notes of the Angelus bell had entered the calm air, drop by healing drop, drifting over the heedless, irreligious roofs

of the town below, as they did every day. I found Brady in
his usual smoking-spot, sitting on a stone behind the cypress trees that flanked the sandstone wall along Byrne
Street. He was alone, a cigarette between his lips.

When I greeted him, he looked at me without smiling.
There was something about the blankness of his eyes that
made me know he had changed; in some way, he had
ceased to be a boy.

'Hello Miller,' he said. 'What are *you* after? Can't you
see I'd rather go solo Pat?'

I quailed inwardly; but I squatted down nevertheless.
'Thought you might like a sandwich,' I said, offering him
one from my lunch tin. Brady raised his eyebrows and took
one in silence, stubbing out his cigarette; boarders were
always hungry.

'That wasn't right, that back-hander he gave you,' I
said.

Brady looked at me, chewing. Then he said softly:
'He'll never make me crack though, the bloody pig.'

He seldom spoke without a joke in his voice, and this
intensity was new. Perhaps he felt he could show it to me:
his crippled cousin. Silence fell, and extended; but he
didn't seem to mind my being here.

From where we sat, hidden from the steeple and its
cross, we looked down on the chirruping, ochre-and-grey
town, and the funnels and derricks of the ships lying in
port, past the stone tower of the GPO. The breeze had
dropped, and it was warm and still; the chugging of a
fishing-boat floated up on the miles of air. I could pick it
out, moving down the glass of the estuary towards the
D'Entrecasteaux Channel, leaving a V of wake. Beyond
was the grey-blue eye of the Southern Ocean. Round hills,
empty and golden-grassed, on the far side of the river,
were in another land to which I might some day escape,
and the dark green foreshores of the suburbs of Sandy Bay
and Taroona, with their cypresses and red-and-white houses,
didn't look like part of Hobart at all, but like places in
Europe: Italian hill towns, perhaps.

From the chapel, the sopranos of Brother Kinsella's

junior choir could be heard, singing 'Panis Angelicus'. The Navvy had a hunger in his soul, a lust for beauty, and this was fed by his choirs, which sang a mixture of Latin hymns and old-fashioned popular songs by composers like Stephen Foster. Every boy with a voice was dragooned into them; Brian, who had a remarkably true baritone now that his voice had broken, was in the Senior choir. Conducting, the Navvy displayed a second self, enunciating pedantically like a gross, middle-aged matron with pretensions to refinement. Waving his baton, lips protruding as though for a kiss, standing hugely on tiptoe, he only roared when some bloke sang flat.

God allowed me to pity him, just now, and I said: 'He does a good job with the choir.'

And all of a sudden, sitting here with Brady, our familiar situation's strangeness came to me. Down below, our native town, our small, gimcrack colonial city, on the edge of the Southern Ocean; up here, this magisterial, medieval world of cloisters, cypresses, Latin and the strap. We lived in two dimensions, I saw; and 'Panis Angelicus' woke a pleasure in me that hardly seemed my own. Like 'Star of the Morning', the hymn was anciently beautiful; the whole stern book of Europe was in it, of which I'd read hardly a page. But this mysterious joy was too intense to stay; almost, it didn't belong to me, and certainly it wasn't happiness.

'I'm skipping Benediction tonight,' Brady said suddenly. 'I'm pissing off downtown to see that new John Wayne. You seen it?'

I was saddened by this. I was fond of Benediction, to which day-boys went only occasionally; I liked the Chapel in the evenings, with its red sanctuary-lamp burning in the dimness, the incense more sharp and significant than by day, the veiled air filled with mystery. I liked the sentimental statue of Our Lady, with her blue-and-white robes and serene, northern face; I often prayed for her to intercede for me. I remonstrated with Brian now, telling him he should go.

'What the hell for? It's all rubbish, Miller. There's no

God, or he'd never allow a shit-bag like Kinsella to be a Brother. D'you think the Navvy is a *holy* man?'

I thought. 'No,' I said. 'But I think he suffers.'

Brady broke into jeering laughter. 'Suffers! I hope he does. Look what he does with his bloody suffering. Passes it on. Is that Christ-like?'

'No. But there can be bad Brothers and bad priests—it doesn't change the truth. And there are good ones. What about the Franciscan?'

'The Franciscan?' Brady frowned at me in puzzlement; and then I realised that he had never talked to the Franciscan. He must have been one of the very few blokes in the college who hadn't.

The Franciscan had come to us from Italy about a year ago, and he had been with us for only a few weeks. He had taught no classes, and we never really knew why he was living in the College. It was probably just a holiday for him.

He had preached one sermon in the Chapel, and I remembered little about it, now. It was not so much what he had said that had held our attention; it was his smile. It made the junior boys follow him like puppies whenever he appeared; and seniors gather round as well. I had been one of these; and he didn't fail us, he appeared every day. Unlike the Brothers, he seemed to have all the time in the world, and was ready to give us endless attention. Every one of us received his smile, like a gift to take away for the rest of the day; I was to take it away for the rest of my life.

Of course, the Franciscan was a foreigner, with a brown cassock instead of a black one, and that alone had made it worthwhile for the Juniors to follow him about. But this didn't really explain our interest in the Senior School, or what happened as the weeks went by. Normally, we would have tired of such a novelty quite quickly. Instead, our devotion grew. We stood about in the lunch-hours, keeping our eyes open all the time for the tall, bulky figure in the brown habit to appear in the cloisters, with his sandals

showing clean olive toes, and the cord about his waist like
that of a dressing-gown. When he appeared, a cheer would
go up, and we would move towards him. He would give a
little wave of his hand, smile happily, and continue to
walk, going nowhere in particular, while our procession
followed him; and then he would begin to talk.

I've forgotten his name, if I ever knew it. He spoke
good English, but rarely said more than a few words at a
time, and he spoke very softly. He was somewhere in late
middle age; a big man, strongly built and comfortably
fleshy, radiating health and well-being. He was bald on
top, with a fringe of white hair contrasting pleasingly with
his tan skull and smooth, tan face. His eyes were dark as
sultanas, constantly narrowed as he smiled; and they gleamed
always with a good humour that was not exactly sly but
cheerfully confiding, as though there were one particular
joke about the world we all shared, but about which he
knew a little more than we did.

We were always waiting for him to tell it; but I doubt
now that he ever did. What he told, what he conveyed,
was not done in words. He smoked a pipe, and we liked
his pipe; it was comfortable, like everything about him. He
was comfortable with the world. I see him standing against
the sunlit red weatherboards of the old bicycle shed, in a
corner of the yard, while we press in a semi-circle around
him, waiting. For what? I no longer know. We devour his
brown harmonies with our eyes: his gown the good colour
of earth; his face like warm, baked clay. His pipe-smoke
flies away on the summer air. When I try to bring back the
voices, I find they are almost lost; but snatches of conversation do come back; some of it inconsequential.

Stubby Pat Lynch's voice: *'Do they have big cities in
Italy, Father?'*

And the soft voice answering: *'Some big cities. But
many are small, like yours.'*

'Ours isn't so small.'

*'Well, perhaps not so small. But not too big either. Eh?
You should be very happy, boys, that whichever way you
look, you can see the hills and the country outside. That*

*is how it is in Florence. And that is good for your souls,
do you know that? It was good for men's souls in Florence. They made beautiful things, because beautiful places
were just across the roof-tops: the beauties that are God's.
That is how it is with you—so far from Europe, here in this
beautiful island.'*

And now, my mouth going dry, I decide to ask this man
things I have asked of no one.

I have reached the age of private ecstasies. The visible
world has taken on a whole new appearance, in the past
year; and standing on my balcony at Trent Street, staring
across the valley of Newtown in the late afternoons, I'm
entranced for an hour at a time by Mount Direction: a
mauve, double-humped hill lying to the east. No one, I
believe, has ever loved a hill or a mountain as I do; Mount
Direction is not just a mountain; it's the sign of an amazing Beyond. Smaller and more domestic than Mount Wellington in the west—little more than a hill—it has a cool
specialness, a musing air of marvel the other peak lacks. It
lies sleeping at the gateway of light, and across its double
top, where I pick out the tiny heads of gums on the eastern
sky, there is another, distant dimension, signalled by a
strange green tinge low in that sky at evening. There's a
membrane stretched across the air; if it split, would I see
God's face?

This, in stumbling, inadequate words, is what I dare to
ask the Franciscan, in front of my mates. It's a measure of
the respect he's created among us that none of them laughs
at me; they listen as though to a reasonable enquiry.

The Franciscan looks at me, neither smiling nor unsmil-
ing, seeing me in detail for the first time; he takes in the
stick I still have to lean on, and his gaze doesn't embar-
rass. But what he says is unexpected.

'I think you have difficulty in praying.'

I flush; it's true.

'You need never doubt that God is there,' he says. *'But
remember what it says in the book of Ecclesiastes: "The
eye is not satisfied with seeing, nor the ear filled with
hearing," And think about the things Thomas à Kempis*

said about that. He gave good advice to young men like yourself—young men who are full of wonder and curiosity at the world, as they should be.' (Here a faintly ironical smile comes back, and he puffs on his pipe.) *'He told you to try and withdraw your heart from the love of visible things, and to turn to the invisible. Sensuality, however full of innocent delight to you now, has its dangers. So,* ragazzo mio, *keep your mind fixed on the invisible. It is all around you, after all.'* He extends his palm briefly towards the nearby air, as though indicating a host of angels; then drops it. *'And pray,'* he commands. *'Don't be concerned if God doesn't seem to listen. He does; and in one moment, as à Kempis says, he may give you what he long denied you.* Ecco.*'*

This last, small Italian word, which he often uses, and whose meaning none of us knows, gives great peace; it's like the closing of a small, well-fitted door, and I stand here with a serenity I've never known before: answered, absolved.

Ginger Denis Fahey asks the next question: a prosaic one. *'Would you like to live here, Father?'*

'To live here? I?' He takes his pipe from his mouth, and his smile broadens. *'That would be beautiful. But only for a time. We are like birds, we human beings: in the end we fly back to where we come from. And my nest is in the hills of Tuscany.'*

Tuscany. The strange name hangs in the air like his pipe smoke, and we stare at him almost in awe, saying nothing for a moment. The Franciscan doesn't belong here; he has told us this plainly, and we don't resent it; but all of us have a musing regret in our faces now. Sadness clutches at us, and I'm not sure whether this is because the Franciscan will soon go, leaving us with nothing but Brother Kinsella, or because we want to follow him to unknown Tuscany, to that landscape of cypresses and dreaming bell-towers and mysterious little smokes we've seen in the paintings of Raphael and Fra Filippo Lippi, stretching behind the smiling Virgin and Child, out through arched windows.

The Franciscan will go, and will not be seen again. For

the first time in my life, I know what it is to cry out in my heart against a loss for which there is no remedy, and over which I have not even the right to cry. And his smile seems to understand this. His eyes meet mine, and his soft voice says to me, and to me alone: *'But birds can fly very far: some of them over whole oceans. Some day you may do that, and come to Italy.'*

There the voices of memory fade out for ever; and the Franciscan is gone.

Four o'clock: light rain is falling. Brian Brady and I walk through the front gate of the school together, passing the little thorn tree without a glance. He's offered to walk down town with me—mainly, I suspect, to escape his prison in the college for a time; but also to cement our friendship made at lunchtime.

I've long ceased to need my crutch, but the steepness of Harrigan Street forces me to brace myself on the black-wood walking-stick I've inherited from Karl Miller, who is now three years dead. When we've nearly reached the bottom of the Harrigan Street hill Brady demands a turn with the stick, and spins it like a hoofer in a dance routine. Then he gives it back.

'You'll be able to give this away soon, won't you?'

'Pretty soon.' I put an unctuous quaver into my voice. 'The leg still gets shaky on a slope; then I need my stick. Need it badly, master.' I go into my Quasimodo routine; mouth a-slobber, back hunched, I lurch along like Charles Laughton in the film, and Brady laughs. 'You don't give a stuff, do you?'

'No, master.' I see that he suddenly admires me.

'But you look pretty fit, you know, Dick. No one'd know there was anything wrong, now,' he says.

One leg, hidden by my trousers, is still thinner than the other, and I'll never run fast again; but I like the fact that Brady wants to dismiss this. He's reduced my grandfather's sad old stick to a trivial toy; and as well, he has taken the grimness out of Harrigan Street.

Harrigan Street! Main street of slumdom; street of Second-hand! I've always thought it eternal; I believe it will run for ever, dripping in our souls. As it levels out to meet Elizabeth Street, where I'll catch my tram, the district of Second-hand begins.

This is a zone that's filled with the sweet silver stink from the Gasworks; the gasometer's great red drum rears above the roofs, together with the brick factory chimney lettered UP TO DATE. First of the second-hand shops is Loney's Used Furniture, where decent men in grey dustcoats move about in the aisles; next comes Mrs Madgewick's Good Used Clothing, with dead men's trousers dangling in the doorway; and then we are passing the shop of the Lady Man: a long, narrow hallway, whose walls, from floor to ceiling, seem to consist entirely of paperback books, piled up in hundreds. Among the Westerns and thrillers, there are sunbathing magazines, with nude photographs. In Junior School, these were the most wicked publications that were known to exist, and a group of us once ventured in to look at them. The odd thing was that the shop was always empty: no customer was ever seen inside.

The place had the silence of a paper-lined tomb. Walled in by paper, staring at us from out of his brown gloom, sat the Lady Man: a figure in a green tennis shade and grey dustcoat, with lank, reddish hair and the pallid, hairless-looking flesh that had long ago invited his nickname. One arm rested always on the counter. I opened a copy of *Health and Efficiency,* taking it from the pile we were all furtively attacking—three of us working in silence, like experts at an unexploded bomb. For a few moments, my stomach dropping as though in a fast lift, I was presented with ineffable disclosures of female nudity, the genitals chastely painted out.

Then the Lady Man's pale hand, with a signet ring, came into my field of vision and straightened the pile. We all hurried out, and never went in again; the sense of escaping something there had been too strong.

As Brady and I pass now, the Lady Man looks out at us from his cavern, and I'm troubled by him. Still there, after all these years! How does he live, when no customers come? What is he waiting for? His mystery is like the central mystery of all adult wickedness; and I wonder briefly whether he's damned. I know little about damnation, at seventeen; but I've glimpsed the fact that it has something to do with tedium; and the tedium of the Lady Man, fixed like a fungus in his cavern, is something not to be dwelt on.

'There he is,' Brady says, as though reading my thoughts. 'The tennis champ. Never sells a thing—he's as bad as you, Dick, with all those bloody papers around him.'

I find he's given to these sudden, cruel thrusts, which show a disconcerting perceptiveness; and I know that he's remembering the childish episode of the stolen comics.

When I was fourteen, I asked him to visit me at Trent Street. He came only once, on a Saturday, and admired my vast collection of comic books. But when he'd gone, I found that he'd taken two with him: *Buck Rogers* number 35, and *The Phantom* number 12. And the rifling of these treasures threw me into a frenzy. Like all collectors, I was obsessed; an obsession that went beyond my love of the comics themselves, and revolved around sequences and sets; and Brady had destroyed two vintage sets. Now, our juvenile voices came back.

'Those old comics? What are you wetting yourself about? You've read 'em, haven't you? I'll get you some new ones.'

'You don't understand. I don't want new ones, I want those. They can't be bought any more.'

Brady stared at me then with incredulous scorn, and laughed openly: a crass raider. And I suspect today that his scorn was justified; is justified still, now that we're almost men. I've long outgrown comics, and my library at Trent Street is filled with good books—certainly no collection of trash like the Lady Man's. But isn't Brady right, essentially? Haven't I built a bunker of paper about myself, to escape from crippledom? Haven't I too lived inside walls of paper? Aren't the Lady Man and I perhaps of the same tribe?

No. I reject it.

We talk with animation again, discovering that we both like the new music we listen to at night on the radio: the rock and roll that adults detest, whose messengers, in this year, are Bill Haley and the Comets.

'I'd like to play rock and roll,' Brady says. 'Or maybe Country and Western.'

'Be a musician?' The idea is outlandish; apart from his singing in the choir, Brady has no known musical ability.

But he glances at me with warning calm. 'Why not?' he says. 'I can read music. My uncle taught me. Wait and see, Miller.'

Here is Lovejoy's second-hand shop: the rain is heavier now, and the galvanised iron verandah awning keeps us dry. The green-lettered sign over the open door says, *Music, Books & Antiques. A. (Sandy) Lovejoy*.

It's a large, rambling shop, in the ground floor of an old, two-storey terrace house. We peer into the dusty display window, examining Toby jugs, toast racks, and a sepia picture of a bare-shouldered Edwardian matron in evening dress, whose smile is radiantly mad. There's an array of battered musical instruments; and closest to us, in an open case, is a guitar.

Brady gazes at this, apparently thinking of our recent conversation, his expression distant and serious, while the nineteenth century washes about us like a tide of dirty water. It has cast up in Lovejoy's window these cracked and yellowed salvages; these wretched personal effects of the dead. I don't like secondhand shops, they threaten me with the past; and I'm suddenly anxious to be gone, imagining threat in the air, pungent as the stink from the Gasworks.

'Come on,' I say. 'What do you want with this old junk?'

But still Brady pauses, his eyes fixed on the guitar as though he's trying to read some sort of rune lettered on its varnished wood. 'What's your big rush? Old things are interesting,' he says. 'I'd like to learn to play that thing.'

And now I become conscious that a thin, middle-aged man in a navy-blue belted overcoat is standing beside us, looking into the window too. For a few moments I don't glance at him directly; but when I do, my stomach hollows. It's the Man in the Lane.

* * *

It's a long time ago now, and I was young. If I s̶
alarm at the sight of him, I might be allowing hinᵈ
too much influence. But I do know that his sudden rea̶
pearance, after so many years, greatly surprised me. For
some moments, nothing happened. All three of us stared at
the guitar.

I tried to tell whether it was the same overcoat the man
wore; it looked the same, but perhaps he always bought
the same sort. He had one hand in his pocket just as
before, and his collar was turned up at the back. His quiet
tie and grey trousers were pedantically neat—so neat that
there was something formal and official about him. He
didn't seem to have changed or aged, unless the creases in
his thin cheeks had grown deeper; and perhaps his flat,
black hair was streaked with more white at the sides. His
sombre, melancholy good looks were those of a widower,
or a man with a secret illness.

'Thinking of buying something, boys?'

He was glancing attentively sideways at us, his head
slightly cocked. It was the same hollow, well-spoken voice
I remembered. It had the effect of a famous voice; one I
felt I should know—from the radio perhaps.

It was Brady who answered him. 'Just looking at the
guitar,' he said.

I wondered if the man remembered me. But he made no
sign that he did so, and his eyes remained fixed on Brady.
I still found them different from other eyes, as I'd done at
twelve years old: they were bleak as the spring sky, their
drooping, yellowish lids elegantly weary. 'Ah—the guitar,' he said. 'Why don't you try it out?'

'Do you own the shop?' Brady asked.

The man was still facing the window, and now the thin,
crooked smile travelled up one side of his face. 'Not exactly,'
he said, 'but I know the gentleman who does. Sandy
Lovejoy's a friend of mine.'

His expression was agreeable, and I wondered if I'd
misjudged him as a child. But it worried me that he

wouldn't look at me. It was as though I'd failed some test, all that time ago, and the man had no further use for me.

'Come on,' he said. He jerked his head towards the door, and we followed him.

Inside, the shop was half-dark, without visible limits under a high old ceiling with dirty, decorative mouldings. It was crammed with vast constructions of junk: furniture, and a litter of smaller artifacts like things from a museum, not arranged in any way, but lodged on tables or the floor, or even suspended by wires from hooks in the ceiling. Aisles went off between wardrobes and dressers, and the man's dark-coated back moved ahead of us down one of these aisles. We followed, and he made a sharp turn to the left to get to the front window, where he picked up the guitar. Holding it very carefully, as though it were alive, he blew on it once to remove the dust, squinting along it, and then held it out to Brady, who cradled it awkwardly, half-smiling. I'd never seen quite this expression on Brian's face before, and I became aware that something important was happening; something that seemed to have been planned.

Silence extended among the piles of junk; and then Brady asked: 'What's this hole for?'

'That's the sound-hole,' the man said quietly.

It was as though he'd indicated a secret entrance; staring at the round, tunnel-like mouth, I felt it to be hypnotic, drawing us in. But Brady was looking at the guitar with deep pleasure; and now he drew his thumb across the strings.

The random sound was surprisingly melodious. Deep and high together, the cluster of notes he had released rang and hummed, climbing to the dim ceiling. He looked up, and asked: 'Is this guitar good for Country and Western?'

'It'd be wasted on that. This is a serious guitar,' the man said. 'It's a Ramirez. Spanish.'

'It's made in Spain?'

'That's right. In Madrid. The Spanish invented the guitar. They still make the best.' His melancholy voice was very quiet; but we attended to him absolutely. 'A British sailor brought this in here,' he said. 'It's got quite a reasonable price on it.'

Without taking his eyes from Brady's, he reach
side and picked up a kitchen chair which he placed
front of him. Then, putting one brown shoe on it
resting an elbow on his raised knee, he cradled the guita
expertly and began to screw at the tuning pegs.

'It's got a good sound,' he said, and struck a chord.
This was far more beautiful and impressive than the sound
Brian had produced; but the man frowned, screwed at the
pegs again and struck another chord, while Brady watched
him with the eagerness of a gun-dog.

And now the man began to play. What he played was a
flamenco piece; probably a malagueña, since recollection
tells me there was the hint of a fandango in it. That he
played well was quickly beyond doubt; under the authority
of his long hands there were no fumbled notes. I had never
seen anyone play a Spanish guitar before; and I doubted
that Brady had either. We glanced once at each other in
delight: we would probably have been equally impressed
had the man begun juggling. Brady's gaze was fixed on
the working fingers or else on the man's face, which was
now in profile, its thin nose bent in absolute concentration
over the strings, dark brows drawn together.

He didn't play very fast, and yet the delicate, tripping,
fandango sound seemed to be fast, like a dance. The
strange, broken gypsy rhythms and the halts and changes
in direction kept us in a state of tension, half pleasurable
and half not. The rhythm was compulsive, making us tap
our feet; and the music should have been gay. Yet it
wasn't quite gay; there was an opposite seriousness and
perhaps despair under it, throbbing in the bass strings.
Every so often the man's fingers would leave the strings to
drum on the tap-plate; and just when we were entering into
the ease and light-heartedness of this little Spanish dance—
picked out on the treble strings, high and seductive—there
would be a change again, like those alarming changes in
the man himself. His fingers, with a speed that blurred
them, would attack the guitar to produce a passionate,
almost fearsome thundering, while his face remained ex-

pressionless, coldly controlled. Then, with some final raps on the sound-board, it was over.

He leaned the instrument against a wardrobe, thrusting his hands into his raincoat pockets and looking at us, eyebrows raised.

Brady's tangled curls looked startled; his blue eyes were dark with surprise. 'You can really play,' he said.

'You liked it, did you?'

'I'd like to play like that,' Brady said.

'Would you? Well we might work somthing out,' the man said. 'Can you read music?'

When Brady said he could, the man stared at him for a moment, as though checking the truth of this statement. Then he said: 'We'll talk to Sandy.' And once again, giving us a look over his shoulder, he moved off down an alleyway between the cliffs of furniture. He had opened his overcoat, and it floated out behind him like a cloak.

Dubiously, I brought up the rear. We were being taken deeper into the shop; I touched an old feather boa on a table as we passed, and sniffed my fingers; it had left what I thought of as a grave-smell. Emerging into an open area of floor at the back, we came upon a plump old man in a brown felt hat, seated in a big armchair with a grimy floral cover and nursing a miserable-looking Australian terrier which began to yap as we appeared. On all sides were musical instruments lying on trestle tables and on shelves against the wall. In the weak electric light from a bulb with a white china shade hanging from the ceiling these looked like the corpses of instruments, never to be played again. Near the old man's chair stood a drum-kit, the bass drum inscribed with the legend SANDY'S BANJO BAND, in 1930s lettering.

The dog yapped twice more, and the man in the chair shouted: 'Sarah! Be quiet! Be-have!' Then he smiled at us winningly, with a set of orange-gummed false teeth. 'Who have we got here?' he asked. 'Who are these young gentlemen?' His voice was loud and high.

'What we've got here,' said the man in the overcoat, 'is a young chap who wants to be a guitarist.' He jerked his head at Brian. 'So you'll have to sell him that guitar, Sandy, won't you?'

'Always willing to do that,' Sandy said. This time his voice was quieter and he stroked the dog's head, his worn grey eyes examining us as though to memorise every detail of our dress and appearance. 'But these are St Augustine's boys, aren't they? Yes—I know the tie. Don't get them in here very often. I'm not keen on the black beetles.' He was referring to the cassocks of the Brothers.

Now I became aware that a lanky youth of about eighteen in a grey dustcoat had sidled from behind a dressing-table to move beside Sandy's armchair. He stood smiling there like an attendant, watching us. Thin and pasty-faced, with pimples on his chin and large, projecting ears, he looked as though he'd never gone out of the junk-shop into the air. Blades of his long black hair, stuck together with too much hair-oil, hung across his forehead.

'Here's my nephew, Darcy Burr,' Sandy said. 'He doesn't have to put up with bloody schoolteachers any more, do you, Darcy? He works for me. And he's a real good guitarist, what's more.' He looked from Brady to me. 'So which of you boys is it wants to learn?'

'I do,' Brady said.

The nephew grinned, and I began to see that his looks were not as unfortunate as they'd seemed at first; his thin, white nose was beaklike, but his bony features were otherwise regular, and not unpleasing. His eyes were amber and slanting, like those of a feral cat; and their feline intentness somehow prevented his lop ears from being comical.

'I'm sure this young chap would pay you off each week,' the man in the overcoat was saying. He jerked his head at Brian. 'I know you like to help boys, Sandy.'

'And will you teach him, Brod? The way you do Darcy, here?'

'I might think about it.'

'Well then,' Sandy said to Brian, 'you're a very lucky young feller. Mr Broderick's the best teacher you could find. Not many can teach guitar.'

'But I couldn't pay,' Brady said. 'Unless I can get some money from home. How much would a lesson cost?'

'I'll see what you're like,' said the man Broderick, ignoring the question. 'If you have the aptitude like Darcy here, I'll give you lessons. We'll talk about money later. I'll be able to tell very quickly whether you have the talent. It has to be already in you. If it's not, I won't bother teaching you. How's that?' His cold, weary stare rested on Brady with what looked like contempt, and Brady flushed. 'But my guess is you'll have the talent,' Broderick said. 'Come in Monday of next week.'

When Brady thanked him, Broderick stared at him patiently; and Sandy Lovejoy did the same. Realising that we must go, we turned awkwardly, making our farewells, and edged away down one of the alleyways towards the front.

I glanced back; the nephew was watching us go, but Broderick, talking to old Sandy Lovejoy, was not. At no time during the conversation had he looked at me; I might have been invisible to him.

3

Both our lives were now transformed. Both were now dominated by the guitar: Brady's directly, mine at second-hand.

The old Ramirez became the first object Brady had truly loved, and music now invited his spirit as no learning offered by the school had ever done; the art belonging to the Muses thrilled and possessed my cousin more powerfully than football. He had previously closed his imagination against all learning; even against books. Now, a different door had opened; he walked through it without hesitation, and his life's course was set. He gave to the second-hand guitar from Sandy Lovejoy's shop a devotion as fanatical as mine had been for my toy theatre or my books.

So no one understood his obsession better than I did. Obsession was a condition to which Brian had been a stranger until now, and of which he was at first half-ashamed; it wasn't a condition that his friends in the football team could be expected to understand. But I understood it perfectly; and this drove Brady further into my company. I was the only one who could share his excitement; more, who understood its secret springs. When I would ask him how his playing was developing, he would make what seemed a special sign between us, raising his hand with index finger and thumb forming a circle and then winking, as though to say: *All under control.* And another more practical matter now cemented our association: I was able to offer Brady and his guitar a refuge.

He began to practise at my home in Trent Street, since the school offered a boarder nowhere to be alone, nowhere to do anything so eccentric as working on a musical instrument. So he came every weekend, and after he'd practised, we would talk and listen to records in my room: Bill Haley and the Comets, Little Richard, Lonnie Donegan, and stronger meat from the past such as Huddie Ledbetter and Bessie Smith. The great, far voice of the Empress of the Blues, singing of Mississippi floods and violent passion, created in us both a similar ecstasy, while beyond my dark little balcony the lights winking in Newtown became the light of Louisiana.

From the first, the entry of the guitar into Brady's life had been made uncannily easy. He had telephoned his mother to ask her to help him with the payments, and she had offered to send him the full amount, on the condition that he didn't tell his father how expensive it had been. So the Ramirez was his within a week, kept in his locker in the dormitory. 'It's good just knowing it's there,' he said to me. 'It's great just to handle it, even though I can't play it properly.' His eyes shone; he stared past my shoulder as though at a vision, and new rapidity and life had come into his speech.

The guitar's face of polished spruce was the last thing Brian looked at before going to bed and the first thing he checked in the morning; the mother-of-pearl decoration around the sound-hole was like some rare jewellery to him: he could scarcely believe he owned such a thing. The only boarder who tried to strum it without permission was laid out on the dormitory floor one night with a right to the jaw. After that, the guitar was never touched by anyone but Brady. In that same week, he had begun his lessons with the man Broderick.

A few days after the first lesson, I caught up with Brian by the old bicycle shed and began to question him, standing in the sun in the same spot where I had once questioned the Franciscan. What sort of a man was Broderick? What did he do for a living? Where had he given Brian the lesson? I badgered him with intense curiosity; and Brady smiled lazily, making me wait.

What did I mean, he wanted to know, asking what sort of man Brod was? (I raised my eyebrows at this 'Brod'.) He was a lot of things, Brady said; a guitar teacher, and also a bookseller: the accountant and buyer at Varley's Bookshop.

This was surprising information. Varley's in Franklin Street, just around the corner from Lovejoy's, was the best bookshop in Hobart. I often went in there after school and knew bald Mr Varley well by sight; but I had never seen Broderick there, and said so.

'You're not going to see him serving on the *counter*,' Brady said scornfully. 'He works behind the scenes, in an office down below. And I'll tell you another thing. I reckon he's the real owner of Lovejoy's. I reckon old Sandy just works for him. That Broderick's a brilliant bloke.' He nodded, his lips compressed significantly.

'There's something funny about him,' I said.

Brady stared; and there was a hostile light in his stare which gave me warning. 'Funny? What's funny about him?'

Somewhat feebly, I tried to explain, knowing already that any sort of warning was doomed to failure. I told Brian of my juvenile meetings with Broderick in Fiddler's Lane; I even remarked, without knowing why, that Broderick didn't seem to have aged very much since then. I began to sound silly, even to myself, and I trailed off, warned more directly than before by Brady's hard stare.

'You're talking bullshit, Miller,' he said.

I said I supposed I was. Broderick was certainly a marvellous guitarist, I said; and I added with hypocritical enthusiasm that Brian was lucky to be learning from him. Where was he giving the lessons?

Mollified (he was easily mollified), Brady told me that the lessons were given in the back of Lovejoy's shop. He had no idea where Broderick lived, or even whether he was a married man or not. There seemed to be only a limited amount of information that could be gained about Broderick, even his first name being unknown at this stage. He came and went; he inhabited different and incongruous locations, and I sensed that Brian didn't feel confident enough to try and find out more.

Never very articulate, Brady conveyed things only in carelessly-flung fragments, and I feared to annoy him by conveying any more of my uneasiness; so our conversations were mostly confined to Brady's enthusiastic reports about progress on the guitar. Glimpses of Broderick came through in enigmatic flashes, telling me little, yet intriguing me more and more. It was as though Broderick wasn't a man at all, but an abstraction; sometimes, I still childishly thought of him as the Man in the Lane.

Once I caught a glimpse of Broderick and Brady together, without their knowing; a glimpse that would remain with me. I was going down Harrigan Street late one evening and the two were standing on the corner of Franklin Street not far from the doorway of the Lady Man's Shop, on the other side of the street—so deep in conversation that they didn't see me. It was almost dark, and overcast, the light like the colour of an old mirror; and I hurried on. I sensed that Brad wouldn't want me to stop, even if he caught sight of me.

And the image remained in my mind all the way home in the tram, worrying me: Brady capless, in the grey school suit he managed to make more disreputable-looking than anyone else's; Broderick in his permanent navy overcoat, hands in pockets, slightly bent to one side, peering at Brady as though some serious question were at stake. They entered my dreams that night with such intensity that I started awake.

I was at an age when I intuitively grasped many of the

enigmas the world contained, but in trying to voice them, could only come up with approximations or metaphors for what was really there. And what I said to myself now was that Brady was sinking into the zone of Secondhand: that menacing past whose relics were washed up in the tomb-dry windows of Harrigan Street.

The notion was not entirely simplistic. All enthralment is an arrested past: the prolonged, perverse childhood from which some souls never escape.

4

Brady's afternoon lessons at the back of Sandy Lovejoy's shop were held in the cleared area of floor where Sandy had sat in his armchair, among the second-hand instruments. Brady and Broderick sat facing each other on two hardback chairs pulled from among the stock; it was very formal. All this I extracted bit by bit.

Broderick began by asking why Brian wanted to learn guitar at all.

To play rock and roll and Country and Western, Brady told him.

Country music, American and Australian, beloved by the farming people all over Tasmania, was what Brady had grown up with; his idols were Hank Snow, Kitty Wells and the Australian Reg Lindsay. But the music was regarded by city people as a joke; and Brady waited tensely for Broderick to scorn him.

Broderick didn't, however; he merely stared at Brady and nodded, his sober stare unchanging. 'All right,' he said quietly. 'All you'll really need for that is a few basic strums. But is it really all you want? That and rock and roll? You've got the aptitude for more, I can see that already.'

'I'd like to play like you,' Brian said. 'That Spanish stuff. Can that bloke who works here play it?'

'Darcy? Yes. He's coming on well. But if you want to play flamenco like Darcy, you'll have to learn the guitar properly: not just strumming. It'd give you a big advantage in accompanying yourself, too. Would you like that?'

When Brian agreed, Broderick allowed him a rare, cold smile.

And so they began in earnest. Brady was shown at first how to hold the guitar against his body; and Broderick told him to feel it, to get to know it with his hands. Self-conscious at first, Brady soon became intent on learning to love by touch the dry, light shape of this magical instrument about which Broderick began to talk, and which he then took from Brady and demonstrated.

He told how its remote ancestor was the Greek *kithara*, whose voice had sounded at certain mysterious ceremonies of the ancient world. The modern guitar, Broderick said, came into Spain in the ninth century, in the hands of the Arab singer Ziryab. It was refined, added to; more strings were tried. Perfected, it routed the lute, and had reigned supreme ever since. He looked triumphant; and Brian proudly shared in this triumph, holding his guitar.

In subsequent lessons, Brady was shown how to pluck the individual strings, and was taught the use of the thumb to produce the rich bass notes: a special action in flamenco known as *pulgar*. Flamenco players, Broderick said, had a power that classical guitarists couldn't match. And while Brady patiently plucked the strings, Broderick went on telling him about the nature of the guitar. Occasionally he brought flamenco records to the lessons, some of them old wax 78s, to play them on a massive radiogram of Sandy's that stood in a corner. Brady was introduced to the hollow, wild majesty of the semi-legendary Ramón Montoya; to Nino Ricardo; to Sabicas, the reigning king. And all the time, sitting with his dark raincoat trailing open, sleepy-lidded eyes expressionless, Broderick talked on about the guitar and its history.

He was like a teacher, Brady told me, except that he was never boring; and although he had such a quiet, almost monotonous voice, it somehow made you tingle; you wanted to hear everything. He told how this particular, woman-shaped creature of polished spruce and rose-wood that Brady held in his arms had come from the workshop of José Ramirez of Madrid, one of a line of great guitar makers who had treated the building of guitars as a problem of physics and mathematics, and had set out to plumb the unplumbable: to discover what it is that makes the perfect guitar.

The Ramirez family came as close as anyone, Broderick said; but no one would ever solve the mystery completely; there would never be a perfect formula, and magically perfect guitars would always occur by chance, and themselves would have little imperfections that were part of the secret of their beauty.

'No real mystery can be solved,' Broderick said.

His cold eyes were fixed on Brian; he sat back in his chair, raincoat flung open, hands in trouser pockets, his legs extended in front of him, casually crossed. 'That's why it's a mystery—like those mysteries of religion your Church talks about.' He faintly smiled.

'I don't listen to that stuff any more,' Brian said.

Broderick raised his eyebrows. 'No? Does it bore you?'

'I just don't believe in it now.'

Broderick was silent for so long that Brian grew uneasy. Sitting at ease in the same position, legs extended, the man finally spoke again, in a tone which assumed that Brian would be interested, but which was casual at the same time; almost perfunctory. 'Eventually you may discover mysteries that are less boring,' he said. 'They might make you lonely—but if you're strong enough, they'll make you master of your life, instead of a victim. The Church sees you as a victim.'

What had he meant by this?

I badgered Brady to try and extract a guess; I found his simpleminded casualness maddening. But it was no use; he said he didn't know; and Broderick hadn't pursued the matter.

3
MRS DILLON

And once it fell upon a day,
A cauld day and a snell,
When we were frae the hunting come,
That frae my horse I fell;
The Queen o Fairies she caught me,
In yon green hill to dwell.

1

He came into my room like a marauder, as he'd done when we were children—entering as he always did, by climbing the Himalayan pine and dropping from an overhanging branch on to my balcony. His old black bicycle was left leaning against the tree-trunk below, his guitar and a haversack on the carrier. He wore jeans and a dark pea-jacket, and his eyes shone with the light of some unusual stimulation, half-exultant and half despairing; or so it seemed to me. It was six o'clock on a Friday evening, two weeks from the end of final term.

He lit a cigarette, standing in the middle of my room, and his fingers shook a little.

'What's wrong?' I asked.

'I'm out,' Brady said. 'Finished. Heading back to the farm tonight, on the bike. Want to join me?'

When I began to question him, he said: 'No time to talk, mate. I've got into a bit of trouble. Are you coming, or not? You won't need to bring much.'

I stared at him. 'You mean *ride* up there? Now? It's eighty miles. And I'm taking the exams, even if you aren't.'

'You can swot up there; bring your bloody books, if you must. What's the matter? Too tough a ride for you?' He almost sneered. 'Your leg's good enough to do it, Dick. We'll sleep by the road tonight. Or are you too cosy here?' And his eyes went derisively about the room, reducing to an old woman's clutter my library, my desk, and Pollock's Toy Theatre on its shelf by the radiogram.

I hesitated. The ride would be hard, and I wasn't sure that I could do it; but he was asking me to share, if only at second-hand, the thrilling wind of risk: to give up crippledom.

'I'll come,' I said.

Our ride up the winding East Coast Highway comes back to me now like the memory of some initiation by torture. Exultancy mingles with unvoiced pleas for mercy; beauty is seen through pain, its images floating past a dim window of distress, the one serious reality the aching, weakening muscles of my game left leg, whose strength both Brady and I had overestimated.

On the night of setting out, when we slept after midnight in a barn near the township of Sorell, all went well. I continued to be confident, before sleep—to be filled with jubilation, in fact, as though I'd broken out into the world, never to be confined again. I'd ridden some thirty miles of highway between fields and through sleeping little towns; now, wakeful and shivering under an old overcoat, listening to Brady's heavy breathing and the sighing of the flatland wind, I was proud of my new strength. I saw myself as a rover like him, in the adult future that waited close at hand; a cripple no more.

But the next day, I began to be in trouble. The island's early summer had left us, and as we rode on under a steady drizzle, through sombre, dripping gum-forests empty of towns, my left leg ached and trembled, pleading to be spared. Brady was always out in front, a tireless, powerful, hunched-over figure who never looked back, his guitar case slung across his shoulders; and I began to be tempted to call out to him; to beg him to wait, to rest.

But I wouldn't, I'd sworn it to myself. Desperately, I made my quavering leg push and push, my books and haversack growing heavy on the carrier, my useless walking-stick tied to the handlebars. The road moved inland at times, the white East Coast beaches appearing and disappearing like visions. I grew weak and dizzy, but said nothing to Brady. Occasionally we drank water from the creeks we crossed, walking underneath the little bridges where it smelled profoundly of earth and rotting willow leaves. I was too tired to speak, at these stops. I pedalled on, a soaked animal in harness, my breath coming in sobs, wheeling above ancient, sullen gulleys that were dense with tall timber. The few cars that passed spattered us with mud.

Eventually I found that Brady was drawing away on the long, steep hills. Once he looked back and smiled cruelly, and I hated him, deranged by pain and exhaustion. Perhaps he'd always resented my grandfather's prosperous house, I said; maybe he'd envied me the comforts I enjoyed, while he must endure being a boarder; and this was his revenge. Had he lured me on this ridiculous ride simply to torment me, now that his final exam was thrown away?

Towards five o'clock, pushing deliriously up yet another hill, I knew I must soon give up. But then my agony ended.

Clearing the brow of a final rise, we'd come out of the hills and the enclosing gum forests, their metal-green ramparts left behind; we coasted downhill, freewheeling, in a long, splendid arc of relief, where my leg need pump no more. At the bottom, we were out on to a white, straight road that ran above the beaches near Swansea, in open, moor-like, tussock country of she-oaks and tea tree, with no human signs except phone wires, and the dry-stone walls along the paddocks, built by the pioneers. The rain was over, and these sweet, pale spaces lifted my heart.

I called out wordlessly to the distant Brady, like a young hound barking, and my cousin waved back, showing that he understood. A clean, easterly wind blew in gusts, and the small, deserted beaches and grey ocean, with spray gesturing above East Coast granite, were not forbidding:

they were pictures of the wild future; Brady's future.

He'd assaulted Brother Kinsella.

This enormity had taken place yesterday afternoon in the empty dormitory, where he'd gone to practise his guitar. The dormitory was off-limits at that time; but there was nowhere else to practise, he said. He had sat on his bed, tuning; and after a few moments had looked up to find that the Navvy had come in the door at the far end.

Brother Kinsella had demanded that Brady surrender his guitar; and Brian had refused. The Navvy had insisted, saying that the instrument would be confiscated; and he had then tried to seize it; to lay hands on the sacred Ramirez.

'So I sank my right in that bloody great gut,' Brady said; and now I had to imagine the unimaginable.

At first, gasping for breath, holding his belly with both hands, Brother Kinsella had looked studiously at the floor. Then, picking up his glasses, and drawing wheezing breaths, he had shuffled up the aisle towards the door, not once looking back. In three more minutes Brady was away.

Far ahead again now, on this straight, white road above the sea, he bent low over the handlebars, tangle of hair fluttering, the guitar bumping on his back. He pedalled into the gusty twilight towards home: the farm called Greystones, near Swansea, where a dubious welcome awaited him. Pewter and pink clouds rose ahead of him like portals; dry yellow tussocks bent in the paddocks, and breakers curled and crashed on the latest empty beach. Plover wheeled, urgently calling; everything moved, in this glass-clear, windy landscape that was not like Tasmania at all, but some remote Scottish moorland. He was already riding into territories beyond the island.

2

Set well back from the highway, the Brady house was built of the orange, hand-made bricks of the early days, with a slate roof from which two attic windows peered like eyes. Michael Brady had acquired land here in 1858, some years after being granted his pardon; he and his men had built the house, and had piled up the dry-stone walls in the paddocks. I would pick one of these rocks from its place, and wonder if my great-great-grandfather's hands had touched it.

Greystones was a last little pocket of the nineteenth century, a mixed farm where kerosene lamps were still the only form of lighting. These were maintained because Brian's father, my uncle Mick, refused to pay the government's electrical bills. Short, stocky and powerful, with greying, brutally cropped dark hair, Mick Brady had the snubby face of an Irish boxer: up-turned nose, jaw jutting, dark eyes watching for an opening, harbouring a bitter resentment.

A good deal of this resentment had to do with the fact that his wife took in paying guests for the summer. It wasn't a prosperous property; the thin, sandy soil would never provide rich crops, and a significant part of the farm's income came from its role as Dora Brady's unofficial guest house. This rankled with Mick; he despised the prosperous guests, whose bags he must carry from the bus when they arrived. But his only revenge was to sneer behind their backs at their talk of Greystones being 'quaint'; a relic of the colonial past. 'Like to see those snooty bastards milkin' cows in winter,' he said. 'They wouldn't find *that* too quaint.' He repeated the word with loathing, making it a mincing parody of all refinement. '*Quaint!* Jesus!' He smiled savagely, like a dog.

The guests, for their part, tolerated the farm's simplicity because they valued its seclusion, its deserted beach, and all its simple rituals, like Dora's morning tea on the verandah.

I had the pleasant status of a guest; but Brian, now officially expelled from St Augustine's, had become Mick's farmhand: a servant of the property. His father had told him he could work for his keep, or else leave home; so Brian now laboured a six-day week and a ten-hour day for which he was paid thirty shillings, while I went swimming or walking, or studied for my exams on the verandah.

Uncle Mick was awed by my ability at such arcane

subjects as Latin and History. Gesturing with his fork over lunch in the kitchen, where he continued to wear his grey felt hat, he held me up as an example.

'This boy here,' he said to Brian, 'he's a scholar. Dick knows that learning'll get you anywhere. You'll be digging ditches, or in jail—that's how *you'll* bloody well end up.' He had set his heart on Brian's matriculating; now he brooded over his son with angry disappointment, and he sneered at the guitar as the cause of Brian's disgrace. The instrument affronted Mick; it was a frivolous object he saw no sense in.

'Playing the *gee*-tar,' he said to me one evening. Leering, inviting me to leer too, he jerked his thumb at Brian, who sat practising on the back verandah. 'Look at him,' Mick said. 'Serious as a pig pissin'.' He burst out laughing, while Brian stared coldly into his laughter. 'Serious as a pig pissin',' Mick repeated. The phrase pleased him.

Sometimes I would help them both with such jobs as rounding up the few sheep, or hosing out dung from the bails in the cowsheds; but the surly presence of Mick made me uncomfortable. My uncle wasn't a man who loved the land; the land had betrayed him, and the animals enslaved him. He kicked the reluctant cows into the bails with a personal animosity, menacing in his hat, his stubby figure electric with rage.

The house had two verandahs running front and back, connected by the central hall; and these verandahs, with their green-painted posts of knotted gum-boughs, had always marked out the two natures of Greystones.

The front verandah, with its easy chairs overlooking the sea and its tarpaper underfoot, was the guests' territory; the territory of holiday. It looked east, to where the sun rose each morning above granite mountains called the Hazards, across the bay; lavender peaks which always suggested the remote South Sea islands, beyond the sun's glittering track. Each morning, as I walked up the dim hall, these peaks and the dark blue bar of ocean waited, framed in the open front door; and stepping into the sun on the verandah, I was greeted by the scents of hot tarpaper, melting butter, and the roses and honeysuckle in Dora Brady's garden.

The back verandah, looking towards the dark green inland hills and the bush, smelling of sheepdogs and cream from the separating room, was farm territory; Mick's territory. Every evening, he still lit the kerosene lamps there which he gathered from every room in the house, setting them up on the rail in a row. And seeing him, squat and solemn, carrying out his ceremony while big shadows sprang around him, I would recall how Brian and I watched when we were small; when the lamps had been like signals in the vastness of country night.

'Stupid old bastard,' Brian said. 'He spends as much on kero now as he would on electric power, if he got connected. He's mad.'

In my room at night, where we sat and smoked, Brian confided his plans. When he was ready, and when he'd saved a little money, he would go away. What he really wanted to do was to go on studying with Broderick; to master the guitar. Then, eventually, he'd escape to the mainland, and get into the country music circuit. For now, he practised his guitar in every spare moment.

Meanwhile, I worked at my books. I was only there for a fortnight, at the end of that November, before I had to go back to take my exams. But the odd thing is that in retrospect it seems much longer, that period at Greystones; or else it seems to be outside time altogether, a place where time became suspended. Perhaps this is because of all that eventually happened; but I suppose too it was the nature of the place itself.

Before things began to happen, I was already in a curious state of mind. I found myself thinking of demons, as I moved about the property; and this was partly because I had demons of my own to resist. I had always seen the countryside as sexless; but now I saw that the land was not innocent, any more than the island itself was innocent. Half-seen shapes of lust and fear lurked in the sulking green bush, where I wandered about alone; and at times I caught the land looking at me out of the corner of its eye. Or perhaps something else did, while the bush seemed to sulk, its viscous gum-leaves gleaming like metal, the grey hair of its she-oaks trailing to the ground in what looked like sorrow.

Then I would remember that we were in Van Diemen's Land, where crimes and monotonous misery had made their indelible traces a hundred years ago; where transported pickpockets from the rookeries and thieves' kitchens of St Giles and Camden Town had yearned for a London they would never see again; where the sealers and shepherds and convicts, out of reach of the Government in Hobart, had made slaves and victims of the doomed Aborigines, hanging the heads of the husbands about the necks of the wives, using the amputated fingers to tamp their pipes. And I wondered at times if the spirits that vanished race had believed in, as well as their own reproachful spirits, still lingered here in the gullies or among the dunes.

The Aborigines had been bound in fear by a demon called Rowra, who had to be appeased, together with other evil spirits. Towards the end, when the colonists had hunted them to the edge of extinction, the women began to go off at night and perform 'devil dances'; frenzied moonrites for Rowra, who now required blood: the sacrifice of their infants. The last of her race, 'Queen' Trucanini, had died in Hobart with his name on her lips, calling out in terror for her white mistress to come to her bedside.

'Oh missus, Rowra catch me—Rowra catch me!' These were her last words, poor Trucanini; she had seen him coming, at the end.

Was Rowra still here?

Sometimes, in the bush that began beyond the top pasture, or on the empty beach at mid-morning where middens of shells from the Aboriginal camps could still be found, I imagined that Rowra was watching me, in the simmering silence. Alone in such places, with warm smells of salt and seaweed rising from the ground, I would unexpectedly find my groin hollowing, and images of naked girls would arrive. But no live bodies were here; only the giant, warm body of the land, above which crows were calling, with a sound like ugly infants. I would think then of Hazel Pearce.

Hazel was Dora Brady's hired help. She lived in, working in the kitchen and cleaning the guests' rooms. About the same age as Brian and myself, and shy to the point of being mute, she was simply referred to by the Bradys as 'the girl'. She was never included in conversations; she spoke only in monosyllables, and ate her meals alone. St Augustine's had given me little experience of talking to girls; but once I'd opened the kitchen door for her, and she had smiled sideways, quickly. She was one of the Pearces: a large family who lived on a small farm out in the hills, where the soil was poor and a few families went on scratching out a bare subsistence—milking small herds of cows, keeping pigs, drinking and feuding, cousins marrying cousins. Grotesques were said to be produced out there among the hillbillies; and Mick told the story that a certain Cooper family had a boy who barked like a dog, and was kept chained up at night. Once, on a Show day, Mick said, the boy was taken in to Hobart and led through the streets on his chain. The dog-boy was one of the few things that made Mick amused.

But Hazel was not grotesque; she was small and pretty, with a trim figure, a cloud of heavy brown hair, a delicate, pointed chin, and green eyes that I thought beautiful. She moved always in the background, in her cheap print dress and fawn cardigan, shoulders bent; curiously neutral, here and yet not here, sweeping in dim corners of the house, picking up sticks for the fire, or filling a jug at the water-tank.

3

Thousands more stars stream across the sky here than in town, white and big on glass-thin blackness, brighter by far, in the island's thin atmosphere, than the glimmer of the township up the coast. Head back, I grow giddy staring at Orion's belt, and the Milky Way; I stride among tussocks,

in the empty midnight moorland of Greystones, where
plover pipe their old, wild loneliness.

Coming back to the house, I catch sight of the couple in
the shadows of the back verandah.

They are standing against the water tank, outlined against
the silver gleam of the corrugated iron; and they don't see
me because they are kissing. Brian is so much taller than
she that her head is craned back as far as mine was to look
at the stars; and in the moment that I see them, their faces
separate, and they stare at each other as though trying to
fathom some question.

I step on to the verandah and cross to the open back
door without their seeing me. But not before I've heard
their whispers—trite and unforgettable.

'You're beautiful.'

'An' you're handsome. An' that's no lie.'

I lie sleepless in my room, whose window opens on to
the front verandah. The night stays unusually warm. Through
the window, the sounds of Greystones come: the sighing
roar of breakers, and a far-off crying heard nowhere else:
two long notes, high and then low. Its source baffled me,
once; now I know it to be fairy penguins, down on the
rocks. But their crying tonight has a tragic urgency, not
like birds' voices at all: a drawn-out plaint like wind on
rock, immensely far, summoning me out of the room.

I climb through the window in my pyjamas, cross the
front verandah, and limp down the three steps into Dora's
front garden. The bright new moon is high. Below the pale
sacking of the paddocks and the dry-stone wall of the
garden, the sea can be sensed, rather than seen: a dark,
giddy opening in the wall of the world. The booming of
the waves is imperative and crisp out here, and the crying
of the penguins more distinct. Without thought, I wander
round to the southern side of the house, where the kitchen
and bathroom are, above a small gulley.

An old wooden gutter carries water from the bathroom
and the kitchen down into the gulley's depths, and there's
the rank smell of the drainwater here. It's not a place to
linger in. The bathroom light is on, even though it's so

late, laying a yellow rectangle across the ragged grass. I begin to skirt this, glancing briefly and with little curiosity at the window, whose blind I expect to be drawn. But it isn't drawn: it's up, and the window as well.

A narrow stage-set alight in the dark, the green-walled chamber at first appears empty. The deep old country bath with its wood-chip heater can't be seen from where I stand; but faint steam is drifting from it. On the marble wash-stand is a wicker bassinet, and I can see an infant's kicking feet and one reaching hand. I hear it chatter, and can hear too the splashing of the occupant of the bath. Then there is the sound of released water gurgling and the faint thud of feet on the floor. I know I should move on but don't; and the first naked woman of my life runs lightly into the frame. My heart leaps as though in terror.

Golden, beautiful, her pale hair drawn up in a bun, she shines in the light of Mick's kerosene pressure lamp above her head, her body white as its flare, white as the breakers on the beach, whose sound comes muffled here. She is real and yet not; she may vanish; and her reality is made more unlikely by the fact that she's a stranger.

I've never seen her before: not about the house, nor on the front verandah where the guests gather in the mornings. She must have just arrived, on the evening bus. Shining with water, veiled in her own steam, her flushed, exquisite face bare of makeup, gracefully trailing a green towel in one hand, she comes to a gingerly halt on the balls of her feet, fully presented to the window, and smiles with her face in profile to the unseen baby. Her face is young, her waist frail and tender; but her breasts, which jolted and lunged as she came, are not tipped by the pale, demure pink buds of the women in paintings, but by big magenta circles: maternal fruits whose ripeness is both noble and appalling. Slow as a dream, in her frame, she is otherwise the twin of one of the nude divinities in the books on my grandfather's shelves: those sombre volumes dealing with Greek sculpture and Renaissance painting. It's only when she bends over the bassinet and murmurs to the infant that I finally admit that I'm not spying on a vision: that I'm not intended to see her.

I back away towards the edge of the gulley; and as I do so, she stands erect and looks out the window directly to where I am, her light eyes narrowing.

My nerves shrill their alarm. Has she seen me? Panic making me stumble, I limp away fast into the dark.

4

The sun stood high above the Hazards.

Mrs Dillon sat reading a book on the verandah of the guests, silky blonde hair spilling forward, her baby sleeping at her feet in its wicker bassinet. I took a chair nearby, not too close, and pretended to study my History textbook. It was the second morning I had done this.

Questioning my aunt with sly casualness, I had discovered all I could about Deirdre Dillon. She came from Sydney; her husband was a wealthy businessman who had not accompanied her. She had been coming to Greystones, although I hadn't met her before, from girlhood; and she had grown up in Hobart, where her father Robert Brennan owned Brennan's Sporting Goods, the biggest store of its kind in the city. And there seemed little connection between this well-turned-out matron and my vision in the bathroom window. Her hair, instead of being piled up on her head, was now centre-parted and worn shoulder-length, in two correct, smooth wings that rolled under at the ends. Even her face was different: she used eye-shadow and bright lipstick, like a model; and like many mainlanders, she wore clothes that were subtly smarter than those of most Tasmanian women. Even in the casual dress suitable to holiday, she had the formal look of a woman born to money.

Today there was no one else on the verandah; the other guests hadn't yet come up from the beach for their tea and scones. She and I read in silence.

Then the impossible happened; Mrs Dillon spoke to me.

'How is your leg these days?'

It was a low, well-spoken, authoritative voice, and I

looked up in startlement. It seemed that our acquaintance was beginning in the middle.

'It's getting better,' I said. My tone was abrupt; I hardly used the walking-stick at all, and felt entitled to have my limp ignored. A breaker fell distinctly on the beach; then it could be heard sucking back. There were crickets beyond the walls of the garden.

'I know all about you, from your Aunt Dora,' said Mrs Dillon. 'I'm glad you're getting better. You must have had to be brave, when you were small.'

I was embarrassed by this, but the smell of hot tarpaper was incense now. Did she know about the window? Unthinkable. Yet her light blue eyes were studying me with odd intentness. They were well-spaced eyes, with clear whites; and the way she had widened them gave her the look of a solemn, surprised, small girl, or of one of those expensive dolls small girls carried about: a Dutch doll, I decided. It was suggested by her fair skin, which looked as though it was never in hot sun, and by her features: the short nose; the mouth of exactly the right fullness, and the firm, round chin that I found perfect; and it was emphasised by her skilfully darkened brows and lashes, and the smooth, flax-blonde hair falling to her shoulders.

We began now to talk more easily. She looked at my books, and asked about my final exams, and St Augustine's. She was a Catholic too, she said, and had gone to the nuns for Sunday School as a girl. But her schooling had been at an Anglican Ladies' College; her father had thought they turned out a better product. She looked sly at this, prepared to joke at herself. Finally, at something I said about the Brothers, she threw her head back and laughed. It was a clever, pleasant laugh, and seemed to me very sophisticated. She was amused by my description of Brother Kinsella; I had compared him to the Beadle in Oliver Twist, and now did an imitation of his voice.

'You should be an actor,' she said.

Carried away I almost considered bringing in my belch; but I thought better of it.

'Would you like to be an actor?' she asked. *'Wonderful, if you were. I love the theatre, don't you?'*

I told her of my ambitions. I wanted to act, I said, but I wanted most to be a producer; I believed this was where my real talent lay. She didn't laugh at me; she nodded shrewdly, and looked impressed, as though these dreams were possible. Then she said: 'Why don't you come over here? It's such a strain, *shouting* like this.' As I lurched to the chair next to her, we both laughed at the drolly deep, exaggerated intonation she had used on the word 'shouting'. We had the same sense of humour, I thought, and grew absurdly elated.

'I was an actress, once,' she said, and nodded quickly, like a child wishing to convince. 'Nothing important—just amateur dramatics. I was in the Hobart *Repertory*.' Her deep stress on the last word signalled amusement again. 'But it wasn't a bad little company,' she said, 'and we did do some good things. I was supposed to be rather talented, and my father sent me to drama school in Sydney for a while—but then I met my husband, and that was *that*.' She sighed, her mouth made small, her voice taking on a childish note, her eyes round and regretful: the Dutch doll's. There was a hint of doll-like fatuousness, as well; but it didn't lessen my adoration. I began to see that Mrs Dillon had two faces, which alternated unpredictably: an indulged, precocious child's (the doll's), and a mature, cultivated woman's, used to having her whims obeyed.

And she was two people in another way, I thought. Beneath her respectable blue cardigan and tartan skirt, she was the other, nameless woman in the lit window; that frame which had held her beauty as my toy theatre had held Titania's. Shame and tender amazement filled me at this; but she smiled with friendly interest, not dreaming that every line of her hidden body was known.

'So now I'm a wife and mother,' she declared. 'No more acting.'

'Wouldn't your husband let you go on with it?' I asked.

She stared at this boldness. 'Not *him*.'

Her tone didn't invite further enquiry, and we both fell

silent. I knew that Aunt Dora's morning tea-time must be close; that soon we'd no longer be alone. I could see the pygmy figures of old Mr Chandler the bank manager and his wife toiling up from the beach through the lower paddocks.

'I might be able to give you a few hints,' Mrs Dillon said suddenly. 'About acting, I mean.'

I thanked her, calling her 'Mrs Dillon'.

'Please stop calling me Mrs Dillon. Call me Deirdre. You haven't learned elocution, have you? I thought not. Your accent's good, but you've got a bit careless with those vowel sounds. I could help you brush those up.' Her own accent, like that of most women of prosperous backgrounds in that era, was middle-class English; no doubt largely produced by her Ladies' College.

'I'll see you here tomorrow,' she said. 'Shall I? You can read to me, and we'll work on your voice. Come an hour before morning tea—then we'll be by ourselves, until the boring *guests* arrive.'

I was flooded with delight, and flattered by the implication that a special, shared difference made Deirdre Dillon and myself more interesting than other people.

How was I to wait until tomorrow morning?

That night, Brian Brady left home for good, riding his bicycle back down the highway to Hobart. He didn't say goodbye to me, and I only found out about it the next day. A quarrel had taken place between him and Mick, the details of which I never learned.

Mick had been getting uglier towards Brian. Sometimes his complaints were open; at others they were grumbled behind Brian's back. (*'That bloody boy. Didn't strip the cows properly yesterday. Useless.'*) And Mick's animosity had been increased by Brian's affair with Hazel Pearce. He wasn't sure that anything serious was going on between them, but he plainly suspected it, and forbade Brian to have any more to do with the girl than was necessary.

But Brian had taken no notice. On a recent afternoon, I had seen him with Hazel in the barn, playing his guitar to

her: the full cowboy lover, I said. But my amusement had
been feigned; I had looked at them with quite another
emotion.

It was the first time I had actually heard Brian sing. The
sound came to me as I crossed the yard; I had peered in the
open doorway of the barn and waved; but they hadn't seen
me. He sat on an apple box, one foot propped on a
kerosene tin, accompanying himself on the guitar, a shaft
of late sun through a crack in the boards catching one side
of his face and tangled hair. Hazel Pearce, standing against
an old tractor, small in her cotton dress of faded blue and
white, was plainly nervous at being truant from the kitchen,
and had the stance of someone who had merely paused
there. But her face was alight, her eyes fixed on Brian as
though what he sang contained all the rhymes her life
would ever need.

Already his fingering on the guitar was good, and the
maturity of his deep voice was surprising. He was singing
'Lonesome Whistle'—one of the Hank Snow ballads often
on country radio stations, about which I grew sarcastic.
But I had to admit he sang it well. He didn't imitate Hank
Snow's American drawl; he had a plangent resonance of
his own which made the ballad personal: his own song of
vagrancy and train-cry, where Carolina became Tasmania.

His voice followed me across the yard.

> 'All I do is sit and cry
> When the evening train goes by;
> I heard that lonesome whistle blow . . .'

Sitting in my room, I said that I didn't envy Brian and
Hazel. But the sight of them had pierced me with a sort of
abstract longing: a simple, silly wish to be what they were.
I was already cleverer than Brady; I knew things he would
never know; but I would never sing 'Lonesome Whistle' like
that, and little Hazel would never be my girl. My regret
carried a mournful pleasure that would lead to many things.

*   *   *

5

'You stay, son, if you want to,' my aunt said at breakfast. 'Just because Brian's been driven out of his home doesn't mean you have to go too.'

Dora banged one of the lids down on her black, wood-burning stove. Her far-staring eyes, which were Brian's, were red-rimmed; her big chin thrust out, she looked at her husband in a way he avoided, and Mick moved out of the kitchen with the quiet of an invalid, his hat pulled low.

So now I was left here alone: a guest. This morning, my lessons with Deirdre Dillon would begin.

Mrs Dillon disliked the verandah when it grew too hot.

'I'm not going to be boiled like a lobster, thank you very much,' she said. She nodded with humorous emphasis, in her parody of a wilful child. And she asked Dora for the use of the small, private sittingroom; a room hardly ever used, and closed to guests.

It had a window on the verandah but this was always closed, its heavy brown curtains drawn, protecting the Genoa velvet of its armchairs and couch. Deirdre Dillon and I were alone in its dimness every morning, and I read to her there from novels she produced, as well as from unread books of English verse we found in Aunt Dora's glass-fronted bookcase: Keats, Tennyson, Longfellow, Masefield. There was a fragrance of varnished woodwork pickled in ozone.

Deirdre was serious and efficient about these lessons, stopping me with mock-severity when she considered my 'a' or 'i' sounds too crudely Australian. And she taught me how to produce my voice from the diaphragm; how to project it as an actor should.

She was kindly, humorous, yet apparently serious about me, as few other people had ever been, and I tormented myself constantly with the question: *why?* I was sometimes humiliated by the idea that Dora Brady had told her to be nice to me; people were always being sorry about my leg. Or perhaps she was bored, and enjoyed the diversion of a seventeen-year-old courtier, whose worship must have been plain in his eyes.

'I know I just didn't *grow,* until I got out of this bloody little island,' she said. 'You'll have to come to the mainland, Richard. It's amazing that a boy can be so intellectually advanced, stuck away in Hobart, and going to those thuggish Christian Brothers. You'd have gone to the Jesuits, if *I'd* had you. That's where my son Patrick goes.'

'Have you got a son, as well?' I was horrified. She was too young.

'He's my stepson, really. My husband's first wife died. Patrick's sixteen—almost as old as you, dear. So I could be *your* mother, couldn't I?'

This was untrue; ridiculous, I said.

I could see that Deirdre Dillon was still in her late youth, and scarcely marked by time. In fact, she was twenty-eight, but looked no more than twenty. Sometimes, in my secret thoughts about her, I would say: *She's just a girl;* and this formula, this fiction about a youthful matron, placed her almost within my reach. My infatuation had reached that point.

'I was twenty-two when I married,' she said. 'Dadda said that was too young. But my husband was a very strong-willed man—and determined to marry me.' Nodding once, mouth small to indicate something was settled, she looked to one side in a way that didn't invite further questions.

On most of these mornings she had the baby Fiona with her, and when I came in, exactly at ten o'clock, I always found her there before me, the baby usually asleep in its bassinet. But on some mornings she would nurse it, sitting sideways. Refraining from looking, I would sit in the chair opposite, and read aloud to her. It was usually a bright day outside, but in here it was always dim, only a panel of sun coming in through the curtains. It smelled like one of those mysterious little boxes women kept on their dressing-tables: boxes that gave out a faint scent, but which usually proved to be empty. It recalled the sewing-room at Trent Street.

She would speak of her lost stage ambitions. 'I was told

I could have done rather well,' she said once. 'I had a very good figure, Richard, believe it or not.' She sighed, gazing down on the baby in martyred reverie. 'But once you're a mother, your girlish figure's gone.' As though to confirm her words, she lowered the infant to her lap, leaving her deathly, blue-netted breast quivering and bare; and now she and the woman in the bathroom window were one.

'I don't think your figure's gone,' I said. 'I think you're beautiful.'

She looked across at me, her eyes paling. 'Thank you, Richard,' she said. 'You're very gallant.' Her green blouse quickly done up, she reached for her packet of Craven A cigarettes, and lit one. I disliked it when she smoked; her face became harder, her eyes squinting.

'By the way,' she said, 'tomorrow morning we'll have to skip our lesson—I'm playing golf with Mr Gibson. I'm sure you'll be glad of a break from your ageing actress.'

6

At the hour when we'd usually have met, I went down to the beach and swam far out into the breakers, chopping furiously into their bottlegreen sides. There were no guests on the sand; the dazzling white curve was deserted. Soon I was past the line where the waves curled and broke, lying on my back in the swell and staring up at the sun.

I had been told not to come out this far: there were undertows. But water was the element in which I was as fast and strong as the most athletic man on land: my years on crutches had given me powerful shoulders. Nothing else mattered but the sea, with its masculine bite of salt, its feminine loll and sway. Drifting and dipping, its big hand under me, I moved towards the line of the horizon.

But this morning, something went wrong. I had turned, and was swimming back towards the beach; but the hand underneath continued to move me towards the horizon. I swam harder; but when I paused and looked up, the beach and the slate roof of Greystones were alarmingly far off.

I wasn't really afraid of my favourite element; I swam

seriously, head down. But then I began to tire; I took a mouthful and gasped, and the sea became a cold, vindictive vastness. I entered a state of weakness that instinct told me was the prelude to drowning; and fear covered me now like a glass dome. I swam on, without hope.

When I put my head up again, it was to see that the beach and the grey roof were much closer. The hand had relinquished its grip.

I limped up the beach, the warm, domestic smells coming into my nose like baking cakes, filling me with humble gratitude. Shuddering, I made my way through marram grass over the low dunes, leaving behind me the iodine-smell of danger, the breakers and the cries of gulls; hearing instead the sweet chitter of landbirds. I went on up the gentle track through the paddocks, beside the hawthorn hedge.

She was waiting for me where the sandy track came to the first dry-stone wall, smiling calmly from under a white linen hat.

'Were you in trouble out there?'

'I got in a rip.'

'I thought so. Mr Gibson and I were watching from the verandah. He said you'd be all right, but I wasn't sure.'

'Aren't you playing golf?'

'I didn't feel like it.'

I began to go on up the hill, limping in my swimming trunks and old sweater, and she walked by my side. She should have been less calm, I felt.

'You're a very strong swimmer,' she said. 'Aren't you? You looked like some sort of wounded hero, walking out of the sea. Byronic, with that limp. I adore Byron, don't you?'

'I prefer Shelley,' I said pompously; but she wasn't discouraged.

'Wonderful Shelley,' she enthused. 'Have you read "Queen Mab"? "How wonderful is Death, Death and his brother Sleep!" ' She broke off, and laughed. 'Shelley was mad about the sea like you, and *he* drowned. Lost in his yacht, in a storm off Viareggio, and they burned his body on the beach. Byron plucked his heart out of the fire. Who but Byron would have done that?'

And I was filled with excitement. This was no longer the east coast of Tasmania, it was the Mediterranean; and the whirring of crickets was a dry yet frantic chorus, telling me how love and death were linked.

Suddenly she asked: 'Do you really want to go on with my silly coaching lessons?'

They weren't silly, I said. They were the best things that had ever happened to me.

'I lik them too,' she said softly. 'But I wonder if they're good for us? You mustn't get too intense, dear. Nor must I.' She stared, her eyes large; her face had become the Dutch doll's. And then, pushing the hat from her head so that it hung behind by its strings, she leaned and rubbed her cheek against mine, one hand on my arm, the silky strands of her hair tickling my neck.

What was she doing? In icy amazement, I put my hand on a shoulder left bare by her green and white sun-dress; but now she moved away and drew me on up the hill, holding my hand.

'Why don't we go for a picnic tomorrow, just the two of us?' she said. 'Dora will pack us sandwiches, and mind Fiona for me. There'd be no harm in that, would there?'

7

She sat erect in pale, dry grass on the headland above the beach, legs crossed in her full skirt, combing her hair, which blew sideways in the sea breeze. Then she replaced her white linen hat.

I was glad she wore the same hat and the green and white sun-dress, whose broad straps crossed her shoulders. These belonged to the time that had begun yesterday, and like all lovers I was superstitious about such things. An empty vacuum flask stood beside her in the grass; we had drunk our tea, and the afternoon of the picnic was already late.

'You really should come to Sydney,' she said. 'You

can't waste yourself here, Richard, if you want to get into the theatre. The only good drama school's there.'

Was this an invitation?

'My husband and I could help you, if you came,' she said. 'Michael has influence everywhere.'

'What does he do—your husband?'

'Oh—he has a lot of *interests*.' Her voice deepened on this word, to make business interests comical. But when I still waited she lapsed into her childish accent, her eyes becoming round, looking out vaguely over the sea. 'I don't know about those things,' she said. 'What he does is very boring.'

'But you must have some idea.'

She shook her head. 'No, it's all very boring. Stocks and shares and things. His father was a millionaire, you know. You must have heard of old James Dillon. No? I thought everyone had. He came out of the slums and made a fortune in property. He owned coal mines and newspapers and things, all over Australia. He was a fearful old man: a fanatic about the Church; gave it scads of his money. Michael did what he said, *I* can tell you.'

I detected a note of contempt in her voice, and probed. 'Is your husband older than you?'

'He's fifty-five,' she said, and I stared at her appalled, while she looked back without expression. But there was a faint nod, as though she conceded that I should be appalled.

Despite her hat, her nose had turned pink, like that of a child who had played too long on the sand, and I treasured this, as I treasured anything that made her look immature. I was now pretending that she wasn't really a young matron of twenty-eight, but a girl who had grown up too soon. I ignored the first fine lines at the corners of her eyes; the faint beginnings of a second chin. I squeezed the twelve-year difference between us into nothing; I willed her to be seventeen, and in the grip of this madness, I blurted out: 'Why did you marry an old man?'

'I felt sorry for him,' she said calmly. 'His wife had just died—and he had Patrick to bring up. I'm very fond of

Patrick, he's a sweet boy. Very sensitive—the opposite of his father.'

'Are you happy with him—your husband?'

The small girl's voice and face vanished, to be replaced by a tone that was cold, brittle and deliberate. 'He's a drunken, coarse boor,' she said. 'Of course I'm not happy with him.'

I stared at her. 'But why do you stay with him?'

'You don't leave a Dillon very easily,' she said. 'Nor a Catholic marriage. Besides, there's the baby now. And my stepson needs me—he really does. You'd *like* Patrick, Richard, you and he are very similar. He and I are a great comfort to each other. He loves music and literature, just as you do: we have wonderful talks.' She giggled. 'Sometimes I think Michael's jealous of us. When he's dead drunk, we can forget he exists. Patrick loathes him. He calls him the Red-Faced Ogre. We shorten that to the RFO.' She laughed again, and would have continued; but I wasn't interested in stories of her stepson, whom I mentally brushed aside.

'You should leave him,' I said. 'You should stay here.' I knew I could say anything, now, and grew drunk with it.

But Deirdre Dillon seemed indifferent to her own atrocious unhappiness. She put a hand over mine, and spoke with discouraging calm. 'If only I could,' she said. 'But you mustn't talk like that. You must forget I ever spoke like this, Richard. It's been such a lovely picnic, hasn't it? And soon we must go.'

She was right. Soon we'd have to walk back to the house, leaving behind the most important afternoon of my life. The time, on her little gold wristwatch, was after six o'clock; across the bay, the Hazards were turning purple, and the island's glass-thin summer light was on the turn, as the tide was. The waves were drawing back, below on the empty beach—an end where no one swam, since the current was treacherous. On our little headland here, above the big rocks of ochre East Coast granite, we were out of sight of Greystones, and of all human eyes; and an immense change was overtaking the landscape. Not sunset, nothing so gaudy and obvious; the island's long summer twilight, subtle and profound. Everything was slowed and transfigured by a deceptive, honeyed radiance that minute by minute made each object unnaturally distinct; and a huge tension began.

It was the dangerous time, when the extraordinary might happen. Seagulls became brilliant as creatures sculpted from snow, wheeling above tangles of iodine-coloured kelp; and the rubbery green creeper called pig-face, with its blazing pink flowers, glowed among the rocks like no earthly plant. Spirits were watching us from the marram grass, I thought, and the salt-white chain of beaches, going north up the coast, reached amazing distances: tiny, uttermost territories of spume and violet mountains, no longer part of the island, nor of any ordinary world.

'I *do* love it here,' Deirdre said softly. 'When I'm home, I never want to go back to Sydney.'

'Don't, then,' I said. 'Don't go.' And then: 'When *are* you going back?'

She didn't answer for a moment. 'Don't ask that,' she said. 'Don't let's spoil things.'

It was she who made the first advance, as before, this time kissing me on the mouth, her lips larger and warmer than I'd expected. When she drew back, the face that reappeared in front of me, like an image on a screen, was the Dutch doll's, blank and solemn. Giddiness made the grass go white and the sea darken to indigo; its horizon revolved. I returned the kiss, gripping her bare shoulders; and I saw that her expression was changing imperceptibly as the light, registering alarm. But I sensed the falsity in this. I was made to know that very few initiatives could be mine; that few things were allowed. I might hold her decorously; I might kiss her and wait to be kissed, and that was all.

'*Now* look what's happened,' she breathed. And: 'You have to be like a son to me, Richard—no more. I'd love to have a son like you.'

But I knew this was nonsense; I was no son. I would come to Sydney, become a great actor, love her with pure devotion until her aged husband died; then I would marry her, I said.

She put her fingers over my mouth. 'Stop,' she said. Then she sat up, and pointed. 'Look at the sea.'

Sunset had finally come, thick in the olive western ranges, and the sea was dimming; but far out, there were light streaks of green. 'It looks like land out there, doesn't it? If only we could go there,' she said. 'Far enough to be safe from everything. From all the people who don't want us to love each other.'

Those were called the Green Meadows of the Sea, I told her. I had found them in a book of Celtic fairy tales: they were a place for souls not quite good enough to enter heaven.

'Only you could have known that,' she said. She laid her cheek against mine, staring out. Even inside happiness, I felt that she revelled in her own fervency, playing a part she had long ago chosen for life.

'You're the one I always waited for,' she said. 'Why did you come too late? Why didn't you come when I was a girl?'

8

And so began my enslavement to the past.

We went to the headland every afternoon for the next four days, with our sandwiches and tea. From their chairs on the front verandah, the old couples watched us go, murmuring.

'Old fools,' Deirdre said. 'They think we're lovers. What do they know about us?'

As soon as we were out of sight of Greystones, we held hands. I was still allowed no more than kisses. Once, when my hand moved on to her thigh, she said: 'How dare you,' and removed the hand. Her clothes were always perfect; passion smelled of fresh ironing. We would kiss for an hour, lying in the grass, and she would dart her tongue into my mouth. But then she would gasp, and say: 'This must stop.' She was like a nubile girl playing sexual games; our delight must always be mingled with guilt, and sometimes she would say: 'I feel someone's *watching*, don't you?' But the beach, and the moorlands of dry grass and tea tree, were always empty.

Deirdre was a shape-changer; I never knew which woman I'd be meeting. On some afternoons it was the child, with her loose flaxen hair hanging about her shoulders, her blank, wondering face, and her small girl's voice; on others, it was the shrewd Sydney sophisticate, hair drawn back in a *chignon*, wearing a smart tweed suit with walking shoes. Her voice then could become severe, making me half afraid that she had grown cold towards me; or else it could be hard and humorous, and she would tell stories about her snobbish Sydney friends, or her husband's obtuse business acquaintances, and go into spasms of laughter, smoking a lot, and coughing and wheezing from the smoke. In this mood, she walked with a comical, energetic motion, arms working, exaggerating the roll of her somewhat short-legged gait, enjoying some private joke on herself. At such times she appeared very Irish, and her eyes reminded me of pale blue seashells. We talked about our ancestry, and decided that our Irish great-great-grandfathers had known each other. The first Brennan here had kept a hotel in Launceston; Michael Brady would surely have drunk there, we said, and this drew us closer, I thought, in a way that her rich mainland husband could never compete with. Her third aspect, the one I longed for but which came very rarely, was the one which denoted true feeling: her face solemn, devout, immobile as a carving's. But it came only seldom, and usually at twilight, when it was time to go back to the house.

Certain things she said stayed in my mind to disturb me.

'*You're such a beautiful boy—I love to kiss you. I hate my husband making love to me—grunting and panting.*'

'*A boy is so pure. What we're doing isn't adultery, darling, is it? Only we know that.*'

'*Being crippled refined you spiritually, Richard. Don't be hurt. You're not normal, of course—and that's why I love you. Neither of us is normal, darling, admit it. I can't bear bloody normal people.*'

'I must go and feed Fiona now. My breasts are aching.'

She talked often about her girlhood, to which, it seemed, she wished to return. We shared the fatal love of lost time: we conjured up the decades of her girlhood, and an earlier one still; the 1920s.

'I *love* the twenties, don't you?' she said. 'People had such fun. My Dadda was a wild young man, then!'

We found we both loved the whole yellowing myth: the Charleston; Scott Fitzgerald; gay young things; Rudy Vallee singing through his megaphone: that decade whose last years had seen her infancy, before I was born. Sometimes, I would suspect she needed to escape reality as much as I did; that she too had been crippled in some way. And in the end, I grasped the fact that if she had lived in the twenties, she would truly have been Dadda's girl . . .

Her father, Robert Brennan, the man she always called 'my Dadda' was never far from her talk. His big store in the middle of Hobart had been familiar to me all my life. I had seen Brennan about the store: a big, florid man with black hair and the same light blue eyes as his daughter. He had always been successful, but in recent years, according to my mother, his heavy drinking had endangered the business. Deirdre laughed about this; for her, the boozy Irish boy who would always come out on top.

'I wish you were still Deirdre Brennan,' I said. 'Then I'd ask you to marry me.'

'Please—don't talk like that. I'm an old woman, and you're a child.' She looked twenty as she said this; she was the young girl today, pale hair floating about her shoulders.

'When are you going back?' I demanded. 'You never say.'

For many moments, she failed to answer. We were walking along the evening beach, which was empty, and clothed in a warm stillness. The surf was small, this evening; the waves fell thoughtfully, and small orange clouds were becalmed above the Hazards.

'Friday' she said and stamped on one of the grapes in a pile of kelp.

'Friday! But that's the day after tomorrow!'

'I know. I didn't want to spoil things.' She moved close, and put her hand on my arm, her voice dropping to coaxing intimacy. 'There's still tomorrow. And we'll see each other again. I'll come to Hobart, to visit my parents. And you're coming to Sydney to be a great actor, remember?'

But now I was shouting wildly. Why hadn't she told me? She mustn't go; she mustn't rejoin a man she didn't love. And I cried out other absurdities I'd rather forget.

Her white face grew indistinct, gazing at me with calm sadness from the deepening dark; her face retreated, and I almost doubted its reality. 'I'll write to you,' she said, and the words seemed to come from a distance.

We were standing near the point of granite rocks below our headland, at the end of the beach. Facing me, she stood with her back to one of these giant, ochre boulders: a long, barrow-shaped edifice as high as a house. Some vast, aboriginal mournfulness gathered here, making her expression seem stricken; but the light was too deceitful for this to be certain.

'I have to go up now,' she said. 'I have to see to Fiona. But I'll meet you back here at eight o'clock. Just this once, we'll go for a night-time walk.' She had never agreed to this before; because of what she called 'appearances', she had only met me by day.

Back at the rocks after dinner, I waited, pacing the few yards of sand while the sea went black and the foam of the waves shone in the dark like phosphorous. I didn't dare leave the spot; I was fearful that she would somehow miss me in the dark.

But this was unlikely. The beach was lit by a full moon, its silver disc standing high and cool above the grassy headland: that headland which had seen all our happiness; that place where our Irish great-great-grandfathers had wanted us to lie; where we had not been ourselves, but other people: she no married woman, I no silly boy; truly lovers, not guilty, free.

The only sounds were the hollow crumpling of breakers, and the piping of plover. Uncannily, the red clouds above the Hazards continued to glow like coals in a grate, even after the peaks had turned black; then they were slowly extinguished. I waited in despair and hope, my true bondage just beginning.

She comes when I least expect it, materialising behind my back as though she's emerged from a cleft in the granite barrow. She's wearing a green cotton dress, and holding a beach-bag: towels, she says; she's brought towels, so that we can swim.

I have to swallow before I can speak. Will we swim without costumes?

Yes, she says, we'll swim without costumes. She has a strange, patient, motherly authority that is different from any way I've seen her. No one from the house ever comes here at night, she says; we'll be perfectly safe.

We walk along the beach to where a little creek runs into the sea: she feels safe in the shallows here, she says; she's not a swimmer. The place is under a huge dome of sky, and the shallow stream makes collapsing sandbanks and multiple runnels; hundreds of seashells stud the wet sand, gleaming in the moon, and the waves boom and sigh far out, their white tops hurrying wildly where the currents meet.

She hands me a towel. 'Keep your distance, remember, and don't look. You've already seen me once.'

'Have I?'

'Yes. Do you think I didn't see *you?*'

She turns away, walking off the sand on to a level place of tussock-grass, where she stops by the dead, silver shape of a fallen gum. And now, some twenty paces off, she ceases to be Deirdre Dillon. The figure by the grey, dead tree, which I covertly watch through my lashes, unbuttoning my shirt with shaking fingers, has changed its shape again, and is no mundane form: distance makes her an image without sound, and removes all personal qualities; even in the bright moonlight, her expression can't be read.

She undoes her green cotton dress, under which she proves to be naked.

Lightly, on the balls of her feet, she runs towards the water, holding with both hands the breasts that make her top-heavy, whose fruits are dark as plums. Night makes her a woman in majestic black and white; even the cirrus of hair between her thighs is ashen. Out in the hissing channel where the creek meets the sea she wades ahead of me, and I'm filled with awe once again by her long, frail waist, by the wide, perfect urn of her hips, and her truly amazing whiteness. She is white as the breakers in the dark; white as driftwood; not just her body, but her hair. Its floating web makes her look both ancient and young; a thought that suddenly repels me, and has to be put from my mind.

She doesn't swim; she wades in the estuary only to the verge of the waves, stooping to scoop up water and let it run down her body. Once, and only once, she smiles across at me. I swim, and don't approach her. When she leaves the water she stands on the sand and briefly raises her arms above her head, as though reaching for a high shelf. Then, before I can reach her, she's turned and is walking back to the fallen tree.

I limp after her, one hand foolishly shielding my groin; when I come close, she's standing with her towel held in front of her, staring at me, her eyes blank and seemingly scornful. I expect her to reprove me; but she lets the towel drop and hang from one hand, holding out the other dead-white arm in silence.

'You're shivering, aren't you? You're cold. You'd better come and dry yourself.' She smiles.

Only the tussock-grass is real, and softly prickles: her flesh is warm in parts, in others, cool from the sea. And the Elle-maid and the farmer's boy, not thought about for years, flit through my head as I tremble. The Elle-maid was hollow behind, like a dough-pan; that was how the boy knew that she was one of the Elle-people, and would bring him sorrow; and he tried to get away. But so great

was the enchantment behind what she did, that he had no
power to resist.

Her face looks down, full of calm majesty. Sand grits
on her skin; from between her parted lips, a gold filling
gleams in a tooth; the gold of her wedding ring glints near
my face. Reality: things of the world.

4
THE BASEMENT

And pleasant is the fairy land,
But, an eerie tale to tell,
Ay at the end of seven years
We pay a tiend to hell;
I am sae fair and fu o' flesh,
I'm feard it be mysel.

1

During the eighteen months I spent at University, I drifted apart from Brady, and saw nothing more of Darcy Burr.

When Brian had come back down the highway from Greystones, Sandy Lovejoy had given him a bed and a job. Once I met him by the doorway of the shop when he was loading furniture into Lovejoy's van. We talked, but were both constrained; we now had so little in common. I seldom passed through Harrigan Street any more, and Brady had now retreated there, in my thoughts. His future as a wandering musician didn't seem to have happened; perhaps he'd remain a second-hand man.

I was doing an Arts-Law course, and had passed my first-year exams with a number of distinctions. This had pleased my mother, who worried about security; she had only a war-widow's pension, and had taken in lodgers at Trent Street, a tedious, childless couple who complained about the heating. But my potential as a breadwinner meant little to me; I still wanted to act. Lessons from a private drama coach had given me some skill; I was prominent in the University Players, and beginning to be given parts in Hobart Repertory productions. Walter Thomas, the drama producer in the Tasmanian section of ABS, the

national broadcasting company, was also giving me parts
in his radio plays, some of which were broadcast nation-
ally. It all ought to have been satisfactory; but it wasn't.

It would be wrong to picture myself as unhappy, at
nineteen; I had plenty of friends at University, and my life
was a full one. But it wasn't the life I wanted to lead; it
wasn't going where I wanted it to go. My ambition to
become a professional actor hadn't changed; I had no real
desire for the substitute theatre of the Law, and I grew
more and more impatient with amateur dramatics in a
small town. What I wanted was to audition for the drama
school in Sydney: the mainland metropolis where life and
competition were serious. And I had tried to persuade my
mother to let me go, using the modest sum of money
which Karl Miller had left for my education.

But my mother, who controlled my inheritance until I
was twenty-one, wouldn't let me use it in this way. Grandfather Miller had wanted me to do Law, she said; those
were the terms of his will, and I must honour them. My
mother quite enjoyed the Hobart Repertory, and was pleased
at my success there; but she refused to take the theatre
seriously as a profession: she saw it as a refined, spare-
time amusement for accomplished people, and no occupation for a grown man. Besides, lawyers made money, and
actors starved. She had all the Victorian prejudices intact,
mixed with some Irish ones. There was a lie at the heart of
acting; and she feared that lie. She thought she was keeping me safe from it.

What gave away my inner discontent at this time were
my periodic drinking bouts. Most of my friends at University were enthusiastic drinkers, but my outbreaks were
different in their excessiveness: I would drink until I was
ill, or passed out; and I did this with dedicated intensity.
Once I woke up at dawn in the dew-wet grass beside a
tram-shelter: I found I was at the Glenorchy terminus, but
had no idea how I'd got there. My student friends pretended to admire prowess like this, but their faces were
secretly dubious.

At times I liked to drink alone, and I did this in seedy,

out-of-the-way pubs where University people didn't go;
'working men's pubs', as they were thought of then. I had
some callow notion about plunging into Low Life, like
Dorian Grey; in such moods, I wanted to discover Hobart's equivalent of the stews of Limehouse, in the dated
British fiction I'd read as a boy. I would drink with
labourers, and have long, solemn arguments with them.
Finding I was a student, they addressed me as 'Perfesser'.
Some of them wanted to beat me up, but my leg usually
saved me; they were chivalrous about it, as my mates at St
Augustine's had been. Then I gave up saying I was a
student and masqueraded as a labourer called Arthur, who
worked at the IXL jam factory and had caught his leg in a
machine. I was then accepted totally, since Arthur's accent
and vocabulary were produced with perfect accuracy.

It was on one of my nights as Arthur, alone and begin-
ning to be drunk, that I encountered Darcy Burr and Brian
Brady again, at the Sir Walter Masterman Hotel in North
Hobart.

It was good to be at the old Sir Walter, a working man's pub
if ever there was one. I'd come away from a rehearsal of
The Importance of Being Earnest by the University Players,
where the producer, a tall, balding third-year Arts man
who wore careful cravats, had kept saying: 'Yes, but what
would *Oscar* have made of this interpretation?' I was tired
of him, and tired of our village hall standard of acting.

I sat over my fourth beer at a laminex-topped table in
the Sir Walter's crowded lounge. At the time, pub lounges
were for women and couples, while the bar next door was
all-male; but I liked to come in here to listen to the
music—usually produced by a skinny old lady in a hat,
who played the piano. She was here as usual thumping out
'Just a Little Street Where Old Friends Meet', while drunken
voices raggedly sang.

As she finished, the frosted-glass doors to the hallway
opened and two young men came in, carrying guitar cases.
I recognised Brian Brady and Darcy Burr.

Both were over six feet tall now, with large hands that

looked used to physical work. Both wore jeans and turtle-neck sweaters: Brady's grey, Burr's dark blue, like a uniform. They set down the cases by the piano where a single microphone stood, sat down on hardbacked chairs there, and began to tune their guitars. They hadn't seen me, since I was sitting by a back wall.

Their tuning didn't take long; they launched fairly quickly into 'The Blue Velvet Band', an old country and western song about a girl who died after her lover went away, beloved in Tasmania for years. Both accompanied on guitar, but only Brady sang. Despite the bathos of the song, I was impressed; he'd improved even more since I heard him sing 'Lonesome Whistle' to Hazel. His deep, resonant voice was a man's now, produced with ease, thrilling in the low notes, and filling the room. The people here plainly liked it; the women especially, who smiled on him dreamily—even the old ones, their glasses of port and gin suspended in their hands. And the men didn't resent him, as they might have done; his broken nose made him one of them: a battler.

In between some of the verses, Burr and Brady played melodic passages of a complexity seldom heard in Country and Western songs, and certainly never heard in places like the Sir Walter Masterman. I was startled at their technical virtuosity; there could be no doubt of Broderick's skill as a teacher. These were simple people in the lounge of the Sir Walter, and they liked simple music; but soon they began to understand that they were listening to some-thing special. Next to me sat a short, wiry old man with faded eyes and curly grey hair; he suddenly barked with laughter and banged the table with a large, gnarled hand, addressing the air and then me. 'By Jesus, these fellers can play,' he shouted. 'Eh?' He challenged me to deny it.

What they played next was daring, especially in a pub like that, where music of any complexity was talked down. The song was a pleasant, somewhat haunting American pop ballad with a Mexican flavour called 'Johnny Guitar', which Peggy Lee had put out a few years before. The crowd knew it, and hummed along with it, and some of the drunks tried to sing too, staggering close to Brian to peer closely into his face as he sang, as though they might discover there some vital clue that would release their own talents. But when the song was ended, the guitars didn't stop: they took up the refrain, developing and then transforming it; the Spanish flavour grew, and now they had climbed without pause into something else: into flamenco.

They were playing a *bulerías*, that most virile of flamenco forms, and they changed to a fast, piston-like clip. The power of their attack and the ringing volume of the two guitars became electrifying, and the lounge clapped along in clumsy approval. The sound travelled to the passageway outside and into the bar across the hall; startled faces appeared around the frosted glass doors, which were now pushed open, and a stream of men from the bar lurched into the lounge, in their grey cardigans and checked shirts and worn suits. Some looked delighted, others confused; all were aware that something remarkable was happening, as the clapping increased. I thought they might turn hostile, as they were inclined to do towards anything unusual, but they tapped and clapped, apparently bemused. And Brady and Burr nodded reassuringly, smiling and winking as they played.

More people came in; they were coming off the street, the lounge was packed, and still the *bulerías* didn't stop, but kept on building. One guitar was percussive, while the other traced the melody; then they would reverse positions, always understanding each other perfectly, coming together in one of the long flamenco rolls that blurred their hands. And just at this moment of completion, before another build-up began, they would pause and nod with grave satisfaction, smiling at each other in profile, beaked nose pointing to broken one, in perfect achievement's thin air.

I waited for that moment to return, and it did. They looked at each other again, like scientists at the conclusion of an experiment (beak nose, broken nose), and it was then, inside the music's jubilation, that I first had a fervent wish to join them; to bind my life to theirs. As though through telepathy Burr looked up and recognised me; he smiled and nodded as he played, with a look of complicity. Then he nudged Brady, who grinned across at me too; and when the *bulerías* was completed, Brian stood the guitar by the chair and gave me his old signal, winking lugubriously with extended index finger and thumb crooked in a circle. *All under control.*

There was violent applause, peppered with wondering exclamations; and the crowd began to call out requests, while the two re-tuned their guitars.

Brady, screwing at his tuning-pegs, suddenly looked up at the audience. 'I'll sing you a Tasmanian song,' he said.

There were scornful guffaws.

'What Tasmanian song?'

'There bloody aren't any!'

But now he began to sing 'Van Diemen's Land'.

The guitar accompaniment was slow and rudimentary, like water falling on stone; and Darcy Burr had taken out a mouth organ, playing it very softly, producing a long, high plaint in the lounge's stillness. Brian Brady, his tangled brown head thrown back, his eyes closed as he sang, suddenly looked Irish to me, not Australian; he was no longer my cousin but someone else, from a hundred years ago.

> '*As I lay in my bunk last night,*
> *A-dreaming all alone,*
> *I dreamed I was in Liverpool,*
> *Away in my own home.*
> *With my own true love beside me*
> *And a jug of ale in hand;*
> *I woke quite broken-hearted,*
> *Lying off Van Diemen's Land . . .*'

I had no idea he could sing like this, or knew such songs. I've responded often enough to his voice since, urging him on under studio lights, or in front of a concert audience. But it can never be like that first time in the Sir Walter Masterman, with its laminex tables and dowdy window curtains. The half-drunk faces were watching him as though he had woken them from sleep. Some were obtuse; but most of them were good faces and I was fond of them, as one is fond of difficult, incorrigible relatives. They had never heard it before, this Irish ballad from the days of transportation; this song of their own great-grandparents. The folk revival had scarcely begun in that year, and such songs had yet to be heard again. I looked from face to listening face, these faithful images of ancestors, the pickpockets and sheep stealers who had arrived in the estuary of the Derwent not a half mile from here, chained below decks on the stinking brigs of despair. It was all not so long ago; not long enough. Did they remember? Would they turn ugly? The old man with the curly grey hair was listening and watching intently, a look of puzzlement on his face, as though he were trying to work something out. Did he remember his ancestor's song? Was he growing angry?

But when it was over he applauded like the rest, clapping with his large, gnarled hands.

Nothing's changed, at the rear of the shop; time has been wound backwards here. The bass drum lettered SANDY'S BANJO BAND is sitting in the same position. The other musical instruments lie for ever on their trestle tables, under weak electric light; the depths of the shop are unplumbable. Outside in Harrigan Street, up which Brady and Burr have led me through thick fog, there is the silver stink of gas. The sign above the door, more faded than before, says: *Music, Books & Antiques. A. (Sandy) Lovejoy*.

We sprawl in aged armchairs. Old Sandy is also unchanged, carefully pouring beers for us at the sink by his glass office. He wears his brown felt hat, a grey dressing-gown and striped pyjamas; we have got him out of bed, but he doesn't seem to mind. Sarah the terrier lies at his feet, her nose hopefully directed at the one-bar radiator. Sandy catches my eye and winks, handing round the beers.

'Soon as you want a refill, you've only got to say! Thirsty work, playing in a pub. Bloody terrific musos, these two boys. Am I right, Dick? Play "Danny Boy", fellers!'

Darcy Burr groans at his uncle. 'Not that bloody corny thing, Sandy!'

'Danny Boy' isn't played; the gleaming guitars stand silent against a wardrobe. Instead we talk; and as we do, I find myself envying Brady and Burr.

I suspect that the wages Sandy pays them are low; but they have a home here, and they can come and go as they please. Brady goes off for weeks at a time, working on coastal fishing boats; and Darcy divides his days between here and Varley's Bookshop, working part-time for Broderick, packing books in the basement. And all the while they are practising their music, and playing at night in the pubs. Sandy's junk shop is their base; the place where they are building their future, which will eventually be realised on the mainland. When they're ready, they say, they'll go to Melbourne or Sydney and make a full-time living as a guitar and vocal duo.

They practise in every spare moment, until their fingers are sore, working on blues, country music and pop. Darcy is even working on rock and roll material, and has bought an electric guitar. He is fascinated by Elvis Presley's 'Heartbreak Hotel'.

'That's a great number, Dick,' he says to me. 'Really original. Brian doesn't want to know about pop, but I do. Elvis shows you just how far you can go; and Elvis started out as a Country and Western singer, remember, just like Brian.'

Brady grins drunkenly, sprawled in his chair. 'I don't need that Yank music any more Darcy,' he says. 'I've found we've got some of our own.' He looks at me, rolling a cigarette. 'Did you know most of the old Australian bush songs have Irish melodies, Dick? A song like "Moreton Bay" goes back to the Battle of the Boyne. It's all the one tradition. I just want to dig those old bush songs up and sing them, and travel the country. That's all I want out of life. Pop music's nothing but concocted crap. But Darcy here wants us to be bloody pop stars. The bastard's ambitious.' He winks, and licks his cigarette paper.

Burr smiles; it's plain he defers to Brady. 'What this bugger doesn't realise,' he says to me, 'is how good he is. With his singing, and my backing and arrangements, we can't miss. And what he also doesn't realise is that you can still succeed by playing the music you care about. That isn't selling out. That's just sense.' He has spoken quietly at first; but as he goes on, his nasal voice takes on intensity. Leaning forward with the beer bottle and refilling my glass, he is looking up at me from under his brows, his amber eyes still resembling a feral cat's; an effect that's emphasised by their faint slant. He appears to me nearer thirty than his true age of twenty-one, but his looks have improved. The pimply junk-shop boy is gone, and his mane of black hair, greaseless now, disguises his overlarge ears. Perhaps it's the white, beaked nose that makes him look cunning; but I don't hold this against him. Since hearing him play, I've decided I approve of Darcy.

'What Brian also doesn't realise,' he confides, 'is that the sort of music he wants to do could get *big*.' He gives the word magical importance.

'And when'll this happen?' Sandy asks. 'When are y'se going away?'

'Six months, I reckon,' Burr says briefly. He doesn't look at his uncle.

'Six months? You're going in six *months*?' Sandy's quacking voice rises in alarm. Brian and Darcy ignore him; but he goes on. 'You young blokes don't want to be too confident. It's not easy, breaking into show business.' He jerks his head at the drum kit, and then addresses me. 'I should know: I had a band once, y'know. Sandy's Banjo Band, in Melbourne, before the War. We had a lot of success, but it didn't come easily.'

'We know,' Darcy says wearily. 'You were the Paul Whiteman of Melbourne. Now you're the biggest antique dealer in the southern hemisphere.' He gestures at the towers of furniture, the hopeless confusion of small objects on tables, the cartons crammed with historic rubbish, and his upper lip lifts in disgust. 'Look at it, Sandy. Do you know what's under all this?'

Sandy looks offended. 'There's nothing y'could really call *under*,' he says, and Brian bursts out laughing.

'Oh yes, I'm just a tired old number to *them*,' Sandy tells me. His sing-song voice rises. 'They don't listen. But I know the score, believe me. They can't go expecting those doors on the mainland to open just like that. Talent's not enough—it's who you know. And it's hard, on the mainland. They'd be better off here, is what I reckon. They're always welcome, Dick—both of them. This is their home. I've looked after Darcy a long time, since my brother-in-law ran off on him—and I gave Brian a leg up, too. Now I need a bit of help from *them*; and I'm glad of their company.'

Brian looks uncomfortable; he and Darcy are both looking into their beers. 'There's no bloody future here Sandy, you know that. We can't hang about in Hobart, for Christ's sake. We're going on the road.'

'If you boys go, there's nothing for me here,' Sandy says, and his worn eyes are pleading. 'How do I manage on me own?'

Suddenly Darcy looks up at him, and his face has entirely changed. To my amazement, it's rigid with fury, the lips a compressed line, the eyes gleaming with the same intensity as his former enthusiasm. 'Go to bed, Sandy,' he says. 'Stop trying to tie us down. We've heard it all too often.'

Sandy begins to speak again, but now Darcy shouts, making me jump. 'Go to bed, you silly old bastard!'

His brutality shocks me; I don't know where to look. But Sandy stands up in dignified silence, setting his hat straight on his head. Finally he speaks, in a small, chastened voice. 'No heart, these young fellers,' he says to no one in particular. 'They come to you when they're in trouble, and you do what you can—then they leave y' for dead.'

He picks up Sarah in his arms. Ancient and threadbare, the dog blinks at us: a little old woman uncertain of her

own reality. 'Thank goodness I still have my little dog,'
Sandy says, in an unctuous chant I feel must often be
heard. He hugs the terrier tightly, drawing a miserable
growl from it. 'Yes, I still have *you*, Sarah darling,' he
says. 'I suppose that's something. You'll always care about
your Sandy.' He smiles piously, while we all sit silent.
'Well, I'll say goodnight.'

He turns and shuffles away, in his brown felt hat and
dressing-gown, carrying the sorrowful dog, and vanishes
through a dark doorway by his small glass office. I called
an embarrassed goodnight.

'Jesus,' Brian says softly. He grins faintly at Darcy.
'Now we're going to have him doing the Prima Donna all
day tomorrow.'

'He'll get over it,' Burr says. 'He's going to have to
learn to be on his own for a good long while. I gave him
enough years, among this junk.' His face shows a pitiless
coldness.

We went on drinking for perhaps another half hour after
that, sitting in our circle of armchairs. Brian's eyes were
hooded, and so were mine, I suspect; only Burr seemed
sober. Affecting to be impressed, they both questioned me
about my life at University; and in my tipsiness, I told
them how little it meant, and what I truly wanted. When
the time was right, I said, I'd drop out of University and
try my luck at acting in Sydney.

'And when will *that* be, Dick?' Darcy's voice was
perhaps sceptical.

As soon as I had enough money, I said. There wouldn't
be much work, at first, and I might have to survive for
months.

'So what you need is money,' Burr said. 'That's all
that's trapping you here, is it?'

I said I supposed so.

'I've got an idea for you, mate,' he said, and leaned
forward again. His confiding tone and smile were back,
and his cruelty to Sandy might never have happened. 'If

you want to save money, I think I can find you a job,' he said. 'I reckon Brod would take you on.'

'Broderick?'

He nodded and smiled. 'I can talk to him about it,' he said. 'I'm sure he'd get you into Varley's Bookshop. They need a new assistant. An educated bloke like you; well-read: they'd snap you up! And you'd really like working with Brod. There's your answer.'

He sat back and grinned. It seemed churlish not to share his triumph, but I stared at him in amazement, trying to look polite.

The idea was outrageous: to drop out of a Law course and become a counter-hand; but I told him I'd consider it. Privately, I had no real intention of doing so.

2

But I did consider it, as the weeks went by. Examining Darcy's logic, I found that it had force; and I began to think seriously of giving up University. Only the thought of my mother's laments made me hesitate.

From the time of that first meeting with Brady and Burr, University had ceased to be real to me; I began to skip lectures, and to call around to Harrigan Street during the day. Lovejoy's second-hand shop was becoming the only place that was real to me, the one place where I was truly content. I would help Darcy and Brian sort through purchases of junk, or load Sandy's van with deliveries of furniture. Often they'd be practising their guitars out the back when I came, and threading my way through the mazes of wardrobes and dressing-tables I would feel my spirits lift at the throb and twang of the two guitars.

They wouldn't stop when I appeared, but would grin at me and go on playing, perched on kitchen stools, cocked heads nodding in concentration. And this was the heart of my contentment: simply to be accepted here; to listen; to be touched by the force and vigour of their drive towards Darcy Burr's dream. They sensed this, and were pleased by it. Lectures on Jurisprudence or Ethics had now become ridiculous and irrelevant.

I often went around in the evenings, as well. One night, after a rehearsal of *The Importance of Being Earnest*, I came very late, at about eleven thirty.

I knocked on one of the glass panes of the street door, and peered in. The winter night was rainless but freezing; an icy wind was coming up from the Channel. After a time the shape of Darcy Burr appeared, making his way between the wardrobes.

'G'*day*,' he said, and waved me in. His eyes glinted with secret amusement; he always used this greeting, whether it was day or night—the droll emphasis on 'day' like a suggestive joke known only to the two of us.

The area at the back of the shop had been made cosier than usual. A log fire had been lit in a fireplace opposite Sandy's glass office, and a soft light came from a table-lamp set on a sideboard. I was shown to a chair at a polished dining-room table of Tasmanian blackwood, one of Sandy's most expensive items.

Sandy himself had gone to bed, and I found myself with Burr, Brady, and a twelve-year-old girl in a long white nylon nightdress and red slippers: a sad-looking child I'd never seen before, with cropped hair like dry grass, worn in a fringe, and a short upper lip that made her vaguely rabbit-like. Her name was Denise; I gathered she was some sort of cousin of Darcy's and a niece of Sandy's, who had come here to stay for reasons that were not made clear. She was painfully shy; her head was constantly bowed, and she rarely spoke. I wondered why she wasn't in bed.

But she was clearly included. As I sat down, she moved about the table laying out pieces of cardboard that were pencilled with the letters of the alphabet, and with numbers. Two others bore the words *Yes* and *No*. The table was otherwise empty, except for an upturned wineglass standing in its own reflection. Denise hurried importantly, like a child chosen to be monitor in class, darting quick glances at us, her small, furtive face bent, never meeting our eyes. I had the impression that she was afraid of something; or perhaps of everything. But my attention was mainly on the cards.

'What's this?' I asked. 'A game?'

Darcy and Brian were quiet, leaning back in their chairs. Now Burr smiled at me with an air of great significance. 'No game, mate,' he said quietly. 'This is a seance. Ever been in a seance?'

I hadn't, and felt partly contemptuous, partly curious. It was Broderick, I learned, who had introduced them to seances, and they appeared to take it seriously; Darcy with enthusiasm, Brian with an embarrassed air. The idea that spirits of the dead could be contacted in this way wasn't one I was prepared to entertain seriously; nevertheless, I did as I was asked, and put my outstretched finger with the others on the base of the upturned wineglass in the centre of the table.

For a moment there was silence, while we sat with our arms extended like the spokes of a wheel. The little smiles of people who expected the impossible touched all our lips. Denise smiled too, her tiny upper lip disappearing, her mouth like a hurt (even smiling was some sort of penalty), her cloudy, greenish eyes looking at Burr from under the fringe of hair. He caught her glance and winked. She looked down again quickly, wriggling with pleasure, her thin, bare arm obediently outstretched. Skinny as a boy except for the hinted swellings of her breasts, she hitched with her free hand at the strap of the nightdress, which kept slipping from one bony shoulder. When her smile had gone, sadness resumed in her face. And there was something abnormal about her, I decided. Trying to sum her up, I described her to myself as schizoid—being given to the glib use of clinical categories, as most of us were at University.

Burr now tilted his head back, closing his eyes as though in prayer. 'We're all waiting,' he said to the ceiling. 'Is there anybody there?'

For a few moments, nothing happened. No one spoke or moved; a log collapsed in the fire, whose flames caused large shadows to leap on the walls, and to lurch like creatures among the junk. Then the glass began to move: slowly at first, then faster, so that we all had to lean to keep up with it. It slid across the polished surface, coming to a halt finally in front of the card marked *yes*.

An ancient sensation of cold crept up my back, overflowing like water on to my neck. 'Come on,' I said. 'Who's pushing the glass?'

'No one pushed it, mate,' Darcy said.

I looked at Brian, who shook his head seriously.

Denise spoke for the first time, her voice so soft it seemed to come from the shadows of the furniture behind her. 'No one's pushing it,' she said. 'It's the spirits.' She peered half-defiantly from under her fringe, her small upper lip setting into place again.

Darcy looked at her with a fondness I'd not seen him show before. 'Denise knows,' he said. 'She knows all about the spirits. She's our medium. They come for her.'

As the glass travelled about the table, spelling out its messages—seeking the letters with little halts and hesitations and sometimes with impulsive rushes, like a blind man feeling his way—a strange assortment of people arrived in answer to our questions; the shadows who always turn up in seances and who end by being tedious. But that night it was all novel to me, and I had some difficulty in maintaining my scepticism, even though I couldn't share the enthusiasm of the others. These strangers from the dead who spelled out answers and warnings seemed worrying souls, with little to say that was helpful or cheering: a drunkard called Ray who had died in 1942; a Rumanian who spelled out endless obscenities; a woman called Jean who had committed suicide in Sydney.

One of them however I did find interesting, in spite of my reluctance to believe in him. This was Michael Brady, born in County Clare, who said he had come to Van Diemen's Land as a prisoner in 1848.

'It's our great-great-grandfather,' Brian exclaimed. 'Yours and mine.' He stared at me, his eyes bright in the half-light.

'You're pushing the glass,' I said; but he protested that he wasn't.

Burr raised his head to the ceiling. 'What did you want to say to us, Michael?'

The glass then moved about the letters to spell out EVIL.

I felt the wave of cold again, at this. 'Who's evil?' I asked.

But now the glass behaved strangely. Moving into the centre of the table, it began to describe circles, so fast that we all had to lean and lunge to keep up with it.

'Jesus,' Brian said. 'What's this?'

We all stared at each other over the glass's vortex; even Denise's gaze remained fixed.

'He doesn't want to answer,' Burr said excitedly. 'You've upset him.' He frowned as though I'd transgressed in some way.

The glass stopped.

'Is there anyone else there?' Burr asked.

'I think we should stop, Darcy,' Brian said. But the glass had already begun to move, and spell out a name. For a few moments, I stared at it without recognition.

HAZEL

'Right, that's it, Darcy,' Brian said loudly. 'She's back! I told you if she came back I'd be out.' He stood up, towering over the table, his face reflecting the fire.

Darcy was expressionless; Denise sat with her head bent.

'Hazel Pearce?' I asked. 'But she's not dead.'

'Yes,' Darcy said softly. 'Dead.'

Brian bent over to peer into Burr's face. 'No more of this shit with spirits, Darcy! You and Brod both—you can court me out of it. I'm going to bed.'

He made off quickly down the room, disappearing through the door by Sandy's office. For a moment, there was silence. Then Burr spoke softly to Denise. 'I think you'd better get off to bed too, kid.' He leaned and kissed her quickly on the cheek, one large hand about her waist, and I saw her flush. Then she shuffled away in her red slippers, grassy head bent, to follow Brian out the door. As she passed the fire, the gown became transparent, disclosing the pathetic thinness of her legs.

'You'd better stay the night, Dick,' Darcy said. He

spoke as though nothing had happened. 'It's late, and bloody cold.'

'How did she die?' I had wanted the glass to answer more questions, and now felt ashamed of my gullibility.

'Hazel?' Darcy asked. 'She died having an abortion, about a year ago. A back-alley job in Launceston. She bled to death without telling anyone.'

I could say nothing for a moment. Then I said: 'It was Brian's kid, wasn't it?'

'That's right,' Darcy said, and nodded brightly. 'When she got pregnant, the Bradys sent her back to her people. Then she wrote a letter to Brian. She wanted to come to Hobart and see him—but she didn't say she was pregnant. I don't think Brian answered the letter. He only found out what had happened later. He won't talk about it much.'

'And now she comes in the seances,' I said.

'She wants to talk to him,' Darcy murmured. 'It's natural.'

I made a sound of disgust. 'I don't really believe in this stuff, Darcy.' I used my Psychology tutorial manner, and expounded. Brian felt guilty, I said; so when they played their games, he unconsciously selected the letters. 'You both do,' I concluded.

But Darcy merely smiled, leaning back in his chair. It was the sort of smile I had seen on the faces of funda-mentalist believers: Salvationists or Plymouth Brethren. 'The spirits were *here*, mate,' he said. 'Just above your head—and you know it.'

I had actually had this illusion when Darcy looked towards the ceiling, but I shook my head. 'Sorry. I don't believe it. And if Broderick believes in this stuff, he's a nut.'

Burr stared at me without answering for a moment, and I wondered if he was about to take offence. There was something vaguely threatening about him at times, even though he wasn't openly aggressive. But when he spoke, his tone was restrained. 'Yes, Brod taught us about the spirits,' he said, 'and a lot of other things besides the guitar. We went to a different university from you, Dick.'

There was nothing I could say to this that wasn't rude,

and we both fell silent, staring at the fire, towards which
we had turned our chairs. Something seemed to be moving
in a dim corner of the shop; glancing from the corner of
my eye, I saw that it was one of the large shadow-
creatures created by the firelight. It was very quiet, now;
in all the piles of junk, not a sound or a creak. Finally, I
asked, 'What sort of things did he teach you?' Something
made me hostile to the idea of Broderick's wisdom, and I
adopted the languid and skeptical tone of one of my lectur-
ers. 'What sort of special knowledge does he claim to
have? He's just an accountant in a bookshop, isn't he?'

Darcy grinned, legs extended towards the fire, hands in
his pockets. 'You blokes who go to university think you've
got a monopoly on learning,' he said. 'Don't you?' Before
I could answer, he said: 'The best thing about working for
Brod in the bookshop was that I learned to *read*.' He
grinned slyly. 'I got an education there. I'm not saying a
university education isn't worthwhile: no knowledge is
useless; knowledge is power, as they say. But how much
power is there in that knowledge they give you at university?'

I said nothing, and waited.

'Broderick could have been a great guitarist,' Burr said.
'Or a scholar. Anything. He knows more than all your
university professors put together. But instead he picked
the path of obscurity—he went for secret knowledge.'

He'd said nothing, really; he was absurd. And yet I was
reluctantly impressed in some way. I reminded myself that
Burr was half-educated, and therefore an easy mark for odd
ideas. But he had a confidence that troubled my compla-
cency; the raw intensity of the untutored, the self-taught,
beside which the respectable certainties of the expert can
suddenly seem feeble. The fact that his dramatic delivery
was plainly calculated didn't lessen its effectiveness; it was
helped by his cold, beer-coloured eyes, which were constantly fixed on mine, as well as by the shop's ancient
gloom, where the years were congealed like drain water. I
edged my chair nearer the fire.

'He taught us about the road to the invisible,' Darcy was
saying. 'He taught us about the Demiurge.'

'The what?'

Suddenly, from somewhere among the groves of junk, a clock began to chime, and I jumped. It struck two, and while it did so, wheezing between each strike, Burr and I were silent. It was growing colder in the shop, and the fire seemed to do little to warm it; I got up and threw another log on.

'I'll put just one thing to you,' Darcy said. 'Is there an unseen world?'

'Of course.' I was standing with my back to the fire.

'And how do you get in touch with it?'

'Not through seances. Through prayer.'

Darcy laughed sneeringly, as though I knew this to be foolish; and now I grew irritated.

'Where do these spirits of yours come from?' I asked. 'The souls of the good aren't hanging around, are they? They're united with God.' My irritation had drawn this from me in spite of myself; I was fast becoming agnostic, at university.

'Don't tell me you still believe in that Catholic bullshit? Brian doesn't,' Darcy said. 'He's grown out of those fairy-tales. So should you.'

'But you believe in spirits that talk to you through a glass. Isn't that a fairy-tale?'

Darcy stood up. 'Time to put you to bed,' he said. 'Brod'll make you understand, when you go to work for him. Have you made up your mind about that yet?'

Yes, I said; and I suddenly found I had.

He didn't ask me what my decision was; he seemed to know, and his grin grew broad. 'Terrific,' he said. 'I knew you had more guts than to stay a respectable middle-class shit. You have to jump, Dick, if you want anything worthwhile. You'll be in Sydney within six months. We'll all go together.'

He began to move away into the dimness beyond the fire; but on reaching the door he paused, and looked over his shoulder. 'I hope you don't have bad dreams, mate.'

*   *   *

I did dream that night, under Sandy's worn grey blankets. But it wasn't a dream I thought of as bad; in fact, it was like no other in my life.

I still found it hard to get warm; and as well, I was oppressed by the musty old shop which had always troubled me, its tall shapes of furniture all around, the fire creatures leaping on the wall. They leaped in my sleep; and I dreamed. It was one of those dreams that don't seem like dreams at all, but a reality more intense than waking life. It seemed to have come from somewhere else.

I was in a crowded place; a large, cave-like room filled with people I didn't recognise. They were discussing somebody who had died. I became confused, and walked into a smaller room which was empty and featureless, with a floor of bare, dusty boards.

The room was filled with wind, coming through a window somewhere. And I heard a voice say: *'She's in the West Wind.'*

The wind became stronger, and ineffably thrilling. I wanted to go back and tell the others what was happening, but I couldn't move. The wind increased to an almost unbearable pitch; it touched my nerves with needles of ice, yet still I thrilled to it.

And now, as I stood stock-still in the room, facing the source of the wind, a set of icy lights appeared in the air just above me. *'It's no dream,'* I said; my body knew in sleep that this was happening. The lights moved and glowed like fireflies, and then they congealed and took form and changed into the lost girl, the beloved, whose small face was ordinary yet beautiful, whose wide mouth tenderly smiled, and whose brown hair was blown sideways. She was the lights, and the lights were she. They pierced me; they were returning, as the wind rose and rose; and the girl was fading. The lights danced and shifted, and her image became uncertain.

She was gone, and I was filled with unbearable grief, unbearable joy, the needles of ice all through me. *'Yes,'* I said, and woke up saying it, to find myself in the cold of the shop, with its dark and jumbled shapes, its dying embers. *'Yes,'* I said. *'It was her. She's in the West Wind.'*

The district of Second-hand claimed all three of us, in our youth: Burr, Brady and myself. But since Brian wasn't a thinker, I believe it affected him less than Burr and me. Despite my condescension about Darcy's lack of education, he and I proved to have much in common. Both of us had lived a good deal in territories of paper.

Darcy's I found, was in the basement of Varley's Bookshop, that territory which was presided over by the man called Broderick. Mine was at Trent Street; and at least one wall of my paper prison was composed of Deirdre Dillon's letters.

My ambition to go to drama school in Sydney and to survive there as an actor was genuine enough. But I have to admit that my longing had a double edge to it—since to reach Sydney, I thought, would reunite me with Deirdre.

Her memory, now over eighteen months old, was constantly tended. She was now only partly real, and yet more important than reality; she drained reality of its savour. I told myself again and again that I had no business dwelling on an adulterous love; before I began to lose my faith, I had even disclosed it in Confession, listening humbly and hypocritically in the dark box to the priest's reproaches. I knew, even as I listened, that I'd made a bad confession, since I wasn't truly repentant, and since my longing would continue the moment I left the box.

'You must stop dwelling in your mind on this association,' the husky voice whispered through the grille. It was accompanied by a smell of cough-lollies; the priest had a cold. 'You are lucky that temptation is out of the way, since you say the person concerned is in another city. But you must be careful of building a false desire, a false image of this woman. Such desire can never be satisfied—not just because in your case it would be sinful to do so, but because we don't find ease of it through lust, or even through what you think of as love. The desire you feel, although you don't recognise it, is really the desire for

God. Being united with Him alone can satisfy those long-ings which are never satisfied, and which pursue us all our lives. Remember that; ask forgiveness; ask God to take you to Himself.' Soon afterwards, he gave me absolution, his voice trailing away in muttered Latin, the smell of cough-lollies persisting.

I had begun to go out with girls—most of them fellow-students—but this meant little to me. Brief moments of promise, brief interludes of physical excitement, were al-ways followed by the decision that my partners were drab and trivial. No one could compare with Deirdre. Besides, the prettiest and most sought-after girls were not interested in me, and for this I saw my limp as being to blame. It was only slight, now; I scarcely ever used the stick; but it prevented me from dancing, and the most vital and popular girls liked to dance; they liked unimpaired men. But it didn't matter, really; nothing mattered but Deirdre Dillon, who should have been Deirdre Brennan.

She had never made her promised visit to Hobart; in-stead, I had her letters. These came regularly in answer to mine, always in the same expensive blue envelopes, ad-dressed in her round, regular hand, in violet ink. The letters had two aspects, as Deirdre had done. There was a light, gossiping tone and a tone of high romance. I was allowed glimpses of Deirdre in isolation—washing her hair, sitting in her garden above Sydney Harbour, reading her books—a young, dreaming girl in an isolated house; a figure in a Brontë novel. And once she had sent me a photograph, which I treasured. On the back of it, in her violet ink, she had written: *The twenties!!* The picture had been taken at a fancy-dress party to which Deirdre had gone as a twenties flapper; headband, beads, an absurdly long cigarette-holder in her mouth. Mooning over it with double nostalgia, it seemed to me that she had actually lived then; and the picture became a sacred relic, an artifact that not only proved Deirdre had existed, but framed her in our lost decade.

At times, in answer to my declarations, she grew almost erotic—and then drew back. They were almost love letters, but not quite; she didn't say 'I love you,' but merely, 'love, Deirdre'. And once she said: *'I can't say that; I mustn't. And you mustn't write to me as you did last time. It makes me long for you too much. I think so often of our lovely beach.'*

Her husband wouldn't open my letters, she said; I could feel safe on that score. But she asked me not to grow so serious—for my own sake. This, of course, did nothing to dissuade me. I lived for the mail. And yet, despite the way in which these letters brought the tones of her voice into my head, she grew less and less real; she became another figure; and this figure took on a new and complex dimension, which Darcy Burr would soon help me to understand.

3

'And how are you liking it here? Any regrets?'

Broderick leans back in his swivel chair, half-turned towards me from his rolltop desk.

'It's a means to an end. I appreciate your taking me on.' This is the first time I've been inside his office since I began work at Varley's.

'It must be a bit of a come-down, after the undergraduate life. And I'm told you went well in your exams.' His tone is neutral, his voice cold as ever, and his blank eyes remain attentive on my face. Their pupils are very small, the yellowish lids drooping in a more accentuated way than I remember. I pause, wondering whether I should sit down; I've only come in here for some catalogues. But now he swivels right around and extends his legs in front of him, his back to his desk, blowing a thin stream of smoke from his cigarette. He seems to intend that I should stay and talk.

'You did metaphysics, Darcy tells me. Did you get much out of it?'

'I liked it, but I didn't see much point in it. In the end, classical metaphysics only told me something I already knew.'

'What was that?'

'That the whole visible world's an illusion.'

He raises his eyebrows as though I've said something that impresses him. Then the crooked smile travels up the side of his face; it gives him a look of cold kindness. 'I'd certainly agree with you there. And what next?'

'Pardon?'

'Where does that take you to?'

'I'm not sure. I'm agnostic about everything at the moment.'

He says nothing to this at first. Formal as a banker in his dark blue three-piece suit, he gets up and crosses to a little table where a bottle of whisky and some glasses stand. He pours two, telling me he keeps it here for the publishers' reps. On a Friday night he always allows himself one; will I join him?

I take the drink with a sense of being favoured, and discreetly look about me, in this narrow, windowless office which is situated at the foot of the basement stairs. There's a worn Persian carpet on the floor, making it intimate and comfortable. A guitar stands in one corner, and the walls consist entirely of books. Many of them look old, and deal with music and art; others deal with philosophy and occult topics, most of their titles conveying nothing to me. It resembles the room of a university lecturer; yet in some way I can't analyse and is probably my own imagination, it seems more suggestive of esoteric knowledge than any lecturer's study. Perhaps it's simply the fact that it's located under ground.

Broderick sits at his desk again and sips his whisky. I take a chair by the bookshelves, but his empty gaze makes me as cautious as it did when I was standing. Now he says musingly: 'Let's sum up the position. People like Locke and Berkeley and Kant have told you that perception's a deceiver; that your senses trick you.'

'Yes.'

'So as far as ontology's concerned, we don't really know what's outside us, do we?' His voice remains hollow, faintly regretful, but friendly now. 'It's just a skin, everything that we see. The question is, what's really out there? Or who? How do we pierce the skin? Did they teach you that, at university?'

I smile, waiting to see what all this will lead to. No doubt some hackneyed theory or outdated system, presented as fresh discovery. But Broderick remains impressive, and I wonder if he remembers our meeting in the lane. His next remark, made casually, is bizarre.

'I'd suggest to you that we're watched all the time from out there. By enemies and allies.' He seems to be gazing just past my shoulder—perhaps to no particular purpose, but despite my incredulity at what he's said, I have the sudden sense of a dark shape standing behind me. I cast a stealthy glance aside, feeling foolish; it's Broderick's overcoat, hanging behind the door. Upstairs, the shop will be closed and empty by now, the dustcovers over the counters. Turning back, I find him watching me with melancholy amusement, and his sad handsomeness touches me as it did in the lane; I'm irrationally flattered by his wish to talk to me.

'You once believed in angels,' he says. 'Or I presume you did, since your Church does. Why shouldn't you believe in other entities?'

'You mean demons?'

'That's a Christian term, with silly associations. I can't take Christianity very seriously, I'm afraid.'

'Why not?'

'Christ was a clown.' His tone is off-hand. 'He died a clown's death. You remember his last words on the cross?'

'They were natural. He took on human flesh.' In spite of my new-found agnosticism, I find I'm still uncomfortable at hearing Christ mocked.

'No true redeemer would take on human flesh, surely? Divine beings are supposed to be pure spirit, aren't they? And the birth of a divine child wasn't new. You've heard of the Eleusinian Mysteries?'

I admit I haven't.

'The divinity then was Dionysus, and his virgin mother was the goddess of the sea.'

He lights a fresh cigarette; he's a chain-smoker, and his

thin fingers are orange with nicotine. As he smokes, he allows the ash to grow longer and longer, inhaling very seldom. Then he asks: 'Haven't you ever suspected that the universe is double?'

At this I experience a small shock, and I ask him what he means. But instead of answering, he glances at his watch, stands up with an expression of forbearance, and favours me with his brief, crooked smile again.

'It's after closing time.' He takes down the dark blue coat from the door; I've been dismissed.

I had very few conversations with him after that; perhaps half a dozen in all, and they were usually brief. He was always pleasant, in a tolerant way, but he would never let me stay for long; he would hint that he was busy. And since I was usually in his office playing truant from my job serving customers upstairs, I had no justification for lingering.

Broderick was only seen in the shop when he passed through the low door behind the sales counter that led to the basement stairs; he never served customers, and bald, portly old Varley, who I suspected did little work any more, seemed to depend on him to run the essential machinery of the place. So the sales staff were in awe of the accountant, growing quiet when he went by; he was like the shop's true owner, coldly calculating its fundamentals, down below.

He was nearly always to be seen through the open door of his office at the foot of the basement stairs. Sometimes, after hours, he would be heard softly practising his guitar. In working hours, bent over his ledgers and catalogues, his cigarette with its long, suspended ash always between his lips, he seldom turned around. But when I came clattering down the narrow wooden stairs to fetch some stock, he would sometimes smile at me over his shoulder. It was a strange smile, melancholy yet remote. He seemed to be waiting poignantly for me to understand something; yet I never met a man less approachable.

I would sometimes lurk about his door at closing time

on a Friday night, hoping to be asked in for a whisky again. There were occasions when he did so; more often he didn't, and sometimes he wasn't there at all; he went to the mainland on buying trips. But when he did talk to me, it was with self-contained brevity, and usually in a sort of riddling style. These conversations, with the exception of casual exchanges about new stock or the business of the shop, were nearly always an expansion of our first one: a sort of dialogue in serial form. But he always proceeded through hints; nothing I could say would make him expand on his ideas for very long. When he wanted me to go, he would look at me as though he wondered what I was doing here, and I would flush, and stand up. I was still not twenty, and found it difficult to judge when I'd worn out my welcome. Sometimes Darcy Burr was here too, for one of his afternoons of work; then we would talk to Broderick together. Looks of complicity would pass between these two; I felt that he had explained much more about his notions to Burr than he had to me.

Once, and only once when I was talking to him alone, he showed a sort of scorn. I had been trying to question one of his remarks, no doubt using the pedantic tone we'd all done in Philosophy tutorials, when he put down his cigarette and looked up at me suddenly, his face severe. 'Look young fellow,' he said. 'You really know nothing.'

His use of 'young fellow', rather than the statement itself, was like a slap; I stood flushing, my dignity affronted.

He went on in a softer tone. 'University gave you plenty of information, I'm sure. But that's just shit.' In his mouth, the word was unusually obscene; he rarely swore. 'Real knowledge is to *know,*' he said. 'A fellow like Darcy understands that. He understands it in the same way he understands music.' He paused, and watched me. 'In pop music, the tunes are the whole thing. But in complex music, the melodies aren't there at the beginning just for what they are. They're there for what they'll become.' I expected him to go on, but he sat back and fell silent, drawing on his cigarette, staring in front of him and taking no more notice of me. It was time for me to go.

I didn't question him much after that, or visit him uninvited. But a certain pattern had emerged from his talk, and I would sometimes prod Darcy to elucidate it, since it became fairly plain that Burr regarded himself as the guitar teacher's disciple. The picture was shadowy, and disconcerting. The material world, it seemed, was in the grip of powers over which God had no control, and this made the idea of fleshly sin ridiculous. There was no sin. Only the spirit mattered; but the spirit was imprisoned in the body. There was hope, but where it lay was never made clear. Deeply curious, I questioned Burr closely about this, and he hinted at intermediaries; supernatural entities of great power who could be invoked as helpers. Then he closed up; but not before hinting that such helpers might actually be available to Broderick. Darcy at that age was often ingenuous and naive, and I didn't take this very seriously. Broderick was another matter; I couldn't dismiss him so easily, and his remarks continued to startle me. Once he remarked that the Holy Spirit was not male but female—a statement I found shocking.

I remained reluctantly fascinated by him, and sometimes, in the night of the basement, I would feel an actual sense of threat. These were heresies he was proposing, after all; trained early to resist them, I found them threatening even now; and what was most disturbing, if they were actually to be taken seriously, was the denial of God's sovereign power. If what Broderick hinted at was true, then there was no assurance of the defeat of evil. There was no happy ending.

Despite his politeness, the bookshop's accountant didn't invite any sort of personal confidences or enquiries about himself. I questioned Darcy closely about him, but could discover only the barest facts. His full name was Clive Broderick; he had once been married, and was now divorced. Darcy believed that he must sometimes have affairs; his looks would surely attract women, Burr said, but he had never actually seen Broderick out with one. The accountant made long phone calls though, and Darcy imagined these were to women.

He was a native of Hobart, but Burr knew of no relatives; Broderick had lived abroad for some years after the War, and had studied guitar in Madrid. Why he hadn't pursued a musical career, and what had driven him back here to the obscurity of the island and Varley's Bookshop neither Darcy nor Brian Brady could say. He lived in a flat in West Hobart, but they had never been there; he gave them their guitar lessons in Sandy's shop, or sometimes, after hours, in his office. And Broderick somehow belonged in those places, I thought—both of which were cave-like, without windows; he was at home underground, and I was somewhat surprised when I saw him in the street. It was hard to imagine Broderick doing everyday things; I could barely picture him shopping, or cleaning his teeth, or even eating. I had never seen Broderick eat; he never brought sandwiches into his office, but disappeared to a solitary lunch in some unknown restaurant. No doubt it was expensive, since Broderick was plainly fastidious.

He moved with extraordinary quietness. I had been startled many times to find him just behind me, in the shop or in the basement.

'Brod's got powers,' Burr said. It was one of his casual workdays here; he and I were alone in the basement, packing books into cartons for the country at one of the long trestle tables. Broderick was absent from his office, away on a trip.

The basement was a gloomy place, yet I rather liked it; I welcomed excuses to escape down here from serving the customers. Darcy and I lurked here like trolls, and furtively read the books. The building Varley's occupied was old, and the basement was like a catacomb: dim perspectives of whitewashed brick pillars; smells of earth and mould; bare electric bulbs hanging from wooden rafters. Not all of these lights were kept on, and there were recesses that remained dark. The island's early summer was here now, but the basement was always cool.

'What sort of powers?' I asked.

He hesitated, and I had the impression that he'd considered some important disclosure and then decided against it. Then he said: 'Brod can travel.'

He and I had recently discussed the subject of astral travel: the possibility of getting the soul out of the body at will, and transporting oneself somewhere else. But I had treated this as folklore, not to be credited as fact.

'It's true. Brod's been seen in one place, while his real self's in another,' Darcy insisted.

I scoffed at this. 'Pull the other one, Darcy.'

His eyes glinted with amusement; he thrust out his neck like a goose. 'Listen, mate, what if I were to tell you that yesterday I saw Brod in his office?'

'You can't have, he's in Melbourne.'

Darcy smiled knowingly, and said no more.

Despite these lapses into superstitious games—games he may or may not have believed in—I found Darcy Burr an interesting companion at that time in our lives, mainly because he and I were being drawn together by our interest in faery lore.

He was very well informed on this subject, being the only adult I'd met who didn't dismiss it. He was particularly interested in the true nature of the Queen of Elfland, and we talked about this topic at length; I never tired of it, in that time when I lived for Deirdre's letters. Queen Titania, he said, had evolved from the goddess Artemis. She was really the third aspect of the moon goddess: the enchantress, Hecate.

We stood by the trestle table, Darcy in his dustcoat (uniform of the worker below ground), myself in the blue suit and tie I must wear for serving customers above. I wasn't packing today; I lingered down here without cause, and at any moment the mincing voice of the senior salesman Mr Pringle would summon me up the stairs, his rimless glasses flashing from the top. (*'Richard? Are you serving?'*) Meanwhile, Darcy gossiped away about the nature of Artemis as Fairy Queen, displaying the learning he'd got from books Broderick lent him, and showing a sly, eager interest that was the closest thing to warmth he

could demonstrate. It wasn't the warmth of ordinary friendship, Darcy was too enclosed for that; but it did create a
sort of conspiratorial closeness, down here. At times I
wondered whether I was truly listening to Burr, or to
Broderick; and it spurred me to do some reading of my
own.

Artemis, as Darcy had reminded me, was both virgin
huntress and goddess of childbirth—her paradox symbolised
by her plant, artemisia, whose juice is 'the milk of the
virgin'. Desiring to be untouched, she'd never marry; and
yet Diana of the silver bow had been transformed into
Diana of Ephesus. ('The one with all the tits,' Darcy said,
and leered.) Like the fairy women of legend, she promised
fruitfulness and ecstasy—but only at one remove, never in
reality. And in Hecate, goddess of crossroads, the link
with Faery became clear. The underworld that claimed
Persephone, where Hecate nurtured the poppy, the flower
of forgetfulness—wasn't this also the Faery Otherworld?

Very likely, Darcy said, since the Otherworld was the
land of the dead; but weren't fairies perhaps those spirits of
the dead unable to leave the earth?

'Have you ever seen a fairy, Dick?' He demanded this
seriously.

I told him I'd had an imaginary companion as a child
whom I'd thought to be a goblin. 'He had a suit of dried
leaves,' I said. 'I probably got him out of a story book. I
called him Pooka.'

'Really? Now that's very interesting, Dick. Have you
heard of the Phouka? That's his name in Irish. And his
English name's Puck—who lives in the forest, and has
goat's legs. And do you know who *that* is?'

He paused dramatically. 'Yair—he used to be called
Pouk. But he's not your Devil at all. He's the old god of
nature.'

One afternoon, in a rash moment, I told him about my
affair with Deirdre Dillon. I gave few details; I somehow
felt that to reveal any intimacy to Darcy was to give him
an advantage he might use. But he questioned me eagerly.

'So she's Bob Brennan's daughter,' he said. 'Lots of money there, mate.'

This brought me up short, filling me with disgust. We were no longer discussing Artemis; we were merely two poor young men in a menial job, gossiping of things beyond our reach, in our cave under the streets of the town; a town where Deirdre's father was a merchant prince.

But soon I'd escape; I'd reach Sydney within a few months, I resolved, even if it meant starving there. Then, Deirdre would become a reality.

4

I still went round to Lovejoy's on most evenings, and we continued to have seances, always with Denise in our circle. I kept up my air of scepticism for a time, but it was more and more a pretence; I had entered a frame of mind where I assumed the spirits were real. I looked forward to each session with a secret, inward tremor, as though I were involved in a perversion that answered some need in me. I told myself it was mere curiosity, but it was more. I'd made contact at last with the unseen, I said. God didn't reveal himself, but the spirits did, signalled always by the delicious and authentic sensation of cold, flowing over my neck.

One night when Brian was out with one of his many girls, I found myself alone with Darcy, who offered me a cup of coffee. We went to his room, which I'd not seen before.

It was upstairs at the back, and its single, tall old window looked out on to the clotheslines and brick out-houses of the Harrigan Street backyards, and the nearby red drum of the gasometer. But it contrasted strongly with these and with the jumbled shop below, since Burr had managed a sort of seedy elegance here, furnishing it like the den of an Edwardian gentleman, with a rolltop desk like Broderick's and a leather couch. An old lute hung on the wall.

I was particularly interested to see an array of pictures tacked to the pine wall next to the desk, where Darcy sat in a swivel chair—also like Broderick's. Some were figures from the Tarot cards: the Fool, the Empress, the Magus. Others were pictures of fairies, taken from books illustrated by the Victorian and Edwardian artists I knew well: Rackham, Doyle, Dulac, Huskisson, Simmons.

Following my gaze as we sat with our instant coffees, Burr said: 'You probably know most of those fairy pictures.'

I said I did, and went on examining them as we talked. One of them troubled me; it didn't quite fit with the others. Then I realised that it wasn't an illustration at all, but what appeared to be an actual photograph of a fairy.

I peered more closely at this naked child with flowers in its hair, kneeling in grass, buttocks on heels, arms extended behind it in order to lean on its hands, its body arched; not quite child, not quite woman, neither sexual nor asexual. The face, turned slightly downwards towards the left shoulder, seemed to muse on something bewildering, something sad, locked outside life; and the grainy, ethereal quality of the black-and-white print almost made me believe that this picture, like the others, was Victorian or Edwardian; something from Sandy's junk-shop. But the small, hurt mouth and the faint, injured-looking swellings of the early breasts had a remembered, worrying pathos. The circlet of flowers didn't look festive; it might almost have been placed in her straight, grassy hair against her will.

Turning back to Burr, I found him watching me, as always. 'Her mother's a drunk,' he said softly. 'Her old man ran off a year ago. Just like *my* bloody parents. Her teachers keep telling Sandy she's got mental problems. But I know that's bullshit. They don't understand what she is. She's really a changeling, Dick.' His tone grew confiding and charged with significance, as though he tried to draw me into a crime. 'That's why the ordinary world's too difficult for her; that's why she knows too much. *You* should know about changelings. They ought to have a special meaning for someone who's had Paralysis.'

'What do you mean?'

He must have heard the dryness in my voice, but his

smile didn't go. 'You really don't know? You've had Paralysis, and you don't know what they used to do in Ireland?'

I shook my head.

'A hundred years ago, kids who had Paralysis were thought to be changelings. People said the fairies swapped the changelings for their true babies—so they'd throw the kids on the fire. The idea was that since they were fairies, they'd fly up the chimney.' He chuckled. 'You were lucky not to be born in Ireland, weren't you Dick?'

I stood up, and said I must go. I wanted to get away from him; to be gone from his room and his photograph, and the smells of mildew and gas.

For a week after that, I didn't see him. I didn't call round to Lovejoy's, and Burr didn't come in to work at Varley's. I was glad of it. The notion that he and I were kindred spirits had now become repugnant to me.

Finally though, on a Friday, I went around to Harrigan Street again—mainly to see Brian Brady. It was a warm evening after work; late sun flowed into Sandy Lovejoy's door, which was still open. There were customers: a man peering at a dressing-table; an old woman suspiciously turning over crockery. But no one was in attendance; there was no sign of Sandy, Brian or Darcy.

I made my way through the corridor of wardrobes to the area at the back, beginning to suspect that something had happened, that things were no longer the same. I found Sandy sitting in his armchair, his brown felt hat on as usual, the dog Sarah huddled on his knees.

He glanced up, but didn't smile or move. 'Hello, young Richard,' he said.

I asked him where Darcy and Brian were, and he shook his head as though I'd asked something in bad taste. The dog, in deference to her master's mood, remained as still as he did, her muzzle resting on her paws; only her eyes moved, rolling sideways in my direction.

'They've gone,' Sandy announced. 'Gone to Sydney, two days ago. Didn't Brian contact you? He said he would, or else he'd write.' His voice took on its old sing-song, almost accusing. 'Well, what d'you expect? That's what they're like, those two. It's off with the old, on with the new.' He compressed his lips and nodded, glad that I must share his disappointment.

'Why did they go so quickly?'

He stared at me in silence, as though trying to formulate an answer, and I sat down on a bentwood chair and waited. Sandy was a talker; his grief and resentment wouldn't let him be silent for long.

'Just as well they went,' he muttered finally. His mouth pursed, and I saw that he was fighting against grief, like a child meted out unfair punishment. 'As far as Darcy's concerned, it's good riddance. I won't miss him, Dick, even though he *is* my nephew. I knew he'd bring me trouble.'

'What trouble?'

'Young Denise,' he said abruptly, as though we'd already discussed her. 'I can't get her to school any more, Dick. Not now he's gone. She was always hanging around him.' He shot a quick, apprehensive glance at me; then he stood up, holding the dog. 'Come and see her,' he said. 'You might know what to do.'

He led the way past the glass office into the ground-floor rooms at the back. We passed down a high, dark hall, and Sandy peeped around an open cedar door.

'Here's Richard come to see you, love,' he said.

But the invisible occupant made no sound.

He jerked his head at me to go in. 'She might talk to you,' he said; and I went in ahead of him.

The room smelled stale. It had a tall old wardrobe and an iron bed, and the window looked on to a brick wall. The child sat on the edge of the bed in the white nightdress she had worn at the seances, hugging herself with crossed arms. A plate with crusts of toast sat humbly on the bedside-table.

She darted a look at me from under her thick, fair fringe, and I greeted her. Her mouth winced in something like a smile, and she threw her bare arms back and leaned on her hands. She suddenly looked older then twelve; there were shadows under her shifting eyes.

'Hello Captain,' she said, and licked her lips.

'Well at least she's talking now,' Sandy said. 'But why are you calling Richard Captain, dear?'

'He's the Captain,' she said. 'But he's not the Prince.'

She continued to smile at me, and arched herself provocatively, her small, sad paps showing through the nightdress like bruises. Then her face became expressionless; her head dropped, and she hugged herself again, beginning to rock to and fro. She said no more, but hummed a tune under her breath. I tried to talk to her, but she wouldn't speak again.

'She'll be like that for hours,' Sandy said. 'I can't do anything.'

He led me back down the passage to the shop. 'It's Brian I'll miss,' he was repeating. 'He was a marvellous feller—like a son to me. But he's off to lead the big life now, and not a bloody thought for what I've done for him, I suppose.'

He sat down in his chair, embracing the wriggling Sarah who yapped protestingly, and his voice resumed its self-comforting sing-song. 'Well, I still have my little dog,' he said.

Two days later, Deirdre Dillon's final letter came. I found it in the post-box on my way out to work in the morning, and read it on the tram.

When I got to the shop, I vanished into the basement, going deep into the tunnels between the pillars. Switching on one of the bare, dangling lights there, I sat on a crate.

She had used the same blue notepaper as always; the violet ink.

Dear Richard,

We must stop writing. My husband is beginning to suspect something, and it's not good for either of us—especially not good for you, darling boy.

You have to forget me. I'm just a silly, ageing

*woman—so you should be able to manage without me.
You'll find some nice, normal young girl, won't you?
I shan't write again. All my love always.*

Deirdre

I put my face in my hands. I could hear Mr Pringle's
mincing voice, calling me from the top of the stairs.
'Richard! Are you *serving?*'

I didn't want to leave the basement; I didn't ever want
to go above ground again.

5

There's a state of peace following despair which is like the
aftermath of an accident. It was in this state that I walked
across Newtown on my last afternoon in Tasmania—making
for Quarry Hill, through an afternoon of clear spring sun.

Wielding my grandfather's stick, which I'd need on the
slopes, passing through districts of peaceful tedium, I was
filled with wonder at the continuing calm of the world.
Changed, I walked through all the small streets that were
stitched into my spirit: rows of neat bungalows whose
styles ranged from the leadlight glass and terracotta tiles of
the Edwardian era to those weatherboard economy boxes
of the Second World War which Karl Miller had despised—
houses which were of no style, and shrivelled the heart.
But I said goodbye to them all.

I had decided not to wait; not to save any more money,
but to leave for Melbourne. I had no further interest in
Sydney, now that Deirdre was lost to me. Walter Thomas
had recommended me to his Drama Department colleagues
in the Melbourne branch of ABS, and this would be
enough to give me a start as a full-time actor: or so I
hoped.

Half an hour later, toiling up a stony, deserted bush road
between gum-covered slopes, I had reached my private
hilltop, just beyond the limits of the last suburb: a place I
shared with no one.

Quarry Hill was one of the highest bordering the town:
the first of the lower foothills of Mount Wellington. Its

larger, olive-coloured brothers and the blue mountain itself rolled upwards to the west behind it, densely grown with gums, drooping grey she-oaks and gold-flowering wattle. Rising above an old quarry, it was made still higher by a great barrow on top: a sort of flat-topped earthwork like those of the ancient Britons, created over the last fifty-odd years from deposits tipped there by the quarry-men. A rough dirt road for their trucks ran to its edges; yet I'd never encountered a truck here, or a single human being.

I limped up the last incline, panting, pushing heavily on my stick; then I was out on the open, grass-grown top: an area about the size of a football field, scattered with yellow everlastings and Scotch thistle. Halting on its eastern edge, I breathed in the air-currents of late afternoon; and a quarter of the quiet island lay at my feet. Southwards, the Derwent's silver bends uncoiled towards the city and its port; on the other side of the valley of Newtown I could pick out the orange-tiled roof of my grandfather's house. My spirits expanded; I threw my stick into the grass; I had a sense of liberation, as though I were flying.

Quarry Hill was extraordinary: not just because it commanded all this beauty, but because of something else. There were fields of unknown force, unknown meaning, running through the body of the island. They gave to certain valleys, certain hilltops, a power and mystery that could plainly be sensed; that could almost be heard humming, like electricity. I had known of it since childhood; I even knew which points in the landscape were within its invisible tracks. There was no discernible reason why a particular hill, or a rise of dry grass to which a few last houses clung, should have this power. It was simply something that could be felt; and I had always had passionate prejudices about the landscape and its compass-points.

The west had never invited me. There, hidden behind Mount Wellington, rolled the wilderness: five thousand square miles of majestically rotting rain forest: unexplored catacombs of Antarctic beech and Huon pine on which it rained and snowed eternally, its cold coasts unvisited, the long waves that rolled from Cape Horn booming on its empty beaches. The west was death. But the east was life: the mild, open east of farms and settlement. Out there, Mount Direction dreamed, its twin humps serenely enigmatic as ever; and the line of power ran straight across to them, and on to the eastern barrier of mottled ranges—cutting through the point where I now stood. That was the secret of the hill. Standing on the edge of its magic grid-line, looking north-east, I saw right to the centre of my mountain-haunted island: a hundred miles of green, farm-nested valleys, musing pastures and navy peaks. Neither Broderick nor Burr would ever know about this landscape, I said: this was a mystery of which they'd stay ignorant.

I sensed something behind me, and spun round. I had a fear that someone was looking for me, following me.

But there was no one here: no figure of retribution. Instead, I was confronted by what had happened to Mount Wellington, towering behind my back. The Organ Pipes, those fluted volcanic rocks on its pinnacle, were touched with pink; and the advancing sunset had deepened its colour to an astounding composite of blue and violet, deep as fathoms of water—so close, I could almost dive in. Nothing stood between me and those fathoms: up here on my barrow, I'd become the centre of some vast process of transfiguration.

The island was saying goodbye to me.

BOOK TWO

THE ABYSS

Nothing is more beautiful than
a guitar—save perhaps two.
  FREDERIC CHOPIN

In the fogs of that winter
Many hundred ships were sounding;
the DP camps were being washed to sea . . .
the misemployed, the unadaptable,
those marked by the Abyss,
friends who came out on the *Goya*
in the mid-year of our century.
  LES MURRAY, *Immigrant Voyage*

5

ON THE ARCADE

1

Is there really some hidden significance in the number seven?

It crops up again and again in the great ballads of Faery, those ballads the Rymers would revive and transform: seven sons, seven daughters, seven knights; seven years of penance; seven years of absence. Spans and combinations of seven were integral to the Faery Process. Seven was the number of years that Hind Etin kept his earthly mistress in Elmond's wood. Seven years was the length of time the Great Silkie told his earthly wife to nurse his son, before he would return to claim him. A seven-yearly sacrifice of one of their number was made by the fairies to Hades; and seven years was the time that Thomas Rymer of Erceldoune spent in the Otherworld, with the Queen of Elfland. Yes, it was always seven years that mortals spent in that place, and always through wishing for what was forbidden— entering the spell which halts time, which turns reality to gauze, which thrills the nerves with a beauty dimly longed for and never found until now; a beauty like the inside of music, a dream that none could bear to wake from, but would wake nevertheless—to find reality shrivelled, savourless and dead. Seven was the penalty; seven was the payment; seven was the key. Pythagoras considered it the number most compatible with the Divine; and our bodies renew themselves every seven years.

Certainly I had renewed myself by the end of the seven years I spent as an actor in Melbourne.

I went there as a youth; I left as a somewhat disen-chanted young man, harbouring that coldly passionate de-termination to change his life which so often comes at twenty-five. With the exception of six dull months work-

ing in an office, I actually managed to survive as an actor
through every one of those years, getting by almost entirely through radio work. But survival was all it had been.
I lived in single rooms: in bed-and-breakfast guest-houses
smelling of floor polish and despair; in rooming houses in
St Kilda, Caulfield and Fitzroy, where I shared dark bath-
rooms and ancient kitchens mysterious with grease. A flat
was beyond my pocket; I never knew from month to
month whether I could still go on covering basic rent and
food. That depended always on the whims of radio producers—at whom, like all actors, I must smile and smile.
They were the princes who totally controlled the livelihood
we made from fantasy, and who could always take it
away. An offhand tone from one of them produced a small
pang of worry; a frown chilled the guts; no calls for a
fortnight spelled doom. And yet we were always light-
hearted; it was the great compensation of the job. We were
in show-business, God help us, high above the grey chan-
nels of the workaday world, sharing our actors' jokes and
show-business gossip and bitchery, each man keeping up
appearances in the studios with his one set of elegant
sports clothes, his one good suit; each of the women in her
smartest suit, her sexiest dress, her most expensive make-up.
Only the two or three top dogs went home to a good
apartment, or a house in the suburbs; there wasn't the
volume of work in Melbourne to keep a large community
of actors prosperous. For that, you had to go to Sydney,
up north in the sun; but Sydney, the nation's biggest city
and the show business capital, whose sub-tropical hedo-
nism made staid, cool old Melbourne envious and contemptuous, also meant fierce competition.

   For a long time I was happy in Melbourne, despite my
insecurity—diverted by occasional interesting parts in local
theatre productions, and by a number of inconclusive love
affairs. But by the time I was twenty-five, the iron had
entered my soul. In that year, when I decided at last to
leave for Sydney, I'd come to certain conclusions.

   My hopes of a big career in the theatre were futile; I saw
that now. I was given good character roles now and then,

but no leads; parts for an actor who limped were limited. At twenty-five (the age when boyhood is truly gone, and when life stretches ahead like a planned holiday—still lengthy, still full of the possibility of surprises, but its endings now actually conceivable), I saw that I must make decisions.

Acting wasn't for me, I decided. I knew now what lay in store for ageing, failing actors. I drank with some of the old ones in the pub—actors like Tom Gordon, whose noble nose was rosy from too many nights here; whose eyes were lost and bemused. He was given to sudden rages; he talked about the successes of his youth, and railed at the stupidity of the producers he fawned on in the studio. Most of the old ones were like Tom. They snubbed the young ones like me to compensate, and were bitter about their more successful colleagues in brassy Sydney. Their hands shook as they held their scripts, these old, drunken actors with their well-polished shoes and good tweed suits; they worried about missing cues as they nursed their hangovers. They still lived in rooming-houses like mine, or in cheap, sad flats with their old wives. They had given their life to the glamour of well-spun illusions, but they had not been rewarded, I saw; and now I made up my mind that I would not end as they had.

This didn't mean I had turned against illusion as a way of life. I had given my life to illusion; what did other people do? Clerks, executives, bank managers, politicians, businessmen: what did they all yearn for, freed from their day in the real world, growing drunk or earnestly thoughtful, opening their souls? I had met them in clubs and hotels and at backstage parties and had seen the look in their eyes at such times, half wistful, half pathetic: the child peeped out then, and asked for stories; fairy food. But the child inside such people was sadly stunted, and it was up to people like me, who dealt in the food of Faery all the time, to bring some back for them. Why not? They wanted to be what I was, but without the cheap rooming-houses and the lack of money. We each paid a price.

So what must I do, at twenty-five?

I wanted to direct actors, I said, not to be one; I wanted to create illusion, not to be one of its tools. And I must do this, I decided, on the handsome salary paid to a producer in ABS, the national broadcasting service. What I secretly wanted, saying this, was entry into that world I had glimpsed in the Red Room: the purring, comforting ether behind the yellow-lit radio dial, where reassuring voices gave all the world's disasters a cosy respectability; where all cold poverty and dismalness were shut out; where Aunt Susan and Uncle Charles lovingly conducted Children's Hour, and privileged, brilliant people adapted *Oedipus Rex* for broadcasting.

It wouldn't be easy. Vacancies for producers in ABS Drama came about rarely; hundreds competed for them, and the organisation was leisurely about making any appointments at all. But I learned at last of an imminent vacancy at Head Office in Sydney, and wheedled a letter out of Rupert Jones, the ABS Drama man in Melbourne who had been my patron when I arrived from Hobart. The letter guaranteed me nothing; but it was sufficient to give me the nerve to prepare to leave at last, to depart this flat city on the southernmost edge of the continent and to take flight north to the unknown metropolis of sun, with my meagre savings and my two suitcases.

I would survive for a time as an actor, if I had to; but only for a time, I said. I wanted to get into ABS badly enough to believe I couldn't be stopped. I wanted an end to rooming-houses; I wanted an end to fawning makeshift; I wanted other actors to smile on me as I now smiled on the producers who kept me fed. I wanted control, and the high, far ether I had seen in the Red Room as my future. I would do anything to get it. Seven years in Melbourne had made me hungry.

2

William Street was my entrance hall to Sydney. A boulevard linking the city and King's Cross, it carried me down into a tunnel of hotels and pawnshops and then climbed the Darlinghurst ridge. I had taken a taxi directly from the airways office, since the Cross was where most actors and show people were said to live.

Scalded by the vinyl of the seat, riding through an air that smelled like tin, I seemed to be wrapped in sacking. I had never been so hot in my life, and it was borne in on me that I had come to a foreign latitude, not very far below the Tropic of Capricorn. The taxi driver wore a T-shirt, thongs and indecent shorts, and was glancing sardonically at my heavy southern suit.

'You better get outa that gear, sport, or you'll turn into a grease-spot.'

Sydney's surfaces were all strange after the cool south; it was nearing sunset, and a hot, honey-thick light coated the low brick business buildings with a weird density, and was reflected in the Cross's hillside windows up ahead, making them flash blinding messages. Strangest of all was a line of three-storey Victorian terraces at the top of the hill, which was the junction of the Cross. Rearing on the skyline, their fantastic arches and spires half colonial-Gothic, half Oriental, these buildings had a worrying, even nightmare quality; they suffered, melting and mouldering in the heat like ancient wedding-cakes, trapped in the wrong hemisphere. Painted in hideous colours, degraded in every way that simple imaginations had been able to devise, they were covered over every inch of their facades by advertisements and neon signs: new, faded and almost invisible, going back to the twenties and perhaps even earlier. One of them said: *Hasty Tasty*. Highest of all, on the pinnacle of the Cross, was a giant bottle of sherry tipping its neon liquor into a glass. It faded out when the glass was full, only to reappear as we passed, like the Cheshire Cat's smile; like a rune of the city I'd need to decipher. I fingered my letter of introduction to Martin Gadsby as though it were a talisman.

At six-thirty the next morning, I woke to find myself in the Sydney of my expectations: a room in Elizabeth Bay.

The place was called Beaumont House, and the bed I was in pretended to be a divan. In fact it was simply an old wooden base set on blocks on the floor—an example of Mr

Beaumont's flair for economy. But I was happy with it,
and with everything else here. I saw that I was living
almost out of doors, in Beaumont House: Sydney Harbour
was half in the room. The sun, already gathering strength,
was streaming through a pair of french doors opening on to
an arcade verandah; and since these doors were the room's
only source of ventilation, I'd been forced to leave them
ajar during the night. Now they framed the giant arch of
the Harbour Bridge, and a blue segment of water.

I'd been woken by the little crashes of breakfast trays,
set down on the tiles by Bela Beaumont, the house's
Hungarian manager, who brought tea and toast to all the
doors. There were five rooms on this long back verandah,
mine being the last, and I could hear his rubber-soled shoes
advancing in a series of hissing rushes. He appeared at the
doorway, setting down the tray on the tiles like a man
doing exercises. Straightening, he paused, and looked across
at me in my bed. 'Good morning, Commander.' He gave
this title to many people, I found.

'It looks like another hot day,' I said.

'Hot—yes, it will be hot again. It is too much for me,
this time of year. I cannot get used to your summers.' His
voice was fast, loud and confident, and everything about
him gleamed: his sculptural, receding black hair touched
with grey in the right places; his tanned forehead; his
electric-blue sports shirt. His almond-shaped brown eyes
were friendly and inquisitive, and he had an almost military fitness, despite a slight thickening of the waist. I saw
him as an officer in a Viennese operetta—a supporting
role, not the lead.

Without a pause from his previous remark, he asked:
'And what business are you in, Mr Miller?'

'I'm a radio actor.'

He threw back his head and laughed on three notes,
while I waited with some irritation for an explanation of
his mirth.

'I am sorry,' he said. 'I am not laughing at your
profession—but so *many* people in show business are staying
in this house! It was once owned by a great theatrical

manager, you know. Yes; and I myself have been in show business. Well, I hope you get plenty of work. You must be able to pay my rent, eh?' He laughed loudly again at his own joke. 'You get plenty of jobs?' he asked.

'Quite a few.' I tried to strike a note of off-hand confidence.

'Good. Excellent.' His white shoes moved like a dancer's; he was taking off. 'Enjoy your breakfast,' he said. 'Ta-ta.' In his mouth, the colloquialism sounded oddly foreign. He disappeared from the doorway like a puppet jerked offstage. Then, just as rapidly, he reappeared. 'You should meet some of the other theatre people here. Remind me to introduce you.'

Sipping my tea, I reflected on how uncomfortably accurate his guess about my rent potential had been. It was almost as if some sixth sense had told Mr Beaumont I had yet to get work at all.

3

We were all refugees, in the Cross.

Dormitory of Displaced Persons, New Australians and old, King's Cross was a ghetto for those on the run: from wives, from husbands, from jobs; from that past where they'd once been respectable. Roosting on its hill above the city centre, this junction where five roads met was so small it had no official right to separate existence. Mini-village in the ward of Fitzroy, gaudy patch on the slum-grey ridge of Darlinghurst, it existed through force of personality, and was more than a district. The Cross was the capital of deviance, and Australia's most densely-populated square mile.

Back in the twenties and thirties, in the era of mutton chops and meal tickets, of the famous Arabian coffee shop and the poets Brennan and Slessor, this had been Bohemia; a southern hemisphere Montmartre. In the summer of 1964, when I first came there, it still wrapped itself in the tatty dressing-gown of these pretensions like one of its own landladies. But by now it was a teeming rookery of male and female prostitutes, show people, failed artists, suc-

cessful criminals, and the wrecked and displaced flung to
Australia from Europe after the War: people like my landlord, Bela Beaumont.

Elizabeth Bay rents were high, and so were his. The
geography of the area entitled them to be so. The
Darlinghurst ridge went on from the Cross to poke a long
finger into the Harbour, becoming the fashionable village
of Potts Point; below the ridge on the city side lay the
dockside slums of Woolloomooloo, and on the other was
expensive Elizabeth Bay, inviting as a dream of pre-war
Hollywood, from which it took its style, with its white
Spanish villas, gardens on the Harbour, and apartment
towers. However diverse, the three districts were essentially one, connected by a maze of streets and lanes; but
Potts Point and Elizabeth Bay, the Cross's smart sisters,
breathed a different air; and this was the air I'd decided
was for me.

I was beginning as I meant to continue, and Bela Beaumont's establishment at the terminus of Elizabeth Bay
Road was no ordinary rooming-house, in my eyes; I saw it
as Sydney's version of a Venetian *palazzo*. In actual fact,
it was a two-storey Victorian mansion come down in the
world, carved into a warren of arty bedsitting-rooms such
as mine; but saying so can't change the way it seemed to
me that summer: it remains in memory a musing *palazzo*,
whose rent was beyond my pocket. Unless I got into ABS
quickly, I'd soon be in trouble; but I'd left my letter of
introduction with Martin Gadsby's secretary, and all I
could do now was wait. I knew no one in Sydney, and I
began to sink into a sense of isolation. But on the third
morning after my arrival, I had a small encounter.

I went out on to the arcade after breakfast, making my
way towards a shower-room at the end. There was no sign
of life. In front of the other four doors, four trays still
stood untouched in the sun, covered with white napkins. I
half hoped to see one of the inmates emerging to claim
one, but it didn't happen. I seldom saw any fellow-guests,
and Mr Beaumont had not carried out his promise to

introduce me; the place was silent as though it were deserted. And yet others must be here; hidden.

Bird cries; the eternal cooing of pigeons from the gardens of Elizabeth Bay, murmuring about a cook in the rich silence. There was a sense of secret events gathering; a feeling of being watched, as I moved across panels of sun laid down through the arches, the figured mosaic tiles warm under my feet. A ginger tom-cat dozed on the balustrade halfway down; I greeted him, and he blinked tolerantly.

The shower-room was in a sort of annexe. Like my bedsitting-room, whose thin wall partitioned it from the one next door, this place was obviously the work of amateur handymen: possibly of Mr Beaumont himself. It had two improvised shower-stalls fixed against one wall, made of cement sheeting. They somewhat resembled voting booths, or perhaps confession boxes. A faint tang of ozone flowed across the bricks, so that I was still half out of doors here; and this had in it all the sub-tropical novelty of Sydney. Over everything, in this great port city of the Pacific, lay the pale bleach of Holiday; nothing was coldly earnest. I hooked shut the rickety door of my booth, and turned on the water.

Seconds after I did so, the clacking of shoes sounded on the bricks in the room outside. The lightness of the steps made me suspect a woman, and I listened tensely. Surely she'd retreat, when she saw my shabby male shorts on the bench? When I came out of the shower, I'd have to cross the full width of the chamber naked, to reach this bench— the only place where clothes and towel could be laid.

But the flimsy structure shook as someone secured the door of the other booth, and a young woman's voice suddenly spoke through the partition.

'What is the water like this morning?'

Amazed, I took some moments before answering. 'Fine,' I said.

'That's good,' the voice called. 'Sometimes it's lukewarm, and that's terrible.' It was a pleasant, friendly voice, free of frivolity or coyness, and with the hint of a foreign accent.

The other shower was turned on and the voice fell silent; I heard a faint hiss of breath. I was now acutely aware that she and I stood naked a few inches from each other. I was unattached, having broken off a recent affair in Melbourne, and women had been on my mind in these last three days. Here in the Cross and Elizabeth Bay, attractive young matrons walked the baking avenues half-naked, stepping across violet carpets of jacaranda blossoms in high-heeled sandals, two-piece swimsuits and sun-hats—or in shorts that left their buttocks half bare, the creases under the cheeks exposed. I kept getting little shocks; one was not allowed to forget the body, in this latitude. All the byways and shops and buses jostled with segmented nudities: thighs; bellies; dewy armpits. City of water, and semi-nude flesh! It still maintained urban formalities of dress downtown, but another, near-naked sub-group wandered among the suits and ties: a race of white Polynesians. The taboos of the Anglo-Saxon grandfathers were slowly fading, as the zone muttered its demands for nudity; youths sat in city buses naked to the waist, pubic hair curling above their belts: narcissists of the sub-tropic of pleasure.

Product of an era and a region of cold-zone conventions, I was still digesting all this; and I was deeply surprised by my invisible neighbour in the shower. Was mixed showering usual, in this strange rooming-house? What would happen if we decided to come out of our booths at the same time?

Now the voice called to me again. 'Are you late for work?'

'Not really,' I said. I didn't feel like explaining that I had no work.

'I'm *always* late for work,' the voice called. 'But I'm not going to hurry my shower.'

I came out of the booth, dried myself quickly, and pulled on my shorts. A pair of white, rather shabby sandals stood on the bricks: on the bench, neatly folded, was a dressing-gown of dark green satin, embroidered with roses. It seemed silly to say goodbye, and she didn't speak again.

I had an intense desire, going back to my room, to know who she was. It seemed unlikely that I'd ever find out.

That afternoon, I phoned Martin Gadsby, the senior producer in ABS Drama. He'd had enough time to digest my letter of recommendation, I thought.

His voice on the phone was small and cold and elderly, and he didn't offer to meet me immediately.

'I'm impressed that Rupert Jones thinks so highly of you, Mr Miller, and of course you're welcome to apply for the vacancy here. But you must understand we'll have a lot of highly-qualified people interested. Are you going to do some acting up here? Good. I'll contact your agency, and book you for my next suitable show. That way, I'll see what sort of talent you have, and we can discuss other possibilities afterwards. Goodbye.' Abruptly, the voice was gone.

The next two weeks were spent waiting in vain for Gadsby's office to give my agency a call.

The agency got me two commercial radio jobs—small parts in soap operas—and the rest was emptiness, while my savings began to dwindle. I walked the streets of the city, calling in at the offices of the commercial radio producers to remind them of my existence. I seldom got past their secretaries; but it had to be done. The rest of the time I waited for the phone, which stood upstairs in the front hall. Mr Beaumont usually answered it, darting out of his nearby office; down in my room on the distant arcade at the back I couldn't hear it ring, but he'd promised to bring me any messages.

There was no other way than this, no alternative to waiting, day after empty day, not just for Gadsby, but for other acting calls. The first step on the road to failure was to take a part-time job; I'd learned that when I started in Melbourne. But Melbourne had been easier. The pool of actors was smaller, and there were no agencies. Sydney was the only city in the nation where enough radio and

television was produced to keep a legion of actors fully
employed, and a number of agencies going full blast; so it
was all more impersonal, you had to have an agent or you
weren't considered. There was a hard core of relatively
famous full-time professionals, and a fiercely jostling outer
circle, whose ranks were constantiy thinned and replen-
ished; I must join this outer circle, and then bore in
towards the centre. But if I got into ABS Drama, I said,
I'd be doing the hiring; a whole different story would
begin.

Meanwhile, I had to survive, and every other day I went
in to Metro Casting in the city, to be told by the secretary
that ABS hadn't yet phoned. She was always hopeful for
me, though.

'You mustn't get down*cast*, dear. I've known young
actors to take months to get their first job. There's so
many hammering at the *doors*, in this town. It's lucky you
can still do juve parts—there's a shortage of good juves.'

Middle-aged, with greying, upswept hair, upswept spectacles and a motherly veneer that totally disappeared during certain steely phone calls she made, Miss Morton
seemed to me like Fate, seated in her cubby hole over her
three phones and her huge typewriter, surrounded by casting lists, and publicity shots of Sydney's famous and
half-famous actors.

'If Martin Gadsby said he'll use you, I'm sure he will,'
she said. 'He's the king, in ABS Drama, and ABS Drama
is what matters.' She lowered her voice. 'Most of the
actors hate him, of course, he can be such an old swine.
You'll just have to get on the right side of him.' Mouth
pursed as though sucking back a smile, hands poised over
the keys of the machine, she looked at me slyly. 'I'm sure
you'll manage that, Richard—you're young and good-
looking.'

I stored this up, as she meant me to. And I waited for
Gadsby's call, in the city of heat and daydreams.

Provincials from the bush or small towns arrive in the
great city of Australia with a projected world in their
heads: a world they believe stretches in wait for them

outside their rented rooms; an impossible cityscape of ethereal encounters, which fades eventually, to be replaced by the real one. The real one is no less strange; but who's to say that the other city doesn't exist somewhere—that city glimpsed in the mind? In those first weeks of my arrival, there were two Sydneys: a mythical Sydney lay somewhere in the heat, out beyond the verandah's arches.

Slowly the real one would begin to reveal itself; but for now, boredom and imaginary excitement squatted side by side on the deserted arcade: two shabby, heraldic beasts. Soon enough, footsteps would sound on the tiles out there; my visitors would begin. But this was hard to believe, just now.

The only human being I saw frequently besides Bela Beaumont was a tall old man who looked like a Russian, with a white moustache, a shock of white hair and blue-tinted glasses. He would often pass me in the verandah or the front hall, carrying in his arms a crippled boy of about twelve, whose rubbery legs dangled uselessly. Each morning a minibus would pull up in Elizabeth Bay Road outside, with other disabled children smiling at its windows; then the old man would appear, pushing the boy to the gate in a wheelchair, and would lift him into the bus. That this was an event in my day was a measure of its emptiness.

But the evenings were the emptiest time, especially Saturdays, when the world was preparing to go out. Then the party was held in Berkeley Towers.

This was a tall apartment building next door. Like so many apartment blocks in the eastern suburbs of Sydney, it had been built in the Jazz Age: one of the last periods to allow whimsy and story-book fancy into the design of large buildings. Built of gleaming clinker brick, it had arched windows with brick sunbursts above them, and was topped by medieval-looking turrets; and although only sixteen stories high, its lines were so dramatic that it seemed like a skyscraper, dominating Elizabeth Point. At exactly eight o'clock, and not before, the Saturday night celebration would begin there; and it always began with an explosion. I would be shaken in my room by sudden and thunderously amplified rock and roll music.

I began to wait for it; always, without fail, it was 'Twist and Shout'. The first time it came it seemed to me to emanate from somewhere in the upper levels of the air—shocking, in this otherwise peaceful district—and it continued, with a counterpoint of exultant party voices, for an hour. Then, just as suddenly, the music stopped, though the voices continued.

The next Saturday night, staring up from the verandah, I located the source: an open window on the fourteenth floor where figures moved to and fro and lights were already on, although the fast sub-tropical sunset wasn't yet completed, and gardens, buildings and water were all sunk in pink. When it was over, at about midnight, the sounds of the Harbour came up with greater distinctness than before. Gulls fought over food-scraps down there, and their explosions of angry screaming startled me; eventually they settled down, and quiet returned.

But late in the night, lying almost asleep, I was disturbed again.

A woman's voice and a man's began to murmur to each other through the wall, and I sensed that they were in bed together, quite close by. I still had no idea who occupied the room next door, never having seen anyone enter or leave, and I strained to distinguish words. The talk was too muffled, and I could make out nothing; now and then there was soft laughter, and eventually they relapsed into silence. I began to sink into sleep; but suddenly I was jerked back to wakefulness by the woman's voice; and this time, although the words were indistinct, I believed I could make them out.

'No. No, don't make me do that.'

This was followed by what sounded like a moan; but perhaps I was mistaken. Then there was silence, and I slept.

I now entered my third week of waiting; and still no call had come from Martin Gadsby. Apart from Miss Morton,

Bela Beaumont, and the actors I'd met in the studios, I'd spoken to almost no one since my arrival. I began to feel unreal; I was in a sort of Limbo, and my hopes were draining away. I'd been foolish, to think I could crack ABS as a producer, I said; I didn't have enough background. I could see myself struggling to survive here as just another actor; perhaps I'd even be driven back to Melbourne.

I've said that I knew no one in Sydney; but of course I knew Deirdre Dillon. This fact loomed larger in my mind with each drifting day. In the hours when I lay in my room, my thoughts kept turning to her; and I was tempted again and again to dial her number in wealthy Point Piper. I'd looked it up in the phone book; even seeing the name there, *Dillon*, had made my heart beat unevenly and my mouth go dry. But I wouldn't ring; it was futile and I knew it, as I'd known it all these nine years; I hadn't attempted to contact her since her final letter, and I wouldn't do so now, I said. But I grew intensely curious. She would be thirty-seven: almost middle-aged. What would she be like? She was here, quite close by, in these eastern suburbs on the Harbour; and yet she was less real than she had ever been.

Finally, on an empty Saturday afternoon, I walked out to Point Piper and searched out the Dillon house in Wolseley Crescent, which proved to be on the very tip of the Point.

It was a childish expedition, and I wouldn't have made it had it not been for my unnatural isolation; had I not been endlessly in waiting on the arcade. And I wasn't merely waiting for the possible, any more; I was waiting for things that could never materialise. I wasn't quite normal, in that third week: the true and deceitful were merging; present and past blurred into each other.

It was a lovely, blowy day of sun and shadow and fast-riding clouds: the big Saturday racing yachts were out, bending and tacking beyond the rich gardens. I could see the tiny figures of the crews working on the sheets; hear the flap of the giant sails. Green, choppy water; pale gold sunlight coming and going in waves, filtering through the sails like white wine. Everything moving, like the yachts and the clouds; yet nobody moving in the houses. On the other side of the Harbour, miles off, were grey-blue headlands and the north shore suburbs. Green Shark Island was close off-shore, at the bottom of the Dillon garden, the white dome of the beacon off its rocks like the temple of a dwarf race.

As is so often the case in wealthy suburbs, there was no sign of life in this cul-de-sac of mansions: no one on the footpath; no car on the road; no face at any window. A sign said, NO THROUGH ROAD, and I stood in the silence like a burglar, on the other side of the street.

Deirdre was here, after all these years: thirty-seven years old. She was somewhere inside this white, imposing two-storey villa, whose style was Sydney Spanish Mission. I studied its every detail: its big, steep roof of terracotta tiles; its barley-sugar columns and arches; its black iron grilles that protected the windows from intruders like me. A stand of palm trees rustled near the front door. At the back, I could just glimpse a high, dreamlike terrace and a formal garden dropping in stages to the water's edge. Lawns; a pool; a few thin rosebushes; a tamarisk. The gardens were sparse here, struggling against the harsh salt air. A Jaguar purred by, and turned into a driveway.

What should I do?

I did nothing; I walked away up the hill.

Monday afternoon. I lie on the makeshift divan in my shorts, felled by the heat. Not a breath of air comes through the glass doors. Gadsby will never call, I say, but it doesn't matter; nothing matters but the heat, and I enter a state of stupefaction.

Before I came to Sydney, I imagined the sun as a luxurious bath; like all natives of cold climates, I daydreamed over pictures of palm trees and tropical sunsets, longing to escape into such images. But the reality isn't like that; the heat isn't a bath, but a burning, wheat-coloured force. The temperature is in the nineties, and going through the streets is a test of endurance.

But at four o'clock, something begins to happen to the burning world outside: a change.

Below the verandah's arches, the jacarandas, camphor-laurels and ragged palm trees have all begun stirring and hissing, as though coming to life. And with queer suddenness, a human voice sounds close to my open door: the voice of a middle-aged woman.

'The Southerly's arrived!'

Another woman's voice answers. 'So it has. Well *that*'s a relief.'

The Southerly has arrived. Patron sea-breeze of Sydney, for which this marine city waits every afternoon, it blows at the curtain of heat. Its first delicious breath strays through the doors and cools my flesh, and the voices of the invisible women, exchanging remarks I no longer take in, recede down the arcade; one youthful and faintly foreign, the other middle-aged, pleasantly nasal and Australian— touching me with a nostalgia for familiar things, for a life with calm and steady connections. I resist a ridiculous impulse to run out and see if they are real.

But I needn't feel so desperate. These have merely been the first players strolling on to the deserted stage outside; already the hissing shoes of an important envoy are approaching my room.

'Excuse me, Commander. Good news!' His loud tones make me jump; as he speaks, he raps on one glass door. 'A message has come,' he announces. 'Your agency.'

I get up and pull on a shirt, intending to come upstairs to the phone, but he holds up a peremptory hand, his fast voice rattling on, speaking in exclamations.

'Don't worry, Commander, you can rely on me—I am an old theatre man myself! You have a part in an ABS radio play! Mr Gadsby is the producer! You must be at the studio at seven o'clock on Thursday evening! Pick up your script from the ABS office! Congratulations! Now you can pay my rent, can't you?'

This time when he laughs I join in; and he lingers, delicately refraining from crossing the threshold. 'Now you are in work, you will be able to socialise,' he says. He looks masterful. 'Do you know that right next door to you lives a beautiful young woman who is very lonely? Yes, a girl of style and character. That's right, Commander—and Bela will introduce you! Ta-ta!'

He disappears abruptly, as though jerked away on a wire, and I stare at the doors in pleasant bemusement, and burst out laughing. The world has speeded up at last.

4

The studios of a big broadcasting organisation at night have the hush of a deserted church. But underneath this is a low, thrilling hum, like that of a ship at sea; the corridors are empty, but you know the organism is alive.

On the hot January night of Martin Gadsby's production, the dim little foyer of the ABS building in William Street was deserted. The commissionaire was away from his desk, on which he had left his girlie magazine and a packet of cigarettes, and I pressed the lift button with a sense of trespassing. Someone had thrown a cigar butt into the ashtray by the lift and the smell lingered. Down a corridor, an illuminated globe of red glass glowed above a door, lettered ON AIR. But that wasn't the studio I wanted; the big drama studio was on the second floor.

The lift was an ancient one; I could hear it groaning and wheezing down to get me like a peevish old man. My hands were sweating and I wiped one on my trousers, my script clutched in the other. It would be nice to recall that night simply as one which rewarded me with success after years of struggle. But it's coloured with someone else's pain: that of poor Phil Desmond, who would die some two years later of the overdose of sleeping pills so clearly in his destiny.

Pretending to study my script, I sat on one of the tubular-steel chairs against the studio wall, keeping an eye on the window of the control room opposite. The place smelled of stale cigarette smoke and clean carpet. Screens stood about, and the odd equipment of the Sound Effects man: an electric buzzer; plates to rattle; a door in a frame, on wheels.

We were doing Rattigan's *Ross,* so the cast was all-
male; and none of the other actors seemed particularly
disposed to be friendly. Having found out which agency I
was from, they ignored me—except for a man with a bitter
upper lip who asked me suspiciously if I belonged to
Actor's Equity. On finding that I did, he resumed the
study of his script. The talk and laughter was muted and
flat in this sound-proofed chamber, and I was glad not to
be drawn into the talk, since I wanted to eavesdrop on
these voices—many of which I'd first heard on the little
Bakelite radio in the Red Room. I took a private pleasure
in the fact that I was joining their owners at last: the best
pros in the country.

There, leaning on the grand piano, was Dr Fu Manchu,
who had laughed maniacally from behind the glowing dial
when I was ten years old: lanky old Eric Mawby, with
arched black eyebrows and avuncular glasses, whose rich,
melodramatic bass I recognised instantly. But what he was
saying now, instead of uttering frenzied Oriental curses,
was: 'Beatrice? Beatrice was pissed out of her mind. Someone had to get her outside and give her three black coffees
before she could go on. Afterwards, she had no idea
whether she'd played Lady Macbeth or Little Red Riding
Hood. She did it beautifully, of course.'

A plump man standing at the piano bent slightly at the
waist, going pink with laughter. He was about forty-five
and had wrinkled, thinning red hair and a snubby, good-
natured face. 'But of course,' he said. 'Poor Beatrice.
Eventually she *will* play Little Red Riding Hood, I'm afraid.
Only Children's Session will hire her.' His cool, beautifuly
modulated voice was familiar as a relative's, and I realised
I was looking at boyhood's lean-jawed hero with the steel-
blue eyes: this was Bulldog Drummond, and the Saint, and
every Nick and Simon and Ralph who had ever mastered
danger—whose real name turned out to be Ronald Porter.

The voices and the laughter began to become spas-
modic, in the private, motionless air. There was no air-
conditioning in this aged studio; instead two giant electric
fans on standards as tall as men revolved full blast at either

end of the room, and as the silence took over I became conscious of their humming. People were glancing at watches; rustling scripts. It was now nearly fifteen minutes over starting time for the rehearsal and obviously this wasn't usual. Cautious glances were cast at the control room window.

Motionless at the producer's desk, Martin Gadsby sat bulkily hunched in there, a cigarette between his lips, surveying us with a sulky expression. He was somewhere in his early sixties, with a clipped moustache that made him resemble a British Army officer, an effect that was partially negated by dyed blond hair worn in an artistic fringe. He turned to speak to the panel operator, while the Sound Effects man stooped over his line of turntables like a chef preparing sauces. Because of the soundproofing it was all in dumb-show; under the fluorescent lights of their cabinet, the three looked super-real: wax figures in a showcase. But it was we who were in the showcase, since the control room could hear us on the stand mike, while we couldn't eavesdrop on the control room. That was one of the ways in which Gadsby's power was defined.

'Who's not here?' Eric Mawby asked. His perfectly produced, hammy old voice had the authority of special eminence.

They all began to compare scripts and talk at once.

'I'm Dickinson.'

'Who's doubling as Parsons? You, Fred?'

'I'm Allenby,' Eric Mawby said. 'And you've got the plum of course, Phil.' He was looking at a sad-faced man of about forty who sat by himself, and who looked up at Mawby with eyes that appeared to have been drained of their colour by some sort of violent excess. I guessed at a nervous breakdown, or alcoholism.

'That's right Eric,' he said. 'That's if you call a masochistic queer who gets buggered by Turks a plum part.'

There was a burst of laughter around the studio but the sad-faced man didn't smile. He had a beautiful voice, and now I knew who he was; I'd been trying to remember. Philip Desmond was the closest thing Australia then had to a star. He had done two films and a good deal of stage work; his Shakespearean performances were revered. But this made no one a living: like everyone else, Desmond made his living in ABS radio plays like this one, and in the big commercial soap operas *(When a Girl Marries; Reflections in a Wine Glass)*. He still had the remnants of those matinee-idol's good looks that had been fashionable here and in Britain in the 1930s: dark brown hair parted on one side; wide-set eyes whose straight top lids made them look 'steady'. But all the lines of the face were drawn down by a weary melancholy, and there were unusually emphatic pouches under his eyes. Tonight he would play the clinically depressed Lawrence of Arabia; type-casting, I thought.

A huge, hollow voice sounded from a monitor the size of a packing case, over by the door. It was Martin Gadsby from the control-room.

'What we're waiting for, *mes amis*, is Simon bloody Harrington, who has simply not turned up, and who *was* to have played the Turkish General.' He stood up; a few seconds later the hushed double doors of the studio opened, and he was moving across the carpet towards us, script in hand: shorter and stockier than he had seemed through the glass, in a pink shirt and old-fashioned red bow tie. He took the cigarette from his mouth, holding it away from himself as though it were about to explode. 'Unreliability is becoming a *disease*,' he said. 'I'll give him five minutes more, and if he doesn't come I'll have no choice but to cancel rehearsal.'

The regretful expressions around the wall were false; we would still have to be paid for this call. There was a silence.

'I think I could do it,' I said.

All the faces around the wall looked at me; Gadsby, the cigarette back in his mouth, pivoted slightly and raised his eyebrows. His elderly eyes were of an unusual forget-me-not blue: the eyes of an ageing beauty queen. Like the startling blond hair, they were in blatant contrast with his grey moustache and sagging, disciplinarian's face. 'Ah.

The new man from Melbourne,' he said. 'Showing commendable ambition, eh, dear boy?'

There were small chuckles—some of them malicious. Gadsby turned the pages of his script, squinting through his smoke. 'You're doing the lecturer,' he said musingly. 'Only one scene. Very well; we'll relieve you of that, and see what you make of the General. But if you can't give me what I want, Richard, we abandon rehearsal.' Silence returned, during which eyes hovered about me like mosquitoes.

We halted for a coffee break at the end of the first act, at a point where I'd appeared in two scenes, but not yet in the key one where Lawrence was tortured.

'Your General is interesting, so far,' Gadsby said to me. 'But let's wait and see what you do with his big scene.' He turned to Phil Desmond. 'Phil, your Lawrence is too camp.'

Phil Desmond raised weary eyebrows. 'Well, he *is* camp, Martin, isn't he?'

'That doesn't mean you play him as a trissy little queen, dear boy.'

'I believe that's how Guinness played him.'

Gadsby took the cigarette from his mouth and stared as though he had been affronted. 'I doubt that,' he said. 'I really do. But whatever the case may be, would you mind playing it *my* way?'

Phil Desmond now had the expression of a brave boy being rebuked by a cruel teacher. 'Which way is that, Martin? You haven't told me.'

'Some things surely don't need pointing out,' Gadsby sighed. 'Lawrence was a man of action and a hero. Would it be too much to bear that in mind, Phil, or beyond your powers to convey it?'

Desmond's eyes dropped to his script, and he said nothing. Gadsby stood up; and with an air of relief, the others began to get up too, and straggle out through the double doors for coffee.

On my way back to the studio I went along to the washroom. Large, blue-tiled and brightly lit, it was empty except for a man who stood at the row of washbasins, hunched over with his back to me. When I came from the urinal to the basins he was still there, stooped in the same attitude; and something about his stillness made me curious. I looked up at the reflection in the big mirror above the basins. It was Philip Desmond, and he was crying.

The reflected face looking back at the reflection of mine was crumpled into a mask of tragedy, tears running down his cheeks. I let liquid soap trickle slowly from my hands, and gazed at this unbelievable image. The red-rimmed eyes didn't seem to expect me to look away; seemed, on the contrary, to want my attention to their woe. I swung sideways to take in the real face, half-hoping that the mirror had misrepresented it, and that he merely had grit in his eye.

But no; he was silently crying, and looked more than ever like a schoolboy who had just been caned—or would have done, had it not been for the heavy bags under the eyes, the deep lines from the nose to the corners of the mouth. The tears ran into these furrows. 'If—Mr—Martin—Gadsby,' he said, spacing the words, 'is—rude to me—again, I shall bloody well—walk out.'

I could find no answer to this, but tried to look sympathetic. I felt infinitely sorry for him, and infinitely contemptuous. Desmond was the best actor in Australia; was this all he could do with his success? He swayed a little, and I caught the smell of liquor. He blew his nose; the sobbing had abated.

'You're just starting,' he said. 'And you're pushy enough to make it, young Miller—that's obvious. Take some advice.'

'What's that?'

'Get out.' He smiled: a falsely winsome smile. 'Get out, sonny boy, or spend your bloody life recording commercials for toilet paper, and being insulted by talentless old shits like Martin Gadsby.' His voice rose now, booming in the echo-chamber of the washroom; no longer the small voice of suffering but the huge, effortlessly-projected voice of the stage professional, heavily and bitterly hammy. 'Do you re-ahlly want to be an *ac*-tor?'

He burst into breathy laughter, staring at me expectantly. Then his eyes filled with tears again, and I turned towards the door.

As I did so, his voice rang out again. 'Oh, *General!* You're going to arrange for me to be *broken,* when we go back in there, aren't you? "Bodily integrity violated, will broken"—isn't that how it goes? Will you enjoy that? Martin will. He's looking forward to this scene. Oh, by the way, he *likes* young actors. It's just the old ones he gets sick of.' He began to laugh again, and I let the door swing shut.

Lawrence, it may be recalled, doesn't actually speak to the Turkish General in Rattigan's play; so I didn't at any stage exchange dialogue with Philip Desmond. Lawrence is tortured and sodomised in an outer room, while the General, within earshot, discusses it with a young Captain. Then Lawrence is dragged in; he lies on the floor semiconscious, and the General speaks to him; but he can't respond.

The only actors at the stand mike now were Roy Taylor, a cheerful man with a large Air Force moustache who played the Captain, and myself. Desmond sat on his chair by the control room window, his eyes still pinkish from crying, and seeming to ask for mercy. It was probably my private knowledge of his suffering that enabled me to play the scene as well as I did. I worked very close on mike, giving the General a soft but penetrating voice, with a suggestion of sibilance. It helped to make him sound delicately obscene, under a perfectly civilized and intelligent surface.

At the moment when Lawrence was dragged in and flung on the floor; at the moment when the General leaned over and pulled Lawrence's head up by the hair, I couldn't resist a quick glance at Phil Desmond.

' "You must understand that I *know,*" ' I said. I was telling him that I knew what had been revealed by the rape: in the general's words: 'Bodily integrity violated, will broken.' The silence in the studio had deepened two layers. As I looked up from my script, I caught a glimpse of Gadsby through the glass. He was sitting very still, watching me as though trying to work out a puzzle. The smoke from his cigarette went straight upwards.

When the rehearsal was over, he shuffled into the studio and moved directly across to me, ignoring the remaining actors.

'Congratulations, dear boy, that was splendid.' He patted my shoulder twice, blinking rapidly; friendliness made his eyes look beseeching instead of threatening. 'And now I think we should talk. Have you time for some supper? There's an excellent place up in the Cross. It serves the most wonderful cream cakes.' He gave me a confiding smirk, as though divulging the whereabouts of a brothel for special tastes.

He led me along Darlinghurst Road, main street of the Cross, through the quarter's unsleeping carnival. It was after ten o'clock, but many of the coffee shops and patisseries and delicatessens were open, and the pavements crowded; life quickened on this little hill, while the city slept below. Gadsby's hand was under my elbow, steering, making me feel uncomfortably like a bride being given away by an aged father. We moved through a close, warm stillness like that of a circus tent; one seemed to catch the odours of canvas, and the dung of herbivorous animals, mixed with the Cross's real smells: grilling hamburgers; cut flowers, coffee. Gadsby led me around the corner into Macleay Street, crossing that invisible line where the Cross proper becomes Potts Point.

There was a sort of elegance here, under the plane trees and awnings; an elegance deriving from a wistful dream of continental Europe. Gadsby's goal proved to be an outdoor café on a flagstoned terrace, whose strings of coloured overhead lights lit the pale green plane leaves. When we sat down under a multi-coloured umbrella, served by waiters in mess jackets and red cummerbunds, the dangerous, drunken shouts and car-horns of the Cross became safely remote; sounds from a distant fairground.

Gadsby had begun to praise me for my interpretation of the Turkish General.

'You've played a man twice your age impeccably, and got right under the skin of a sado-masochist. Only a very few could do that, Richard—I wonder how *you* did?' He chuckled, watching me try to look modestly non-committal; then he leaned forward and patted my hand. 'There there, dear boy, I'm sure you don't share the General's proclivities.'

His warm, somewhat moist old hand remained on mine, imprisoning it on the table. I froze in appalled embarrassment, but I didn't try to escape, and controlled my expression. The moment was crucial; if I showed even a flicker of disapproval, I might very well see the door I'd so long waited to get through slammed shut; and I had no intention of causing that to happen. I'd eaten too long from the greasy bowl of failure to be so squeamish; I was prepared to endure a good deal of petty discomposure to give up that brew for life.

Gadsby now fixed me with a serious yet almost tender gaze, and spoke softly. 'So you want to be a producer. Can you tell me a little more about yourself?'

My hand was still trapped, but I isolated its plight in a corner of my mind, organised my thoughts, and began to speak, my tone one of friendly formality, as though our loving attitude were perfectly normal, or had escaped my notice. It was very important, in putting my case, that I shouldn't appear to be just another actor; I had to produce a background that qualified me to enter Gadsby's magic realm of control. I spoke about my university years, and dwelt on the theatrical direction I'd done for the University Players—subtly adjusting my vowel sounds so that my accent, like Gadsby's own, was the one which at that time still signalled a calm expectation of privilege. But now there was a little setback that sent a chill through my bowels.

'You didn't take your degree,' Gadsby said, and frowned.

No, I told him, theatre had been all I cared about; and I gave him my most frank smile.

He patted my hand rhythmically, seeming to brood. Then, he smiled back. 'Never mind,' he said. 'I haven't got a degree-either. No bloody academic qualifications do much to make a producer, do they?'

Now a diversion arrived: the cream cakes. Multi-coloured childhood concoctions were wheeled up on a trolley, and Gadsby, freeing my hand at last, blinked upon them with thinly veiled gluttony. Although I wasn't fond of cakes, I feigned polite enthusiasm as he pondered over a choice for me.

'Why not try *that* one, son? With the marvellous cream topping? A young fellow like you doesn't have to watch his waistline. This is very naughty of me I'm afraid, but one can't be Spartan *all* the time.'

An indulgent aunt with a sweet tooth, he now became quite appealing; but I still saw authority in the sag of his cheeks, and remembered Phil Desmond's tears. Gadsby wasn't a kindly aunt; yet although he'd said nothing to commit himself, I had a premonition of success—that assisted leap for which so many wait in vain; and I breathed in the odours of cigar-smoke and coffee now with cautious exultancy.

'How old are you, Richard?' Gadsby asked suddenly. He was leaning forward over his cake, forking it in with great dexterity, dropping not a crumb or fleck of cream. When I told him, he sat back and stared, wiping the cream from his moustache with a clean handkerchief.

'You've got it all in front of you, son—haven't you?' His pouched face had in it now an intimate, naked wistfulness; it was as though he had dropped a mask, out here in the warm night, and had plainly told me that he saw in me his own youth; that I stood where he longed to stand again. The surprising moment didn't last long; he cleared his throat, finished his cake, and changed to a dry, almost official tone: one I was sure he used in the office. 'I'm glad Rupert wrote to me about you—he described you as brilliant, and I think he was right. But tell me—why don't you want to go on acting? Why do you want to produce? Is it because of the limp? That wouldn't stop you in radio.'

'It's not that,' I said. 'It's because of the way I am. Some people are raw talent—others are best at managing talent, and putting a frame around it. I believe that's the category I'm in.'

He nodded slowly. 'Then you're like me. You live off the beauty of others; and you may make a producer.' He lit a cigarette and became curt again.

'I can't promise you anything yet; but I'd like to see you in the Department. It won't be quick or easy, and other people will decide as well as me. Meanwhile, I'd like you to meet a few friends of mine. I'm having a party next Saturday night—will you come?'

We parted with a handshake, standing on the footpath again. He had someone to visit in the Cross, he said, and turned on his heel, his smile already fading like a faulty bulb, moving off up Macleay Street under the plane trees and red brick apartment buildings: an elderly man in a navy Bermuda jacket, with a pot belly and dyed blond hair—changed and reduced by the frame he moved in. How few transformed the frame!

5

The following evening I had my first visitor, on Bela Beaumont's arcade.

Beaumont House was set back from the water, up on Elizabeth Point; but at night the Harbour's noises were so magnified that I seemed to be suspended just above it, and the sudden squabbling of the gulls could still startle me. It was one of their outcries after a long period of silence that made me look up from the script I was studying. The glass doors were open as usual, and I found that a tall young woman with her hair drawn back in a bun was standing on the dark verandah, looking in at me.

She knocked lightly on the door-frame and cleared her throat, holding herself very erect. 'Excuse me. May I come in?' It was a quiet, rather high voice, but it made me jump. It was also foreign, although the accent was very slight.

I got up from the rickety little table I used as a desk, murmuring some sort of assent. She stepped into the room, holding a black leather handbag protectively against her stomach with both hands, and glanced back over her shoulder so that I half-expected someone else to follow her in. But no one did, and we faced each other awkwardly in the muted orange glow from my table-lamp, with its aged paper shade. The overhead light was off.

'Thank you. I'm sorry to invade you like this,' she said, and smiled. The smile was professionally friendly and infectious, her wide-set grey eyes bright and intent; she waited as though explanations were due from me, and not from her. It was impossible not to smile back, but she made me very conscious of my crumpled white shirt and old grey slacks, since everything about her was formal: her erect posture, tight-waisted black frock and high-heeled shoes of black patent leather.

It was a European formality, and in these first moments I thought that she might be German. She was attractive, but seemed somehow old-fashioned, as so many of the migrants did who were currently coming into the country: her dark blond hair in its *chignon* was from the Weimar Republic, her wide face dramatically pale, and her straight nose perhaps capable of being earnest.

I gestured at the one easy chair, with its stained pink cover. When my visitor sat down on it she gave it dignity, sitting erect and expectant like someone about to impart some piquant scandal—or perhaps to hear it. Her high-arched brows were darker than her hair, and gave her a look of pleasant surprise.

I've been waiting for you, I said; but I didn't say it aloud.

She glanced behind me; then she said: 'I know this may seem strange—but would you mind shutting your doors?'

I stared at her in amazement; but I did as she asked without comment, returning to sit opposite her on the hard dining-room chair beside my work-table.

'I live next door,' she said. 'You're the radio actor,

aren't you? Bela often talks about you. I thought you wouldn't mind helping me.'

'How can I do that?'

'Just by allowing me to sit here for a moment.'

Now the arched brows seemed serious; she cleared her throat with a hint of tension, and briefly licked her lips. 'There's a man coming down here in a few moments I want to avoid: a friend of Bela's. He said he'd call on me, and he knows I'm in the house. I'd just like to hide here until he gives up. Can I do that? Does it annoy you?'

Immediately following this question, a rapping sounded from outside as though on cue, clearly audible through my doors. She put a finger on her lips like a schoolgirl.

'He's knocking on my door,' she whispered. 'He'll soon go away.' Her eyes held mine in silence; we waited, staring at each other, and the rapping sounded again, louder this time.

'He's not a very nice fellow,' she whispered. 'He's a *Pole*.' The smile assumed I knew all about Poles.

Footsteps receded on the arcade, and she looked up again, continuing to listen carefully until the sound had gone. Then she spoke in a normal tone. 'That was very kind of you. I don't usually burst into men's rooms.'

She stood up, and I did the same. 'I'm glad you did,' I said. 'It was time we met.'

When she was gone, a few minutes later, I sat still for a long time, listening to the silence and the wild altercations of the gulls. She had taken her immigrant intrigue away with her, and I had a sense of anti-climax: a baffled, formless excitement that wasn't helped by knowing that she was still nearby, just through the wall.

6

Beaumont House was a foreign country, like many others around the Cross. The district had become a ghetto for the wave of post-war immigrants from Europe.

The refugees from World War Two had begun to outnumber the native-born, in this part of Sydney; they had gravitated here as though by instinct, and the old Australia's stenches of beer and prawns had been replaced—not just by the foreign tang of garlic, but by the tragic aroma of memory. Lost Europe and lost dignities were preserved here, in the Cross; heart-numbing relics were hoarded in the tops of wardrobes, and under rooming-house beds.

The newcomers ran many of the quarter's restaurants and delicatessens; or else, like Bela Beaumont, they managed rooming-houses. For a time that can never be repeated, the Cross became exiled Europe in microcosm, and the air of Darlinghurst Road and Macleay Street was murmurous with re-run Continental intrigues and Continental betrayals: those passionately preserved hopes and causes that even the crassest Australian could see were broken and devalued for ever by the War; baggage that should have been left behind. The native-born eyed these people with mingled condescension and suspicion; the pain the Displaced had emerged from, the pain they carried in them always, meaning nothing. Australians could make little of them, this tribe from Eastern and Central Europe, in the first two decades of their coming: women with formal, old-fashioned dresses and strangely braided hair; shabby men with fanatical, pale blue eyes, in the jackets of old suits teamed with sad, neat sports trousers, carrying executive briefcases in which there were probably bombs, or books that no one would want to read. The native-born dubbed them Reffos, or Balts; and in the coffee lounges, the Reffos confirmed all suspicions by endlessly reviewing their broken lives, railing against the Machiavellian leaders who had sold them out, so that now they found themselves here, in this flat, huge country of flat, emotionless people who knew no other language but English, at the end of the world. Sometimes a Balt or some other refugee would go mad, succumbing to the wartime blackness he had carried to the southern hemisphere in his brain; would shout and rave, standing alone in the street of meaningless sun, his pale eyes coldly crazy, his flood of foreign words proof of his insanity. Then the police paddy wagon would come from Darlinghurst, and the big Sydney cops in their dark blue caps would haul him away, their disgusted faces saying: *A Reffo. What else can you expect?* They would look inside his briefcase, when they got him to the station up at Darlo; they would finger his foreign books.

Only a few of the Displaced were truly Balts; they came in fact from every nation in Europe where the century's two great tyrannies had squatted. But my neighbour, the young woman in the room next door, was a true Balt, I found: a native of what was now the Soviet province of Estonia, whose name was Katrin Vilde.

I began to plan ways to further our acquaintance; I lurked on the arcade in the evenings, hoping to intercept her. But for the next two days, I met with no success; there was never a sound from the adjoining room, and I began to wonder if she'd moved out.

On the third morning, when Bela Beaumont brought my tea and toast, he lingered in the doorway to talk, and I sensed that he had a purpose. Bela had a masterful way of asking cheeky personal questions—helped, I felt, by his upright position at the doorway, spruce and shaved, while I reclined slothfully in my bed on the floor. This morning he somehow extracted the information from me that I had a chance of joining ABS Drama—and then became exclamatory, while I sipped my tea.

'But this is wonderful! You have a big future in front of you, Commander, this is obvious! To be an actor is one thing—but a producer in an important organisation like ABS, that is another! You are a very fortunate young man.'

I protested that I hadn't got the position yet, but he brushed this aside. 'You will get it. And now it is time you had more social life. You are too much alone. I should like to introduce you to the Vilde family. You have already met Katrin, I believe.' He gave me a special glance, lifting his chin and narrowing his eyes. 'Did you know I also have her grandfather and brother living upstairs? Very sad,' he said briskly. 'The boy is crippled. The old man is very good with him. Tonight at eight we all meet in his apartment for a few drinks. These are cultivated people— people you will like. You will come?' Before I could answer, he became cheerfully imperious. 'Of course you will come. That is settled. Ta-ta.'

He was gone.

'You know why I have taken the name of Beaumont?'

Perched on a small, straight chair, Bela Beaumont paused for effect, a square of cheese upheld like a little flag in his left hand, a glass in his right. His white shirt gleamed; his grey trousers were knife-edged; he wore a tie. 'Because bloody Australians cannot pronounce my real name,' he said. 'So when I bought this house, I thought: good; an elegant Anglo-Saxon name, very snooty. My house and I will share it.' He led the laughter, loud and confident in the flat he let to Mr Vilde, on the first floor at the front.

Mr Vilde proved to be the old, Russian-looking man with the thick white hair and moustache whom I'd seen carrying the crippled boy in the mornings. We three were the only men here, and there were two women: Katrin Vilde and Bela Beaumont's wife Maria. All of these people sat with very straight backs, and all plainly wore their best clothes, as though these few drinks were an occasion. Was I the occasion? I couldn't quite believe it; but they began to make it plain that this was so, and I felt I should have worn a tie myself, instead of an open-necked sports shirt.

'We wanted to have you up long ago, and get to know you,' Katrin said. 'But we didn't know whether you'd want to come. I'm afraid this flat is very small and crowded—I hope you don't mind.'

I protested, telling her insincerely that the place was charming; but to call Mr Vilde's living quarters a flat was to put a strain on the term: it was another of Bela's makeshifts. I gathered that Katrin spent a good deal of her time here, only using the room next to mine to sleep in. There was no bathroom, but a tiny kitchen was built into a porch off this living-and-dining-room. Through the open door of the one cupboard-like bedroom, I could see Katrin's brother Jaan, who was paraplegic, propped up on pillows in a double bed. Presumably he slept there with his grandfather. His long, intelligent face had the pallor of chronic illness, with dark circles under the eyes; pale brown hair fell on his forehead.

There could be little doubt that the Vildes were poor, yet it didn't seem like poverty. We were drinking imported vermouth from expensive glasses; they kept up appearances in a way that was more impressive than affluence, and that made me half admiring, half uneasy. The room was fanatically neat, clean and foreign; we might have been in Eastern Europe, an illusion completed by the nineteenth-century moulding around the ceiling and the unfamiliar black bread that went with the cheese and pickled cucumber. There were smells of sour things like sauerkraut, and over all was the faint mustiness that always hovers about old people. Mr Vilde and his granddaughter had set up lost Estonia here: tablecloths woven in traditional geometric patterns; framed Estonian woodcuts on the walls. There were a few chairs, an aged sofa and a cheap round dining-room table, all carefully crowded together; an old kitchen dresser served as a china cabinet. An upright piano stood in one corner, polished like a mirror, with a runner on the top in the same Estonian pattern.

'Yes, I have put a lot of work into this place. Put me anywhere and I will survive,' Bela Beaumont was saying. 'Property is the answer. No investment can touch property. Bricks and mortar! That you can touch, and know it will stay.'

Chewing, he squinted appreciatively at the high Victorian ceiling with its central rosette, while old Mr Vilde, dressed despite the heat in a heavy grey suit of 1940s vintage, watched his landlord gravely through the blue-tinted glasses that brought to mind an old-fashioned anarchist. He was lean, dignified and imposing, but he'd scarcely spoken at all: perhaps he had little English.

'Listen to how Bela boasts,' Maria Beaumont apologised, and smiled at me for indulgence. Her black Hungarian hair gleamed as though lacquered; she was plump and tightly corseted inside a close-fitting knitted dress.

'All right, I boast,' Bela said, his fast voice rising. 'But where would you be without your boaster, Maria? We have survived.' He pointed at me accusingly. 'For this young Australian here, survival has never been a problem.'

The old man spoke for the first time, his deep voice quiet and slow. 'We must not be sure of that. He is an actor. They do not survive so easily.' He smiled at me, and raised his glass.

Bela raised his own glass in a toast. 'Ah, but soon he will be a big producer of drama in ABS radio! Your lame leg will not matter then, Commander.'

I felt myself grow stiff, but I continued to look bland.

'Oh Bela,' Maria said. 'You must not be so *personal*.'

He waved his hand. 'Richard doesn't mind, Maria. He and I are friends—and the world is his oyster. It wasn't so for us. Eh?' He pointed to old Vilde and looked at me sternly, raising his voice. 'This man was a university teacher in Estonia—a mathematician. Now he has lost his country and his career; the Soviets seized Estonia, and his son was shot by them. So there are worse things than a bad leg, am I right?'

Vilde spoke softly. 'I still have my granddaughter and the boy. And for this I thank God.'

I had grown uncomfortable at Bela's insensitivity. Exercising his privilege as landlord, he seemed to be treating the old Estonian and his family as exhibits. Vilde sipped his vermouth quietly and said no more; but Katrin, holding her glass with both hands, now cleared her throat with a small, feminine sound of warning. She still wore her hair in a bun, exposing a long, white neck which I found remarkably beautiful.

'I'm sure Richard doesn't want to hear about our troubles, Bela.' Her tone was low and calm, but it nevertheless made Bela look cautious.

'But I really am interested,' I told her.

'It isn't very cheerful,' she said to me. 'Some other time, perhaps.'

Her face abstracted, almost blank, she picked briefly at a nail, then stopped: plainly a nervous habit. I had thought

her about my own age when I first met her; now, covertly
studying her, I decided she was older, perhaps twenty-
eight. Her skin was flawless and unlined, but I sensed a
greater maturity than my own: it was in her dignified
manner, her careful control, and certain small, shutter-like
changes in her eyes, manifesting many levels of concealment. She awed me a little, and I tried to be critical: her
face was too broad by Anglo-Saxon standards; her Cupid's
bow lips a little too full. But these things were in fact at
the very heart of the attraction she had for me, and in
trying to disapprove of them, I merely played a game,
postponing assent. The short-sleeved, grey linen dress she
wore tonight, buttoning to the throat, made her seem
somewhat prim. I doubted that she was prim, but there
was something closed about her.

'Katrin is a wonderful artist,' Bela was saying to me,
seeking to mollify. 'A singer. In any other country, this
girl would be a star! But here she must work as a hotel
receptionist by day, and sing in the migrant clubs at night.
This is a problem, Richard. She can only sing to Russians,
Estonians, Germans—Australians don't want to hear her
material.' He stood up and crossed to the Vildes' piano,
throwing it open with a masterful gesture. 'Please, Katrin—
Richard must hear you sing.'

She didn't protest in the usual manner; she got up,
smiling at me as though seeking sympathy, and said something to the old man in Estonian, addressing him as
'Vanaisa'. He shuffled over to the piano to accompany
her.

She began with two Estonian folk songs, while we all
sat straight and attentive on our chairs. She had a good
soprano voice, very clear and true; at times almost like a
boy's. But the melodies were trite, and since the words
were a mystery to me, I was secretly bored.

Clapping, Bela called: 'A Russian song, Katrin! Sing us
a Russian song!'

After a murmured conference with her grandfather, she
sang 'The Little Bell'.

The long notes swooped and soared, dwindling off into

distance and then swelling again, while Vilde produced deep, crashing chords on the piano, bent forward so that his moustache almost touched the score, peering through his tinted glasses. Then, in this stuffy little flat in the Sydney heat, I saw the land of their longing, where the ringing of the bell on the night-time sleigh carried far across the snow: not the grim Soviet Union that had swallowed their country, but the Russia of legends; a Russia that had perhaps never existed, outside the song. It was a hymn to the lost hemisphere; her spirit went speeding to its mark, the wineglass grew warm in my hand, and I remembered that I'd seen this night before, in the dream of the skates.

It had been a recurring dream when I was first crippled; I'd forgotten it until now. In it, I found myself at the edge of a vast, frozen lake in the north of Europe, near the Arctic Circle. Pine-skirted, it extended past towns and villages into a night of gem-hard cold, and I sat in powdery snow at the edge, trying to fasten on a pair of bright silver skates. My frozen fingers trembled at the fastenings; my crippled leg bent awkwardly; voices urged me on, but I couldn't do it. Then there appeared in front of me a tall figure in a belted jacket and heavy trousers, without clear features. He had long, straw-coloured hair and a green muffler wound about his neck. He didn't speak, but conveyed cheerful encouragement, and he bent on one knee and swiftly adjusted my skates.

Within seconds, side by side, we were skating the lake. I leaned far forward, arms working in rhythm; I was propelling myself on the marvellous skates, and the figure a little way ahead turned and smiled at me over his shoulder. At this, crouching and thrusting out with a new strength, I found that I could skate with majestic skill. A magic force spun me away; I was crippled no more; I flew across the ice, my legs pumping like the pistons of a powerful machine. I caught up with my companion and passed him, skating off alone into the great night of the North, into a realm of pure speed.

Far away on my right, little lights were twinkling like fallen stars; breathing black air, I smiled with joy. Were these the lights of Rainbow Bridge? Or just a village at the lake's edge? I was leaving behind log fires; mugs of coffee; good, spicy food. Was love left behind there too? I skated on and on into the blackness, where the only lights were stars: freed into the utmost North, the world's high rim, beyond all human comforts; freed into the territories of my fate: the outland of fairies; furies; gods.

Pausing between verses, Katrin Vilde bent to look over old Vilde's shoulder at the score. The curving white line of the back of her neck was perfect as her far, extended notes had been, and a hollow opened inside me like longing. It would be simple and pleasant to say that I fell in love with her then; that it was then that I resolved to marry her. But nothing is ever that simple. In fact, I was reverting to type, among these refugees: a member of one of the most insecure tribes on earth. I secretly saw them as representative of old, subtle Europe, beyond my scope; I respected and yet mistrusted them, and struggled not to find their tragedies excessive; I thought them possibly calculating, and even wondered if Bela Beaumont might be match-making, and whether they had all frankly discussed me as a possible husband for Katrin. She was perhaps at an age when marriage had become crucial; and I suspected Bela had talked about the high salary an ABS man would get; he was capable of it.

A little later, Katrin and I walked down to the verandah together, bound for our respective rooms.

'It's easy to see you home,' I said.

'Very convenient.' She grew stiff, and I wondered whether she found my remark gauche. I couldn't tell whether she liked me or not, yet I sensed that I was important to her in some way. We paused on the dark arcade outside her padlocked doors, and her face grew more striking and exotic than it had been in the light. Her features, which I saw as German mixed with Finnish (knowing nothing of Estonians), were touched by a ghostly Mongolia, the wide-set grey eyes and strong cheekbones fleetingly Oriental.

'Bela talks too much,' she said. 'He shouldn't have said that about your leg. You had polio as a child?'

They were very personal and direct, these people.

'Yes. Don't worry about Bela,' I said. 'I like him. Besides, I'm used to it. I've been crippled a long time.'

'*You* aren't crippled.' She sounded suddenly almost angry, and I saw that her moods changed by the moment. 'You scarcely limp at all,' she said. 'Look at Jaan. He was knocked down by a car when he was six, and he'll never walk again. He was a perfect little boy before that. You should be thankful, not sorry. Calling yourself a cripple may make you become one.'

She couldn't see me flush, in the dark. There was a sudden outburst of seagulls' voices from below on the Harbour, and we both started.

'They fight over scraps,' I said; I hardly knew what I was saying, and she looked back at me solemnly.

'I think we should say goodnight.'

She unlocked her glass doors; I unlocked mine. It was ridiculous, and perhaps she thought so too. Glancing sideways, I saw her glance back; she released a faint breath of laughter, and went in.

7

Martin Gadsby's party was at eight o'clock. I discovered that his apartment was in Berkeley Towers, whose high, orange-tiled rooftop and little turrets, cut against the Harbour's many-coloured skies, I had so often contemplated from my humble niche on the arcade. The coincidence didn't surprise me, it was the sort of address I expected him to have; many broadcasting people lived in this area.

On Saturday night, 'Twist and Shout' thundered out over the district as usual just as I finished dressing, and the festive voices began to murmur in the upper air as sunset tinted my room. It took me only two minutes to walk along Elizabeth Bay Road to Berkeley Towers, passing the *Keep Out* sign by the wrought-iron gates. Making my way down a half-timbered hallway on the fourteenth floor, I found this level to be filled with the same amplified rock music—much louder now. The tune had changed to 'All

Shook Up'. Was it possible that it came from Gadsby's? Why would an elderly director of radio drama be playing rock music at his party?

My knock was answered by a big, fleshily handsome man of about thirty-five, holding a drink. When he flung open the door the noise was deafening.

'Rich-ard Miller! Yes? We've been expecting you. I'm Rod Ferguson.' He was like a joyous butler, his pink face glowing with controlled delight; he radiated pink and silver, his beautifully-barbered hair ash-blond and grey. He ushered me in, shouting in my ear. 'Sorry about the show. I hope you don't mind watching.'

When I looked bewildered, he gestured across the large, dim living room towards a TV set, on which the contorted face of Sydney's favourite rock star, Mick Jordan, was coming to climax in close-up. So it was from here that the music emanated, and not from a record-player. ' "Eight O'Clock Rock",' Rod shouted proudly. 'My show: I produce it. We always watch it go to air at Martin's. He loves it.'

'I never miss it either,' I shouted. 'I couldn't if I tried.'

He pointed his finger in mock horror. 'You live down below, don't you?'

Martin Gadsby appeared in front of us, his gleaming white shirt fresh from the iron, a Paisley scarf knotted at his throat. He shook my hand, and held it. 'Hello, son. You look startled. I hope you're not snobbish about rock and roll? We love it. And Mick Jordan's *marvellous*, don't you think?' He made further remarks, but I found it difficult to concentrate on what he was saying, being distracted by the scene at his back; then he was gone again. The room was very large; its only light came from the fast, spectacular Sydney sunset which was reaching its penultimate stage of deep orange, out through the big windows. Twenty or so people were standing about with drinks, most of them actors and actresses I recognised, dressed with carefully casual smartness. But among them danced limber, alien figures who appeared at first to be naked.

The girls wore minute bikinis; the youths had on briefs

that were little more than G-strings. Oblivious of the stares and smiles that followed them, they writhed and twisted about the room, and made wild cries in worship of Mick Jordan. They only looked self-conscious in the intervals when the music stopped.

Talking with Rod Ferguson by the windows in one of these intervals, I watched a nude, self-conscious youth with tattoos on both arms being engaged by the perfectly-dressed Gadsby in measured conversation; uncertain of what to do with his hands, he began in desperation to twirl the hair in an armpit.

'How do you like our rockers?' Rod asked. 'We always get a few up here for the show. They're a good guide to how the programme's going. If they like it—' He raised his thumb, and smiled.

'Where do you get them from?'

'Around the Cross. We bring them off the streets. They don't give any trouble, or else they don't get asked again; and they want to be asked. Martin insists they wear the swimsuits—it gives us a free floor show. They get issued with them at the door.'

I began to question him about the techniques of television production; from this we passed on to theatre, and found our opinions compatible. We talked for perhaps half an hour, drinking scotch, during which time I was constantly conscious of the height I stood on. It was like being in an airship, up here near the turrets of Berkeley Towers, and the view was even more spectacular than I'd imaged below in the arcade; Beaumont House with its slate roof and Italianate tower looked small from up here. Sydney is a city of hills, but all of them are low, so that the only way to see its extent is to get on top of a high building. From Gadsby's apartment, the sheer, intricate size of the land-locked Harbour was opened out: the whole twenty-one square miles of bays, urban headlands and peninsulas of olive-green bush, unravelling to the Heads and the Pacific. Although electric lights teemed on the many foreshores, the vast, milky blue of the water with its traffic of ships and small craft could still be made out, as well as the orange roofs of terracotta suburbs, drowning in twilight.

'Eight O'Clock Rock' was over; softer music came from a record player to which the naked rockers still writhed, and Rod Ferguson's voice, speaking directly in my ear, was now more distinct. What he said startled me; but since I was somewhat drunk, it seemed to come to me through a baffle.

'So you're going to join us, Richard. Another recruit for Aunty ABS.' I looked at him; his theatrical jollity had vanished; his gaze was fixed on me with the professional interest of an executive. Suddenly I was being interviewed; or was it a parody of an interview? My head swam with whisky.

'There must be plenty of others in the race,' I said. 'I'm not counting on anything yet.'

'I don't think you understand, Mr Miller.' He beamed with quick, well-crafted benevolence, his gaze insistent. 'I'm on the interviewing committee, and I'm prepared to take Martin's word about you. He's very impressed. The rest is formalities.'

I stood still, trying to look gratified and sober; what he had just said would sink in fully later. Darkness had set in, and the only light in the room at our backs came from a single standard lamp. Still standing by the window, we were looking through our reflections into the sky, where stars rose and burned. Far below on the Harbour a thicker light glowed in ships' portholes: Navy destroyers off Taronga Park; freighters from Europe and Asia anchored off Cremorne Point. Ferries scurried quickly to the north shore and back, like lit-up clockwork toys.

'It's a great town, isn't it?' Rod said, and his congratulatory hand fell briefly on my shoulder. Without a pause, he went on: 'ABS is a funny place, matey. You may begin by directing everything from the kiddies' serials to King Lear. But where you go from there is up to you. Maybe you won't get stuck in radio for ever—even though Martin thinks it's the only artistic medium.' He smiled. 'Don't misunderstand me—Martin's a great old radio man, and I love him—but television's the future. It's hard for the older ones to adjust who grew up with radio—but a young bloke like you would be crazy not to go with TV eventually. If you ever get interested, come and see me.'

He was looking out through the glass, or perhaps at our reflections, his patron's hand on my shoulder, his bulk making me look thin and starved: the Prince in his tower, being munificent to a vagabond.

Some time later, when the party had ebbed a little, I found Gadsby at the open door of a bedroom off the hallway, handing out briefs to a new crop of male rockers who had come in late. Nude figures laughed raucously in there, capering about while he stood in contemplation—cigarette in mouth, now and then releasing a discreet little cough, or patting his bleached yellow hair.

'Hello, son. Would you like to slip on a pair yourself?' He chuckled through his cigarette, and then looked faintly embarrassed. 'No, well perhaps not.' He became suddenly serious, a hand under my elbow, leading me away from the doorway of temptations.

'I'm glad you've got to know Rod, he's important to you. We'll be writing to you soon. I think we'll have you with us in the Department.'

I began to thank him, and he patted my arm. He was more fatherly than lascivious, I saw; the beseeching look of friendliness had come back into his eyes. 'Enough said for now. We've still got to go through the hoops: an interview and so on. But your life ought to change, soon. No more hand-to-mouth, eh, dear boy?'

He was uncomfortably perspicacious, I thought; he knew exactly what he was rescuing me from, and the importance of what he was giving me.

'You live in that seedy guest house next door, don't you? Bloody eyesore; used to be a fine old house. These scruffy DPs will ruin the district before long,' he said. Like many of his generation, he was a xenophobe about foreigners, it seemed; Bela's *palazzo* was dismissed.

'You'll soon be out of there when you join Aunty. I think you'll find the salary we'll give you will let you do better.'

I made no comment; I was able to half enjoy his snob-
bery, since this was my night of triumph. But it appeared
that there might soon be appearances to keep up in my
private life, and I was touched with a faint unease; I'd
grown fond of Beaumont House, and just for a moment I
thought of the Vildes, and felt obscurely ashamed.

As we went back into the living-room, Gadsby said:
'Rod can teach you a lot, even though he's a TV man—
keep in touch with him. But for God's sake, don't think of
going into that vulgar television yourself.' His expression
had become almost threatening; had he overheard us talking? Carefully, I assured him I was only interested in radio
production.

'Good,' he said, and his face softened again. Cigarette
in mouth, his fast mutter went on. 'The bloody morons
want to turn on pictures now the way they turn on hot
water, and have all the work done for them. But to listen
to words and build everything from sound: that takes
imagination. There must be a few people left with imagination, mustn't there, son?'

As I came back along the arcade to my room, I saw that
someone was standing by the balustrade down at the end,
looking out over the Harbour. None of the rooms showed
lights through their doors, so I came quite close before I
recognised Katrin Vilde.

She wore the same close-fitting black frock as the other
night: perhaps she'd just come home from a singing en-
gagement in one of the migrant clubs. She turned as I
approached; it was too dark to see her expression clearly,
and yet I had the impression that her smile was willed.

'You're all dressed up,' she said. 'Have you been to a
party?'

I told her I had; I even pointed up to Gadsby's lighted
windows, and told her about him. I was full of whisky and
elation, and found myself announcing that I had the ABS
job.

She grew animated at this, her face lighting up as
though the good fortune were hers. 'I knew you'd get it,'

she said. She asked many questions; they weren't insolent
and probing as Bela Beaumont's were, but I felt purpose
behind them; her high-arched brows betrayed small, enigmatic assessments. 'Won't you have to compete with others, before this position is decided?' she asked.

I told her what Rod Ferguson had said, and she listened
carefully.

'Yes, it's quite plain. The old man has a lot of power,
and he is giving you the job because he finds you attractive.'

In spite of the truth of this, I grew somewhat nettled.
Gadsby could hardly appoint me if I had no ability, I said,
no matter what his sentiments.

'Of course not,' she said calmly. 'He appoints you
because he can see you have talent, but also because
you're attractive to him. Both things are true. There's
nothing wrong with it. That's how the world is.'

This revelation of European realism both mollified and
impressed me. Then her mood changed again.

'You'll forget your poor migrant friends,' she said,
'now that you're becoming a big producer.' The joke was
not just a joke; I heard wistfulness in her voice.

I seized my opportunity, and asked her to come out to
dinner with me the following evening.

8

For nearly nine years, the memory of Deirdre Dillon had
prevented me from caring permanently for anyone else.
Not a month had gone by in all those years when I didn't
think of her.

This isn't to say that I lived always in a state of hopeless
yearning, or that I didn't otherwise enjoy life. But Deirdre
was always there, in the back of my mind. I would take
out her photograph sometimes and study it, and she would
smile back at me roguishly, poised with her long cigarette
holder, creating exquisite regret. As I read the inscription
on the back of the black and white print, it was as though
she spoke in my ear, in her low, intimate voice. (The
twenties!!) Her twenties headband and beads, as well as
the deep swell of Time, reduced the reality of this figure,

as the years went by. A strange young woman at a party, she looked at me from out of another decade, another life: someone I should long ago have forgotten. Yet my love affairs all came to nothing, and every girl was measured against the image of Deirdre Dillon. If I finally drew back from a relationship, Deirdre was the reason; and if a girl grew tired of me, it was because she sensed the presence of Deirdre—or so I told myself. Even then, I sometimes suspected that the memory I nurtured with such sickly care was no real memory at all, since memory implies reality recollected, and this was something else: something other; something more and something less. But then I would dismiss the thought; I would summon up my devotion with renewed intensity; I would patch any weak point in the wall of my obsession.

At the time when I met Katrin Vilde, I was still privately casting myself as the survivor of a blighted love affair; and if anyone had told me that there really had been no love affair, I would have grown angry. I thought then that my fixation had begun at Greystones, when Deirdre and I had met. It was all very simple, and appealingly wistful; she and I had been ideal lovers, barred from each other for ever by her bad marriage, and by the gap in our ages. But I was wrong, hopelessly wrong. I should have looked much further back: I should have recalled the Red Room, and the Mask of Paralysis, which had spared me so narrowly. I ought to have thought more deeply about the Barrow World of Faery, and asked myself why I had longed for it, and why I had cast Deirdre as its queen.

When Katrin and I began to go out together, I realised that she was someone whom the image of Deirdre was unlikely to devalue; and I began to think myself cured.

There were certain people, I believed, who made us know instantly that they would change our lives, and that our depths were known to them. These were people who were descended from what I thought of as prototypes; figures from another time. And the little shock we experienced on meeting such a person was in fact the recognition of the prototype: that other image behind the face in front of us, seen as though through a distorting glass.

Where had we first encountered these prototypes? In dreams; in an earlier life, I said—never in this one. I thought about this often, on Bela Beaumont's arcade, as my feeling for Katrin Vilde grew. Perhaps it was when one met and recognised the descendant of a prototype that one truly fell in love;' and the experience was all the more intense when the loved one was superficially different from oneself. Opposites did attract, but only when commonality was hidden underneath. This was the paradox that made for fatal piquancy and force: the long-beloved face beneath the new beloved's mask; the marvellous subsoil of the familiar, recognised with joy, shared like childhood, potent as ancestry: the prototype whom our own prototype had known.

On our first night out, I took her to a Hungarian restaurant in the Cross. It was cheap and musty, with an aggrieved waiter, hard wooden seats and candles stuck in Chianti bottles, and we were perfectly happy there. We began a dialogue which continued without flagging over the next few weeks—sometimes in the restaurants and streets of the Cross, sometimes in her grandfather's flat, where she invited me frequently for coffee.

Although we were foreign to each other, we had significant things in common, we found. Our different childhoods, in a small city in Tasmania and a town in South Germany, were like two shards from the same pot. We came from the same temperate zones, at opposite ends of the earth—touched by soft, elusive lights unknown in Sydney. We were both strangers in this latitude, we said, whose radiance in the end was like the glare of delirium; we shared the same homesickness.

Katrin and Jaan and the widowed Andres Vilde had come out to Australia in 1951 on the *Goya:* one of those warships the Americans had converted into crude passenger liners for the transport of refugees. Painted white for its new role, the *Goya* had carried East Europeans to Australia from the DP camps of Germany; and the Vildes came from a camp in Dillingen-on-the-Danube. In Vilde's cramped flat, seated on a straight-backed chair, sipping Katrin's coffee, I began to understand their past. The old man nodded and made brief interjections, usually in Estonian, prompting Katrin. Once, I had longed for unknown Europe: the Tuscany of the Franciscan, and Fra Filippo Lippi; the Germany of forests and castles, in my books at Trent Street. Now here was Europe in exile; Europe at second-hand.

She made me see the red-brick barracks of the Camp on the edge of Dillingen, and the town gate and its clock, and the poppies and cornflowers growing in the fields by the Danube in the summer; she summoned up the cool scent of lilacs in private gardens at night. She brought out a cracked, sacred, black and white photograph that her grandfather kept between the pages of an Estonian Bible—a small girl in plaits, sitting in a field among the poppies. I could smell the summer scents of Dillingen: the field flowers, the dry stalks of grass on her favourite walk by the river. I missed it with all the pangs of loss, as though that past were my own.

'I liked it in Dillingen,' she said. 'For my grandfather and mother it was miserable, but I was happy. I could walk in the town and by the Danube, and there was always another country out of sight. I used to think it was just past the edge of Dillingen, where the road went. The road was long and straight, and the horizon was very low. I could glimpse it in the distance, past the houses: another land. Goethe wrote about it. Have you read Goethe? *''Kennst du das Land, wo die Zitronen blühn—?''* No; you don't speak German. How strange, when you have a German grandfather. But you understand what I'm saying, don't you? You are the first Australian I've met who does. I knew you might, when I first came into your room.'

Katrin's formal education, carried out in the Camp, had ended at sixteen, when they left Dillingen; yet her reading was wide. In the Camp, books had been precious, like those of the Middle Ages; hoarded, lent only to those you could trust not to damage them. She regretted certain lost books even now. Some she and her grandfather still had; torn, dog-eared and treasured, printed on cheap wartime paper.

She didn't speak of the boy Jaan very much, but when she did it was with tenderness, almost as though he were her own child. Once, when I called early at the flat to take her out, the old man answered the door and beckoned me in, and I found Katrin in the bedroom pulling a sweater over the boy's head. The practical action was startlingly maternal in its style; she glanced up at me and smiled, and Jaan smiled too. His eyes, unlike Katrin's, were hazel, but widely spaced in the same way. She spoke to him in Estonian, and I listened in fascination to the liquid flow of this tongue from the North's utmost edge, a language she had told me was not even Indo-European, but related to Finnish. She was most foreign to me, speaking it.

When we had been going out together for nearly a month, she had still allowed me no more than to kiss her goodnight.

'It's so obvious, getting involved when we live side by side. I don't want to provide you with a convenient affair,' she said. She was very much a product of the fifties, as I was; it was indecent to rush. But sometimes I wondered if she would become involved with me at all. In a curious way, despite our affinities, I still didn't really know her. There was a part of herself and her life that she wasn't showing me, I thought. She seemed very proper; but who was the man I had heard through the wall? And why was she still unmarried, at nearly thirty? Did the old man and the boy keep her tied to them? What was wrong with her?

Outwardly, there was nothing wrong with her. Big-boned, energetic and cheerful, she seemed absolutely normal, her wide, well-trained European smile unfailingly confirming life's goodness. And yet I asked my questions.

Then, on a hot night early in March, the phase of decorum she insisted on came to an end.

I had taken her to the theatre, and we had said good-night at her doors as usual. For over an hour, I lay naked and sweating on my bed, kept sleepless not just by the heat, but by that huge, insupportable hunger which seldom comes again, after twenty-five: a hunger not just for sexual homecoming, but for the flowering of some sort of myth, yearned after with every nerve, to which the desired woman is the key.

The night was breathless; a banked-up fire burned in upper levels of blackness. My doors were open; big white stars stood in navy sky, through an arch. Her doors must surely be open too; she lay and breathed not eight feet away, and I knew if I were able to hold her, I would hold strange old Europe and the world. The Harbour and the city were inside me; thwarted yet exultant, I was filled with all its snaking, dark green foreshores, where yellow lights from bungalows spilled down sandstone headlands; I could see the Pacific breakers thundering like trains on all the northern beaches: on the pepper-coloured sands of the Peninsula, with its far, expensive suburbs like California. Uphill in the Cross, crimes were being committed, in rooms smelling of beer and dust—the dust that was every-where in Sydney, its sterile pollen collecting on the ragged leaves of palms; on window sills and verandahs.

Were her doors open? They must be; her room, like mine, had no window, and it was too hot to close them. Was she asleep, or lying awake? What sort of faint-hearted creature was I, that I let her lie there alone? Truly a cripple? But Katrin, unlike Deirdre Dillon, refused to see me as a cripple.

I got up, pulling on a pair of shorts, and went out on to the arcade. I'd go in to her, I said. Perhaps she'd dismiss me with contempt and sadness; but I no longer cared.

At first, I didn't approach her doors; I walked to the balustrade and leaned on its warm stucco, my mouth dry, the old ceramic tiles tepid under my feet. A faint coolness rose from the Harbour, and the sky was clear; I could pick out the other Cross, with its cold white pointers.

Her light was out; her doors were open. As I walked towards them, my heart jolting, she materialised in the frame like a figure developing in a photograph, standing straight and still in a pale blue nightdress. Her dark straw hair was down, falling to her shoulders without a wave, giving her a look of serious sexual intent. Long, bare arms of extraordinary smoothness went around my neck as I kissed her, and the tang of perspiration came to me.

I'd never imagined finding such an odour more exciting than scent; it was frank yet haunting as the sour smells in her grandfather's flat upstairs: that strange, sad capsule of lost Europe. Breathing it in, I was breathing in life; and as we struggled to hold each other closer, I was held by a joy that made me know that all other joys had been a child's fragile fancies.

There was silence from ABS for over a month. I hadn't yet been interviewed, and the appointment began to seem somewhat less certain to me. But I had acting engagements from the commercial radio stations to keep me going; and I had Katrin.

On the arcade, coming and going between one another's rooms in the new cool of autumn, maintaining a fiction of separate lives in front of Bela Beaumont, we saw ourselves as comrades, not just lovers; poor yet happy outsiders at the foot of the city's cliffs, preparing to climb. Hand in hand, we wandered through the underside of the unsleeping Cross at all hours of the day and night, every yard of it as familiar as the objects in our rooms: the red-brick apartment blocks of the prosperous, and the smelly old terraces of the desperate, with their balconies of grimy wrought-iron.

We despised none of it, the tough old Cross. Walking home in the early hours of Sunday from a party, or from one of the migrant clubs where I'd watch Katrin sing, I'd even persuade her to call in for a coffee at the Hasty Tasty, the cavernous, supernaturally ugly hamburger café in one of the Victorian terraces on the junction, where the neon bottle of sherry was poured against hot sky. Open at all hours, the Hasty was the district's true pivot; legend said that it hadn't been closed for an hour since 1927.

Familiar spirits of the Cross passed us here. There went the sinister Mr Smith, who dressed always, even in mid-

summer, in a tweed overcoat, felt hat, woollen gloves and
dark glasses; and here came the Duke of Darlinghurst
Road, with rat-sharp grey eyes, sharp nose and bald top-
knot, in his huge, tent-like, grease-grey coat and multitude
of waistcoats, sniffing along the gutter on the lookout for
treasures, all to be secreted in his dozens of pockets. And
in a closed fruitshop doorway on the corner at night sat
Wenceslas Kupka, a skeletal, thinly bearded Czech in a
beret, selling books of his own poems and essays, all
printed by himself, which expounded monotonous theories
of conspiracy, and made lurid accusations against publishers who refused him. He never spoke, and people never
bought; haughty and contemptuous of mocking passersby,
Wenceslas seemed placed in the doorway against his will,
and one felt that he would have despised the vulgar act of
selling a book. He was there every cold autumn night, his
yellow face drawn with enigmatic suffering, his dark,
mittel-European eyes pleading, accusing and angry, looking out from his wayside shrine among the books. I called
him Saint Sebastian, since he seemed to long for arrows;
but I laughed because he troubled me, and Katrin wouldn't
hear him mocked.

'He has been driven mad,' she said. 'He is not able to
write in his own language: what hope does he have here?
He can only look ridiculous; he is lost, like my grandfather.'

There was a seriousness about her which I put down to
her Lutheranism. Her grandfather was very devout, and
Katrin only slightly less so. She was a mixture in equal
parts of sensuality and old-style propriety, a mixture more
common then than it is now. The two parts co-existed in
equal balance: a tension that could perhaps only be ended
by marriage. She didn't want her grandfather to know how
things were between us, and avoided coming out of my
room at compromising times. Her bed next door was
seldom slept in now; but early in the morning, before Bela
arrived with his breakfast trays, she would slip away to
maintain a fiction of 'respectability'. No doubt Bela made
his assumptions, but he contented himself with significant
smiles, and small references. (*'Your Katrin sleeps late,*

this morning—I cannot get her to answer her door.') He
was smugly proprietary, and sure enough, began to make
broad hints to me about marriage. (*'This girl is in love
with you, Commander.'*)

I discouraged these advances firmly. I was not ready for
marriage; I didn't yet know whether I wanted to marry
Katrin Vilde, even though I was irrevocably in love. I still
wasn't sure that I knew her. When we weren't making
love, there was a paradoxical maidenly quality which I
couldn't find believable; it was as though her life had been
arrested, somewhere; there was a lost section, which perhaps accounted for the fact that at twenty-nine, she looked
no more than twenty-two. I had tried to question her about
earlier love affairs, but she had closed up. There had been
very few, she said; and why should we discuss them? I
saw that she was easy and flirtatious with the immigrant
men in best Saturday suits who came up and spoke to her
in the clubs where she sang; and I wondered then if her
lovers had been many. These were shabby thoughts, and
only troubled me occasionally; but the mystery of her lost
years nagged at my mind.

We seldom closed my doors at night, since no one ever
came to this end of the verandah; and the outbreaks of
squabbling among the gulls, coming up through the darkness, were a constant accompaniment to our talk and our
lovemaking. Those voices, rising and bursting like bubbles
from the Harbour, buoyed us up many times to a plateau
beyond passion; and hearing them at other times, we would
glance at each other and burst out laughing.

Yet sometimes a heart-stopping gulf would yawn beneath the long glide of pleasure, not so much threatening it
as giving it a keener edge, accompanied by crude whisper-
ings in corners of my mind; whispers of guilt inseparable
from the era. *She shouldn't be here, in this room. What if
she gets pregnant? Are you going to marry, or not?*

Her taut, strong, long-waisted body had reached that
moment in its history which is as near perfection as anything
in nature can be: a marvellous white arch between youth
and maturity. My instincts warned me that failure to reach

its natural goals would be disastrous; it had to be taken seriously, this body, and I was already half-responsible for it.

Her skin had a different grain from an Australian girl's: a sort of dough-like smoothness which was both exciting and sobering. *'You're made to have babies,'* I said; the remark had jumped from me before I knew it, and the effect on her was startling; her smile was extinguished, and her shocked face went blind as her arms wound about me. Yes, there was something still not in focus; her body had an unknown history.

On the day the letter came confirming the ABS job, I asked her to marry me.

We went out into the Cross for supper, and drank champagne to celebrate. I made her laugh a lot, that night. But when we got back to my room, her mood changed.

We had stopped just inside the doors, hand in hand, not turning on the lights. The red beacon on the arch of the Bridge winked and winked like an inflamed eye; and suddenly, she began to speak about Estonia.

Although she had talked often of the camp in Germany, she had seldom mentioned her homeland; now she entered the topic obliquely. 'You will make me a home Richard, won't you?'

I laughed, and said I would. Didn't everyone make a home?

She touched my face with tenderness and amusement. 'What a sheltered life you've led in Australia. Nothing really worries you. But I've never had a home; not really. Not since I was nine years old, when we escaped from Tallinn.' Her voice went dry; she twisted her mouth into a smile, as though to apologise for inappropriate feelings. 'Estonia was beautiful,' she said. 'We had a house then. I loved our house; it had decorations carved on the eaves, like in a storybook. I remember when we ran away in 1944; Grandfather said we must take only what we could carry, and I took my doll.'

The Russians had been bombing Tallinn day after day,

she said; the noise never stopped, and she began to scream. Her mother had to calm her. She saw ships burning in the harbour as the Germans retreated; the railways were destroyed, and the roads were crowded with trucks and with people pushing carts and carrying luggage—all running away.

'We knew we must go too,' she said. 'It had been bad enough under the Germans—my father was a patriot, and he had been in trouble with them for opposing the occupation; he wanted our country to be free. The Soviets had occupied us before the Germans, in 1941. Now they were back, and we knew how it would be. There would be no hope for people like my father—people who didn't know how to be cunning, and fit in. He had been lucky not to be taken before. The Russians had deported people from all along our street, in 1941. Anyone who spoke against the occupation might go. They took wives from husbands, and children from parents; they took them on trains to Siberia. But my father refused to run. He would stay, he said, and fight for a free Estonia. The Americans and British would save Estonia when they won the war, in a few months' time. That was what he believed.' She bent her head, and seemed to consider.

'He was foolish, I suppose,' she said at last. 'Not long afterwards, we heard through friends that the Russians had shot him. My mother hadn't wanted to leave, but Grandfather persuaded her; we would soon be able to go back, Father had said so. We only just got out in time; we caught the last Red Cross ship out of Tallinn, carrying back wounded to Germany. I remember it was fired on by the Soviets, and their planes still went on bombing the harbour. We thought we were lucky: but I knew then I'd never see Father again.'

Cossetted child of a land of safety, where such things never happened, I murmured vague comfort. But Katrin ignored me, looking out over the Harbour; she seemed compelled to speak on, telling me all that she had never told before, making me join that past. Staring into distances I couldn't plumb, she cleared her throat.

'I had to leave my rocking horse,' she said. 'That was what I hated most. It was beautiful—it had real fur. I wonder what became of that rocking horse?'

Suddenly she was crying, and I knew these were child-hood's tears, released at last. She stood clasping her hands hard, gasping as though in pain, unresponsive to my attempts at calming her. Then she stopped, and raised her head to look at me.

'I have to tell you something,' she said. 'Jaan isn't my brother.'

9

On that summer night in 1944, when the train drew into the station at Munich, she had just turned ten.

Her mother and her grandfather sat very straight on the padded seats of the compartment, holding badly-wrapped paper packages of possessions that would not fit into their two suitcases, and wearing the grave, stricken expressions that had now become habitual with them. On her mother's face this expression had replaced a calm smile; on her grandfather's it had replaced authority.

It worried Katrin, this gravity without authority; it made Andres Vilde look bewildered, and this frightened her; she would not let herself think about it. She said to herself that it was a temporary thing, like the worn cuffs on his one remaining suit: he was still only fifty-five; not yet an old man. When he had gone to his work at the university in Tallinn, her grandfather's suits had been perfect; and they would be perfect again, she said. She was tired of being tragically unhappy, and refused to be so any more; she resented it. Kneeling on the well-sprung German seat, she bounced up and down on her knees, looking out the open window.

'We're here, we're here,' she said. 'In München, in Germany! Mother? Grandfather?'

The sad faces showed no response to this; it was almost as though she had shown gaiety and excitement in church. 'Travel,' her mother said tonelessly. 'We have done too much of it, Katrina. Get your things together. Have you got your doll?'

But Katrin ignored this, and went on bouncing, leaning out of the window as the train slowed. The inexplicable sounds of a great station at night closed around her: hollow hoots and clangs in tall grey-green caverns like entries to forbidden dreams. A porter standing close to the platform's edge as she went by frowned frighteningly as a high official; but a passing *Wehrmacht* officer winked with special friendliness at this little foreign girl with her pigtails, Baltic-grey eyes and open smile. He was handsome, in his peaked cap and field-grey uniform; his eyes were of the German cornflower blue, and Katrin would always remember him, because he had welcomed her. And so the Vildes entered Germany of the War.

When they got out on the platform, she forgot to be so elated, and took her grandfather's hand. *'Will someone look after us here?'*

Andres Vilde looked up the platform, standing next to their rope-tied, humiliated suitcases. His eyes roved carefully behind their blue-tinted glasses, but his deep voice was reassuring. *'Oh yes,'* he said. *'God will look after us, Katrin. We are here because the Germans fought over us, and now they have to do something with us. They think we belong to them; but we belong only to God. He will provide.'*

The Germans called refugees like the Vildes *'Die Vertriebenen'*: the driven-out. Katrin became used to this label. They were helped to find lodgings in a house in an outer suburb; she went to a German school there, and Andres Vilde found a job as a labourer in a bakery. There was a shortage of labour, with so many German men at the front.

And so Katrin's important grandfather, who had worn dark suits with flowers in his buttonhole every day to the university, now worked in a singlet and old trousers at night, wielding a long shovel in the bakery's hot, floury dimness, taking the rye bread out of the ovens for the Germans to eat at breakfast. When Katrin saw him there, visiting the bakery, she wanted to like it, but couldn't. He was a tall, lean man, who had grown strong on his father's farm when he was young, and he could do the work; but he slept a lot by day, and grew more and more silent, although he still read Katrin stories. He had tried to get a job teaching maths in a school, but had been told such jobs were only for Germans. His hair and moustache were already mostly white, with only a little of their rusty blondness left. Frau Forster, their landlady, said Andres Vilde was 'distinguished'.

'Your grandfather wasn't meant to do this son of work, at his age,' her mother told Katrin one evening; and suddenly she began to weep, and walked out of the room.

Because they had so little space here, in this fusty, cabbage-smelling apartment, Katrin slept on a camp bed in the living room behind a screen, while her grandfather slept on the couch. The allied bombing raids were frequent, and she waited every night for the droning of the planes, the terrible wailing of the sirens, and the explosions; she would pull the bedclothes over her head, knowing that searchlights were stroking the harm-laden dark, and that soon she would have to get up and go down to the cellars.

On nights when it was quiet and she was meant to be asleep, she would hear her mother and grandfather talking beyond the screen.

Grandfather Vilde's voice rumbled useless comfort. *'We have to hope, Leenu.'*

'Hope?' Her mother's voice rose, and Katrin could imagine the red-rimmed, slanting grey eyes, the brown, strictly-parted hair streaked with grey, the wide mouth that once had smiled easily. *'What have we to hope for, with Arvo murdered by those animals?'*

'We will go back.'

'We will never go back. Estonia is finished. We have no home anywhere.'

'Then we must manage here. The Germans—'

'The Germans have made you a bakery hand—and they will give you nothing else. You and Arvo both made it plain what you think of them; do you think they don't know? They wanted us to be German, and we wouldn't; we are Balts.

And we Balts are to do their dirty work, that's how they see us. And they are losing this war of theirs, which is a filthy war. What will happen here then?'

Her mother's voice, which had risen, now broke, and her grandfather's rumble went softer, and Katrin heard no more.

But she had heard too much; things her mother had never said to her. They had both told her constantly they would go back home soon, to join her father. Now, pulling the bedclothes over her head, she saw with horror that this had been just a fairy story, to keep her happy. Her father was dead; and she would never see again the carved eaves of their house; never again, her rocking horse; never again, the old storybook towers and wooden houses of Tallin, or the long, long beaches of the Baltic, with their pearl-coloured distances of sky and water and the thousands of racing, white-capped waves, where she and her friends had paddled and swum and dreamed of mermaids, in the short, mild summer: the magic, grey-green Baltic, like no other sea, where amber came out of the foam, and wizards from the Gulf of Finland brewed up storms, whirling them in from the Arctic Circle.

Crouched there, clenching her teeth behind the screen in Frau Forster's flat, she began to ask God questions. *'Who will look after us now Father is gone? And where will we go? If Grandfather and Mother don't know, who does?'*

It was the United States Army and the International Refugee Organisation which ultimately answered these questions. A little over a year later, the Vildes found themselves in the IRO camp in Dillingen—on-the-Danube, in the United States zone of broken Germany.

Die Vertriebenen had a new name now; they were Displaced Persons, and must wait in their camp until the world found places to put them.

They waited for four years, during which she left childhood's edges. In many ways they were happy years for her; but they drained her grandfather of the last of his prime, and killed her mother. The big old three-storey barracks of mellow red brick on the edge of Dillingen, surrounded by willow and linden trees, became her home. She was fond of it, in the end, and living here was not a suspension of life for her, as it was for her mother and grandfather; it was strange and interesting, like being in a boarding school. She even loved its yard in front, snow-covered in winter, patchworked in summer with yellow grass, where she met her friends under the big willow tree in the centre, and they filled jugs at the taps.

The camp was life. There were many nationalities there, including Estonians, and she now had friends: the children were a secret society in the Camp, where each national group had formed its own community, each having its own school, its own church services, its own community group. Leaders appeared; failures and successes; there were worlds within worlds, in the Camp. Precious commodities were hoarded and traded: chocolate, coffee, soap. They even managed to print their own books, on yellow wartime paper. Smart operators ran rackets, and negotiated with local farmers; the lost committed suicide or went mad; the studious sat with their texts. Surrounded by people at all times, Katrin became accustomed to the lack of privacy, and to group living.

In the great, echoing brick-walled dormitory with its immensely high ceiling, the Vildes like everyone else had their own little living space, with beds and a few pieces of furniture and blankets hung up for privacy. And Katrin had found that it was possible to be private with a minimum of means. As she got older, and her figure began to develop, male faces began sometimes to peep at her through gaps in the blankets, when her mother was out; putting her clothes on under another blanket became second nature to her. She learned now that if she wore certain dresses men would stare at her intently, with expressions that no longer saw her as a little girl, but not as a person either; and they would come and try to talk to her, their eyes probing her clothes in a way she hated. She detested these men, and avoided wearing the dresses; and she flattened her growing breasts under her clothing with strips of cotton binding.

She wasn't ready to be a woman; her hair was still in plaits, and she still took her doll to bed; the one she had brought from Estonia, on the night they had run away. She knew this was silly, at fourteen; and when her mother laughed at her, she pretended it was a mascot. But Lottie was all that was left of Tallinn and childhood; and she whispered to the doll about those times they had shared at home in Estonia, when her handsome father was alive.

Her mother and her grandfather watched her all the time, and forbade her to speak to men, telling her stories of rape. But these warnings weren't necessary; she had nothing to do with boys, except when she talked to them in mixed groups about the Camp; she accepted the strict moral code of Lutheranism without question, and listened with respect when her grandfather read aloud from his Bible in the evenings in their blanket-room, while her mother sewed.

The Vildes knew that refugees must never lose their pride; must never drop those standards of cleanliness, dress and morals without which they were truly lost. Look, Andres Vilde said, at what happens to those who let themselves go here: the men who have become drunkards and gamblers and adulterers; the women who have become loose or slatternly. Such people have forgotten what they are, have given up. Katrin saw that this was true, and already she was calmly aware of the whole range of human viciousness; nothing could be hidden here, since the Camp was a peepshow, giving glimpse on glimpse of vice, of inner collapse between the other walls of decency and stubborn hope. Desperate, furtive couplings by adulterers in doorways, or in grass by the Danube; raving, murderous quarrels between husbands and wives who had descended into hells of hate; the frown and bluster of the male or female bully, which must be met without compromise or fear; the dry, empty grin of prostitution; the anxious smiles of old men who fondled little girls: these things were all part of the broken world.

Yet childhood persisted, like the Limbo of the Camp itself. The vocation of DPs was to wait, until they could be

offered escape on the converted wartime troop ships: to
America, Canada, Argentina, Australia. They must wait
for years.

Katrin's mother was now a woman who had forgotten
about smiling. Not all the Camp women were like that; a
lot of them were jolly, gathering together in groups and
shrieking with laughter. But these women had husbands,
while Mrs Vilde still mourned hers, and would do so to the
end. There were people who could not be displaced, and
she was one of them. Such people had lost interest. True,
they carried on; but life was never again a thing to be
enjoyed; merely to be endured.

Then, when Katrin was still fourteen, her mother grew
ill, and took to her bed behind the blankets, growing
steadily thinner over a number of weeks. She was taken
away to the hospital in the town, where her father-in-law
sat constantly by her bedside, as she slowly became a
skeleton woman, calling for water. The doctors said she
had cancer of the stomach; but Katrin knew her mother
was dying of sadness. Leenu Vilde was still only thirty-eight.

For nearly a year, Katrin was inconsolable. But she was
still glad to be here, in Dillingen-on-the-Danube, which
was full of consolations. She loved to walk from the Camp
past the high, grey ramparts of the yeast-smelling brewery,
which was like a medieval castle—past the yellow *Gasthaus*
and all the small houses with shuttered windows, and on
through the medieval gateway into the main street of the
town, with its old clock tower, its delicatessens and dress
shops and bakeries. American soldiers wandered there,
and patted displaced children on the head and gave them
bars of precious chocolate. She liked the rich Americans,
who were always smiling and generous; and in the town,
she went with her girl-friends to American films, and
sighed over Stewart Granger. This dark, Hollywood-British
film actor was Katrin's first love; in the darkness of the
cinema she told herself that he would be the sort of man
she would marry when she and her grandfather went to
America: the land of their first choice.

But did she really want to leave Dillingen and Europe? How would they ever get back to Estonia then? Lost Estonia had become lost Paradise; it was a landscape that glowed with impossible loveliness, with the crystal, transcendant light of the ultimate North.

Ghosts of Dillingen-on-the-Danube! Ghosts of the Camp! She sat in summer grass so tall that no one could see her, putting poppies in her hair. In the black and white photograph Andres Vilde kept, her clear, expectant smile was that of a child at a party; she looked out into marvellous vistas, joyously confident, a child who had known no agonies at all.

In the summer before she turned sixteen, she was filled with a love that had no human object. She loved lost Estonia; she loved the knights in the fairy tales; she loved Stewart Granger; and sometimes she dreamed of a gypsy. She learned singing now, from an old teacher in the town called Professor Broch. Because they were *Vertriebenen*, he charged very little.

And Dillingen waited. It seemed almost unscathed by the War, and by the secret horrors of the ruined Reich. It was a decent, tranquil farming community, its light summer air full of calm and peace. But there was also a strangeness in the air; the scent of a permanent dream, mingling with the scent of lilacs, filling Katrin with hunger. It was a smell like hay, like dust, like pollen, but sweeter than any of these. It was perhaps the smell of distance, and Dillingen was a place of distances: its roads ran far between corn fields and pastures to places beyond the day; past steep-gabled farm-houses near the flat horizon, led on by the weird threads of telephone wires.

In the June of 1950, just after her sixteenth birthday, she went to a dance with her friend Friida, a blonde girl with gullible blue eyes, who was said to go petting with boys by the Danube at night.

The dance was held in one of the big dining-rooms on the ground floor of the barracks. Coloured paper lanterns had been hung around the old brick walls, and

a Hungarian band on a small platform at one end played
a mixture of polkas, waltzes, traditional Hungarian dances
and stilted attempts at American swing. Katrin and Friida
were approached immediately, and danced for an hour
with a number of different partners.

Then a dark, wide-shouldered young man of about twenty-
four appeared on the platform, standing by the microphone
while the other musicians remained seated. He was dressed
in Hungarian national costume; all in black and white, like
Hamlet. The master of ceremonies spoke into the microphone. Geza was the finest gypsy violinist in the Camp
and perhaps in Germany, he said, and now he would play
a *czardas*.

Geza Lukacs wasn't a true gypsy; he was a Hungarian
motor mechanic and part-time dance-band musician who
had fled the Russian advance on Budapest in 1945 when
he was twenty, wearing a strange assortment of German
and Hungarian uniforms and carrying his fiddle. He survived in the woods on beans and mushrooms; then he
made his way to Vienna and thence to Munich, where he
worked in a garage. With the defeat, he had found himself
in the Camp.

But for Katrin that night, he was a gypsy; and as she
watched him play, the jaunty, suave rhythmns of the *czardas*
made her heart falter and her feet tap and the colour mount
to her cheeks. Her grandfather would disapprove of Geza
when he met him, mistrusting his appearance at a glance;
the dark, wavy hair that was too long on the back of the
neck, and the loose, slouching way Geza carried himself,
his shoulders slightly hunched, like those of an American.
And in fact, he was always talking about America: that
great Otherland where everyone could succeed, and where
he planned to find fame as a violinist. His dark eyebrows
arched upwards in a way that seemed to signal a joke.

Head bent in controlled frenzy over his fiddle, hair
swinging, Geza Lukacs played faster and faster, while
Hungarians of all ages danced their native *czardas*, and
other nationalities clapped in rhythm. The two girls stood
directly under the platform as he played, and Friida looked
up at him like a worshipper, with her gullible blue eyes.
Katrin was too dignified to do that; but Geza caught sight

of them both and winked. Then he came to a slow passage, the halting *czardas* rhythm that maddeningly postponed a return to speed and frenzy; and he looked into Katrin's face, not Friida's, with a sudden, sombre question.

Thrillingly mournful, his violin moved on tiptoe, climbing back towards the wildness and joy that everyone knew it must reach; that everyone longed for; that was almost unbearable to wait for.

Katrin was a child of Geoffrey of Monmouth; of Chrétien de Troyes; of Eleanor of Aquitaine.

The legend had become a cartoon; the sweet self-torment of Heloise and Abelard and the yearnings of the Troubadors had been made safe for democracy: Tristan was played by Stewart Granger. And yet, in that halfway year of 1950, the legend wasn't dead; it was still dangerously alive, and such things as the far gleam on water, or the scatter of distant light at night, promised a saga of love that was only half physical: the territories of ecstasy. Out there, just past these flashes from the edges of the Otherworld, the unknown beloved was waiting, impossibly pure of spirit, and completely hers.

But the legend and the ecstasy had their price and their casualties, and Katrin's optimism and capacity for dream— the long fantasy born in the twelfth century and only discarded in the late decades of this one—were both her strength and her weakness. New sentimentalities, new capacities for disaster, have replaced the old ones—and the new sentimentalism sees inevitable destruction for a child in poverty, anxiety and privation. But Katrin had come out of the vortex of the century's greatest disasters with her tranquil hopes, her capacity for joy, her self-respect untouched; Andres Vilde saw to that, holding to the belief that almost anything could be endured if the family endured, if God was trusted, and if discipline and a plain knowledge of consequences were maintained. Faults in the wall would open up elsewhere, if they were to open at all.

Child of the Camp, as well as of the Troubadors; aware in theory of every vice; realistic and even cynical about the inevitable weaknesses of human beings, Katrin Vilde was nevertheless young for her age when she met Geza Lukacs:

a disastrous mixture of tough caution and sentimental naivety.

'Whenever he played that fiddle, I knew what a soul he had,' she said to me, and laughed. 'I was such a fool. He did have a soul, but it all went into his playing—the only true part of him. We were going to marry, and then go to America together. Grandfather could come too, Geza said. Geza would play his violin and I would sing and we would all be rich. But two days after I found I was pregnant, he disappeared from the Camp.'

I could reconstruct little of their passion. They would walk by the Danube after dark, on paths that went out of the town; I pictured her lying with him there, in that poppy-grown field that had fermented her childhood dreams—drifting into a narcoleptic trance, while scents of ineffable promise floated across the flatland dark, in the mild South German summer.

Why had she ever trusted him? How had he ever broken into the Lutheran capsule that enclosed her?

But I learned little more of Geza Lukacs, who was swallowed up forever by ruined Europe, and from whom she had never heard again. It was all a long time ago: in the year that she had met him, I had met Broderick in the lane, in my island on the safe side of the world. The Hungarian fiddler's memory was a dormant illness, I thought, offering us no threat.

That was before Darcy Burr reappeared.

6

THOMAS AND THE RYMERS

1

He came at around four-thirty on a Saturday afternoon, in May of the following year.

Katrin and I had been married since January, but we were still living on the verandah of Beaumont House, saving to furnish a flat. When he appeared, I was polishing a pair of shoes in what had once been my bachelor bedroom; Katrin was upstairs with her grandfather. Kneeling on the floor, intent over my work, I didn't hear his footsteps; I recall the sun glinting on the shoe I held in the way that one remembers unimportant objects seen in the last few moments before an accident.

'*G'day.*'

No one else said it like that. The insinuating downward inflection made it both a joke and a password, calling up complicities that only he and I shared.

He leaned sideways through the doorway, grinning down at me—only his top half visible, like a spy in an old British comic paper, the fingers of one hand curled around the frame. The thumb of the other hand was hooked into the strap of a guitar-case, which was slung over his shoulder like a rifle. Both of us stayed motionless. I continued to kneel, staring up at him.

'I hope I'm not disturbing y',' he said, and his grin broadened, as though at a piquant joke.

He stepped into the room, divesting himself of the guitar, which he lowered to the floor. Somehow too large for the room, he looked like a vagrant, in frayed, worn-out jeans and a khaki military shirt of the sort sold by disposals stores. His lank black hair was what struck me first; longer than convention would have allowed when I last saw him (seven years ago? eight?) it was cut in the new, mop-like fashion of the Beatles, and hung to cover his ears, making him somewhat resemble a Red Indian. He looked older; but the feral gleam of his slanting eyes was just as I remembered. He was like no one else, this gleam told me; and his sly plans included me. This notion was entirely irrational; but Burr had brought the irrational through the door with him.

I stood up, finding that my heart was hammering ridiculously. 'Hello, Darcy,' I said. 'How did you find me?'

My abruptness and lack of enthusiasm seemed not to disturb him—or perhaps not to register. He went on grinning, big hands dangling, poised on the balls of his feet, alert for either welcome or dismissal. But this was a joke; either way, his expression said, he would stay. He was back, and I wouldn't get rid of him; he would always turn up, and my surge of apprehension was mingled with a cold and dubious excitement.

'How did I find y'?' he echoed. 'I can always find y', Dick—there's nothing easier than *finding* people.'

I looked at him for a moment in silence, not answering his smile with one of my own. I didn't want him to stay; I didn't even want him here, I thought, but I gestured at the old pink armchair, and told him to sit down.

'Thanks.' He lay back at his ease and stretched his legs in front of him, crossing one scuffed, elastic-sided bush-boot over the other, his expression of secret amusement unwavering, the brightness of his beer-coloured eyes reflecting the sun through the door. He reminded me of Clive Broderick, whom I seldom thought about now; it wasn't just the association, but something to do with the way he sat.

'Been a long time,' he said And then, as though reading my thoughts: 'Eight years, eh?'

I asked him where he'd come from, and he seemed to consider.

'Come from a lot of places,' he said. 'We got in from Queensland a week ago. We reckon we're about ready for Sydney.'

'We? Is Brian with you?'

'Of course he's with me. We've been working together for years, on and off. We used to do the Country and Western circuit: called ourselves the Brady Brothers. Got quite well known around the back-blocks.' He straightened in his chair and leaned forward. 'But that's all over, mate. Folk music's what's in now; and Sydney's the place to make it.' He broke off, then peered at me alertly. 'And how about *you*, Dick? A big-time producer in ABS! You really got there, eh?'

I showed no answering warmth. Instead, I asked him how he knew I worked for ABS.

'Easy enough.' He looked evasive. 'I just phoned around a bit. Phoned your office yesterday, and they gave me this address.'

'Did they? They're not supposed to give out addresses.'

For the first time, my unfriendliness seemed to penetrate, and he frowned. This frown was faintly alarming; it changed his appearance. Things had happened to thin his mouth and to narrow his big white nose; and instinct told me that these things, whatever they were, had been drastic. There were lines in his cheeks and about his eyes that made his face look too old for the youthful Beatle-style hair; and the total effect was one of formidable hardness. It was like a second face, and for some reason I thought of a standover man.

'Why shouldn't they give me your home address?' He had spoken softly, almost in a whisper. 'What sort of bullshit is *that*, Dick? Don't you want to know us? Brian and me?'

I hesitated, looking for a suitable answer. But before I could speak, he said: 'It's about Denise. Right?'

His tone had changed to one of perverse gentleness, trying to draw me in. I didn't reply, since no reply was necessary; eight years no longer existed, we were back in his little room over Sandy's shop.

'You don't want to be worried about that,' he said. 'Not after all this time.'

Again I made no answer, and I found that my heart was beating unevenly. Burr now dropped his head and studied his joined hands, as though reading a message on the thumbnails. 'You shouldn't hold things against people, Dick. Things that can't be helped, or aren't their fault.' He was speaking almost under his breath. 'Besides,' he said, 'you were in it too.' And he looked up and actually smiled.

'What's that supposed to mean?'

I was startled; almost alarmed. But I already knew what he meant, and his stare told me that he was aware of this. I wasn't guilty; I'd done nothing to harm the child, he knew that. And yet he somehow knew as well that there was a sense in which I'd always been guilty: guilty when I set up my fairy books in the sewing-room; guilty when I played with my toy theatre; guilty when I talked to him in Varley's basement, dwelling on the Faery Process. I was the one who had understood him, he was saying (but not aloud); I had encouraged him, and we two were the only ones in the world to whom Faery was real. Yes, we were accomplices: this was what his smile had always been trying to tell me.

When he finally answered, his voice was soothing. '*You* wanted the seances, Dick, just as much as she did. Remember? *You* were interested in the spirits.' And now his smile of complicity came back; he turned it on me in full strength, and I found it impossible to resist. With shame but also with relief, I reluctantly smiled back; and at this, he gave a little sniggering laugh through his nose. He had offered a diversion, with this talk of the seances, and I knew I'd accept it; he was prepared to admit to me a minor, counterfeit guilt, if the other guilt needn't ever be acknowledged. That crime had never been committed; we could both pretend so. After all, I'd never known its details, and it was now such a long time ago.

'Yes,' I agreed. 'I was interested in the spirits.'

The tension had gone from the room; the sun's yellow light congealed on the shabby furniture, and we relaxed into a little silence.

'Nice spot, this,' he said, and looked about inquisitively, dwelling on Katrin's dressing-gown with its pattern of roses, hung on a chair. He'd won, and we both knew it.

I wouldn't dismiss him; he was in my life again, and I wasn't sorry. To tell the truth, I was half glad. How can I defend this, even to myself? Does it explain anything if I say I found him interesting? He was more than interesting; he was like a part of myself, just as Brian was.

I asked why Brian wasn't with him.

'He's not far away. We've rented a pad in the Cross—in Victoria Street. You'll be seeing him soon,' Darcy said, as though offering me a reward; and his grin hinted now at good things to come. 'That's one of the reasons I called, mate. We're doing our first gig in Sydney as a folk group tomorrow night, and we want you to come. It's at the Grain Loft. We call ourselves The Tinkers. And I'll tell you what: we're going to the *top* here.'

'You'll need to be good,' I said. 'Folk singers are coming off the walls, at the moment. Anyone who can strum a guitar.'

'We're different,' he said. 'Wait until you hear us. Will you come, Dick?'

I saw urgency in the corners of his eyes; and suddenly I felt almost sorry for him, in his worn boots and vagrant clothes: twenty-eight, already looking old, and talking about going to the top. What 'top' did he imagine they could reach in folk music?

Yes, I told him, I'd come.

He stood up to go, peering delightedly into my face. 'Good on y', mate. Brian's really going to be pleased. Bring your wife.' And he winked.

I hadn't yet told him I was married; he'd found this out from somewhere as well.

2

It was always half-dark in the Grain Loft. Orange candles like little pumpkins flickered on rustic wooden tables. No liquor was allowed; our entrance tickets entitled us to one free cup of instant coffee, served by girls in cheesecloth dresses and waist-length hair, whose pale, stricken faces hinted at sorrows worthy of a ballad. The air was spiced with marijuana, as Sydney's pioneer hippies took their first dangerous inhalations.

Mellow acoustic guitars and banjos began to tune up, strumming and tinkling from hidden points in the dusk to create the little thrills of anticipation we all felt then, no matter how poor the singers—bards who would dredge up memories not our own. It seems remote now, that ancestral excitement; commerce has sucked the ballads dry, since the sixties. But they'll rise fresh on other lips, as they always do.

I came here quite often with Katrin, who had begun to be fascinated by the folk boom. The British, Australian and American songs were an alien tradition to her, but she now talked about learning them. She'd begun to realise she must join the Anglo-American world, if she wanted to succeed as a singer; the Baltic clubs, with their audiences of exiles, were the past, while places like the Loft, and the many little coffee-shops that had sprung up around the city featuring folk singers, were the future. I was sympathetic to these hopes of hers, but a little dubious about her ability to adapt; I had no premonition at all that night of what might happen.

The Loft was the hub of the Sydney folk scene, and any folkie who wanted to make a name in the city had to perform here. Three stories above the Darling Harbour docks, it really had been a grain loft, years ago. Gordon Cartwright, the middle-aged ex-carnival man who ran it, had leased the top floor of one of the old brick warehouses here to cash in on the folk phenomenon that had arrived from the northern hemisphere—doing little to change the place except to build a stage at one end, and to put up poster-sized pictures of the gods and goddesses: Joan Baez, Pete Seeger, the Clancy Brothers, the Seekers. A heavily symbolic sack of wheat hung near the stage. Nearby, in the western wall, a door opened on to space. Its old loading platform and beam-and-tackle were still suspended three floors above the lane, and an appropriate nineteenth century portscape glimmered out there, like Doré's London: the lamps and stone mushrooms of the Pyrmont Bridge; the lights of wharves and ships.

There was no sign of Burr or Brady, although Katrin and I peered about constantly in the gloom, seated over our coffees and our pumpkin candle. The first few singers were uninspiring: a Joan Baez imitator without the voice; a pedestrian, middle-aged clone of Ewan MacColl, who sang unaccompanied with his hand over his ear; a youth with Woodie Guthrie material who assumed an Oklahoma accent and played a very rough banjo. But then Gordon Cartwright bounced on to the platform, clutching his list of artists in both hands and exuding the special excitement he manufactured whenever he had new talent to introduce. Wiry and bald in his youthful green T-shirt, gym shoes and jeans, he crouched anxious under the spotlight like a servant, craving his audience's tolerance, darting quick glances everywhere, hoping the fumes of grass wouldn't be sniffed by police. The next group was appearing at the Loft for the first time, he said, and he named Brian Brady, Darcy Burr, and their female partner, Rita Carey.

'The Tinkers are new to folk music,' Gordon explained. 'They've been playing the country music circuit until now.'

He had to break off, as derisive groans broke out. The folk fans were very puritanical in that year; Country and Western was despised, as was most pop music. The purists who came to the Loft, ranging through all ages, were here to listen to traditional ballads and protest songs—British, American and Australian—performed either unaccompanied, or with the instruments they thought of as traditional: acoustic guitars, banjos, concertinas. Electric instruments were anathema.

Gordon's grin became even more fixed and placatory; elbows raised to the horizontal, he held his list as though it were a tray. 'Come on,' he pleaded. 'Musos have to earn a living how they can, don't they? We're going to hear Brian Brady sing solo, first. Brian's been abroad a few years. Before he came back to Australia, he worked as a seaman, and he spent some time in the UK, and saw a bit of the folk scene there. Brian Brady.'

Gordon jogged away, clapping, and the crowd soberly joined in. These were excellent references for a folkie, and Brady now had to be given a fair trial.

When he walked into the lemon spotlight, carrying his guitar by the neck as though it were a shovel (still the old Ramirez, I saw), it gave me the same small shock as seeing Burr had done. Like Burr, Brian had aged a lot in eight years; certain lines in his face made him look older than he was. His hair wasn't as long as Darcy's, but the tangled curls were certainly more profuse than before, as a gesture to the sixties. His broken nose had become more noticeable, but I saw that he was attractive to women; a little breeze seemed to stir through the row of girls who always sat at the front (groupies of the folk scene, in uniform cheesecloth dresses and beads), causing their heads to nod.

'That's your cousin? He looks like a roughneck,' Katrin said. But when I glanced at her profile, in the dark, I saw that her expression was both inquisitive and indulgent; the look women wear when they are only pretending to disapprove.

Brian went through the same routine as every other folk singer, seated on a wooden stool under the spot: screwing at the tuning-pegs of the guitar; cracking jokes. There was always aggression in the air at the Loft, especially when an untried singer came on. Brady was like a fighter whose opponent was the crowd, and I began to be tense as though I were up there myself. But he projected a cheerful pugnacity that got him through the first few minutes—doing it by sending out signals of warning.

A voice called: 'Where's your mates?'—and Brian's light blue eyes searched the room, giving the impression that the owner of the voice might be unsafe if he found him. But then he smiled, and said confidingly: 'I could do a bad thing to Darcy. I could tell his joke, before he gets on.'

This got a laugh; they began to be on his side. And I saw him through Katrin's eyes: a roughneck. Where most other Grain Loft performers looked like singers dressed as labourers, Brian looked like a labourer attempting to be a singer, his short-sleeved shirt of faded blue towelling displaying biceps enlarged by hard work.

'I'll sing you an Australian song,' he said. 'We do have a few, besides "Click Go the Shears".'

He began on the convict ballad 'Moreton Bay'. Badly sung, its pathos is merely tedious; but Brady sang it well, and the Loft went silent. He was better now than when I'd heard him in the Sir Walter Masterman, his voice rough-edged but true; the last eight years had given him deep bass notes that went straight to the pit of the stomach. His guitar work was on a different level from anything the average folkie was capable of, lyrical and assured, producing a hush of respect.

The applause was whole-hearted, and I had a rush of possessive elation; I peered at Katrin in the dark as we clapped.

'Well? Is he good?'

She smiled. 'You're proud of him, aren't you? Yes, he's good.'

Now Darcy Burr came on; there was still no sign of Rita Carey. Dressed just as he'd been yesterday evening, in khaki shirt and jeans, Burr carried an electric bass guitar which he set about plugging into an amplifier at the rear of the platform, going quietly about his work like a tradesman, Indian hair swinging.

Small murmurs had begun at the sight of this forbidden instrument, and now some of the audience actually began to hiss. I quailed inwardly, but Darcy appeared unaffected; he bowed and grinned with cold insolence.

At this, an aggrieved male voice called out: 'What *are* you? A bloody rock and roll group?'

Darcy leaned into the microphone as he'd leaned around my door, his eyes glinting in the spotlight. 'You can make up your mind when you've heard us. All right, Sunshine?' He still grinned, but he gave out a small charge of menace, and nobody else called out, although low mutterings continued. 'What a strange-looking man,' Katrin said. 'He looks like a goat.'

Brian, in the meantime, had been fitting a pickup on to his guitar and had plugged this into a second amplifier; now he looked up at Burr. For a moment, Darcy went on tuning, striking deep, resonant octaves, and the depth of sound after an evening of acoustic instruments was brutal and startling. Then the two of them froze for a moment, catching each other's eyes like men ready to plunge into dangerous action. Darcy nodded, and they launched into 'The Leaving of Liverpool'.

Standing up to the two microphones, they sang it at a fast, rocking pace, without the distortion the audience had feared. Their treatment was entirely traditional, Brian taking the verses, Darcy joining in the choruses; but the accompaniment transformed it. Burr's bass guitar, throbbing under the electrified Ramirez, gave the song a whole new attack; a dimension unknown at the Loft. The impact was instant, jerking heads up all over the room, kindling amazed smiles, setting feet tapping; and within a few verses, I knew that the objections of the majority were being swept aside. And watching Burr grin and sway cunningly over his bass guitar, I admitted that a good deal of their success was due to him, and his instrument's subterranean power.

Rita Carey came on now, and she and Brian sang a number of the traditional Irish songs the Loft approved of, made popular by the Clancy Brothers. Her intonation still carried traces of her years in Country and Western: certain plangent last notes were country, and so was her frilled white blouse, with which she wore a black velvet skirt; so was her wide smile, which appealed for friendliness. She was small, with a small-chinned Celtic face and a mane of waving copper hair falling to her shoulders; her voice was quite good but somewhat frail: a dependent voice, which seemed uncertain when it wasn't blended with Brian's. But the Loft was prepared to like her, and applauded at special length when she sang 'Aileen Aroon', which she did as a solo, the two male guitars gently following after. She sounded curiously alone, as though singing on a moorland; and the song somehow fitted her. I guessed that she and

Brian were lovers; he stood close and proprietary, his size exaggerating her smallness.

The last song, 'The Bard of Armagh', was Brian's solo. He went back to acoustic guitar, and Burr abandoned the electric bass for a penny whistle—its aged piping mingling perfectly with the Ramirez. The last of my hostility towards Darcy now ebbed away, as he piped with eyes closed, white nose pointing. How could anyone vicious produce these far, sweet sounds? The feeling I'd had long ago in the Sir Walter Masterman came back: I wanted to interweave my life with theirs; more: I wanted, irrationally, to raise them high. We would all live inside their songs, and their simple yet enviable talent, the raw matter I lacked, would be half mine too: I would contain them all in my own life.

I knew all this was absurd; but as long as the music lasted, common-sense was cancelled. And as Brady performed the song which would become his signature, head thrown back, eyes half closed, he was no longer anyone I knew: I saw him as the line of girls at the front were doing—the groupies in their cheesecloth dresses who had become his first fans. His tangled brown hair and broken nose were not of today at all; he had come from somewhere else: the ageing harper of the ballad, marked out by Sergeant Death. Soon, too soon, he would disappear, no matter how much they yearned for him to stay.

Under the applause, I looked at Katrin, who was clapping hard. She was quite unaware of my glance; her face, still turned towards Brian, could perhaps be called thoughtful, and there were tears in her eyes. This didn't startle me; she had a Slavonic readiness for tears, especially when music moved her.

I led her over to the wooden barrier next to the stage which hid the singers waiting to come on, and behind which the group had vanished.

Brady and Burr were crouched in a corner, packing away their instruments; Rita Carey wasn't to be seen. Darcy caught sight of us and waved, his expression slyly elated.

Straightening up, Brady looked surprised, then delighted.
He advanced on me, his face adopting an expression of
mock menace, waggling in his hand a phantom strap.

'Assume the position, Mr Miller. A little taste of Doctor
Black.'

I held out my hand and he gave me two phantom cuts.
We doubled with laughter, while Katrin stood waiting. I
was glad to see him as I'd seldom been glad to see anyone.

'Jesus, you were good,' I said. 'How did you get so
good?'

'Introduce us to Mrs Miller,' he said. He was looking at
Katrin over my shoulder, and I saw her as he must have: her
courteous smile and firm, friendly gaze a little too formal
for the Loft.

He almost certainly perceived her as someone more
correct than he was used to dealing with; when I'd introduced her, he put a hand to his mass of curling hair. 'Take
no notice of the hair,' he said seriously. 'It's a wig.'

She burst out laughing, and I was pleased; I wanted
them to like each other.

3

Peak hour at the Hasty Tasty, the Cross's roaring vortex;
the permanent, seedy midnight of the old Australia.

The pubs are closed and the drunks are in; the Beatles,
Elvis Presley and The Beach Boys wail and thunder from a
giant, glowing jukebox in a corner. A sign on the back
wall announces ambiguously: WE NEVER CLOSED. Up under
the canopy of the vastly high, slaughterhouse-pink ceiling,
it's still the nineteenth century, the ancient mouldings
defeating all trivial attempts at modernisation. But down
below here it's 1965, as sailors, derelicts and prostitutes
jostle by the door for hamburgers and steak sandwiches,
visit each other's booths in the restaurant-section like Hollywood celebrities, or fall dead drunk off the stools at the
counter. In the big window on the street, watched through
the glass by a knot of appreciative spectators, a little man
in a cook's hat makes the hamburgers, flipping them in
rows on a big black hotplate, distributing watered-down

tomato sauce from a basin, toasting the buns. Shrieks and growls rise from the arena behind him; Navy men locked in combat writhe past him like blue eels, but his starved comedian's face remains sad and tolerant, presiding over the Hasty's hearth.

Oblivious of the din, Brian Brady and I sit talking in one of the booths, drinking the Hasty's terrible grey coffee.

It's a cold night; rain whips along Darlinghurst Road outside. Brady is hunched in a navy-blue pea jacket, both hands locked around his cup, looking like a figure from one of the ballads he sang two nights ago; for me, he's still enclosed in their echoes. Close to, I find more lines in his face than I saw at the Loft: he looks thirty. There's a redness about his nostrils, perhaps from cold.

Passing here half an hour ago, walking home from a late production in the William Street studios, I was startled to see him sitting in the booth alone, and came in to join him. The Hasty seemed an odd place for him to be at this hour, especially when the Victoria Street flat that he and the other two shared was three minutes' walk away.

'Rita's out this evening,' he told me. 'And I needed to get away from Darcy for a while.' He grinned to take the edge off this, in a way that invited no further discussion.

I questioned him about his life over the past eight years. I was glad of the chance to talk to him, and interested in his time as a seaman, when he worked on overseas freighters. I was ready to see this period in a romantic light; but he dismissed it.

'All you see is the bloody ports. And most of the time on ships I was scraping paint off the sides. No sea shanties now, Dick.'

He spent a year surviving in Britain, he told me, where he sang in pubs and clubs as the folk revival was born; it was there that he built his repertoire of traditional ballads. Then he came back to Australia and eventually found Darcy Burr again. At present, he said, he and Darcy and Rita were only just surviving; they had one regular job, playing flamenco and sentimental Spanish songs in a small restaurant in the city for a miserable fee.

'The flamenco still comes in handy,' he says now. 'It impresses them in the fancy restaurants. I'm glad Brod taught us.'

'What became of Broderick?'

He looks at me from under his brows, sipping coffee. Then he puts down the cup. He doesn't answer at first, but glances across to the doorway, where the crowd struggles at the hamburger counter. Mr Smith appears outside, halting in front of the window in his dripping felt hat and eternal, mask-like sunglasses. His age is hard to tell; perhaps fifty. He's said to be an Englishman of good background come down in the world; his mouth is refined and superior, and he surveys the Hasty with an unpleasant smile, hands in his overcoat pockets, detained by this onion-smelling turmoil of the vulgar, and the hamburgers sizzling on the iron. Then he moves on through the rain, in his broken sandshoes.

'Brod?' Brian says. 'That was a bit queer. Brod disappeared.'

'Disappeared? How?'

'He vanished about five years ago. Old Sandy told us about it. No one knew where Brod went, or why; he didn't tell them at the bookshop he was leaving. He got listed as a missing person by the police, eventually. But Darcy's sure he's dead. I am too, actually.'

'How do you know?'

He begins to roll a cigarette; then he looks up at me sharply from under his brows, the half-made cylinder gone still in his hands, as though he's wondering how far I can be trusted. 'We know because Darcy calls up his spirit. He comes pretty regularly.'

Seeing my expression, his hungry blue eyes drain of friendliness; or at least become empty. 'You don't believe it; but it's true,' he says. 'Brod gives Darcy advice. Darcy says that when we play he can feel Brod helping us. I've felt it myself. You can say what you like about that, mate.'

I can think of nothing to say to this; I'm embarrassed. These are callow games that should have been left behind in Harrigan Street; but they are still plainly real to Brady.

He lets a small breath of laughter escape him now, and says: 'You didn't like Darcy contacting spirits, in the end, did you, Dick? Neither did I. But that doesn't mean it doesn't happen.' He lights the cigarette abruptly, and something in the tightening of his cheek-muscles makes me realise that he's tense in some way; his eyes avoid mine. When he speaks next, his glance warns me not to disagree. 'Darcy's got a lot of strange ideas, but he's also got a lot of talent. I need him. Rita and I really want to succeed with this group, and it's Darcy who's going to get us there.' Under his worn, newly adult face, I see the boy's looking out half-defiantly, as it once did in the St Augustine's yard in front of the old bicycle shed. The image is projected on the noisy air between us, while the Everly Brothers wail from the jukebox.

'But you're the real talent in the group,' I say. 'It's your singing that does most to carry it, Brian.'

He shakes his head. 'It's Darcy who pushes us. He learned a lot about scoring music from Brod, and he's got a real flair as an arranger. He can play any instrument he picks up. And he's the one who handles agents and managers. I don't want to know about all that commercial crap. Darcy's sharp.'

'Yes, he's sharp.'

'He's been into some strange things. He even worked in Scientology once. And he went away for a year.'

I look blank.

'He did time a couple of years back, in Melbourne. A restaurant-owner owed Darcy for two weeks' work playing guitar, and wouldn't pay him. So Darcy beat the shit out of him, and cleaned out his till. He got a short spell in Pentridge for that.'

He looks towards the door again, and I seem to see a shadow cross his face. 'Here the bastard is now,' he says. 'He must have followed me out.' His tone seems cheerful enough; but I wonder whether it's natural.

Burr is moving towards us between the booths; and his appearance is changed. He's taken to wearing rimless glasses, which give him a stern, almost schoolmasterly air.

There's something pedantically neat about him, no matter how shabby his dress; I feel sure he would have been neat in prison. It's difficult to see him normally, now, knowing he's been in that netherworld; but as he slides into the booth and grins at me over the table, I smile back as naturally as I can.

'Well mate—what do you think?' He radiates anticipation; he's referring to their performance at the Loft.

'You were terrific,' I say. 'You'll be regulars there now.'

But he shakes his head in happy dismissal. 'No, Dick, no. *That's* not what we want. We're aiming for something a whole lot bigger.'

I sit back, retreating a little from his stare. 'Lots of luck,' I say. 'What is it you want?'

He goes on smiling with an air of triumph. 'Our own show on ABS TV,' he says. 'And you're going to get us there, Dick.'

I laugh outright, and look at Brian, but his serious face already knows about this; he watches Burr. And in spite of my resentment at Darcy's cheek, I feel an insidious excitement begin to churn in me. Isn't this what I wanted, watching them at the Loft?

'Your own show? That's impossible,' I say. And I bring out all the reasons, talking like the smooth ABS executive I'm becoming.

'To get an appearance on TV, let alone a show of your own, you have to have a big reputation. But you and Brian aren't even known. Besides, I'm not even a regular television director; I'm a radio man.'

'But you could do it if they let you, couldn't you? You *could* direct a music show, couldn't you, Dick?'

Yes, I say patiently, I've done a few TV productions; but what he wants can't happen. A group would have to be extraordinary, to be given its own show.

'*We're* extraordinary.' Burr's smile has gone, and he leans towards me with his elbows on the table. When he becomes emphatic, he still cranes his neck like a goose; it emerges now from his black rollneck pullover, and his face comes close to mine. He peers, his myopic gaze almost threatening behind the new glasses, which I'm sure he doesn't intend.

'I'm telling you, we're like no other group. We're going to be terrific.'

His nasal voice gives the last word magical importance; he emphasises key phrases like a salesman, creating a hypnotic effect; I can't look away. It's a performance I half admire, despite my resistance.

'You saw why we're different,' he says. 'The *electric backing*. No other folk group uses that, right? We're no dreary ethnic folkies; we'll get the rock audience as well as the folk audience. The people who listen to the Beatles will listen to *us!* So what do you think about that?' His air of triumph has a deeper current beneath: fanaticism, perhaps.

'I'm not denying you're good. I might even be able to get you an appearance,' I said. 'But not a series, Darcy. Be sensible.'

'There'll be a series.' He's absurdly confident; he glances at Brian with the air of one who confirms something, and Brian's look is respectful. It's as though they both knew I'd come in here tonight.

The din of the Hasty grows louder: it's time to go. On the jukebox, the Beatles are singing 'Love Me Do' for the third time; and in a booth across the aisle, a middle-aged derelict with thick grey hair and a face the colour of dough and raspberries is beating time frantically with two teaspoons, lost in an ecstasy of second-hand creation. For him, the Hasty is a no-land of no hope; when the jukebox stops, he'll know it once more.

Burr and Brady have as much chance of their own show as he does, I think. But I find myself agreeing to get them an appointment with Rod Ferguson.

4

The Australian Broadcasting Service was a nation within the nation. Inside her capacious empire, Aunty harboured many territories and breeds; and the producers and journalists who were the organisation's aristocracy were seen in those days not just as broadcasters but as part of the establishment that ran the country. Mechanics of dreams with permanent tenure, we inhabited a world of make-believe on Federal Government pay, with full superannuation on retirement. What could be more desirable? I grew sardonic about this at times, but mostly I appreciated my luck.

To Burr and Brady, I could tell, my situation was entirely enviable, and they probably had a childish belief that I could do anything for them I wanted to, no matter what I might say. But by the Monday afternoon following our meeting in the Hasty, when they were due to call in at my office, I'd begun to cool on the situation.

I'd set up a meeting for them here with Rod Ferguson, and now I half regretted it. Theirs simply wasn't the sort of group that ABS would mount a show for, I thought, and Rod would probably see me as the type who went in for nepotism; I'd told him Brian was my cousin.

The phone rang; it was the secretary in the main office. 'There are some people here say they've got an appointment to see you, Richard. A Mr Burr and his friends.' Her voice sank, dubious and inviting family confidences; forty-ish Penny was a typical ABS vestal virgin. 'Have they *really* got an appointment, dear—or are they off the streets?'

We both knew what this meant; it was a standing ABS joke. People were always trying to get in off the streets to the corridors and studios of dreams: actors and writers who would never act or write, as well as the purely deranged, trying to climb out of the Cross into another life, as I'd done. Wenceslas Kupka had once got as far as the Director of Radio Features, brandishing wads of poems and inflammatory pamphlets; a uniformed commissionaire had escorted him shouting from the building.

'They're OK. Send them along,' I said. A winter downpour was filling the gulch of William Street, seven floors below; waiting at my desk, I sat and watched the cars sending up bow waves.

When they straggled in, making the small room seem overcrowded, I became even more convinced that the whole thing was a mistake. It was hard to believe that this was the group I'd found so enviable under the lemon spotlights at the Loft. They all looked bedraggled, plebeian and pallid, and they made me acutely conscious of the formal suit and tie that ABS expected its production staff to wear. At the same time, looking around them curiously in their worn jeans and damp dufflecoats, the two men made the office fussy and sterile. They stood against the bookcase with a dubious respectfulness and examined the tall radio monitor in the corner.

'What's this, mate?'

I explained.

'Jeeze. Looks like a coffin.' They kept their voices low, as though in church, while I phoned Rod's office to let him know they were here.

Rita Carey sat timidly in front of my desk, legs crossed, having given me her wide stage smile. I would catch her watching me as though trying to guess what I might do; plainly, there'd been much discussion. She was pretty, I thought, and somehow likeable, but she lacked the glow she'd had on stage, and had the hinted melancholy of those who are determinedly cheerful. Her mane of copper hair didn't look very well-brushed, and her pale blue dress had a dingy look. Her white legs were bare, and the sandals she wore despite the rain were plainly at the end of their life.

Darcy had brought a demonstration tape, and when Rod Ferguson came, pink and grey-suited, beautifully tailored, giving off an aroma of Old Spice aftershave, we all listened in absolute silence. Rod sat beside the desk, while I remained in my chair behind it; but it was clear who now had the central place in the room.

The group had recorded a number of the songs they'd presented at the Loft, as well as some flamenco pieces Brian and Darcy did as a duo; and while the tape was playing, I found I believed in them again, however unlikely ABS was to want them. I began to be ashamed of my embarrassment.

Rod's response was hard to judge; he remained professionally poker-faced, his large eyes fixed, the clean whites shining, listening with care. When the tape was done, he smiled from one to the other as though to tell them they'd won some prize. But the compliments he paid them had no offers appended, and began to sound merely polite. Darcy had already spoken for the group, so it was to Burr whom Rod mostly addressed himself, using his most mellifluous ABS voice.

'I *loved* it, Darcy' he said. 'You're marvellous musicians, and the electric backing's really unusual.'

I sighed inwardly as he paused, knowing already that a put-down of their hopes would follow.

'The trouble is,' Rod said, 'we have these terribly stodgy programme executives higher up, some of whom came out of the Ark.' He became flatteringly confiding. 'I've told Richard: all they want to know about is schmaltzy show bands and vocalists imitating Frank Sinatra. I had a hard enough time getting 'Eight O'Clock Rock' to air—and I just don't think they're ready for a whole series using a folk group, however good. Even if they were, they'd ask why they should let comparative unknowns have their own show.'

Rita Carey spoke for the first and only time. 'We're not entirely unknown,' she said. Her small, husky voice rose as though asking a question. 'We're known in the country. We've been doing Country and Western tours for two years; we made a record. They like us, out around Tamworth and those places.' She looked wistfully at Brian as though for help; she waited for others to give her answers.

'That's right,' Brian told Rod. 'We've even got a few fans. Or don't you count country people?' He grinned without resentment.

'Of course,' Rod said; he spoke as though to someone a little backward. 'But that isn't the mass audience, is it? And our programme executives have to be convinced you'd get that audience.'

'We can convince them,' Darcy cut in. He couldn't disguise his hunger, or the amber coldness of his stare, which was fixed on Rod. I glimpsed the standover man; he exuded a faint yet almost physical intention to coerce, his neck beginning to extend in the goose-like way that brought his face nearer to Rod's; and suddenly I realised what I'd let loose: if Darcy became aggressive and wouldn't take no for an answer, it would reflect very badly on me.

'We're not just ordinary folk musicians,' he was saying. 'We're a whole lot *more* than that.'

Rod's expression became blander; he leaned back and clasped his knee. 'I'm sure you are,' he said pleasantly, and changed the subject, plainly preparing to end the interview. 'Are you from Tasmania too, Darcy?'

'I'm a gypsy,' Burr said. He was looking at Rod with perfect seriousness, and I sat astounded.

'Really?' Rod glanced at me, asking whether to laugh or not, but my expression remained neutral. He turned back to Darcy. 'A real one?'

'A real one,' Burr said flatly. 'My father was a gypsy. You don't meet many of us about these days.'

Rod became respectful of Darcy's peculiar ethnic status. 'That's unusual. I suppose that's why you play such good flamenco.' Picking up a pencil, he sat tapping it lightly on the desk, staring at Burr now as though at a rare animal.

But Darcy made no acknowledgment of this new interest. 'What I'd like you to do,' he said, 'is see us perform at the Loft. You can't get an idea from a tape. Folk groups get major audiences overseas, but not here. That's because no one here's professional enough to deliver the goods. We are, you'll see that. We'll get the majority audience for you—not just the folk fans. We're working on material that's never been done before: it'll need a very special presentation on TV—and Dick and I will work on it together. That's why he ought to produce the show.'

Rod raised his eyebrows and glanced at me, but Darcy was still talking, his eyes unwavering.

'Why don't you take a risk? Why does ABS always have to play it safe?' He was frowning almost fiercely now, and I waited for Rod to react; to dismiss him. But then Darcy broke the tension by winking, with a sly, grossly exaggerated expression of invitation. 'We'll be

new,' he told Rod. 'Like nothing you've ever put on.'
Grinning, he repeated that statement he'd made in the
Hasty Tasty. 'We'll be *terrific.*'

It ought to have been crude and embarrassing; instead
he'd somehow made it funny, and Rod Ferguson laughed.

'You're almost starting to convince me,' he said. 'All
right—I'll come and see you.'

Darcy had made an old technique work, and I'd suddenly seen the power of his will. Arriving at a brink of
impertinence, he had disarmed his subject by making himself a jester at the last moment—as mendicants like him
have always had to do. It hadn't entirely hidden his aggression, but we're all titillated by a little bullying if it's
followed by a signal of capitulation, and Rod had proved
to be no exception. A bachelor of unknown tastes, seemingly adored by a series of women but probably enamoured
of neither sex, he was fairly tough under his ebullient
manner. I'd watched him produce his shows, and had seen
him quell performers and technicians alike with occasional
displays of soft-voiced firmness, pink executive jaw out-
thrust. Yet Burr's shabby intensity had broken through to
him; it wasn't to be stopped, for all its crudity.

I walked them along to the lifts.

'What's this about new material, for God's sake? There
isn't any, is there?'

Darcy grinned sideways, pressing the lift button while
Brian and Rita watched him in awe. 'I'm working on it.
And you're going to help.'

'And what's this about being a gypsy? Don't bullshit
me, Darcy.'

He winked. 'My old grandad was Scots. But let Rod-
baby think I'm a gypsy if he likes to, right? I'm whatever
anyone wants me to be.'

5

Our marriage was entirely happy, in those first six months
before Burr appeared at our door on the arcade.

A few weeks after he and Brian and Rita arrived in
Sydney, Katrin and I moved from Beaumont House to a

flat in Potts Point, taking Jaan and old Vilde with us. So I
now had a family, with a family's routines—even if these
weren't quite usual.

Every weekday morning at eight o'clock, I'd come out
into the glassed-in kitchen-verandah above quiet Challis
Avenue, and put on the kettle for tea. The two-bedroom
flat was on the second floor of an old, mustard-yellow
terrace a few doors from the corner of Victoria Street, and
as I lit the gas stove I would look across to McElhone
Stairs, the nineteenth-century stone steps going down off
the edge of Victoria Street and the Darlinghurst ridge to
the wharf sheds and funnels of the Woolloomooloo docks
below. Pigeons strutted on the tennis court of the convent
on the corner where the nuns played every Saturday, flap-
ping and calling in their black habits. The plane trees were
bare, imitating winter in Europe.

But I remember those weekday mornings as being always bright, cold and sunny, as they so often are in
Sydney in June. Waiting for the kettle to boil, I'd open the
sliding windows and look out, and the mini-bus from the
school for disabled children would pull up directly below,
the faces smiling at the windows as though on a treat.
Prompt and straight-backed as a clockwork man, old Andres Vilde would emerge on the front path below me in his
shirt-sleeves and blue glasses, waving to the driver. Now it
was time for me to carry Jaan downstairs, and to fetch his
folding wheelchair; and looking down on Vilde, with his
thick shock of white hair and last-century walrus moustache, I would feel a surge of fondness. He was a strong
old man, despite his seventy-five years, and although Jaan
was now thirteen, Vilde still sometimes picked him up and
lifted him into the bus as he used to, despite my protests.

Vilde and Jaan had become central components in my
happiness with Katrin. We were a family, and ate and sat
talking together in the evenings; yet the old man never
seemed to intrude when she and I wanted to be alone. He
was devoted to Jaan, with whom he shared the second
bedroom, and he spent much time walking him in his
wheelchair, helping with his mathematics homework, or

simply watching television with him. To be with his great-grandson seemed to be the main source of Vilde's contentment. He never complained, and spoke little of personal things; at least not to me, which made him comfortably half-real. This was also helped by the fact that he was naturally taciturn, his English remaining uncertain, even though his vocabulary was that of an educated man. But once, just after we were married, he said to me briefly: 'You are good, to take the boy. To be a father to him.' And he took my hand and held it for a moment, peering into my face. Like Katrin, I now called him *Vanaisa:* Grandfather.

'Tere, Vanaisa,' I would say, and he would smile with pleasure and return the Estonian greeting. He began to teach me a few phrases, but I found them difficult to retain.

At night, sitting in a big leather armchair Katrin had bought for his especial use, he would slowly read a newspaper or else his Estonian Bible, using a magnifying glass. He remained a devout Lutheran.

'You read the Bible often,' I said one evening, and he looked at me over his glasses, putting the book carefully aside. We were sitting in front of the gas fire in the high-ceilinged living-room, with its glass doors leading to the kitchen-verandah. Katrin was out, singing at the Estonian club; Jaan was in bed. Vilde always drank a single straight vodka at this time, and I poured one for each of us, setting them down on the coffee table between us.

'Without God,' he said, as though reading some rune from a stone, 'we grow sick.' He picked up the glass.

Perhaps he saw God as a vast medicinal herb; I envied him his faith, but he shrewdly read my expression of complacent neutrality, his eyes narrowing.

'You think this is not so, Richard? It is the worst sickness of all. Many have it now. Adolf Hitler had it, who has smashed Europe in pieces, and who is the reason I am sitting here now. I have heard that towards the end Hitler began to see the Devil. It is an interesting story; perhaps it is true. The doctor would find him on the floor by his bed; he was crouching, you understand, looking at something in the corner of the room. And he was trembling, begging Satan to go away, to leave him alone. Naturally, the doctor could see no one. You will say that Hitler was insane. This is a sentimentality of the present time: to explain all evil as insanity. Not to believe that monstrous things can be done by people who are sane. Hitler was never insane; he was far more serious than that. He had come to an agreement: he had embraced evil.'

For a moment we were both silent, as Vilde sipped his vodka and then put down his glass on the coffee table, wiping his moustache. He sat quite still, no longer quite the helpful old gnome I'd been inclined to see, looking at me steadily through the blue-tinted glasses, his head thrown back. He was always very sparing of his movements, and his low rumble was only just audible; but it now became more fluent, and I recalled that he'd once been a lecturer.

'The Nazis were very much interested in witchcraft— paganism. Naturally; they had denied Christ, now they had need of the Other. The Communists will find the same thing. We think that we can give up the rituals offered to God, but we find that we cannot. It is supposed to be the rational age, this one. But the rational age does not seem to have arrived.'

'Not yet,' I said. 'But it may.'

He smiled in a faded manner, and his voice became tired. 'It will never arrive. Giving up the rituals that are God's, we go back instead to other rituals. I think we go back now to paganism: to magic, fear, witchcraft. I see it in your newspapers, and on the television. We look for the old rituals that lead always to sickness, and to blood.'

It had been a speech of unusual length for old Vilde, and for this reason I remembered every word of it. When I spoke of it half-jokingly to Katrin, she raised her eyebrows as though I were displaying slow-wittedness. 'But of course,' she said. 'He's right. Surely you can see that?'

She had great respect for the old man, and I was wise enough to say no more.

*   *   *

The two of them had boarded the *Goya* for Australia when she was three months pregnant, hiding her condition from the Australian Immigration authorities. Andres Vilde had decided that the child would be passed off in Australia as Katrin's brother, after it was born. He would be its grandfather; no one in the new country need ever know otherwise. Those were the days when an illegitimate child was a deep disgrace, and a barrier to marriage; and Katrin was still not seventeen. Jaan was only told of their true relationship after she and I were married; even now, he still called her 'Katrin'. But in every other way, he had always treated her as his mother, so that little else was changed for him.

I often wondered about all those years of deception, and why she'd remained unattached. She told me of a long involvement with a young German migrant who had been going to marry her, and who had ended by breaking it off some years ago. Jaan was the main cause of this, she said. Dieter couldn't accept him; there were many men who couldn't accept other men's children, and Jaan's becoming a cripple made it worse: he had ridden his tricycle into the path of a passing car. After Dieter, although she went out with men occasionally, there'd been no more serious love-affairs until she met me. When she found that I'd once been crippled, she said, it had been like a sign that I was meant to love them both, she and Jaan.

But I sometimes found it difficult, in those early days on Bela Beaumont's arcade, to believe that there had been so few men before me. In spite of myself, I had the notion occasionally that her nature had been one of secret promiscuity—even though I had no real evidence of it. I still wondered about the man I had heard through the wall, before she and I met; their voices nagged at my mind, and finally I questioned her about it.

She couldn't remember who it was, she said. It would have been a friend visiting, that was all; she hadn't been in the habit of sleeping with men. She grew offended, and I rebuked myself; I was the silly product of a puritan small town, I thought, with all the old prejudices about unmar-

ried mothers implanted in me. After we were married, I
forgot these suspicions; and I grew increasingly fond of
Jaan.

I took my stepson for walks in his wheelchair about
Potts Point and down to Elizabeth Bay; and I sat on his bed
and read to him in the evenings. He was intelligent, and a
good reader, and his taste in books was growing adult. But
he maintained a sentimental fondness for the fairy stories
of his childhood, as I had done; he would still ask me to
read them to him aloud, and Katrin told me it had great
importance for him; it was a ritual affirming some sort of
connection between us. He was perfectly bilingual, and
had a large number of books in Estonian and English.

I often read him *The Wind in the Willows*. He was
especially fond of it, and of the Shepherd illustrations. He
would pore over them with me, pointing to things.

'Badger's house—I'd like to *live* there, Richard,' he
said once, and smiled confidingly into my face, his thick,
dark brown hair falling on his forehead: Geza Lukacs'
hair. And it seemed to me that he guessed I had wished the
same thing myself at his age, and was asking that I remember it, and draw closer to him. But I avoided the gaze
of his intense hazel eyes with their drooping white lids;
they were the eyes not of a child but of someone much
older: a survivor of deeply difficult experience. And instead of entering into the compact he wanted, I retreated
into neutral pleasantness.

'Would you?' I said, and went on reading.

If he was rebuffed, he didn't show it; no doubt such
withdrawals were threaded through his day. To make up
for what he might have sensed, I read to him longer than
usual.

Marriage to Katrin had transformed my life more than
marriage usually does. I'd married Europe as well, I thought:
hers and old Vilde's, with its kitchen-smells of sauerkraut
and borscht, its faint, aged scents of books and sheet
music, its tragic, tall old dreams, its muffled echoes of
gunfire. Loving her, I loved lost Dillingen, and the sub-
Arctic city of Tallinn where I could scarcely hope to go,

locked as it was behind the Iron Curtain. Lying late in bed on Saturday mornings, the door to the living-room ajar, I would listen to Katrin and her grandfather moving about outside, making breakfast, talking to each other in their closed, slurring language which mingled with the cooing of pigeons from the convent; and once again I'd become aware how strange my new wife was to me, carrying her alien past inside her. Speaking Estonian, she became another; fleetingly, I was no longer in Sydney, but in a medieval town on the Baltic. Vilde's voice would sometimes grow vehement at these times; I would wonder why, and then I'd recall that his life had been broken, and that his Lutheran certainties and his discipline concealed many sorrows: for his long-lost wife and son and daughter-in-law; for his lost country; for the crippled boy he had carried about in his arms.

I had begun to learn now what it meant to be married: to become a double person; and I saw that my life had only been half-nourished, before this. The European home-spirit that Katrin and her grandfather created in the flat was like the black Estonian bread they bought in the Cross, baked by their countrymen in exile. Unlike the lifeless white bread I'd been reared on, these heavy loaves were a food one could live on: a staple. She would never see a scrap thrown away; bread should never be wasted, she said. Habits of the Camp, not to be broken.

Sometimes, deep in the night, she would wake crying out of a nightmare, caught once again in the bombing raids of childhood, or putting out once again on the Red Cross ship through blazing Tallinn harbour, knowing that her father was lost. Then I would hold her until she grew calm, yearning to protect her from these perils I'd been spared, and could barely imagine. Our bodies had already become shaped to one another, and I hadn't truly loved before; I'd only known a counterfeit, on the east coast of childhood.

We thought our situation invulnerable; but in fact, it was totally fragile. Our marriage, like most new marriages, was a mixture of passion and game-playing; and each of us

had a childish streak: the result of in-grown imaginations.
This was the situation that Darcy Burr was now invading;
yet had I been told that he represented a danger, even
indirectly, I would have laughed at the idea.

It was after midnight when the phone rang in the living-
room; it woke us both out of the first shallows of sleep.
    'G'*day*.'
    I took a deep breath. 'It's not day,' I said, 'it's the
middle of the bloody night.'
    'Sorry, mate.' He didn't sound sorry; he sounded cheer-
ful. It had been three weeks since our meeting with Rod;
not having heard from Darcy since, I'd half assumed he'd
given up his schemes. I waited.
    'We just knocked off at the restaurant,' he said. 'I forget that
people like you are early to bed. Now listen, Dick, I've got
to see you. Can you come around to the flat tomorrow night?
It's important. Brian and Rita will be out, and we can talk.'
    Katrin looked alarmed, when I came back to bed. Propped
on one elbow in the bedside lamp's half-light, she spoke in
a tone of wifely accusation, as though I were somehow
responsible. It wasn't a tone I'd heard from her before.
    'I don't like people who ring in the middle of the night:
it's threatening. Who does he think he is, this Darcy? And
why must he see you alone?'

6

Victoria Street followed the line of the ridge above the
city, linking the Cross with Potts Point. It was a street of
cheap cafés and tall old terraces: frowning houses in
Victorian bonnets, fallen on hard times, like the muttering
old ladies of the Cross who went through garbage tins. The
place that Brian and Darcy were renting was halfway
between the junction and the corner of Challis Avenue,
little more than two minutes' walk from our flat; yet this
would be the first time I'd called there.
    Something had made me hold back; a premonition that
soon enough, all our lives would be intertwined, and that I
ought to keep clear a little longer.

Why? I wasn't sure. I didn't really mind helping them, even though I still thought that their dream of a television series was hopeless; yet something about the fact that Darcy in particular was now living so close by made me cautious. Once I'd been to see him, I'd probably have to return the invitation; and I was oddly reluctant about having him home. I half feared he'd eventually commit some fresh crime, I suppose; and I already sensed that he'd burrow into my life. The fact that I somehow wanted this only made it more perturbing. He was bringing something back to me, it seemed: something that had been missing from things, even though I'd thought I had everything; something that I wanted and yet didn't want; a factor I couldn't identify. No doubt this was a fancy preserved from the period when we three were boys together, its strong yet ghostly pungency explained by the fact that Burr and Brady had appeared from out of that time, when maturity and the commonplace hadn't yet been earned; when anything was possible.

Their flat was in the ground floor of a narrow, three-storey terrace set back a few yards from the street. It had plainly been allowed to run down for years; the dim mosaic tiles on the front porch were like broken paving from a lost civilisation. The front door was half open; mynahs scolded in the street's big plane trees, in the six o'clock twilight. When no one answered my knock, I walked into the dark entrance and knocked again on another door on my right, which was also ajar. Getting no answer there either, I peered in, wondering if I'd come to the wrong place.

But I was reassured by the sight of the mute guitars. Brian's Ramirez and Darcy's electric bass were propped against a long table in the centre of the room; a twelve-string and a banjo lay across chairs. I went in, to find that the room was empty and half dark. It was large, with a line of tall windows at the far end which looked out from the cliff-edge across the gulley of Woolloomooloo, with its nineteenth-century slum cottages. Beyond, the modern towers of the city were adrift in an apricot soup of smoke

first disconcerted; unsure whether I liked it or not. But I
quickly knew that I would.

'What *is* this?' I asked.

'It's our new sound,' he said. 'Our elf music. *You* know
this ballad, Dick.'

Brian and Rita were singing the verses, taking them solo
by turns, then coming together in unison. The melody
sounded traditional, though I couldn't place it. And I
began to recognise the words, which I'd never heard sung,
but had only encountered before on the printed page.

> *'True Thomas he took off his hat,*
> *And bowed him low down till his knee:*
> *All hail, though mighty Queen of Heaven!*
> *For your like on earth I never did see.*

> *'O no, O no, True Thomas, she said,*
> *That name does not belong to me;*
> *I am but the queen of fair Elfland,*
> *And I'm come here to visit thee.'*

It was 'Thomas Rymer', I said, and Darcy nodded in
delighted confirmation. He'd got it out of Child's *English
and Scottish Ballads*, he said.

'But where did you get the arrangement—the tune?'

'It's *my* arrangement, Dick. My tune.' His glasses flashed
proudly as his head went back. Meanwhile, Rita Carey
was carrying the verse in a high, empty voice, like someone singing in her sleep:

> *'O see not ye that bonny road*
> *Which winds about the ferny brae?*
> *That is the road to fair Elfland,*
> *Where you and I this night maun gae.'*

I saw the extent of his talent, and how it had grown in
eight years. In addition to the electric and acoustic guitars,
there was the piping of a treble recorder (that would be
Darcy), what sounded like a xylophone, and the sly patter-

ing of a finger drum, as the Queen and True Thomas set out on the road to Elfland. And in a solo passage before the voices returned, the little pipe summoned the listener to follow, beckoning the spirit away to the land of green delight with Thomas of Erceldoune. Meeting Darcy's gaze, I saw that he understood what he'd created: music from that country of small, distant lights; music inspired by the Lady who comes to us in sleep, disguised in mortal flesh; music from the Barrow World.

As I digested this, I looked further about his room: it had an underground feeling, perhaps because of its tunnel-like shape, its drawn blind, and murky moss-green walls. I wondered if he'd created this effect deliberately, to reproduce Broderick's little study in Varley's basement; and I suddenly felt certain he had. The dead bookshop accountant was strongly in my mind now; his influence on Burr could still be seen. Darcy sat in an attitude like Broderick's—long legs fully extended and crossed at the ankles—and there was even a similarity about his smile. Some of the occultic books on the shelves had surely once been Broderick's; I seemed to remember certain titles, although I'd never read them: *The Secret Doctrine; The Kabbalah Unveiled;* works by Aleister Crowley. He must have made a gift of them, and I wondered if the chart on the wall was inherited from Broderick too. The names on it meant nothing to me: *Kether, Binah, Chukmah.*

When the tape was done, Darcy listened to my praises in silence, with a one-sided smile which was complacently pleased, legs still extended. Then he said: 'You see why you've got to produce us, Dick. Only you could understand what I'm doing. Remember our talks in Varley's? I thought this group might specialise in fairy material: the English and Scotch ballads.'

I saw immediately that we could do it. The whole show could be mounted on the theme of Faery, and I could back it with visuals; graphics. I began to talk, and his eyes never left my face. I suggested other ballads: 'Tam Lin', 'The Demon Lover', 'Clerk Colvill'. We talked without consciousness of time, as we used to do in Varley's; time was suspended, in Darcy's closed room, and we played the tape over and over. Eventually I'd come to see the Rymers as partly my creation; now, I wonder. It was as though we'd taken some euphoric drug: it all seemed possible; it was going to happen.

'What should we call this group?'

'Thomas and the Rymers,' he said promptly, and we both laughed.

'Who'll be Thomas?'

'Maybe me,' Burr said, and I laughed again, while he poured me another wine. '*You* understand Dick,' he repeated. 'I knew you would. We can make it happen, you and me. The others'll be our instruments.' And he winked.

Later, I'd recall this remark with some dubiousness; now, like everything else, it seemed the simple truth, and I was unable to resist the idea that he read my mind. More: that he read my memory, and saw me in the sewing-room at Trent Street, a foolish elf-boy severed from Fairyland, troubled by those figures, ageless yet pubescent, who flew against the moon. It was still not quite possible to feel close to Darcy, however convivial he seemed; there was always a cold barrier in him somewhere. Yet tonight I felt warmer towards him than I'd ever done: a sort of cerebral warmth.

He was right, he and I would create this together; we'd bring Faery into being, I said. I'd ask Rod Ferguson to let me make a pilot; then I'd propose a series, and see if Rod would back it. I was about to get up and leave, in this happy frame of mind, when Darcy surprised me again.

'There's just one problem,' he said. 'Rita.'

'Rita? What's wrong with her? She's fine.'

'Yes,' he said jeeringly, 'she sounded fine in the end—*after* I'd worked on her for hours, and Brian had persuaded her to keep trying. She doesn't really like this fairy material, Dick—she doesn't have the feel for it. All little Rita cares about is C and W, or else nice, simple Irish songs—about *love*, if possible.' He lifted his upper lip in contempt. 'She's going to drag Brian down. She wants to keep him singing that corny material all his life. She never really wanted to quit doing Country and Western. The silly bitch wants to marry him, of course. She's been hanging on for two years now, but marriage isn't for a guy like Brian: he's got to be free.'

We had to get rid of her, he insisted, she wasn't good enough for the new group. But the brutality of this worried me, and I protested; surely she'd earned her place.

'She'll never make a lead singer,' Darcy pronounced. 'She hasn't got the vitality. It's Brian who's the real singing star in this group—and I'm the one who knows what's good for him.' His eyes had taken on their peering, fanatical look; he'd ceased to smile, and thrust his head forward at me. 'What we want is a female vocalist with *real* talent, who can match Brian, and really feel the fairy material. And I think I've found her.'

'Who?'

'Your wife, mate.'

I put down my glass and stared. He always had the power to disturb me, in the end; and yet I felt a reluctant excitement about this too. 'Katrin? You've never even heard her sing.'

'But I have.' He looked clever and triumphant. 'I went to the Estonian Club the other night. When you told me how good she was, I got curious.'

It was true I'd praised her to him.

'She's bloody marvellous,' Burr was saying. 'That voice! Like a choirboy's! It's perfect for our elf-music, Dick—don't you see that? And can't you imagine her and Brian together?'

I couldn't see Brian dropping Rita, I said, especially since they were involved with each other.

His gaze shifted. 'Leave that to me. We'll keep both women in the group, if we have to. At least Katrin can try out with Brian at the Loft, can't she? You'd like to give her a chance, wouldn't you?'

Yes, I said; but not at Rita's expense.

Things were going a little too quickly for me, and I wasn't sure any more that my enthusiasm had been sensi-

ble. I decided I should dampen his over-confidence a little
before I went.

'All I've said I'll do is try and make a pilot programme,' I told him. 'That doesn't mean that Rod or the
Programmes people will buy the idea.'

'They'll buy it,' he said. 'This is only the beginning.
We'll end up overseas, mate—and you'll be our manager.'

My dubious laugh didn't seem to disturb him in the
least; it was as though he knew my commitment would
soon over-ride all scepticism. Opening the door for me, he
still wore a smile which oddly parodied intimacy, even
tenderness—as though he and I were committing ourselves
to much more than a musical group.

'You know, Dick,' he said, 'this was always going to
happen.'

7

'John Riley' was always the best thing that Katrin and
Brian did together, yet it wasn't included on the LP the
Rymers eventually made, and no practice tape survives;
the only recording that exists now is the faulty one of
memory.

This was one of three traditional ballads that Darcy
chose for her guest appearance with Brady at the Loft, on
the night when Rod Ferguson came there to see the group
work. She and Brian had rehearsed in our flat for a number
of evenings in succession—always placing themselves by
the double doors that opened on to the closed-in verandah,
as though on a little stage. They laughed a lot, I remember; she'd had little to do with Brian's sort of Australian
before, and she found him amusing, like an off-colour
story. At the same time, she had great respect for his
talent; the way it combined with his careless crudity was
plainly intriguing to her. Brady made fun of what he saw
as her stiff formality; when they argued about arrangement
or interpretation, he would call her 'Prima Donna'. But
they got on well, finding accommodation by parodying
themselves: she the starchy European, he the Australian

roughneck, as she called him; she had something of a
penchant for outdated slang, as many migrants did.

Brian accompanied on the old Ramirez. There was a
particular solo passage he always did with great deliberate-
ness, the strings buzzing a little: it stayed in my mind, and
would come to me in moments before sleep; Brian's sound,
summoning up his tangled hair, intent frown as he played,
and out-thrust bottom lip of Celtic fullness.

I recall them on stage at the Loft surrounded by a soft
cloud of darkness, picked out in the lemon spotlight, the
audience mostly hidden. My hands were sweating from
nervousness; Rod sat expressionless beside me. Darcy Burr
and Rita Carey stood at the edge of the stage, and I
wondered briefly what Rita was thinking; she seemed to
wear a doubtful expression. Yet no suggestion, as far as I
knew, had yet been made that Katrin should join the
group.

She waited now while Brian tuned his guitar, her hair
falling straight to her shoulders in the approved manner,
her blue and white dress vaguely Bavarian in style, full-
skirted, with a cross-laced bodice—folkish, yet somehow
making her look doubly foreign among the turtle-neck
skivvies, cheesecloth dresses, coloured singlets and jeans.
There was unnerving quiet as Brady tuned, and I heard
Katrin make her small, throat-clearing sound, touching her
lips with her fingers: a sign of nervousness. But she stood
straight and still and stared the audience down, her eyebrows raised in friendly query. Tall beside her, ready to
begin, Brady smiled in encouragement as though they
were alone; on the mike, I distinctly heard him say, *sotto
voce:* 'OK, Prima Donna.'

A ripple of clapping went through the room as they
began 'John Riley'. The Joan Baez recording had made
this old British ballad popular with the Loft, and studying
the faces about me in the dark, I saw that they were
instantly impressed with Katrin. Although hers was a trained
voice—taboo at the Loft—its natural simplicity helped it
not to seem so; and she had adopted the Anglo-American
folksinging technique with ease. What Darcy called her

choirboy quality helped—it suited the nineteenth-century
ballads, and recalled Joan Baez—but blended with this,
making the colouring her own, was the faint, tantalising
slur of her accent. The mix was just right; and under it all
was the classical soprano's reserve of power. Filled with
the exultant note of loss I'd first heard in 'The Little Bell',
her voice winged upwards, Brady's deep under it; and on
his face and hers, tipped back into the light, looking
somewhere beyond the heads of the audience, there was a
shared expression; rapt, infectious and disturbing.

It made me see how they were matched, for the first
time. Superficially incongruous together, formal European
and Irish-Australian 'roughneck', they'd become the song's
nineteenth century seaman and the patient girl who waited
for him; children of the people, physically vigorous, their
strong, broad cheekbones making it plain that their long-
ings were the vital longings of health, untainted by any
sickly dreams. I felt no twinge of misgiving, that night; I
was proud of them both, and clapped as hard as the rest
when it was over.

Rod Ferguson, still clapping, leaned close to me to call
in my ear.

'They're marvellous, Richard. I'm sold, matey; we'll
make a pilot. But your wife's got to join the group! You
can't keep that girl to yourself any more.'

8

'I'm sorry to come bothering you like this.'

The husky voice was humble, yet it started a singing of
alarm. She'd come into the office without warning or
explanation; after I'd told Penny to send her along, I'd
moved out from behind the desk to greet her, and now we
stood facing each other in the middle of the room.

Rita Carey was even smaller than she looked on stage,
and I suspected she was the sort of person who found it
difficult to keep her life tidy. Reality was difficult; her
low-heeled shoes told you this, out of tune with the good
grey suit and white blouse I guessed to be her best. The

narrow-waisted jacket was well-cut, but somehow didn't fit properly. And yet she had dignity.

'I won't stay more than a moment.' She darted a respectful glance at the pile of scripts on the desk, twisting the strap of her vinyl shoulder-bag between her fingers. Then she looked up at me with the willed, defiant stare of the timid. 'I'm hoping you might help me,' she said.

I asked her to sit down, and she perched on the edge of a chair, drawing her bottom lip carefully under her front teeth. I sat on the corner of my desk, to be informal; but it didn't seem to dispel her nervousness. For a moment she said nothing, her green stare going out the window to the low brick office buildings of William Street. It was a country stare, more like a trance than thought, discouraging all empty briskness. She came from Uralla, a little town on the New England tableland; the biggest city she'd needed until now had been Tamworth, the country music capital. It had probably taken most of her reserves of courage to come here alone—even though she'd smiled for audiences in tent shows and town halls for years. Where she came from, offices were places that brewed trouble: fines, health department notices, hire-purchase demands, unnecessary permits. For her, ABS probably belonged to that whole official world the bush held suspect.

To break the pause, I told her how well I thought the group had gone last night.

'Yes. I'm sure everyone's happy. Your wife's a wonderful singer. She's had training, hasn't she? I never had any training.' She picked at a shred of pink varnish coming away from her thumbnail. Then her head jerked up.

'Maybe you can stop what's happening. I know you're going to get us this TV show. You could stop Darcy from pushing me out.'

I drew a deep breath. 'That's nonsense. No one's pushing you out.'

Her smile was despairing; I couldn't look at it. 'I know this isn't your idea,' she said. 'It's Darcy's. But if there's a series, your wife'll be in it, not me. I know that.'

'Then you know more than I do.'

She had grown very pale, and twisted the strap of the
bag as though to break it. 'Did you know Brian and me
were on the road together for two years, before he met
Darcy again? It's never been the same since. Darcy's got
all these ideas that don't suit Brian—but he makes him
think they do. Brian and me were happy doing country
music, as well as the old bush songs. That's what Brian's
good at. That's what he really likes. This new ghost music
of Darcy's doesn't suit him—but he'll do whatever Darcy
says.'

Taking in her beseeching stare, and her face's outmoded
prettiness, framed in its copper mane, I thought of someone drowning, trying to pull herself over the edge of a
lifeboat. And I saw (as sometimes happens in dealing with
a stranger, encountered only once), that this was a true
crisis in her life, and no manufactured one, and that I was
involved. It was very unwelcome; I didn't want to know
about it, and I inwardly cursed both Brian and Darcy. Her
head was bent, now; tears had come, but they were quiet,
and she was resisting them, blowing her nose. She wasn't
really the sort of person who made scenes, and I wondered
how often she'd been defeated before, resigning herself.

'If there's a series, you'll be in it,' I told her; and I
meant it.

She looked up with faint hope. 'That's good of you, to
say that. But you don't know what Darcy's like. He can't
be stopped by talk.' Then she checked herself. 'I'm sorry,
I know you and he are old friends. And I'm glad you'll try
to help me.'

Then her voice took on a tonelessness which had
recognised the death of love. 'Brian's twenty-seven, but he
still doesn't want to get married. He wants to be free, but
to have things all mapped out for him. Darcy trades on
that, he arranges everything. It's silly, isn't it?'

I saw her to the door, making bland reassurances in an
ABS voice, and watched her retreat towards the lift. She
was weighed down by the shoulder-bag like a child carrying adult luggage.

*   *   *

When I arrived home that night, Katrin was stirring chicken soup in our kitchen on the verandah. She looked up through the steam with a flushed, happy face, and I saw that something important had happened for her.

'Darcy Burr wants me to join the group. He phoned today,' she said. 'He's got wonderful ideas for the material we'll do.'

'I thought you didn't like Darcy.'

She looked faintly disconcerted. 'He's a bit menacing when you first meet him—but he can be quite charming. And you're right—his musical ideas are brilliant. I think the group's going to be extraordinary. I'll work every day to learn those songs.'

She hugged me, youthfully excited. She'd been watching my face for the answering enthusiasm she expected; not seeing it, she leaned back and tried to read my expression. 'What is it? Aren't you pleased?'

I told her about Rita, watching the joy fade from her face.

'But Darcy didn't say anything about pushing her out.' Her voice had become thoughtful and questioning. 'It's possible to have two women in this sort of group, isn't it?'

'It's possible, but that's not what Darcy wants.'

She frowned. 'And what about Brian? What does he say?'

'He doesn't even know at the moment.'

'But surely Brian's loyal to Rita? He must be.'

'I don't know,' I said. 'Brian's always gone from one girl to another. He doesn't like to be pinned down.'

We sat side by side on the couch in the unlit living-room, and she stared at the floor in silence. Her responses had been more or less the right ones, but there had been a flatness in her voice that worried me. Now she asked softly: 'But can't you persuade them to take me on without dropping Rita? After all, you'll be in charge of the show.'

'I can try. But it's not how Darcy sees the group.'

'Darcy thought I'd be just right for the elf sound.' She stared wide-eyed, with a look of farewell, at the light-filled frame of the double doors where she and Brian had practised.

'Yes. You'd be just right.' I put my arm about her shoulders. Her body was stiff and sad, and didn't yield.

'But I have to give it up,' she stated quietly. She was still looking at the doors.

'No. But we can't just forget Rita, can we?'

'They don't *want* Rita!' Her vehement tone made me start; she'd swung around on the couch to face me, in the half-light coming from the kitchen. 'If they did, I wouldn't say any more. But from what you say, there can't really be two of us, and they want the one who has a feeling for this music, isn't that true? And yet you expect me to stand aside.'

'I don't expect that. But Rita's stuck with Brian for years. She's owed something.'

She stared in silence. She was honourable in her instincts, and I saw that she was struggling with herself, breathing deeply. When she spoke again, her voice was quieter, but full of vehemence.

'I'm nearly thirty. I put Jaan first for a long time, and I spent years being something second-rate; a funny migrant, singing songs that your people don't want to hear—songs for those people who have only the past to care about, and no future.' I took her hand, but it was clenched into a fist. 'Don't you see? This was my great chance to break out; and I don't think I'll ever have another.'

She glanced at the doors again; she twisted the wedding-ring on her finger. I had never known her like this; I saw an alien capacity for wild despair that alarmed me, and I also knew that what she said was true: it was confirmed by the first, fine lines at the corners of her eyes. She still looked no more than twenty-four; but for how much longer?

'I'm sorry,' she said. 'You must do what you think right, Richard. But I think you want to please everyone, and that never works. In the end, you may be hated by everyone.'

'Not by you, I hope.'

'Not by me.' She laid her head on my shoulder as though exhausted, and once again we fell silent.

It was a silence I continued to find worrying.

Katrin had taken the enterprise of marriage very seriously. We'd been married in a Lutheran church; I'd agreed to this to please her, since I'd lapsed in my Catholicism, and she'd treated the ceremony with great reverence. For the first few months she'd concentrated on decorating the flat as though it were her whole aim in life. She enjoyed making a home; she enjoyed cooking, and had been filled with pleasure that her grandfather and Jaan lived more comfortably than they'd done at Beaumont House. She'd given up her daytime job as a receptionist, and I'd unconsciously begun to think of her singing at night as a paid hobby; had almost begun to see her as the conventional wife. When I left home in the mornings, she would wave me goodbye from a window of our upstairs verandah, and I would carry away with me up Challis Avenue the image of her broad blonde head and water-grey eyes, watching me go. I would look back twice or more, and when the window gaped empty, I would feel a faint pang. It was the stage of marriage when there could never be enough reassurance; never enough love.

Now, sitting on the couch, I saw that I'd been living in make-believe for these past few months. Singing was no hobby, it was her central passion, and she didn't see herself solely as a wife; she'd perhaps been waiting all the time for just this moment. Maybe she'd almost given up hope that it would arrive; but that only made the threat of its withdrawal all the less bearable.

But our problem was solved very simply. Two weeks later, Rita Carey disappeared.

It was Brian who told me the news. He and I had met in a pub on the Cross for a drink after I finished work. I hadn't seen him for these past two weeks; Darcy had wanted time for them to work on his arrangements for the songs before we met again.

'Where did she go?' I asked.

'I dunno.' Brian drank his middy of beer off in three long gulps and pushed both our glasses across the laminex counter, signalling to the barmaid for fresh ones. He didn't

want to talk about it, and as always with Brian in this
mood, it was almost impossible to extract information
from him.

'So you've broken up permanently?'

His quick sidelong glance was like a warning. 'She's
shot through, hasn't she?' He picked up his fresh glass.
'We weren't jibing any more as musicians, anyway. She
didn't like this new stuff we're working on—she was
getting to be a real pain about it. Darcy's right—with an
opportunity like you're giving us coming up, we can't be
half-hearted, can we? Right?' He looked almost pugna-
cious, as though challenging denial. 'She'll be better off in
Tamworth,' he said.

'Is that where she's gone?'

'No. I told you—she's just disappeared. I've got no
bloody idea where she is at present. I can't find her, if you
want to know the truth.'

He had tried. He had phoned her parents in Uralla, as
well as Country and Western friends in Tamworth; but
they knew nothing. He'd even searched through the Cross
and the city. But she'd vanished, and the short note she'd
left had given him no clue as to her intentions.

'Is this anything to do with Darcy?'

I got the sidelong glance again. 'Why should it be?
Forget it, Dick. Women come and go. Y' can't go on
being serious about them, or you end up in harness, mate.
That's all right for steady blokes like you.'

I suspected pain somewhere; but he remained expressionless, drinking, and I decided to say nothing about her
appeal to me.

'Anyway,' he said, 'the Rymers'll be OK. We've got
Katrin now, haven't we?'

9

Now Burr and I began our planning sessions for the pilot
programme.

Brady and Katrin rehearsed the songs with Darcy at
other times, while I was at work. They weren't much
involved in the actual mounting of the programme,

recognising the fact that Faery was a territory in which Darcy and I specialized. So he and I were left to ourselves there.

Burr was endlessly receptive and deferential to my production ideas. I was now bent on making the main presentation and style of the group revolve around the English and Scots ballads of the supernatural; my desk at work was piled high with books on fairy and supernatural lore, and with reproductions of fairy paintings from the eighteenth and nineteenth centuries, and particularly from the Victorian era: heyday of Faery.

'You'll have to get out of the jeans and roll-necks,' I said. 'You'll need medieval-style costumes, like people out of a Richard Dadd painting. Do you think Brian'll agree? He doesn't like anything fancy.'

'He'll bloody well have to agree, mate. You've got the image we want, spot on; it's your show. It's going to be like nothing anyone's seen. No one but you could produce this, Dick. I was right.'

He was full of glee and admiration. It was partly flattery, of course, I knew this; but I could also tell that he'd made a shrewd decision that my ideas were going to work for him, that they matched his own, and in some ways went beyond anything he could have conceived.

I was working in my toy theatre again.

Darcy's great strength lay in the melodies and arrangements he devised for the ballads themselves; and in this area I deferred to him, scarcely questioning his choices, and returning his admiration. We would pore over Child and other sources together, searching out those ballads of the supernatural that appealed to us; we would decide on the mood and style, and I would leave the rest to him. Sometimes he used traditional melodies; more usually he fitted the words to variants on these melodies of his own devising, with instrumental passages in between the verses that were startlingly modern in their style and in the use of the electric guitars. But it all worked; it had a strange harmony. He was influenced by the British group Pentangle; such things were in the air. But a good deal of what he was doing was entirely new, and his own; when he said it was like nothing else, he told the truth: so far as we knew, some of the Child ballads we were searching out hadn't been performed in recent times, and certainly not recorded.

We thought almost as one, as the weeks went by; we excited each other with constant fresh ideas, and I was infected with Darcy's comical yet dark glee. We laughed like conspirators, as though there were an underlying point to the presentation, never put into words by either of us, which went beyond mere entertainment, and would catch people unawares, subtly undermining their simple enjoyment of a folk group, and drawing them into that Otherworld they thought had no power any more, its messages carried by the weird electric whine of the guitars. Our sessions grew longer and longer; we would phone each other at all hours of the day and night, so that even Katrin began to wonder about the degree of our obsession.

'Listen, Dick: about "Tam Lin". I've got the perfect instrument for the sound of the forbidden wood—a dulcimer.'

'You can play a dulcimer?'

'I can play *anything*.' Gleeful sniggering came down the phone, in which I joined, amused at his swaggering egotism—elated by his enormous confidence that we would enchant the public.

Now that Rod had given me the go-ahead for the pilot, and would let me produce it in September, my interest in the radio productions I was doing became almost perfunctory; I thought of the Rymers constantly, and Martin Gadsby had taken to making reproachful remarks, accusing me of deserting radio.

Rationally, I still knew that the likelihood that Programmes would be convinced by the pilot was slender; there was small hope that they'd launch a whole series for an unknown folk group. But emotionally, I was fixated on our succeeding; I couldn't accept that we would fail. Few men are placed in the position of giving their fantasies flesh, and this was what had happened to Darcy Burr and to me.

But an odd development characterised our planning sessions, concerning which I would have felt embarrassed had anyone else but Darcy and I been aware of it. Much of the time, although we discussed the practical and artistic means of realising the fairy and supernatural themes, we were going beyond these particulars and into the general; we were discussing the mythology and anthropology of Faery, as we'd once done in Varley's basement.

Theory nurtured practice, we said; it gave us ideas. This was true, but I began to admit to myself that we often theorised for the sake of it; that we both had some sort of need of it. And in each session, it seemed to me, Burr took the lead in this theorising, as though guiding me along a path.

The night before we were due to record the pilot, when his nerves and mine were strung to a high pitch, the path came to a gateway. He had wanted to bring me there all the time, I suppose. In some ways, he was very patient.

Our sessions occasionally took place in my office, but mostly they were held in Burr's room in the Victoria Street flat, when Brian was out. We'd be out of Katrin's way, he said; she didn't want to listen to our talk.

It was true; she didn't, any more than Brian did. And although she admired Darcy as a musician, he'd made her uneasy, on the few occasions when he'd come to the flat to visit. 'He makes a funny atmosphere,' she said. 'I feel it for an hour after he goes.'

Darcy had developed a habit. When he wanted to see me in the evenings after dinner, he would walk down Victoria Street to the corner of Challis Avenue and stand outside our gate and whistle, two fingers in his mouth: the sort of whistle once prized by members of street gangs. I would look out from the sliding verandah window and see him grinning below on the path.

It had been like that this evening. He'd whistled me out at about eight; now we sat in his room. The pilot was entirely planned for tomorrow evening's recording: the set designer, the technical producer and the lighting people were all happy; everything was ready to go. Burr and I said that we needed to meet now for a last look through the camera script, but this was just an excuse; our talks had become an addiction, and what we were discussing was the Faery Process again.

'Fairyland's double,' Darcy said.

He was lying back in an armchair beside his desk, perfectly still, legs extended in front of him in their habitual way, crossed at the ankles. As always, the room was half-lit by the tall standard lamp. I knew now what the sweetish smell in the flat was; he'd taken to the occasional smoking of marijuana—a practice that was fairly dangerous at this time, since the police were raiding apartments and houses in the Cross in a hunt for suspected users. I sometimes worried about his getting caught, but he laughed at this.

He held out the damp joint to me now, and I leaned and took it.

He grinned. I'd never smoked pot before, refusing because of a secret dread of losing control. But tonight I drew the smoke in, coughing as its sickly sweetness stung my chest.

'It's double,' Burr insisted, still watching me, his voice croaking a little as he held in his smoke. And a remark of Clive Broderick's came back to me; something about the universe itself being double. It had always lurked in my mind, as the guitar teacher himself had. I was trying to gauge the effects of the pot, but so far, nothing seemed to be any different. Was there an odd clarity about the furniture?

Meanwhile, Darcy was enlarging on his theme, the smoke seeming to affect him very little.

The Faery Otherworld had two aspects: dark and light; Hades and Elfland. It was impossible to know which zone one might find oneself in: the Barrow World of eternal night, or that country whose very air was the bright ether of dream. But Elfland itself was located under hills; under barrows; under ground: and that was where the dead were, wasn't it?

As to the elfin people themselves, who were they? On what level did they have their being, and why did they tease our minds? They kidnapped earthly mothers to nurse their children; they craved our vitality, as malicious spirits did, we knew that: they might well be entities between Heaven and Hell. Lost wives, lost sweethearts who had gone to Elfland were sometimes seen again by those who loved them—but usually only once. And he recalled for me the story of the young Scots farmer whose dearly loved wife was lost in Fairydom. She appeared to him suddenly among their children, and told him he could win her back by waylaying the fairy cavalcade at night. But when he waited for it on the heath, he lost his courage; the troop rode by, his wife wailing among them, and he watched it paralysed, and did nothing. Then it was gone; she was lost to him for ever. He heard the harness bells and the triumphant laughter recede, and I found his pain unbearable; because how would he ever be free of it?

A double world: enchanted and endlessly sweet, its savours never failing; or else dim wastes without hope, where shades went drifting in endless loss. Was this why Broderick's ideas had been so disturbing? Was this why my mind had rung with shock when he told me the universe was double?

There was a fatal moment when people succumbed to the wish for that region, I said; when they reached out for the Otherworld. And then everything was changed. It happened in dream, or else in sickness—at times when the will and the life-force were weak. It had happened to me in the Red Room. Paralysis had put its mark on me, and then spared me; I was one of those who had looked into the grave early, and had then drawn back.

'Brod knew all that,' Burr said softly. 'He knew that you were special, Dick: he told me, once. And he knew that some day you and I would work together.' He stubbed out the joint.

'I didn't trust him.' My own voice was loud and rude in my head; stoned, one spoke only the truth, it seemed.

Darcy's eyes gleamed quick at me behind their glasses,

and I had a stirring of caution; I remembered his capacity for violence. But this thought was silly, and his voice when he spoke confirmed it; he wasn't angry, he sounded gentle and almost cultivated.

'That was a pity. Brod was your ally, and we don't find many. He wanted to teach you all he taught me. Brian was never up with it, because Brian's pretty simple. But you were different. Brod offered you knowledge, and you blew it. You weren't receptive enough.'

'Maybe I didn't want it.' My tongue was slow; it almost hadn't finished this sentence. The hash had unseated the room's perspective. It now seemed as long as a corridor, and Burr was down at its end. I tried not to be alarmed, while he went on talking, watching me insistently. And now, with a logic I found exquisite, making me laugh aloud, he put everything into place.

Of course the universe was double; how could anyone but a fool believe otherwise? Had Christianity ever really justified or explained a merciful and omnipotent God's toleration of evil and pain? Could it even give a reason for one child's death in agony? For villagers being bombed and maimed in Vietnam, even as we spoke? For frightful, undeserved catastrophes, or tormenting disease? For the long chain of suffering—preying and being preyed upon—which was the destiny of all animals on earth?

'That's the natural order,' I said.

Darcy laughed. 'There's nothing *natural* about it, mate. You don't even believe that yourself. It's totally *un*natural. It's disastrous. And it *began* from a disaster.'

I laughed again, but he ignored my laughter; he went on to explain in detail the pre-cosmic calamity through which the material world had been created: not, it seemed, by what we called God at all, but by an inferior and malevolent force—the Demiurge, one of whose identities was the God of the Old Testament.

'So Jews and Christians have both been fooled,' Darcy said. 'The Demiurge thinks he's God, but he's wrong. There was a split, do you see that, Dick?'

Leaning closer, he elaborated. The true First Cause of

things was quite detached from the Demiurge, and from the misery of matter and false Time; it was pure spirit, and its name was the Abyss. As for us, we were all trapped in matter, where we didn't belong. This was what gave our spirits pain; this was why we longed for something nameless, all our lives.

'You really believe that, Darcy?' I remained impressed, but the room's perspectives had certainly gone wrong. The green walls were furry as vegetation; the coloured, comic-strip Tarot figures in Darcy's pictures were threatening and comically alive (the Fool, the Magus, the Empress), and the shaded lamp was bright as a sun. I found I was very thirsty; I wanted to stand up and get a drink, but I couldn't summon the will to do so.

'It's truer than you think,' Burr said. He thrust his head even nearer and frowned, and I half feared this frown; I wanted to placate it. To get free of our prison wasn't easy, he told me—but invisible beings existed whose powers could be invoked; entities of power, who reflected the different levels of consciousness. And always the most potent power that could be turned to was that of love.

'Love,' Darcy repeated, and now he smiled, with what I saw was intended as tenderness. (Was it tenderness? I wasn't sure.) Through love, and through the magic of sex—through direct contact with the divine female force—we could liberate ourselves; we could achieve communion with the Abyss. And we could then rediscover the older Mysteries: the secret knowledge of Eleusis; the rites of Koré, raped and stolen by Hades, like that Scottish farmer's wife lost in Elfland. It all linked up, didn't it? The dual Otherworld waited—where either we were lost, or renewed. He looked at me fixedly, an adult with a wayward child whose attention might stray. I wanted to laugh again, but his face had the shine of fanaticism, which can only be laughed at in the abstract.

'We have to get free of the world,' he said. *'We have to pierce the skin.'*

How? Through magical bliss, he said. The way of Faery; the way of Dionysus. And didn't Dionysus preside

over all magic? No wonder Christianity saw him as the
horned god: the Enemy!

'Look, people still want bliss; they still want the invisible,' he said. 'But Christianity can't give it to them any
more, right? Once that door shuts, it's hard to open again.
And what in the world could be more important?'

He waited; I said nothing; his glasses flashed. 'Maybe
it's especially important *here*,' he said. 'In Australia, I
mean. Because we don't have much to take our minds off
it, do we? People are killing because of that; nasty murders
that we can't see the sense of—have you noticed? Hitch-
hikers get tortued; girls get cut to pieces, out in the bush.
And yet the desert's waiting all the time with the answers.
I was out there once, near Darwin, and I felt it. The
Aborigines found the power-places there; but we don't want
to know, do we?'

I wanted to go, but couldn't summon the will to get up.

'Brod knew all about that,' Darcy said. 'He showed me
the paths of power.'

There was a long silence. I looked at a blue coffee-cup
on the small table beside me, which grew and filled my
vision, calm and still. Then I heard Darcy speaking again.

'He made me see that there were two people inside me:
one who was weak and sentimental; the other somebody
who could be strong enough to make himself free. I made
myself free of my bloody parents, to begin with. That was
the first hurdle. I didn't have to think about them any
more, I could be totally indifferent. I could have watched
them killed if I had to, and not given a bugger.'

'Do you remember much about them?'

'Remember them? Oh yes mate, I remember them.'

His mouth grew abnormally thin, his face was con-
stricted by a frozen, inverted passion; he clenched his fists
on the arms of his chair, and I was sorry I'd asked. 'I
remember them fighting in bed,' he said, 'and fighting up
and down the kitchen when they were both drunk.' He was
looking back into echoing lanes near the Gasworks, and
had suddenly become a small, far-off figure, down the
long hall the room had become. His voice was far off, too.

'But my old man had sense. He got out and took to the road, and I never saw him again. So he didn't have to see my mother dead drunk in the kitchen every night, passed out and pissing herself on the floor. Neither did I, after I moved to Sandy's.'

I couldn't look at his distant figure; I waited. There was no time, here in his room; and Harrigan Street ran on for ever, in the soft rain of the island. I had somehow assumed that Darcy had no hurts; that he felt no normal sadness. Why had I assumed that?

And I knew now why it was so important that the Rymers should lift him free. I smiled at him, and he smiled back with severe calm, still as a storybook king, in his chair.

10

'Take two,' I say. 'Close-up on Katrin and Brian.'

I hunch in my chair in the control-room's semi-darkness as though at the wheel of a truck with ten gears: chain-smoking cigarettes; muttering to the script girl next to me; calling the shots to the vision-mixer; peering at the script under its little lamp. With elated fury I focus on my whole technical orchestra, unable to slacken attention for a second, lifted high on concentration as though on Darcy's hash, willing it all to work.

And there are tensions within tensions in this long, nigrescent saloon with its red and green lights, jigging meters and blue-grey video screens. Although I'm in charge here, my authority is silently in question. I haven't had the production experience to justify doing a show like this, and despite the comparative success of our rehearsals, scepticism floats in the darkness. Rod Ferguson's influence put me in the chair, and the techs know it. On either side, at the control desk, sardonic shadows wait for a mistake to be made: a wrong cue, a bungled sequence of shots. I've ridden some of them hard to get what I want, and they resent it.

Only the sound crew, who have come to admire the group, are probably with us. It's taken us weeks to find the right balance; to get exact, restrained levels with the electric guitars that match with the voices, and blend with Darcy's delicate pipes and acoustic instruments without drowning them. Nothing like it has been done on ABS before, and even as I worry about camera angles, I must listen all the time to be sure that the balance stays right. I know I should trust the sound crew; but I trust no one.

'Take one. Medium close-up. Keep Darcy in shot.'

I have the three in view all the time through the control-room window; the black cameras stalk them out there, and my headphoned envoy the floor manager dodges and crouches in front of them like an attendant spirit, pointing dramatically, leaping nimbly over cables. But it's the black-and-white screens above my head I attend to most: second-hand images more vital than the real one through the window. Brian is working on electric guitar; Katrin is singing, head back, straight as a sentry beside him; Darcy is a little apart, crouched cunningly over the table where his electric dulcimer has been set, working away with his little hammers, mop of black hair swinging. All are in outfits designed to my specifications: the two men in tight knee-breeches, full-sleeved white shirts and leather jerkins; Katrin in a full-length skirt, long-sleeved blouse and a jerkin that complements those of the men. We're using key lights on the studio floor to create an eerie dimness; although we're in black and white, we have coloured gels over these to create studio atmosphere, and they dramatise the modelling of Katrin's face, striking upwards to put shadows under her Estonian cheekbones; she gazes yearningly at Brian as she sings.

It's all working, except for one thing: Brady is drunk.

This has kept me in a state of anguished concern. When they first got into the studio he was grinning loosely, his eyes bloodshot and his speech slurred. Darcy Burr took me aside, his fingers digging into my arm, his face drained of colour, his frown dangerous, his voice hissing in my ear.

'The bastard's pissed! He's been gone for two days: it's because of that little slut Rita. Get some black coffee. Get the bugger sober.'

During the dry run, Brady played some jarringly bad notes, and his attack was less sure than usual when he sang. He ridiculed his costume, which he apparently regarded as effeminate; he made homosexual gestures, and flapped his sleeves like a bird. I took him aside and reproved him, and his face showed a blurred look of shame; he swayed.

'Sorry mate, sorry. Rita's gone, see? Can't find her anywhere. She ought to be here tonight, oughtn't she?'

'Do you want to wreck it for Katrin—for all of us?' I was angry now.

'No Dick, no. It'll be right when we cut. You'll see.'

And it's proved to be true. Now that we're taping, he's performing as well as he's ever done, and I begin to relax. There'll be no second chance. If the Programmes people are convinced by this pilot, it will go to air as the first of a series; if not, it will never be seen.

But it's all coming together, and we've only had to stop the cut once. My fingers are trembling as I yank at the script; fulfilment is unfolding inside me leaf by leaf. We're doing 'Tam Lin', our last ballad but one, and sporadic murmurs of admiration have started in the control room's darkness; the still air tingles with pleasure.

They're good; the Rymers are very good indeed, and below the flickering, multiplied blue images of my creation, I sway and hum now in fervent communion, in rhythm with the music, no longer caring what the techs think. I mutter to myself, I call sudden commands, and the script assistant laughs in encouragement; she's already sensed the flowering of something irresistible. *I've put them inside the frame*, and a magic is taking place; they're more than themselves now, Katrin, Brian and Darcy. I concentrate on calling the shots, as we alternate faster and faster between the studio (where I cut from instrument to instrument, face to face) and the graphics I've matched with the progress of the song: the luminous, semi-nude fays of Huskisson, Simmons and Sir Joseph Noel Paton; the decadent and sinister Otherworld creatures of Fuseli and Richard Dadd; the equivocal Victorian flower-faces of Doyle and Fitzgerald. This is the soul of the show, as brownies, hobmen, kelpies, water-sprites, silkies, bogles flit and pass on the screen; as the slyly ominous heartbeat rhythms and haunting tunes Darcy has devised arrive to persist in the mind. His small hammers on the dulcimer produce notes like water-drops in a cave; his bass guitar whines in a way that would set the nerves on edge, if it weren't seductive. Now he changes to treble recorder, its plaint a variant on Katrin's singing, its far, ominous refrain announcing Janet's arrival in the forbidden midnight wood, and her crucial attempt to rescue Tam Lin, her elfin seducer. I super Burr's piping Pan profile over Brian's working fingers on the guitar.

'Roll credits,' I say, and slump back in my chair as though I've run a race. Brian is singing 'The Bard of Armargh', the farewell ballad that will end each show—if we're ever granted the series. Off camera, Burr catches my eye through the window; he grins and triumphantly winks.

A hand falls on my shoulder; looking up, I realise Rod Ferguson has been standing behind me all the time. Well, he has a right to be here; without him, the pilot would never have been made.

'Congratulations,' he says. 'Lovely production.' His prominent blue eyes are further enlarged with unfeigned enthusiasm, almost, it seems to me, with awe; and the nearest techs imitate his smile. 'It's no ordinary folk group,' he says. 'Watch out though, Dick—you'll lose that beautiful wife of yours to show biz.'

Soft laughter from the darkness. Not malicious; the reverse in fact, since everyone now is scenting a triumph.

7

AND PLEASANT IS THE
FAIRY LAND

1

As the new summer opened like warm newspaper, and the deafening drilling of cicadas began in the plane trees of the Cross, all our lives were changed.

We'd been granted a series of six half-hour programmes, slotted at nine o'clock on Thursday nights. It wasn't a top spot, but by the time the fourth of these programmes had gone to air, in mid-November, the press attention and the ratings we attracted exceeded even Darcy Burr's predictions, astounding the executives in Programmes. They'd only anticipated a minority audience for the series in Sydney; but after the success of the first two shows, they decided to make the series national, and the response in other states was just as enthusiastic. The slot was changed to eight o'clock on Friday nights all over Australia: prime time. A second series was planned for the new year, at a much higher fee for the group.

The Programmes people shouldn't have been surprised. We were not only riding the wave of the overseas folk boom, we were appealing to a section of the pop audience as well, just as Burr had planned. Darcy was ahead of his time, in Australia, and the press and the public were startled and intrigued by a folk group using strong electric backing, and by the ballads of the supernatural.

The Rymers developed a cult following among the young; one of the Sunday papers labelled the group 'electric folkies', and the term stuck. The more trendy magazines began to use the term 'occultic music'. A poster was produced of the group by ABS Publicity which I began to see everywhere, and media gossip pieces in the press began to refer to Katrin and Brian as 'folkie sex symbols'. More and more of the publicity began to concentrate on these two; they were interviewed by a number of magazines, and showed signs of developing into pop stars. Both began to get fan mail; and Brian's female following in particular was steadily growing in size. Large numbers of girls began to hang about the doors of the ABS television studios on the evenings when we recorded, waiting to surround him when he came out.

It was a modest crowd in comparison to the hordes that mobbed overseas pop stars; but on one evening it was large and strident enough to warrant hurrying the group into a waiting ABS car and speeding away into the night of the Pacific Highway.

The urgency of these girls, as they ran after the car towards the gates (all of them calling: 'Bri-an! Bri-an!') was strange and pathetic. As we left them behind, in that sterile suburb of floodlit buildings and giant transmission towers, I saw with amazement that some of them were weeping. Brady, sitting beside me in the back seat and waving back at them, was bemused and scornful. 'Silly little scrubbers,' he said softly.

The fantasies and the group intoxication of popular success didn't seem to move him; he remained a sardonic folk singer, and most of the time scarcely seemed to notice the effect he had on women. He grinned at them amiably, and slid away; it was Katrin's opinion that he was afraid of involvements, and always would be.

Now, watching the running girls recede through the back window, I believed I understood their longing. They wanted nothing less than to stay inside the music, whose high excitement seemed so much sweeter than life. Darcy Burr's wistful recorder and mouth-organ accompaniments had much to do with this, but the girls were scarcely aware of it. Brian was what they wanted; he was one of those in whose face the stamp of the Otherworld was strong: that Otherworld the music summoned up. Yet he himself was unaware of it.

Unable to stay with him there, they wept.

*   *   *

I could hum and sway and be as eccentric as I liked in the control-room now: I was regarded with that awed respect which only top ratings can command. Only Martin Gadsby wasn't impressed, and continued to look at me reproachfully; I was plainly deserting radio, and he shuffled past me in the corridors without a word. I felt briefly guilty about the old man, but put him from my mind.

The show was simply called 'The Rymers'. We brought in a few other folk singers as guest artists, to avoid overexposing the group and exhausting their material; but it was clearly the Rymers' programme. I directed it in the studio, but occasionally, through an arrangement with Gordon Cartwright, it was done as a carefully-staged outside broadcast from the Loft, in front of a small, hand-picked audience. And Burr was 'Thomas'. In what I saw at first as a modest gesture, he'd taken the stage name 'Thomas Darcy', to justify the group's title. I dreaded the day when a journalist would dig up information on his prison term; then it occurred to me that Darcy had more than one reason for adopting his pseudonym.

The supernatural ballads weren't the group's whole repertoire, even though they were central. Brian did a number of solos, mainly Australian bush ballads and Irish rebel songs, which were what did most to build his personal following; and he and Katrin sang a number of the traditional ballads of love and loss—among them 'John Riley'. As well, we usually included at least one guitar duet by Darcy and Brian to demonstrate their virtuosity. Once, they played 'Johnny Guitar', ending with their spectacular *bulerías*— and as they bent towards each other in profile (beaked nose, broken nose, the two guitars raised like obscure weapons), I had a brief shock, studying Darcy on the control-room monitor: just for a moment, I was looking at Clive Broderick, bent over the Ramirez in the back of Sandy's shop. This illusion was momentarily so strong that I was held and distracted by it. But it was simply a trick of the black-and-white image; checking through the control-room window, I found that the resemblance was no more marked than usual. At that moment, sensing my stare, Darcy looked up at me and grinned as he played; he gave me the sensation, as he often did, of having picked up my thought waves.

I'd feared that we might run out of songs, before the series ended; but Darcy's inspiration in producing melodies and arrangements for the Child ballads seemed inexhaustible. He was very much subordinate to Brian and Katrin in the eyes of the public—the cunning instrumentalist who worked in the background and sang only in the choruses; and he wasn't seen to have Brady's sex appeal. But there was no doubt in my mind how much of the group's success sprang from him. Some of his arrangements owed something to Pentangle; others, in weird yet harmonious contrast with the fairy ballad content, had echoes of the Beatles; but many were like nothing anyone had heard. He was influenced by Indian sitar music, as others were beginning to be at this time; he had acquired a sitar of his own, and the quarter-tones fitted perfectly with the pre-Christian and medieval themes of the great Scots ballads of the supernatural. He was also getting stronger and stronger percussive effects with his finger-drums, and with an Indian tabla. But he wanted an even bigger beat, he said; and only his need to play the other instruments prevented him from introducing a snare drum.

We were always together now, the four of us, in one way or another. We had long restaurant meals; we schemed far into the night over bottles of expensive wine, in a state of exultant intimacy that was not of our own making but the show's. It devoured our lives, and Jaan and old Vilde were left a good deal alone. Darcy and I were deferred to as the programme's masterminds, and still spent many hours in planning sessions.

As for Katrin, she had found her true home in the group, singing under the television lights with Brian Brady beside her, the cameras circling them like tall, intelligent insects; she'd never really enjoyed working as a soloist, she said, and Brian gave her the security and confidence she needed.

'He's so simple and easy,' she said. 'He makes me feel nothing can go wrong. We know each other's thoughts, when we sing. He's like family to me; perhaps it's because he's your cousin.'

And certainly Brian was becoming a part of our home life. Although Darcy seldom came to Challis Avenue, Brian was at the flat more and more; rehearsing duo material with Katrin, or eating meals with us, or playing his guitar to Jaan, who was eager for his company, and had the Rymers poster up in his room. Brady was apparently enjoying a series of girls from among his pool of fans, but he never brought them to the flat. He was often half-drunk, although he hadn't come drunk to a recording again. I sensed that he now disliked living with Burr. He seemed somehow oppressed by it, and I guessed that it had been this way ever since Rita Carey disappeared.

She'd left a white slip hanging on a chair in the Victoria Street flat. Like so many other things in that junk-shop living-room, it wasn't moved for weeks. I would wonder whether Brian noticed it, and if so why he didn't get rid of it. I'd never told him of her visit to me, and the slip was like a memento of someone I'd betrayed myself; my eyes would seek it out.

2

'Hello? Richard Miller?'

In the first few seconds, on that hot afternoon in January, I didn't know the voice. I thought it was an actress looking for work, and was half-impressed. It was a period voice, the sort of voice men once couldn't resist: low and beautifully modulated, promising episodes and complicities beyond the humdrum, its associations Noel Coward comedies and songs by Cole Porter.

'It's Deirdre Dillon speaking. You may not remember me, after so long.'

I sat absolutely still. It was a young woman's voice, unchanged; but she'd now be nearly forty.

'I remember you,' I said.

'Do you?' She seemed to have drawn back from the

receiver. There was a brief silence which I didn't break; then she said: 'I hope you don't mind my ringing you like this.'

'No. I'm glad to hear from you.'

I waited, and she hurried on, the humorous undertone entering her voice which I remembered, and now decided was a sign of nervousness. Perhaps it always had been.

'I've often thought of contacting you, Richard, but I could never pluck up the courage; and I didn't really know where you were. Then I read about your show in some women's magazine—so I watched it on the box. There was your name as producer, large as life. It gave me rather a turn. Had to have a whisky as a *stiffener*.' Her voice deepened comically, in the old way; I listened as though to a monologue in a dream, gripping the receiver.

'How is your husband?'

'Mostly bed-bound, I'm afraid. A chronic invalid.'

'I'm sorry. What's wrong?'

'Oh, something quite bad.' Her tone had become light, cool and empty, dismissing a distasteful topic. 'It may be cancer, actually. He's not expected to live.'

She cut short my awkward speech of sympathy. 'I'd love to see you. Can we meet?'

I hesitated, and her delivery became humorous again. 'Fraught pause. I realise you're married—to that interesting Continental lady in the Rymers, isn't it? The magazine told me everything. But this is partly a business matter I want to talk about—and you're not on a leash, surely?'

I made no response to this.

'The only thing is, it's got to be somewhere near here,' she said. 'My husband's impossible about my leaving the house for long; he wants me here all the time. He's made me into his nurse. The prisoner of Point Piper.'

There was another pause, and the low voice of complicity came back, all humour vanishing. 'Please see me, Richard. Just for an hour. I wonder how much you've changed? You sound terribly mature.'

I laughed at the reappearance of the note of caricature

on this last word. But after she'd hung up, I found myself
trembling, which I told myself was ridiculous.

Leaning on the rough wooden rail at the end of the Rose
Bay pier, I pulled off my tie and undid the top button of
my shirt, enjoying the small, humid wind. Tonight was
less oppressive than usual, for January.

The streetlamps and traffic of the New South Head Road
were at my back; in front of me, across black miles of
Harbour, were the distant lights of the North Shore. A
long container ship inched by in midstream, the lamps on
its many derricks glimmering in festive strings, like those
of a fairground. The complex edges of the Harbour were
marked out on this side by other strings of lights: the
windows of Point Piper, Rose Bay, Watson's Bay; the rich
eastern suburbs, which ended where the great, landlocked
water of Port Jackson finally found the sea, between the
invisible Heads the ship was bound for. Deirdre's districts:
that was how I'd thought of them once, when I first came
to Sydney.

We'd arranged to meet at eight o'clock. I'd driven here
from Potts Point after eating at home with Jaan and old
Vilde. Katrin was out singing with the group at a club in
the western suburbs—a frequent situation just now, since
the Rymers had accepted a series of club engagements in
this period before the new television series started. They
were also working on an LP for local International Recording Company release; so I was left to myself quite often
lately. Unless I cared to go along as a spectator, the
Rymers were now leading a life that didn't include me,
and I'd be glad when the series began, and they were back
in my hands.

Twenty past eight, and I wondered if Deirdre would
come. Curiosity made me go on waiting for her, pacing
the pier with all the tension of a lover. Curiosity made my
mouth unnaturally dry. Curiosity was all it was, I said; this
and a faint, irrational guilt, generated because Katrin didn't
yet know about the meeting, and because Deirdre herself
had made it seem like an assignation. She could slip down

here from Point Piper, she said, on the pretext of taking the dog for a walk, and her sick, possessive husband need suspect nothing. I found the subterfuge silly; but it was no business of mine what games she played.

I went on pacing the pier, which was almost empty. Two old men in shorts and towelling hats sat fishing with handlines, plastic buckets of bait beside them; aged boys. When she appeared at the other end, I knew it must be Deirdre because of the big black Labrador straining on a leash beside her. I also recognised her hair, flax-pale as ever, and still worn youthfully to her shoulders. I walked back to meet her, squinting to discern her face, the perspective of empty planks diminishing between us.

Her walk was the first thing that was disconcerting. The faintly rocking gait I remembered, practical and slightly comical, which she'd only adopted in frivolous moods, now seemed to have set and become exaggerated. Or else it was accentuated by the dog's tugging on the lead. A woman of fashionable appearance came towards me, a privileged eastern suburbs matron in a heavy-knit, expensive navy cardigan worn over a white summer dress. Her figure was good, but she was shorter than I remembered, and her full bust made her slightly top-heavy. A filmy white scarf was knotted at her throat, the ends floating in the breeze as her hair did.

Now I made out her face, which peered at me and then oddly looked away, by turns. Yes, it was Deirdre; it was recognisably the face of the girl in the twenties headband, even though there were changes I couldn't yet take in. She was still a strikingly pretty woman, and there was nothing I could do about the ridiculous hammering of my heart, a reflex uncorrected by time. I'd thought about her for so many years, until Katrin came.

She came to a halt in front of me, and the Labrador uttered two pompous barks.

'*Down* Major, be quiet,' she said, and he sat and panted. Her smile was apprehensive, asking me not to judge her new face. I saw its double chin, its tracery of lines, and the papery quality of skin that would never be firm again, and was whiter than before. Her hair's blondness, too, appeared almost white, at close quarters; was it dyed?

'Hello Richard.' Her voice was the same, pleasing as it had been on the phone. 'You've still got your limp,' she said.

'I'm not likely to lose it. You look well.'

'I'm a middle-aged frump, darling. And when you last saw me I was the age you are now.' Her pursed smile was impossible to read. 'But you look just how I thought you would. You've turned into a handsome man. Harder-looking than I imagined. Are you hard?'

She had always been instantly personal; that hadn't changed. But she couldn't sustain the meeting of eyes, as she'd once done; hers flitted away, and then came back almost furtively. It wasn't true flirtatiousness but something else: a new, puzzling evasion. Where was her steady, lucid stare? I had a piercing rush of grief, to see how time had humbled her; if time was what had done this. Then it passed.

'How do you like Major? Isn't he gorgeous?' She patted the dog's head, her voice becoming sentimental. 'Yes, he's my gorgeous boy; my best, big friend. Say hullo to Richard.'

To my amazement, she went on talking about the dog at some length, describing his habits and foibles, while I listened patiently. I had the impression she was starved for company, and would talk like this to anyone who'd listen. I couldn't stop looking at her, my curiosity unappeased.

'I don't know what I'd do without my Major,' she said. 'Sometimes I think he's the only sane person in our house.'

I interrupted. 'Shall we walk?'

She looked at me quickly, breaking off as though I'd caught her out in a bad habit. 'Yes,' she said quickly, and took my arm. Her hand seemed very small and ineffective.

We walked, moving along the promenade beside the New South Head Road, with its curving concrete wall above the small, sour beach. Yachts swayed and rattled at their moorings; headlights swept us; the ghost of an old Empire Flying Boat rode at the Rose Bay base, and our

feet trod the fallen, inedible fruits of Moreton Bay figs—
the grey, spreading, banyan-like trees which haunt the
streets of Sydney, and whose giant root systems make
buttresses and cavities large enough for hiding-places. We
stopped by one of these Gothic entrances, mutually attracted to its concealment from the traffic. It was like
being in a hollow tree; Deirdre stood looking out at me,
Major lying obediently at her feet, and again I had a sense
of the illicit, as though we'd found a place to begin an
affair. I shouldn't have met her, I thought.

'So you see, I'm not in a very easy position.' Having
questioned me about my marriage and my career in ABS,
she had now begun to tell me about her own life, playing
with Major's lead as she talked. Headlights regularly picked
out her upturned face and then let it sink into dimness
again, in the doorway of the tree.

'I've got a girl of twelve to worry about, and a dying
husband who's totally intolerant of his own son. The strain
between them is terrible; I have to mediate. Michael just
won't accept that Patrick's an entirely different type of
man from himself. Patrick's twenty-seven now—a year
younger than you, remember?—and he's never going to be
the sort of Dillon to take over the firm. He's too sensitive
to deal with crass businessmen like his father. He's a
musician. And he loves the Rymers, Richard. He's passionate about them.'

She looked at me as though this were significant. The
light, clear blue of her eyes was beautiful as ever, but age
had changed the line of the top lids, making them coarser,
with a cat-like slant that emphasised her Irishness. It was
as though some ancestral face had made its way to the
surface, and it gave her an attraction of a different kind
than before; less maidenly, more overtly sensual.

'He never misses the show on TV,' she said. 'He's
studied the group in detail. This may surprise you; he got
himself into the audience for every show you recorded at
the Loft.'

I asked her what instrument Patrick played.

'The drums,' she said. 'He's in the King Pepper New

Orleans jazz band—they play at a pub in Paddington. Patrick's a wonderful drummer—everyone says so. He and I love the old trad jazz; we used to spend hours listening to his records and getting tiddly on whisky, when the RFO was at work.'

'The RFO?' Then I remembered: Red-Faced Ogre.

'And of course, Michael hates all that,' she said. 'He threatens to cut him out of his will, for being in the band. Ever since Patrick dropped out of the importing side of the business his father put him into, he's been paid this miserably small allowance, as though he were still a boy. And of course, the band doesn't make much. I have to help him out of *my* allowance.'

'Does Patrick do anything else—besides the drumming?'

'Not really. And it's just as well, since Michael keeps me so confined. It means I have a *companion*.' She'd adopted a parody of formality, saying this; it was the voice of a clever little girl. With a sense of vertigo, the years dissolving, I saw that her face had now become childish too, assuming a blank, wide-eyed solemnity I also remembered: the Dutch doll expression.

'It's very frustrating for poor Patrick,' she said. 'He'd like to work as a professional musician full-time, but there's so little that's worthwhile, here in Australia. He wants to go overseas—we both do—but of course the RFO won't hear of it. Do you know, with all his money, Michael's only ever let Patrick go to Europe once? He won't go again himself—the only time he and I went, he said France and Italy were dirty. *Dirty!*' She burst out laughing, and ended in a coughing fit; from her wheezing, I guessed that she still smoked.

'So Patrick went alone to the Greek islands,' she said, 'when he was twenty-one. He stayed on Aegina for a month, and he's never forgotten it—he's been passionate about Greece ever since; he reads books on Greece and Greek mythology all the time. He keeps saying he wants to take *me* there. But not much hope of that, I'm afraid.'

'He's lucky he doesn't have to work.'

I tried to conceal an unreasonable antipathy towards Patrick; for all I knew, he wasn't as hopeless as he sounded.

'Perhaps I shouldn't be telling you all this.' Her voice had taken on a new and peculiar note of intimacy; of confession. Tilting her head back, she searched my face, her eyes very wide and fixed; and her features had become those of eleven years before, luminous, sad and beautiful in the white beams from the cars. The illusion was so complete that I stared, with sudden fixed attention. She put her fingers lightly on my cheek.

'I was wrong: you *haven't* got hard, Richard. You look just like the boy you were at Greystones. But you've done so much better than Patrick. He's been wasted—and I worry about him, you see.'

'Should he be your worry—at twenty-seven? After all, he's your stepson, not your son.'

For a moment she said nothing, considering. 'Sometimes I think he should get away from home,' she said. 'But I've only a few good friends, I've no bloody social life, since Michael got ill—and I'd miss Patrick awfully.' She glanced across the promenade to where the bare, autumnal masts of the moored yachts swayed in the dark, her eyes fleeing from mine and then seeking them again in the way that was new; then her voice dropped even lower, almost whispering, with an intimacy that approached the sexual.

'Perhaps you're right: perhaps Patrick depends on me too much. I sleep separately from Michael, I have my own room, and Patrick still joins me there whenever he can. Whenever the RFO can't walk in on us.' She looked at me swiftly as though I'd commented. 'It's perfectly innocent, Richard. We talk for hours, and drink a bit of grog and listen to music. But I think that Michael's getting jealous.' Standing close, she murmured as though we'd been confidants for years, creating unwanted thrills of vicarious excitement. 'Patrick was wrapped in me as a small boy; we had a wonderful closeness. He'd even help me choose what to wear, and help me dress; I used to call him my page. But he's still inclined to walk in when I'm dressing, even now, especially when he's been on the grog—and he does hop on to the whisky, lately.' Now her voice took on the hushed, old-fashioned tone of gossip. 'Today I came in from the bathroom with nothing on at all, and there Patrick was, large as life. I had to order him out of my boudoir.' Now she wore a special purse-lipped smile I couldn't return. 'He keeps telling me what a remarkable bosom I've got; and the other day he wanted to help me on with my bra. Well *really!* I wasn't having that. I've become rather large in that department, darling, as you'll have noticed— and Patrick's always been impressed with Rubensesque ladies like me. His affairs never last long, and he shows no sign of marrying; he always says no girl he meets com- pares with me. Sometimes I suspect he's never been to bed with one—that he's still a virgin. Do you think I should be worried about that?'

She looked ingenuous, almost arch; and I looked back as though I'd learned of her death. 'I think I can see why your husband would be worried,' I said.

She didn't like this. I'd been disloyal to childhood's compact, and her eyes gleamed briefly with adult annoy- ance; but she made no comment. Something had made her an infant forever—Dadda's girl; her rich, dying husband's middle-aged baby; her stepson's make-believe mistress, tormenting him with her games. The lights of the cargo ship moved with infinite slowness towards Watson's Bay; the channel beacons winked in the Harbour's secret lan- guage, and we seemed to be held in the landscape of Limbo. She lit a cigarette; laughed at her own jokes; patted the whining Major; became a sophisticated Point Piper matron; became a small girl again; confided in a voice that still thrilled me in spite of myself. I felt sorry for Patrick now, whom I'd never seen. Cruelty had a baby face, and talk was its instrument, with its endless titillations, prom- ises of nakedness, hints of a consummation that would always be denied. A true fairy nurse, she offered nothing but the thin milk of dream, in which there was no nurture, but merely addiction. Adult love threatened her; she cared only for the callow or the handicapped, and I had been both.

To bring the conversation to a close, I asked her what the business matter was she'd mentioned on the phone.

'Well surely you *realise*,' she said, and her voice became cool and practical. 'I'm hoping that Patrick can join the Rymers—that you'll give him an audition. You haven't got a drummer—and he has this theory that a drummer would bring something important to the group. He's absolutely obsessed with the idea. Would you consider it, Richard?'

For a moment, I said nothing; then I burst out laughing. Her look of hurt checked me; patiently, I began to explain. The Rymers weren't looking for a drummer—and even if they were, there'd be scores of top musicians knocking on the door. Patrick's band, as I understood it, played only in pubs. It was hardly a great track record.

Her head dropped. She didn't argue. 'I see,' she said. 'I'm sorry to have bothered you. But I'm glad I saw you, anyway. I've so often thought of you, Richard. Won't you give me a kiss before we go?'

I kissed her lightly on the lips, which tasted of tobacco. Yet even so, the treacherous ghost of desire moved in me.

'You *are* circumspect,' she said. 'You must really love that Baltic wife of yours.'

'I do.'

She said no more; we walked towards my car through the windy dark, Major pulling at his lead. And now I felt ashamed of my bluntness about Patrick.

I didn't really think I could do much for him, I told her, but I'd mention him to Darcy Burr. Darcy might be prepared to talk to him, even though there was almost no chance he'd take him on.

She hugged my arm. 'Will you? That's wonderful. And you'll talk to Patrick yourself, won't you? You'll like him, Richard. He's a vulnerable man, and terribly introverted; he takes getting to know. But he reminds me so much of you.'

Driving home, I felt like a man who had long believed himself to be suffering from a fatal illness—only to find that no such illness existed.

3

A couple of weeks later, when rehearsals had begun for the new series, I found myself looking through the control-room window at Patrick Dillon. Behind his gleaming drumkit, all kitted out in his medieval outfit with its leather jerkin, he bobbed and swayed as though mechanised, cautiously smiling. The Rymers had a fourth member.

I could still scarcely believe it—even though, as Deirdre had promised, he was a very good drummer. But when I'd told Burr about him, almost as a joke, Darcy had responded with extraordinary enthusiasm.

'A *drummer!* Do you realise what a coincidence this is? I'd already started looking for one, Dick. A drummer's what we need, to give us the sound I've been wanting.'

'But we've got your finger-drums and tabla, Darcy.'

'Stuff those things. How can I work on all my other instruments when I'm doing percussion? It's always limited our possibilities. What this group needs is a really big beat. I want that Ringo Starr sound underneath. Think of the power! Think of it under "False Knight Upon the Road", or "The Demon Lover"!' He radiated that instant exultancy which somewhat resembled a salesman's. 'This new series'll *rock* them, mate; the last series was nothing.'

'Snares and a bass drum in a folk group? He'll drown the rest of you.'

'They said that about the electric guitars, remember? It's all a matter of balance, we can keep him down. You and the sound techs will work it out. Remember, folk music's only what we *use*. We can be as big as the Beatles!'

I knew better than to laugh at this self-generated elation of his. Lately he'd become obsessed with the Beatles, and with the legend of their success, which he actually seemed to imagine could happen to the Rymers; I guessed it to be a fantasy with some private meaning for him. The vital, haunting songs and the coldly cheerful northern voices were ubiquitous now, coming from radios all around the Cross and at every party we went to; and Darcy dwelt half gloatingly, half enviously, on the enormous crowds the Beatles had drawn here eighteen months ago, when they

made their Australian tour. Just think, he said, of how fast
they'd come up, and where they'd come from; an ill-paid,
smelly, Merseyside group living in squalor in Hamburg,
playing for a pittance and for gruelling hours in nightclubs
in the brothel quarter, high on Preludin; then, a year or so
later, touching down at London airport to be greeted by a
vast human sea: all for them.

The story seemed to fascinate him, like some vision of
transcendental joy; it could all happen to the Rymers, he
said. Perhaps total fame had dimensions for Darcy I couldn't
imagine, like communication with those spirit entities of
his. Obviously, it was a form of power, and on that scale,
I thought, it ceased to be vulgar and became a sort of
mystery.

But none of us took him seriously—least of all Brady,
who had pointed out to Darcy one night that ours wasn't a
pop group, and never would be, as far as he was concerned. He didn't like pop any better than he'd ever done;
he was a folk singer, and wouldn't be turned into a mon-
key on a stick for teenyboppers.

They'd then become angry with each other, glaring
furiously; I almost feared a punch might be thrown, until
Katrin intervened. Her soothing, motherly remonstrations
made reluctant peace between them, and Darcy avoided the
topic with Brian after that; but he still raised it with me.

I saw now that the addition of the drummer was another
step on the way for Burr: an essential part of his plan to
give a folk combination a pop group's dimension of success. 'All right,' I said, 'I'm prepared to try it; but what
makes you think Patrick will be any good? All he's ever
done is work in a trad jazz band.'

'That's all I need; a good, solid jazz drummer—if he is
one. I'll shape him after that. And besides—think of the
advantages.' He grinned with a hint of suggestiveness; we
were alone in his room at Victoria Street.

I stiffened. 'What advantages? What do you mean?'

'Use your head, mate. What about all that Dillon money?'

'What about it?'

'I've got plans for the Rymers to have a crack at London, eventually. We'll need all the dough we can get, then. Maybe Patrick might like to put some capital into getting us launched, over there.

'You can forget that,' I said; and I told him about Patrick's financial situation, as Deirdre had told it to me.

But Burr wasn't discouraged; the sly grin stayed, while he eyed me speculatively. 'Things can change,' he said. 'From what you say, old Dillon could peg out, soon, and then Patrick inherits—or Deirdre does. Fancy you meeting her again, Dick; I'll bet you're pleased, eh?'

Cold caution went through me at this, and I stared him down. 'I won't be seeing anything of Deirdre,' I said, 'and if I were you, I'd forget the Dillon money. Just take Patrick on if he's a good drummer—okay?'

'Okay mate, okay, but I know how you feel about her—I remember.' He watched me as though from out of a cave, leaning back in his armchair, the faintest suggestion of a grin remaining.

'I don't feel anything, any more,' I said. I sensed it was important to contradict him. 'She contacted me because she wants us to audition Patrick. I've passed the message on. I've also discussed it with Katrin. That's all.'

'Sure. Don't get uptight.' But his grin insisted on knowing my feelings better than I did myself, and for the first time since the Rymers began, I felt I might dislike him, if this were kept up.

Now Patrick was in the group; and I wasn't really sure whether that was a good thing or not. I studied him through the glass.

I don't know what I'd expected. I hadn't expected to like him, but I did. We all liked him. He was so eager to be accepted, so quiet, and so pleasantly modest; the opposite of what we'd imagined, and what our prejudices had told us a rich man's son would be. But then, he had very little money to call his own; he lived always in expectation, poor Pat.

And I remembered seeing him before. As Deirdre had told me, he'd been among our hand-picked audience at the

Loft, whenever we recorded there. He'd always come alone, and had sat in the front row; and his respectful yet insistent gaze would have made him stand out even if his fair good looks and his expensive clothes hadn't done. He not only examined the members of the group with a sort of fixed and yearning hunger, but his eyes often rested on me as well; and I recalled wondering briefly what he wanted, and who he was. This lover-like examination went far beyond the sort of interest shown by a typical folk fan; only Brian Brady's female groupies were so devoted, and their interest was in Brian alone. I'd decided that Patrick might be an agent for the club circuit; then, when he didn't approach us, I'd forgotten him.

His conventional haircut and his clothes had made him incongruous at the Loft; but in most other settings they were pleasing. Of medium height and well-built, he wore quiet, Harris tweed jackets; interesting sports shirts of high-quality linen and cotton; tailored slacks. A little scarf was often knotted loosely at his throat, in the manner of a World War Two air-ace. He was certainly good-looking, but in a way that was going out of fashion; the blond and regular small boy style. His thick, butter-coloured hair flopped over one eye with a dated raffishness, and he looked, if anything, older than twenty-seven; there were heavy pouches under his eyes, and his faintly pudgy skin had a glossiness I suspected was a symptom of his fondness for whisky. Yet the face of a sheltered child looked out from behind the man's features—the sort of blond small boy who'd won baby shows, and now found the world a little difficult. This, and the wide, attractive smile that earnestly asked you to like him, as well as dark eyebrows that contrasted with his hair, gave him a certain resemblance to the faded film star Alan Ladd; a resemblance that some magazine articles would comment on. But I noticed that the smile often left his eyes uncertain; he didn't really have film star blandness, and the eyebrows would occasionally point upwards in some private anxiety, wrinkling his forehead, betraying his vulnerability.

He was always anxious to please, and patently delighted

to be in the group. And he was very quiet; unnaturally quiet, perhaps: he gave no trouble. His open smile and his looks had led me to expect an outgoing nature; but he usually spoke only when spoken to, as though he feared to irritate, or suspected that his position in the Rymers might at any moment be snatched away. Yet Brady and Burr and Katrin had accepted him wholeheartedly; they'd all grown instantly fond of him. Katrin wanted to mother the hard-drinking, delinquent boy; and Brady liked Patrick because he made him laugh. It wasn't that Patrick cracked many jokes himself, but he so much enjoyed the jokes of the others—laughing immoderately, going red in the face—that he created merriment. He always carried a silver hip-flask, in emulation of the vintage jazzmen of the twenties and thirties whom he idolised; he was never entirely drunk and never quite sober, and the sight of him producing the flask from his pocket, taking a little swig and smiling like a blond baby with its bottle, was irresistibly funny to Brian, as well as to Darcy.

Attractive to them too was his knowledge of the old New Orleans and Chicago jazz, and early blues. He was minutely versed in the legends and performances of the titans; his record collection was vast, and contained treasures on wax 78s. He had none of the one-upmanship or snobbishness of the usual jazz *aficionado;* he simply loved the music, and grew quietly excited as we all traded the beloved and ancient names: King Oliver, Tommy Ladnier, Satchmo, Bix, Bessie Smith. His model among drummers was Baby Dodds. We all listened to his Hot Sevens together at Victoria Street, and as Baby Dodds came to a big passage, the pounding West African rhythms would carry Patrick away; sitting on the floor, head thrown back, eyes closed, expert hands pattering on the boards, he would go into trance. But most beloved of all among jazzmen was Jelly Roll Morton. When he was particularly moved by a passage in any piece of music (piano or otherwise, jazz or not), Patrick would growl in his throat: *'Oh, Mr Jelly!'* The incongruousness of this never failed to break Brian and

Darcy up; it became a private joke between the three of them, muttered on stage: *'Oh, Mr Jelly!'*

The 'fourth Rymer', as Patrick was dubbed in the press, created a lot of interest—not only because the Rymers were news, but because the use of drums in a folk group had such novelty then. And to my surprise, the drums and the harder rock style worked; as Darcy had said, it was all a matter of getting the levels right. The new power and excitement of our sound was undeniable; Patrick's drumming, and the way Darcy incorporated it into his arrangements, had a lot to do with the even greater success of the new ABS series. We were certainly capturing an even larger segment of the pop audience now, and there were negotiations for a Town Hall concert.

To get the relationships right, Patrick was set well back on special mikes; and he comes to mind always a little removed, on his own small island behind Brian, Katrin and Darcy, bobbing on his lonely perch behind the huge, expensive kit with RYMERS painted on the bass drum, anxious eyebrows pointing upwards at the corners, asking that his efforts be approved.

'Go Pat, go!' Darcy called in rehearsal. 'Oh, Mr Jelly!'

And Patrick smiled in gratitude, working on his cymbals and snares, wanting merely to survive, to stay inside the circle of the Rymers' magic.

This magic was a fact for him. He took up an interest in the fairy ballads and fairy lore with obsessed enthusiasm; almost with reverence. Darcy and I enjoyed his respectful questioning; we even grew somewhat addicted to it. I think Patrick would have become my disciple, had I let him, but deeper involvement with the Dillon family wasn't what I wanted; I kept him at arms' length, and so he became Darcy's disciple instead. He was speding a lot of time with Darcy. And yet he continued to watch me; his eyes would seek me out through the control room window, or follow me about the studio. Could I have saved him? Perhaps no. No.

His steady beat still sounds in my head, strong yet hushed. We got him to use brushes, in some of the fairy ballads; in others he worked with his sticks on an ancient wood-block he'd used in the jazz band, its delicate racket filling Darcy with glee. *('How about that, Dick? Old Pat going clackety-clack under the penny whistle! Terrifc. Sounds like a bloody elfin shoe-maker!')* He wasn't the world's greatest drummer, but he was good; the steady, muted pulse he provided under the guitars had a trad jazzman's reliable solidity: a strange and effective underpinning to the still-traditional singing of the ballads.

But I think he sometimes wanted to break out of his frame, to burst into big, showy solos like the swing drummers of the forties. Once, for a joke, he did this in rehearsal.

Everyone cheered, in the studio, but it went on too long. Something had taken hold of Patrick, now: the pleasant smile became a grimace; the smooth, flaccid face was suffused with blood; his hair grew untidy on his forehead, and his medieval costume no longer suited him. Shoulders hunched around his ears, he attacked the side-drums as though he hated them; eventually he lost his rhythm, while our barracking died away. Then he broke off and showed us an abashed boy's grin, and it was all right again.

That was the only time I suspected that he was secreting some sort of anger. He had wanted to find his way to real wildness; but something would always inhibit him. He could find no real release; not in jazz, not in whisky, not even in smoking hash, to which Darcy had converted him. (He called it 'Lady Jane', like a period jazzman; even in this, he was out of his time.)

And still he watched me. He seemed to want something, some intimate communication, perhaps, which he was unlikely to instigate, and which I was determined to discourage. I didn't know what Deirdre had told him, and I didn't want to know. Her insistence that he and I were alike was something I found displeasing, in retrospect, to a degree I couldn't account for and didn't want to think about; and I was absolutely resolved that no discussion of Deirdre would take place between Pat and me. Looking back, I can see that the rigidity of my position, despite all the circumstances, was not quite natural.

He only tried to discuss her once.

We'd just finished recording; the others had gone to the dressing rooms to change, but Patrick still lingered in the studio, where a last few staging people were packing up. Waiting for Katrin, I wandered in to talk to him.

'You did a great job tonight, Pat. That brushwork in "The Unquiet Grave" was tremendous.'

'I do ma best, boss.' He gave me the Alan Ladd smile, sitting on his stool by the drums. The yellowish pancake makeup and the rouge on his lips accentuated his tendency to prettiness, making him lady-like; his solemn hazel eyes were those of a Victorian heroine, and now grew solicitous.

'But you look tired, Richard.' Unlike the others, he often used my full name; he'd probably got this from Deirdre, and I wondered again how much she talked about me.

'It must take a lot out of you, pulling the show to-gether,' he said. 'I know I take ages to unwind, after we record. Deirdre says I'm manic for days.'

This was the first time he'd mentioned her since the day of his audition, when he'd done so only briefly; I knew he sensed I didn't want it, and I saw him watch now for my reaction. He was playing with one of his brushes, drawing it through his hands. My lack of expression didn't deter him, apparentiy, and he went straight on, his deep, well-bred voice hurrying the words out. 'I'm really glad she talked to you about me. I wouldn't have dared approach you myself, and it's changed my whole life. She under-stood what it meant to me. Mother's always understood what direction I needed to go in. She's like that, isn't she?' He held out his hip-flask. 'Swig?'

'No thanks.' I ignored his question, looking at him stonily; his sudden use of the title 'Mother' was somehow shocking, and I suspected that my expression was more forbidding than I intended. 'I must be off,' I said. 'Katrin's probably ready to go home.'

His smile was wiped away; two red spots appeared on his cheekbones, through the makeup. 'Sure Dick, sure. See you.' He pocketed the flask, got off the stool, and began to pack up his drum kit, his handsome face gone hangdog.

As I'd intended, he didn't bring her name up again; and I imagined that all contact with her, even indirect, was ended for me.

But I was wrong. Soon after this, her phone calls began. She was to remain in my life as a voice.

She phoned me at the office with increasing regularity. The launching of Patrick in the group was her chief excuse for these calls at first.

'Patrick admires you enormously Richard—you and Darcy both. He finds Darcy fascinating, and so do I. He brought him here to visit me. What an interesting person. I think he lives for the imagination—like us, darling. I can see why you and he work well together. The show last week was brilliant. The use of the pictures is all your doing, isn't it? You always were fey. I love the way those Dulac fairies appear when you do "Tam Lin". It makes me tingle.'

In the end, she did little to cloak the fact that the calls were their own purpose, and I half looked forward to them. She became a diversion, when I wasn't too busy; and I began to realise that she was lonely, and that I was an answer to her loneliness. She wanted to talk about novels she'd read, poetry, plays she'd seen, music; and when she did so, her coy silliness was dropped, to be replaced by the cool tones of an old-fashioned bluestocking— and occasionally by the soulful notes of Victorian romanticism.

'I do love Yeats.' Despite her slight excessiveness, I knew that this was true. *'Do you still read him, Richard? You should quote him in the show: "Away, come away: Empty your heart of its mortal dream." '*

When she had first married Dillon, she said, she thought she loved him. He had been masterful and attractive, and had pretended to take an interest in the arts. Very soon, this pretence had dried up; he wouldn't take her to the theatre, and disliked her friends. He began to resent her bookishness; an old-fashioned Catholic, he had a hatred of books, and even pictures he saw as immoral. *'He burned my copy of Joyce's "Ulysses",'* she said. *'Can you imagine?'*

Despite Dillon's wealth, her life seemed extraordinarily circumscribed. Like Patrick, she had an allowance, which Dillon changed at whim. All their finances were under his control, even in his last illness; she couldn't even sign a cheque. There had never been a joint cheque account, and she had no personal savings or assets of any consequence. She half resented this, but she had a lack of real interest in such practicalities which was sometimes astounding. *'I don't want to know about those things.'* Her voice took on its babyish tone, saying this.

Sometimes, when a phone rings, I still half expect to hear that low, beautiful, cigarette-stained voice. She would come on without announcing herself, without preamble.

'I've been listening to "The Lark Ascending"—the Vaughan Williams: It's so beautiful. I watched a skylark once—I was standing at the side of the road in France, somewhere in the Jura. They don't fly, Richard, they hurtle up and up. Then they circle, pouring out that music. No wonder the poets wrote about them. No bird does that here. Do you think we lack ecstasy in Australia?'

When she wasn't being frivolous, I would picture the Deirdre of eleven years before on the other end. Perhaps she knew this; occasionally she hinted that we should meet again. When I made excuses, she wasn't offended, and I sensed that a physical meeting had little real importance to her; that she'd not really expected one.

'I'm a telemaniac,' she said. *'I'm addicted to the phone, darling. I sometimes spend hours on it, with people I like, even on long distance. I spoke to Madge Allwright in London for an hour, last week. My husband gets these giant phone bills, and goes into a frenzy. It's terrible, I know.'*

She would come on now without preamble. *'Michael's better today. Stumping around the house demanding an elaborate dinner, and wanting to entertain his bloody business friends.'* It was as though I'd become a diary, in which she placed verbal entries. And more and more frequently, she talked about Patrick and his obsession with her.

The idea of incest has a pathos about it; a strange monotony. I categorised their relationship as quasi-incestuous, even though this wasn't strictly true; and I began to be given glimpses of their life that I didn't want. But although I received these coldly, she was seldom discouraged; unwanted verbal vignettes continued to disturb me, in the middle of the office day. I saw them, out there at Point Piper: she lay on her bed in her dressing-gown, or sat at her dressing-table in her underclothes, while her uselessly handsome, baby-faced courtier attended her; they drank Scotch or sherry; they played tapes of the Rymers, or LP records; they mocked the RFO. Occasionally, she allowed a shoulder-strap to slip; a breast or a thigh was bared: rewards for his devotion.

It began to be difficult to know whether it was Patrick she wanted to titillate, or me. A new note was being introduced, which I did my best to discourage: a shared guilt without substance, all of Deirdre's creation.

'Hello darling, isn't it hot? I'm lying on the bed without a stitch on: I hope Patrick doesn't walk in. I've been thinking about you, and I had to call—but I've only a few minutes to talk; Michael could come in at any second. He's hounding me lately, and he'd be furious if he knew this was you on the phone.'

I refused to take this game seriously, which was based on the proposition that she lived in constant fear of Dillon: who was jealous not just of Patrick, but of me. But she persisted. Terrible trouble would ensue if her husband discovered Patrick's feeling for her; or even if he found her talking to any man on the phone he suspected of being interested in her. He knew about me and hated me, she said. (*'You're the real threat, darling. I know I shouldn't say that. He's insanely suspicious of you.'*) Uninvolved with these games—or so I thought—I would tell her that she ought to stop calling me, if she was worried. But she took no notice; or else grew hurt, and I relented.

'I have to go,' she would say, in a low, urgent voice.

'He's coming.' And she would ring off in the middle of a conversation.

Words, probably, were all that she'd ever wanted; she had no real need of anything else. Child of a literary culture, of an island where most of our messages had come through books, she found words endlessly exciting. Child too of Irish Catholicism, she had made the telephone a perverse confessional; a place where lapses into salaciousness or betrayal had neither flesh nor penalties, where faces were hidden, and people were nothing but voices: where fear and lust could easily be dismissed, simply by hanging up the phone.

4

The chronically jealous must live with their demon all the time. For them his every word is law; they're in constant expectation of his whispered, malicious pronouncements, and when these are made, they're seized on with a terrible eagerness. But we others, who are jealous only when we're forced to be, are always reluctant to listen. Jealousy's a bad joke, and we reproach ourselves for our thoughts. Unable even to voice them, we continue in exquisite uncertainty.

Although Katrin and Brian were constantly together, often rehearsing alone in the evenings while Darcy and I plotted at Victoria Street, I'd experienced until now no stirring of suspicion. I saw that they'd grown fond of each other; but that was natural, I said. Inside the ballads, inside the screen, he and she were my ideal couple; and if there was now a special affection in their glances and a special enjoyment of shared jokes, this was natural in musical partners, whose association is that of platonic lovers.

Alone under the flaring lights, their claim on public attention put to the rest each time they sang, they had only each other for support; and when they triumphed, it was a triumph for their shared talent, and the reward for all the hours they'd spent marrying it. Under that ordeal, the brief looks they exchanged had the heightened savour that's only experienced otherwise by those who share danger—

and which no outsider can possibly comprehend. His powerful, masculine fingering on the old Ramirez bore her up; her bright glance thanked him as she sang. They'd proved as well-matched as those fabled creatures, ideal partners in marriage—Katrin welcoming Brian's cheerful toughness in times of stress; Brady turning for help to her shrewdness and musical sophistication. He'd never met a woman like Katrin, and his bantering amusement at what he'd once seen as staid in her had plainly turned to admiration. Now, when they argued about interpretation of the songs with Darcy or me, they did so as one.

Watching them work, I believed I knew everything they felt; I connived in the double desire I saw printed in their faces on the monitors, soon to be repeated in a multitude of living-rooms. Simple dreams! They'd have Europe and America at their feet; they'd taste the essence of beauty itself, they'd race through a stratosphere of melody: a night-ride that could never exist on earth, but which did exist for musicians—while we, their acolytes and manipulators, could do nothing but glimpse it through the glass. I recognised all this.

But on a certain evening in March, towards the end of the series, my peace of mind was ended. It only needed a fragment of gossip, as it so often does.

I came into the control-room early. The doors to the bright-lit corridor hissed shut, and I paused in the dimness, adjusting my eyes. I was wearing rubber-soled shoes, and had made no sound. There were only two technicians at the long control-desk: a bald vision-mixer called Stan, and a lanky boy from the sound crew whose name I didn't recall. They hadn't heard me come in; they sat looking through the window into the studio, which was slowly coming to life. Lights were being carried into place like tall toadstools; the floor manager stood chatting with a cameraman. Darcy and Pat weren't out there yet; Katrin and Brian, already made up and in their costumes, were seated on high stools. Brady leaned close to say something to her, and she smiled up calmly into his face, eyebrows ironically raised: it was the way she often looked at me.

'More of a true romance every week,' Stan remarked. 'And they don't do much to hide it on camera, do they?'

'Some people reckon it gets hotter off-camera. An' that poor limping bugger hasn't even woken up yet.'

They began to chuckle, but then the boy saw me, and nudged Stan.

I moved to the control desk and opened my briefcase, while they greeted me with loud, unnatural affability. Taking out my script, I went though the motions of preparation. I couldn't look at Stan or the boy. The voice of the floor manager in the studio, coming through the mike, was asking me for information; making jokes. I'd come on duty; I was now on the bridge of my ship, which was sinking.

'Tam Lin' opened the show; Brian and Katrin had made it their signature. Tonight it had a malicious, jigging merriment in the fast passages that seemed new; it had become the song of adultery, as iron bands tightened around my head. From where he stood, working on the bass guitar to add to this merriment, Darcy Burr could look straight through the control-room window at me. He did so now and caught my eye, grinning at a joke I must have seen at last.

The following evening he whistled me out into Challis Avenue for a walk.

He had big news, he said: the album the Rymers had just made for IRC, which was shortly due to reach the shops, would now be released in Britain as well. The company's head office in London was apparently impressed with it.

'And that's not all, Dick. I've been talking to Phil Brown, their Artist and Repertoire Manager, and his boss is coming out from London in a few weeks. He's looking for talent, and he wants to meet the group.'

He paused impressively, waiting for me to enthuse, but I said nothing.

'You realise what that means? We could get a tour to the UK. Television appearances—the whole thing.' His sideways glance had never been more triumphant. 'Suppose we get a song on the charts there? We wouldn't come back here at all, then. We'd be on our way, in Britain.'

His dreams of mystical fame were being given substance at last; the human sea was waiting. But I came to a stop, compelling him to pause too.

We'd been walking the narrow streets of Woolloomooloo, in the hot twilight; down in that gulley of slumdom and bad smells, derelicts in other men's suits had tried to beg money, or cursed us. The place depressed me, but Darcy seemed to like it; he often led us there on our walks. Now, as darkness gathered, we were making the long climb back up McElhone Stairs to Potts Point, the lights coming on among the wharf-sheds below us. Climbing steps still gave me trouble; my leg ached, and I'd stopped in order to ease it. But I'd also halted because I was angry.

'Why wasn't I told about this before?'

'Look, I only just heard about it from Phil.'

'But presumably you've had the idea of a tour of the UK for some time.' I had a sudden giddiness, only partly caused by the steps. 'I'm the group's unofficial agent. Don't you think I should have been involved in these discussions?'

He peered at me, trying to read my displeasure. It no doubt seemed excessive, and I heard the pomposity of my own words; but suddenly everything was moving too quickly. Our former positions were reversed; I was importuning, while Burr set the conditions for the future. The Rymers would be out of my control when the current series ended next month; they'd be lost to me, and Katrin might well be lost to me too. She'd go to Britain with Brady; and if they weren't lovers yet, they'd inevitably become so.

This was a prospect of my own invention; a product of my state of mind since yesterday. When I grew calm, I'd see it merely as an exaggerated fear, not fact; and the notion of going abroad hadn't even been discussed with her. But here on the darkening stone steps—empty except for Burr and me—it all seemed likely; it had the certainty of disaster.

'Don't get upset,' Darcy said. His voice was soothing. 'You wouldn't go against a chance like this, would you? Knowing what it could mean to Katrin and all of us? There's no group without Katrin. You wouldn't be against her going, would you?'

'That depends on how long it's for. What are you expecting? That I'd give up my job to follow you, if you stayed? It's a job I like—and it put the group where it is. What would I do over there? Carry the bags?'

My tone was more offensive than I'd intended, and his mouth tightened; it was now his turn to be angry. I saw severe threat in his face, and I understood now how anger had once put him in gaol. 'You'd be our producer,' he said softly.

'Really? What would I produce in Britain? The concerts? The records? Don't con me, Darcy.'

But now he'd regained his composure; his face changed back with great rapidity, and he smiled. 'There are lots of things you could do over there,' he said. 'And if I want you for our producer, you will be, Dick. You and I *make* the Rymers. Brian and Katrin don't really understand that, because they're instruments—and instruments have to be simple.' His voice sank lower. 'You're worried about those two, aren't you?'

'What's that supposed to mean?'

'Nothing, mate—I just thought all the talk might be bugging you. Naturally there are rumours about them. People like to see them as lovers, and they see themselves that way when they're on stage. Well, that's all right—we want that, don't we? They're our lovers—they're what make the Rymers work.'

But I no longer savoured this partnership of ours; his use of 'we' revolted me unreasonably. If he sensed this, he didn't show it; he'd drawn even closer in order to confide, glancing down the steps to ensure that no one was approaching.

'Patrick understands the situation,' he told me. 'So does Deirdre. She and I are getting to be real good friends. She's still in love with you, isn't she Dick? *You're* the

ones who were meant to be lovers.' He watched me with
sly care.

'It's all in the past,' I said. 'I've told you that.' He was
invading every part of my life, and now I wanted only to
get away. I turned and limped up the steps towards the
lamps of Victoria Street—conscious all the while of his
knowing grin, coming up behind.

In a dream that night, he and I stood at the top of the
stairs, glaring at each other in a fury. I punched Burr in the
face; he looked surprised, blood coming from his big nose,
and then I saw that he was Brian Brady.

'You stole my comics,' I told him.

My cousin and I began to fight, grappling beside the
iron spears of the safety fence that ran along the edge of
the ridge. I could hear the hateful thrumming and piping of
'Tam Lin', song of adultery; and now we swayed on the
top step, my fingers around his throat, his big fists flailing
about my body. Below us yawned the well of the stone
stairs, foul with memories a hundred years old. I was
desperate not to fall in, but we both lost our foothold, and
plunged into air.

We were falling, Brian's face hugely surprised above
me. *'She's in the West Wind,'* I said; and his expression
showed that I'd found him out.

Over the years, I'd found that when I was worried, my bad
leg gave me trouble, aching and growing weak so that the
limp became noticeable again. This began to happen now.

I decided to say nothing yet to Katrin about the UK
tour. That discussion would have to come, but I postponed
it; and I tried to assume that Burr had exaggerated, that the
man from IRC would offer no such glory. I knew I
deceived myself; in some form or other, the group's common dream was about to materialise, and my role in it
would be one quite frequent in dreams: that of invisibility;
voicelessness. I would watch their joyful faces unseen; I
would helplessly speak, but no one would listen. I would
not really exist. I saw myself in Britain as the comic,
unemployed husband, the cuckold who followed the group

about, who sat at the edges while people smiled and murmured about the fortunate, famous duo whose money supported him: his wife and her guitarist lover.

Inward anger grew, but it was an anger I couldn't yet voice. If a long-term move to Britain were made, it would have to be without me, I'd already decided that; and if Katrin insisted on going, our marriage would end. But to oppose a short tour would be churlish. As to the rumours about Katrin and Brady, what evidence was there to back them? What would I charge her with? The talk of two stupid technicians?

Over the next few days, I felt ashamed of both my anger and my doubts; she was always affectionate towards me, and I saw that she and Brian behaved blamelessly together. Their moments of almost marital affection would sometimes chill me, and I began to hate the buzzing of Brian's guitar strings. But their fondness was open, never furtive, and to challenge it would have been demeaning.

It was Jaan who first noticed my limp. I'd taken him out in his wheelchair for a walk before dinner, going down around the long, moon-bare curve of Wylde Street to the Garden Island naval base. Pushing the chair back uphill, I found the going unexpectedly hard; the limp was as marked now as it had been in boyhood.

Jaan screwed around in his chair. 'Your leg seems bad, Richard. Does it hurt today?'

'Just a little.'

He remained screwed about, watching with an encouraging smile, his soft brown hair fluttering. As always, his face had a look of adult knowledge. 'I don't often remember that *you* were crippled,' he said. 'You don't usually limp much. Your leg was never crippled properly, was it?'

'No, not really. My spine wasn't affected like yours, mate. The leg just gets tired now and then.'

I knew what he was thinking, and grew uncomfortable. Paralysis had spared me; why hadn't it spared him?

'Katrin says you're all working very hard,' he said. 'She practised for ages with Brian last night. Will the programmes finish, soon?'

He watched me; I made some sort of answer, and he turned to the front again. But a knot had tightened in my stomach. Last night, I'd been working late back at ABS; when I'd come home, Katrin had made no mention of the fact that Brady had been there.

After dinner, when Jaan had been put to bed in his room, and old Vilde had gone in to sit with him, she and I stood in the kitchen on the verandah together, washing the dishes.

'I saw you coming down the street tonight,' she said. 'Pushing Jaan. I watched you from up here. Your limp's very noticeable now. Why is that?'

I didn't answer; instead, I asked: 'Why didn't you tell me Brian was here yesterday evening?'

Her high, surprised eyebrows became more surprised; her wide-set eyes flickered for a moment, dropping to the floor and then returning to mine. 'I didn't think it was important.' Her expression went through two stages: comprehension and tender understanding; a rather deliberate sequence, it seemed to me.

'You're not upset, are you? Surely you're not listening to gossip? We always knew that would be a problem.'

She put her arms around me; my chin rested on the top of her head. I'd always loved her head's generous roundness. It was dark outside, the curtains weren't drawn, and I watched our reflections in the black verandah window, where a faint distortion made her look like someone else: a woman I didn't know, and would never know. I held the real woman tighter, perhaps to prevent her from vanishing.

'I've been stupid,' she said. 'A lot of men wouldn't have put up with this at all. But there's nothing between Brian and me. Do I really have to say that to you? Nothing but the music.'

She looked up into my face. 'He's a very simple bloke,' she said. 'He's unreliable about women, and probably about most other things. I like him, but I don't approve of him. Without you, he'd just be singing in pubs. But when he sings, he's someone special.'

She had dropped her head again, and spoke with her

face against my shoulder, musingly now, as though I'd reassured her.

'I couldn't give this up, Richard. It's everything I've ever wanted. I feel I belong to something now; I never did, before. And Brian and I are such a good duo. We might even succeed in Britain, if IRC back us in the way Darcy wants.'

'He's talking about a big tour over there.'

'Yes.'

'Perhaps even going there permanently, if you make it big.'

'It's possible.' She looked up, searching my face, starting a tentative smile. 'That would be wonderful, wouldn't it?'

'What about Jaan? And your grandfather?'

'They could come.' She had gone suspiciously still, in my arms, and for the first time I thought I heard doubt in her voice. 'We'll make a lot of money,' she said.

'And what do you imagine I'll do there?' I kept my voice light.

Her arms tightened about me. 'You'll be our manager. And we'll all have marvellous times.'

'No,' I said. 'IRC would manage you, not me. I'd be a passenger, and I won't give up ABS for that. So we'd have a problem, wouldn't we?'

Her head remained down. 'Don't say that, darling. You could go into broadcasting there—or theatre. You could do anything, over there. You've always said you'd like to go. But it's all too good to be true, anyway. It may never happen.'

She looked up, smiling again. She didn't really want to hear what I was saying; she was much too happy.

5

'Hello? Richard?'

She hadn't rung for some weeks; I'd begun to think it was a rite she'd grown tired of, and I'd been half relieved and half regretful. But now there was a new note in her voice, making me stiffen warily, sitting at my desk.

'You've heard about my husband?'

No, I said.

'But didn't Patrick tell you? I'm surprised. Michael died a week ago.'

'I'm very sorry.'

'Yes, it's sad. But it had to be expected.' Saying this, her voice grew small, flat and empty; and I was shocked to detect a hint of the small-girl tone, the parody that dismissed all seriousness. Was even death a game to her? But a hint was all it had been; it didn't reappear, and I gave her the benefit of the doubt.

There was a pause. Then she said: 'I'm not going to play the hypocrite, darling, I have to admit it's something of a relief. He was ill for a long time, and you know what the situation was like for me.' Her voice dropped to a level of deep secrecy, alerting my senses in a way I didn't want. 'Do you know what the first thing I thought was, when they rang me from the hospital? If only this had happened years ago, when I first met Richard.' Another pause. 'I shouldn't have told you that, should I?'

She waited, and I tried to put an end to the topic by ignoring it. 'So you and Patrick are free. You'll be able to go anywhere you want soon, won't you?' I thought this dismissal might offend her; but she had the Irish propensity for jumping from subject to subject, mood to mood, without a pause.

'I wish that were true, but it's not,' she said. 'He's left over a million; the house is mine, of course; and Patrick's inherited a house of his own at Palm Beach. I'll inherit a lot; but it's all to be parcelled out to me in dribs and drabs by his snooping brother Paul.' She grew petulant. 'As for Patrick, his miserable allowance stays the same until he's thirty. And if we do things that Paul doesn't like, he can practically cut the money off, do you see?'

'How can he do that? It's your money.'

I didn't really want to know; I was embarrassed by all this, but I was obviously expected to ask.

'They have ways, the bloody Dillons,' she said. 'The money's in a family trust thing, which Paul administers.

He can invest it how he likes, under the will. It's mostly in things called *debentures*.' It was the child's indignant voice that pronounced these key words; grim adult terms she shouldn't have to use, let alone worry her head about. 'It's all been plotted to control me,' she said. 'Michael was worried that I'd neglect Fiona, or take her off abroad or something—bloody old Paul made that plain. Paul's always hated me. Do you know what else he said? "If you play up, Deirdre, I'll reinvest the money in ways that produce no return at all—and your income'll be stuffed." He *said* that to me.'

'But at least you're more free than you were. You can come and go.'

Her voice lost its indignation, and became resigned. 'Yes. But sometimes I get lonely. Patrick's not here as often as he was, and I need him, at present. He spends so much time over at King's Cross with Darcy. I'm alone here today. I wish you'd come and visit me, Richard.'

'That isn't possible. I've got a production meeting in ten minutes. I must go.'

'Don't go immediately.' Her voice was quick, almost panicky, and I waited.

'I wanted to talk to you about Darcy,' she said, and grew conversational again. 'Patrick's become very close to him, and he's awfully impressed with Darcy's ideas; we both are, in fact. Fiona likes Darcy too. She's a precocious child for twelve, I sometimes find her difficult to handle, and he's awfully good with her; he's teaching her the guitar. I'm thinking of letting him move in here. Patrick made the suggestion; he says Darcy and Brian Brady don't get on well any more as flatmates. What do you think?'

I'd grown cold. 'I wouldn't do that, if I were you.'

'Why ever not? You and Darcy are friends, aren't you? Patrick said the two of you think so much alike.'

'Where the show's concerned, we do.'

My negative tone seemed not to trouble her; or perhaps she didn't notice it. 'He's opened up whole new under-standings for Patrick and me. Mysteries.' She capitalised the word.

'Maybe you'd be safer with the Church's mysteries.'

My tone had been one of mild sarcasm; but she took me seriously.

'You do sound a prim Catholic. I thought you gave all that up long ago.' It was her free spirit tone, now. 'What's the Church ever given us? I've had the Micks, darling, they've brought me nothing but guilt and misery. You shouldn't be critical of Darcy, he really respects you.' Her voice sank again, thrillingly serious, almost longing. 'And he approves of *us,* darling, you and me. Do you know he did our horoscopes, and they matched perfectly? What do you think of that?'

'I don't believe in astrology.' I had the sensation of going down in a fast lift; my body betrayed me, when my true attitude was contempt.

'You've become awfully rigid, haven't you? I'm sorry, Richard, I shouldn't say these things, I know. You're devoted to your Continental wife—but is she devoted to you? It's not very fair, the display she puts on with Brian Brady, is it?'

I said nothing, and she sighed.

'Well, that's your affair—but don't be hostile to Darcy; he's really changing our lives.'

'You'd better be careful he doesn't change them too much.' The iron bands were around my head again; I wanted to hang up the phone. I would, in a few more moments.

But she went on as though I hadn't spoken. 'He's showing us ways to be free from repression and guilt. He's making us see how many paths lead to the centre.'

She sounded like a born-again Christian quoting from Scripture; from the faint slur in her speech, I guessed that she'd been drinking sherry, as she did almost every afternoon.

'I've learned to love the physical world, through talking to Darcy. The invisible forces in the earth. I feel them all around me.' She gave a small, excited laugh. 'He told us the other night that the way to make contact with the earth-spirit was to go into the garden naked, and sit on the

ground in a circle holding hands. We did—the four of us.
But only in our bathing suits, I'm afraid; I insisted on that.
I couldn't have everyone starkers, with Fiona there. We
sat under the tamarisk, with the moon on the Harbour, and
we felt this incredible power from the earth go through our
bodies—almost frightening. Patrick said it was like being
back on Aegina, where the old earth-spirits are close.'

Darcy had been moving quickly with his games, I thought;
now he was showing Deirdre and Patrick a way to make
their own games permissible. Did it have to concern me? I
decided that it didn't.

She went on, her voice becoming quaintly and incongru-
ously authoritative. Already, with Dillon only dead a week,
it was a rich woman's authority: one who was free to
pursue whatever whims she chose, and to have others
approve. 'It's known as the ecstasy of the Goddess. Darcy
says only a few people have the talent for it, and that I'm
one of them. He calls me Daeira. Next time he comes, he's
bringing some magic mushrooms. If we eat them, we'll
have actual visions, he says. I'm not sure that I'll risk that,
or that Patrick will either, although Darcy says it's safe.
He's incredibly pagan, isn't he? A Dionysiac. Did he
really leave school at fourteen?'

When she finally went off the phone, I sat thinking. I
believe I had some vague sense of disaster, that afternoon,
but I didn't take it seriously; one seldom does. Looked at
objectively, the situation was far more comic than disastrous. There was no one like an ex-Catholic for responding
to the call of other mysteries, any mysteries; and I glimpsed
what was happening. The circle had been formed; the
hands had been joined; the little gate had been opened.
The sly lane between the worlds stretched away: empty,
twilit, and irresistible, leading back to Eleusis, saying:
Come.

She and Patrick were about to be free; or so they
thought. Their money would make this freedom enormous,
leading them towards limits that few ever crossed. What
mightn't they buy, in the strange old bazaars of the spirit?
Darcy would become their guru; they would join the new

tribe who wandered in search of cut-price revelations:
instant deities and devils, ingested through pills or plants.
She could be the daughter of Oceanus; Patrick could be the
child-god: why not?

But it was now that Burr began to become alarming.

Mass occultism was only just beginning in that year, and
Darcy was one of the first through the door; something of
an achievement for a Tasmanian provincial, and at first it
intrigued people. But combined with his will and ceaseless
ambition, it also began to worry them. Once the notion is
established that someone is dedicated to a strange set of
systems, ease is no longer possible, and a chain reaction
begins. There were people now who were actually afraid
of Darcy.

When we'd begun the first series of Rymers programmes,
his relations with the technicians had been good; they'd
respected and consulted him. But he was becoming more
and more perfectionist; it began to be said that he couldn't
be crossed, and that he flew into rages. Then he conceived
the notion that Len Green, the chief sound tech, was
refusing to get the balance he wanted in certain songs.

Len was more sour and obtuse than self-opinionated,
and he was plainly out of his depth with Darcy's demands.
No doubt Green was irritating and obstructive; but I began
to be really concerned when I passed the door of the empty
studio one evening, and saw them talking together.

Len was standing against the wall of the control-room,
and Darcy was frankly bullying him. Talking hard into the
tech's face, he seemed on the verge of violence; a busy
nerve jumped in his cheek, and he clenched and un-
clenched his big hands. Len had paled; and this was
plainly caused by fear, not anger. Seeing me, Darcy stopped
and walked away.

But later, Green came to me and complained. Burr had
made threats to him, he said, and if it happened again,
he'd ask to be taken off the show.

'That bloke's mad,' Len said. 'I ought to report threats

like that to the union—or else the cops.' His fingers were shaking as he lit a cigarette.

I tried to defuse it; I asked what sort of threats Darcy had actually made; but now Len became evasive and sullen. He didn't want to press it, he said, he just wanted me to make Darcy stop; and I had the impression that he was still frightened.

A week later, he managed to get rostered elsewhere. This was unusual. Technicians were usually intimidated by no one, their union being a strong one; we all trod carefully with them.

I spoke to Darcy about it; but he smiled dismissively. 'Doesn't give us any more trouble, does he?' he said. 'He's gone, right? I can't stand idiots. This show's got to be perfect.'

He seemed to me lately to look unwell; to have lost weight and become more sallow, with dark shadows under his eyes. He was plainly under a tension which swung him in some rhythm between elation and irritability: a pattern of obsession. I imagined that this revolved around the hopes he'd pinned on the IRC release of the LP in Britain, and above all on the talent scout on his way from London.

The album was out in Australia now, and one of the tracks—'Lady Isabel and the Elf Knight'—had become so popular on radio, despite its esoteric nature, that it looked like becoming a hit. The new breed of hippies—mysteriously exact reproductions from originals in California—were said to be finding hidden meanings in the ballad, which were only fully apprehended if it was listened to while smoking grass. But none of this satisfied Darcy. All that mattered now was the marvellous envoy from the northern hemisphere: the man who had the power to transport the Rymers to that zone where ultimate fame was possible, instead of this provincial miniature of it—but who could also shut the door and deny it. Local success hadn't brought Burr contentment, but its opposite; he was tantalised constantly by his dream of swinging London, the great ancestral metropolis which had lately become a powerhouse of pleasure, resonating to the music of the Beatles: that group who were more than a group, who breathed an air of myth.

Would the Rymers breathe it too? Becoming possible, the dream grew tormenting; all his longing was focused there, and gave him no rest.

Another week went by; we were into March now, with only two more shows to record, and the man from the International Recording Company was due in two more weeks. I was curious to know whether Darcy had moved out to the Dillon house as a permanent lodger; I gathered he spent more and more time there with Patrick, but hadn't yet moved in. Meanwhile, Brian Brady had quit the flat in Victoria Street, and had taken an expensive bachelor apartment in a tower in Elizabeth Bay. He could afford this now, he said; and Victoria Street was dreary. But I sensed that there were other reasons for his move, related to Darcy.

Usually, Brian wouldn't talk much about Burr; but sitting with Katrin and me in our living-room one evening, just after he'd moved, he did give some hints. He was fairly drunk that night, and probably said more than he intended.

'I didn't like the set-up there any more,' he said; and he dwelt on the mess the flat was in—all except for Darcy's room, which was off limits.

'He's got these little teenage girls coming in and out all the time,' he said. 'They camp there in droves, as if it's their bloody home. It *is* their home, they reckon. Some of them can't be older than sixteen, and Darcy gives them pot. He'll get busted, some day, and I don't want to be there when it happens. One of them's in love with him. He calls her Pipsqueak.'

We both questioned him. What made the girls move in there? What attracted them? Was it the music—the glamour of the Rymers?

Brian shifted restlessly, not wanting to pursue it, and stirred the coffee Katrin had made him. 'Most of them are in trouble in some way, and they reckon Darcy's got all the answers,' he said. 'They're like bloody disciples. You know how he is. He psychs them out. He keeps harping on things and they believe him. He calls up spirits for them, and you can feel the spirits hanging about the flat all the time, now. In corners of the rooms. It was getting on my nerves.'

Katrin and I looked at each other, as though we were humouring a child. Like Darcy, Brian appeared unwell, lately; he seemed thin, sallow and strained, and had developed a habit of clenching and unclenching his hands that was new. He was doing it now.

'I'll tell you something,' he said. 'The other night I saw a face in the mirror.'

I laughed. 'Anyone we know?'

But he didn't seem to notice my amusement. 'I don't know who it was. It wasn't clear. I'd cut myself shaving, and I looked into the mirror in the living-room to dab at the cut. I was by myself, just on my way out. And I saw two reflections; another one besides mine. There was a bloke standing behind me. But when I turned around, he'd gone.'

'Too much grog and not enough sleep,' I said.

'That's right. You weren't yourself,' Katrin assured him. Moving out to the kitchen, she reached from behind Brady's chair as she passed and straightened the collar of his rumpled jeans jacket; a small, wifely action that brought all my doubts back with a sickly rush. And yet it could have been seen as merely maternal.

Patrick now had a second home, I gathered; he spent more and more of his time at Victoria Street. I seldom went there, lately; but one evening after work I called to leave Darcy a script, and received a glimpse of his new household.

The front door was opened by a girl in the costume of the folk-music groupie: black shirt, long red corduroy skirt, wooden beads, bare feet. She was perhaps seventeen— skinny, small-boned and sandy, with quizzical, empty grey eyes which were not in focus, and a small mouth turned down in a bitter U-shape. I guessed that this was Pip-squeak. A now-familiar smell came to me; she held a joint of marijuana in her right hand, suspending it at shoulder-height like a dart.

I asked for Burr, but she said nothing; instead she examined me with contempt; I wasn't even sure she saw me properly, and I wondered if it was only pot she was using. When she finally answered, her voice was piping and scornful: a weak flute. 'Who wants him?'

I told her, and she smiled. 'Oh, the producer! The *boss* man! Darcy's not here.'

'Come in, Dick.' It was Patrick's voice, calling from the living-room.

He greeted me from a couch where he lay smoking a joint of his own, clad in a long cheesecloth shirt and jeans. On him, this looked like fancy dress; he belonged in tweeds or a suit. 'Darcy'll be back soon,' he said, and I found myself a chair.

The girl sat cross-legged on the stained carpet, picking at the loose skin on her bare foot, drawing on her joint and squinting. Once she held it out to me, but I refused.

'Square,' she said, and appeared to retreat into a trance.

'Dick never smokes it,' Patrick said respectfully. 'You really should try,' he told me. 'It does make everything simple and clear. I've understood myself, now, as well as people I care about.'

A curious conversation followed between the two of us, while Pipsqueak ignored us. He wanted, like Deirdre, to talk about Darcy's visions; he had the blank, joyful expression of the convert, and no cynical comments of mine would stop him: he looked at me with holy forgiveness and love, his soul made beatific by the dope. Much of it I've now forgotten, but fragments remain.

'There's a new age dawning this year,' he told me. 'An old cycle's ending and a new one begins, in 1966. Did you know that, Dick? The earth-forces will come into their own, and people will be liberated.'

He went on expounding his second-hand insights, while I paid them little attention. The year's numerological and astrological significance was his main theme, but I've forgotten the details. A new religion was to be born, it appeared, and Darcy Burr was one of those chosen ones who had grasped it.

When I smiled, Patrick came as close as he'd ever done to being indignant. 'It's true, Richard, don't laugh. Darcy says Australia's especially suited to the new religion. There are places of power in the desert where it can all be understood, where the forces reveal themselves. Darcy's going to take us on a trip there, when the show's all done. He knows the places to look for, out near Alice Springs.'

I smiled at the idea of Burr leading his followers into the desert, but Patrick leaned forward earnestly, propped on one elbow. 'No, but why not here, Dick? Why not here, among these pagan rocks?' I imagined he was quoting; probably from Burr.

'Right,' Pipsqueak said suddenly, and nodded. 'Right. Darcy knows.' She looked at me now, and seemed actually to see me. 'Darcy's our father,' she said. 'He takes us to the circle between the worlds.'

'How?' I asked. 'By dropping acid?'

The emptiness of her eyes became hostile. 'You think you're in charge of the Rymers, don't you, boss-man? It's Darcy who's in charge. He's in charge of everthing.'

Patrick looked faintly embarrassed. 'Pipsqueak's awfully stoned,' he explained. 'She worships Darcy.'

'Tell him I called,' I said.

It was during those weeks that my repeated nightmares began.

Little of their content comes back now, and it's hard to account for the extremity of fear they created during sleep, except to say that a true fear hid at their centre: the dread of losing Katrin which I couldn't even voice, let alone justify.

Somehow this had now been increased because of my talk with Darcy on the steps; and it perhaps explains why he stood at the centre of the whole series of nightmares. But it doesn't explain their peculiar nature.

Even now, I puzzle over the strength of the conviction I developed that these weren't normal dreams; that Burr was somehow sending them to me, telegraphing them into my sleeping brain from the flat in Victoria Street. This notion, ridiculous though I knew it to be, would not be dismissed at the time; and perhaps it took its force from the fact that Darcy addressed me directly in the dreams—in tones which alternated between cajoling and frank bullying.

He wasn't in the forefront of the action; instead he commented on it for me, like the narrator of one of my radio productions. Yet I felt that the action was somehow his to control. He usually smiled, but sometimes he frowned; and I was afraid of this frown in a way I'd certainly never been in waking life. I felt that the dream Darcy was the true one, not the one I met by day; and his frown threatened my whole being. It faced me with dissolution; with the loss of myself, as well as Katrin. I was sinking, and he talked and talked; he never stopped talking, and his commentary created all my terrors and temptations.

The temptations concerned Deirdre Dillon. She appeared in the dreams as often as Katrin and Brian did, and at the heart of each nightmare Burr was assuring me I belonged with Deirdre, not with Katrin, and that I'd already made my choice.

Deirdre stood naked in the bathroom window at Greystones, looking out at me with a light, hard gaze, beautiful as any Renaissance divinity in Karl Miller's books. *'I haven't a stitch on, darling.'* I'd been hearing her voice for some time, mingled with Burr's talk; and now I knew that while I'd watched her, he'd watched me. My longing became nausea then; a nausea quickly transformed into dread. Desire and dread were the same, because what I felt was already known to Burr. I was guilty, and he would make me pay; and all the time Katrin and Brian looked at me with sad understanding from a distance, standing together decently, in their Rymers' costumes. These two belonged together, I was told; I didn't deserve Katrin's vigour, her optimism, her health. She looked at me with tragic regret.

But Brady smiled. He'd raided me as he'd once done in Trent Street—taking my wife with his old, cheerful casualness, as though it were no great thing. If Deirdre had been my waking dream, Brian, I saw now, was Katrin's: he was Geza Lukacs, come back in a new guise.

The panic one feels in nightmare is rarely in proportion to the facts it contains; sometimes, on waking, one can see no reason for the horror at all. This, despite the seriousness of the issues tormenting me, was my case. Little in the facts of the dreams could explain the sheer degree of their terror and oppression, or my certainty that I was lost beyond recovery. When I was fortunate enough to wake, finding Katrin asleep beside me, I would hold her until her body-warmth dispelled the dream's iron truth.

But Burr and his troupe always came back. The dreams continued for many nights, operating now through a sort of shorthand. I had experienced the essentials; there was no need for the actors to play out whole scenes again. They had only to appear in their various guises for me instantly to understand my fatal position. Katrin and Brian always wore their Rymers costumes; Deirdre always roamed naked, in the perfection of her twenties, speaking with her middle-aged voice which, unlike Burr's, rambled towards no destination, no final point.

In those strange weeks, it wasn't dream that imitated life, but life that imitated dream; because Deirdre's phone calls had now begun again, almost as though she'd been prompted. Since her husband's death, she'd begun to allow herself to say things to me she'd not done before: directly erotic hints; frank appeals to the shred of past that linked us. And she begged me more and more frequently to visit that Point Piper villa I'd once longed to enter, and whose interior I'd never seen.

I continued, patiently, to refuse; it wasn't a good idea, I said.

'Patrick now says he's in love with me. He wants to marry me, and take me abroad. Isn't it indecent? I've told him never to mention such a thing again. He bought me a print of a Titian Venus yesterday; he said she reminded him of me. He says I'm his goddess. I told him I wasn't

*quite as overweight as his Venus—that dampened him.
He's getting impossible, lately.*

'*Too late now, I suppose; but it should have been you. I
think of us more and more lately, the way we were. You
were so beautiful, with your poor leg. And we loved the
same things, didn't we, Richard? Remember your Yeats?
"Tread softly, because you tread on my dreams."* '

With the flavour of Darcy's nightmares still in my mouth,
I grew alarmed and finally angry. I asked her to stop
calling me, and she went off the phone, her voice hurt and
frigid. I had finally cut the connection, I thought; it had
been that simple.

And now the dreams changed. Deirdre vanished from
them, and so did Brian and Katrin.

I'm still unable to account for their new content. Where
did it come from? Forgotten reading? Conversations in
Varley's basement, lodged in my unconscious? No doubt;
but at the time, this somehow didn't seem likely; instead,
the sensation of being a receiver for entirely novel messages from Victoria Street became even more intense than
before.

Burr was alone with me in these episodes, talking at me
directly; and I listened to him with a mingled sense of
loathing and boredom so insupportable that I felt myself
suffocating. I would wake in panic, sucking in air with the
most vivid physical relief, as though I'd just escaped
drowning. Yet the extraordinary thing was that Darcy
seemed to be doing little to harm me except to recite
names, frowning as he did so: endless lists of names,
tedious and repellent, all but one of which meant nothing
to me.

'*Bunting,*' he said. '*Puckrill; Fury; Maumet.*' And then:
'*Phouka.*'

He stood in the street and whistled me out, and I looked
down from the verandah window not wanting to come,
while he grinned up at me. I had no such emotion when
this happened in reality; merely a sort of reluctance, lately,
which his perennial air of bringing important news would
quickly overcome. There were two Burrs: the one by day,

and the one in dreams. Yet I sensed they might soon blend
in some way.

'You should give up these long planning sessions with
Darcy,' Katrin said. 'You look drained, after you and he
have been together. Do we have to do so much of this
ghost material? Brian and I would rather do more love
ballads. That's what we're best at—everyone says so.'

6

We had taped the last show, and the Rymers were mine no
longer.

As we went into the last week of March, most of their
talk was of a three-day trip to Melbourne, where they were
booked to do two big concerts, as well as a TV appearance. They were driving down on Wednesday, in a mini-
bus Darcy had bought to take them on tours. All of them
were excited about the concerts, but they were a good deal
more excited by the advent of Roy Slade, the talent scout
from IRC, who was due here from London on the day
before their departure. Uttering his name, their voices
came close to awe; even Brian seemed reluctantly affected.

On Monday, the eve of the northern envoy's arrival, Deirdre Dillon's call for help came.

'I have to see you.'

'I'm sorry, that isn't possible; I'm very busy.'

'Don't hang up.' The voice seemed genuinely urgent,
without affectation, and I waited for three beats.

'I wouldn't phone you if I had anywhere else to turn. I
want you to come over to the house immediately. I'm in
serious trouble.'

I looked at my watch; it was a little after five o'clock.
'Isn't Pat there?'

'I can't *talk*, Richard. Just come.' Muffled weeping
began, and the line went dead.

The sign still says NO THROUGH ROAD. The Southerly hisses
in the leaves of the palm and banana trees. This millionaire's tip of Point Piper is deserted as ever, and when I

slam the door of my car in Wolseley Crescent, the bark of
a big dog breaks the hush. It's Major, staring at me
through the black, wrought-iron gates.

'Hello Major,' I say. He lowers his nose, and growls in
his throat; then he wags his tail twice, and admits me.

The stage is empty, just as it was when I made my
expedition here years ago. The late sun is vacuous and
mild; it's not yet twilight. Silent, the big white villa,
whose chimneys are tall as minarets, wearing hats of
Cordova tiles. The half-glimpsed, half-real terrace still
muses over the Harbour at the back. No sign of trouble:
untrodden levels of lawn go off empty as ever to the
water's edge; the roses and tamarisks nod and writhe. The
Harbour is pale blue as reverie; an oil tanker slides past
Shark Island.

But one thing isn't right: the black iron safety door is off
its latch, and the front door is slightly ajar. I push it open
and step in, my heart thumping as though I'm trespassing.
For a moment, I'm twenty-five again, and her unknown
husband is waiting inside.

On black and white ceramic tiles, I stand inside the
Dillon house at last. There are faint, clean odours: furniture polish, flower scents, and a dry, papery smell which
is the house's individual essence. Airy light fills the entrance hall; I sense that the house is full of light, reflected
off the Harbour, dancing on white walls upstairs and down.
Directly in front of me is a handsome staircase with cedar
banisters.

She's standing on the landing in a belted dressing-gown
of moss-green silk, looking down at me with no sign of
recognition, her face like powder. I feel certain she's been
standing there ever since her phone call.

'Are you all right?' My question is loud, in the clean
silence.

At first she makes no reply, her mouth pursed and
dubious, both hands holding the gown together. Finally,
her voice floats down to me.

'Shut the door behind you.'

She's as solemn as a child in shock, and her explanations can wait. I cross the tiles and begin to climb the stairs. Her blanched hair, which falls loose to her shoulders as always, alarms me with its web-like disorder, and as I climb, she seems formidably larger than her true size: statuesque. But when I stand in front of her, she's quite small again, her uncorsetted figure soft and vulnerable. Only her bosom remains almost massive, her hands still clutching the gown together there: pale, freckled and appalled.

'Patrick raped me,' she says.

It's been uttered so quickly that I almost doubt what I've heard. Without waiting for a response, but giving me a single, swift glance, she turns and makes off towards a hall that opens off the landing.

'We'll go to my room.' This is called over her shoulder, peremptory and abrupt, as though I'm to be taken to task for what's happened. I follow the lustrous, moss-green gown and floating web of hair down the hallway's dimness; she hurries with the certainty and authority of a woman in her own house, but only through habit, I think, since everything is altered for ever.

She lives in this room; I sense it as soon as we come in. I imagine she seldom leaves it, and is seldom out of her dressing-gown either. We sit side by side on a little couch. Still holding the gown together at the throat with one hand, as though for protection, she pours two sherries from a decanter: a good hostess. But her face is still blank, and I fear that in a moment she'll give way. I continue to behave normally, as though this may postpone her hysteria from surfacing. And I look about me, while she sips her sherry in silence; a silence which in her is more alarming than complaint.

Large as a sitting-room, this long-imagined 'boudoir' of hers is furnished much as I would have expected: thick, blue-grey carpet, antique double bed with brass knobs, rosewood writing-desk, a small rosewood table on which the decanter stands. Armchairs, and the couch we sit on, are covered in blue-and-white brocade; there are crowded white bookshelves, and a record-player. It's the bed-sitting-

room of a solitary: a pampered, unmarried girl with cultivated tastes. But although it's clean, and although one of
the casement windows is open on to a view of the Harbour,
a white curtain undulating gently in the breeze, the room
has the fustiness of a place whose occupant has lost interest in order. There are faint food and cigarette smells in
the warm, quiet air, mingled with scent. The bed is un-
made; underclothes lie on chairs. On the long, cluttered
white dressing-table, with its mirrors and battery of jars, a
coloured portrait photograph stands: her twelve-year-old
daughter, whom I last saw as an infant. She's pretty, with
auburn hair, but it's a pale, indoor, Victorian prettiness,
from which her mother's life-force is somehow absent; the
large, dark blue eyes are a disillusioned woman's, rather
than a child's.

I decide to break the silence. 'What happened?'

She turns to me, putting down her glass on the table and
letting go of the collar of the gown so that it gapes,
disclosing deeply divided whitenesses. 'I *told* you: Patrick
raped me.' Her voice rises a little. 'My stepson *raped* me;
and Darcy Burr encouraged him to do it. Otherwise, it
never would have happened.'

I sit astounded yet not surprised. But now she ducks her
head and begins to weep, a handkerchief held to her nose,
hunched forward in profile, gasping. Her whole body shud-
ders, under the gown.

'Where's Pat now?'

'He's gone.' Her voice is squeezed and small. 'Gone off
with Darcy. Fiona's at her uncle's, thank God. And the
housekeeper's away. So I'm here by myself.'

'Have you called the police?'

She turns quickly to look at me, blanched hair swinging.
'Of *course* not. How could I do that?' Her voice is a wail;
the suggestion frightens her, and the open, crying mouth is
a child's: almost square.

'You're not hurt?'

She blows her nose and grows quiet; it takes her some
time to answer. 'He's assaulted me; he was trying to *force*

himself on me. When I screamed, he stopped. It's only my
face he didn't mark, do you see?'

I see, since she's opened the gown, under which she's
naked: a martyr displaying wounds in a sentimental painting, her reddened, sky-pale eyes accusing the world. Then,
seemingly satisfied by my dismay at these few sad bruises,
she wraps herself up again. But my dismay has sprung as
well from seeing what Time has done to the body of the
Elle Maid, making her death-white and voluptuously swollen:
a creature of Earth.

I put my arm about her shoulders. Humbly, she lays her
wet and papery face against my neck; I smell her powder
and the sherry on her breath, and my pity is love's familiar. She has no understanding of why this penalty has come
to her: even now, she doesn't see that her mirror-games
have gone too far. It isn't her fault, it's Burr's fault;
Patrick's fault. She'll run away crying, to tell Dadda. But
bankrupt Robert Brennan is dead now; and so is Michael
Dillon. Both Daddas are dead, and there's only me.

In a muffled voice, talking into my neck, she says: 'He
hurt me, Richard.'

I stayed, my arm still about her shoulders, while it darkened in the room.

Twilight: the dangerous time, when things begin to
change, and no longer seem themselves. The world faded,
through Deirdre's bedroom window; colour drained from
lavish, grass-green water-plains as spacious as her carpet,
extending for miles: a Harbour for the rich, the far, violet
headlands like frontiers, imagined rather than seen. A few
last yachts bent at a distance; a miniscule Manly ferry
hurried towards the city, and the big, empty house on the
point seemed ready to drift away; to sail out on to the
water in the next Southerly.

As she talked, I began to see that she almost feared it
would.

She spoke slowly at first, then more and more quickly,
in full, panicky flight from that land of strange insights
where Burr had been leading them. Patrick wasn't really to

be blamed, she insisted, he wasn't really vicious, it was Darcy. If it weren't for Darcy's influence, Patrick would never have forced himself on her. His whole personality had changed: he only did what Darcy suggested.

'Patrick used to be so gentle. Now he's aggressive and demanding. He's not himself. They're both on that horrible hash, of course; I hate the smell of the filthy stuff. Even Fiona's become defiant; I see Darcy whispering to her in corners. She's infatuated with him. I'm sure it's innocent, but it frightens me.' She blew her nose, while the red-haired girl on the dressing-table gazed at me with her look of precocious disillusion.

'Patrick keeps saying that he and I must marry, and go abroad with the Rymers,' she said. 'It's mad. The family would have a fit. And he keeps wanting more and more money. That's Darcy's doing too, I'm sure. He's taking over our lives.'

The note of panic rose higher. 'He's practically moved in here, and he won't go. He says he's Patrick's guest. Major barks and barks, when he sees him. He's never liked Darcy, from the first.'

She should simply demand that Burr stay away, I said; it was her house. Surely her brother-in-law would help, if there was any trouble?

But now a new agitation gripped her; clearly the worst alarm of all.

'*No*. I can't. Bloody Paul would blame *me*,' she said. 'I asked Darcy here in the first place, and Paul would say I'd created the situation—that I'd exposed Fiona to bad influences. He'd take away my income. He's only wanting an excuse like this.'

The handkerchief went to her nose; she looked out the window in vague and helpless anguish, and I recognised what spectres she was staring at now: the big house floating off, the investments and securities she laughed at and didn't understand bobbing into infinity: lost toys of a fortunate child, who had never imagined the world without them. The room was almost dark.

I tightened my arm about her shoulders; her body-heat

came through the gown, and she turned back to me in mute appeal. The sails of the yachts on the dimming Harbour were like flashes of thought, and I saw that the indistinct face turned up to me was changed by some alchemy of darkness into the Deirdre of Greystones again: a girl in her twenties, her beauty absolute. The wave that went through me was like warning; but its true identity was longing.

'*You* talk to Darcy,' she murmured. 'You can make him leave us alone.'

'I'll do what I can. Now I have to go.'

'No. They might come back.'

'I'll phone in the morning to see that you're all right.'

For a moment, she said nothing; then she spoke under her breath. 'It should have been us. We would have been happy. Stay with me, Richard. I need you to look after me.'

I stood abruptly. 'I'll let myself out,' I said.

She looked at me once more and then turned away, making no response at all. Her expression in the dark was unclear, her face a white blur. Hunched forward, motionless, elbows on her knees, white-blonde curtain of hair hanging about her face like a tent, she neither looked up nor spoke, as I moved to the door.

Outside in the Crescent, walking uphill to my car, I took deep breaths. I wouldn't phone her in the morning; I'd never hear her many voices again. The Hobart girl with the Irish sense of humour; the old-fashioned child; the cool and cultivated Sydney matron; the cruel and lovely Elle-maid: all were gone. I walked quickly; but I couldn't quite leave her behind, no matter how fast I walked.

I wasn't involved, I said. But I knew that my protest was hypocrisy. I'd somehow entered the condition of guilt, in a zone beyond the rational where Darcy's dreams had become reality. I was held by frail webs more enduring than adultery; I always had been, and eventually, I'd pay.

7

All was as usual, in the Hasty Tasty.

The jukebox was playing 'House of the Rising Sun', and under the high pink ceiling, the sailors, rockers and prostitutes spilled out of the booths with an eternal air, as they'd done when I first met Brady and Burr here a year ago. The time was after eleven; it was always close to midnight in the Hasty, and the inmates, although they gave an illusion of coming and going, were constantly here, their din drowning the music. WE NEVER CLOSED. The small man in the cook's hat made hamburgers in the window for ever.

Not far away, in some exalted, deep-carpeted chamber of the Sheraton at Potts Point, blessed by the celestial tinkling of piped music, Burr and the others were at present engaged in their meeting with the man from IRC, over a late supper. Slade was staying at the Sheraton, of course; the Beatles had stayed there.

Their meeting had been set for nine o'clock. At ten-thirty, Darcy had phoned me at home. His voice had been tense, without its usual humour. It contained true portentousness now, I thought; not the kind he used to manufacture.

'We're still at the Sheraton,' he said. 'Katrin and Brian are having a last few drinks with Roy—but the deal's all been settled. You and me have got to talk now, Dick. It's very important. I'll meet you in the Hasty.'

I'd ceased to frequent the Hasty Tasty; the place no longer amused me, and I tried to persuade him to come to the flat. But he insisted; we had to talk alone, he said; the Hasty was best. He still used it as a rendezvous, even though he could now afford the most expensive bars and restaurants in the Cross, and I'd often wondered why. Sitting here now, I came to the simple but extraordinary conclusion that he actually preferred the place; it suited him.

Here he came, peering between the booths, formally turned out for his dinner with Slade in a brown suede jacket and collar and tie. Combined with his rimless glasses, the effect was one of stern responsibility; he appeared to be masquerading as some sort of professional man. Briefly, knowing what I was going to tell him, I suppressed physical fear—its grip unmistakable and humiliating, like that of a schoolyard bully. Then it was gone, replaced by the anger I was nurturing.

It was only when he slid on to the bench opposite me that I found he had Pipsqueak with him; she'd been walking down the aisle behind, his bulk hiding her smallness. Burr gave no explanation for her presence, but behaved as though she weren't here. She was wearing the same black shirt as before, with her string of wooden beads, and her skin appeared greyish in the underwater light. Her eyes, the colour of faded jeans, were still unfocused; she looked at me blindly and briefly, twitching her nose like a rabbit, and I doubted whether she saw me.

Burr ordered two coffees from an elderly, distracted waitress, who addressed him by name and fawned on him; he was well-regarded here.

'We're in,' he said abruptly. 'Slade's giving us everything: The UK concert tour; a British LP; appearances on the BBC: the lot. He wants us in London in a month.' He watched me and waited, and I wondered if he was trembling, on his pinnacle; my own slight trembling was something I managed to hide, keeping both hands beneath the table.

'Right,' Pipsqueak said, and nodded like a doll. 'The lot.' She looked around her dreamily; the Beatles were singing 'Yesterday', and she reverently hummed. Across the aisle, in the booth opposite ours, the same grey-haired derelict as before was accompanying on the teaspoons, drumming away in his frantic private bubble. I thought of those temperate hells in the visions of Swedenborg, which were not imposed on their inhabitants but sought out by them, since the damned wanted only to be there, in foul and frowning houses where they lusted and quarrelled eternally; in lanes filled with ordure, where they preyed and marauded without cease.

'What this means,' Burr said, 'is the greatest chance we'll ever have. But Katrin's very worried—we all are. So I said I'd talk to you.' His eyes, fixed on me in the old insistent way, had a new glassiness, the pupils dilated. He made no attempt to smile, and his face was more drawn than ever; he looked ill, I thought. Fame, real fame, was waiting: the greatest trip of all; the human sea that would offer its worship to the Rymers, raising them into an ozonosphere of power that few of us ever knew. He had overcome every kind of obstacle: the only one left was me.

'Katrin says you're still threatening not to come,' he said. 'That can't be right, can it?'

'How long will the tour last?'

He looked at me with impatience, as though he'd endured me for too long; he blew out his lips, slowly released air, and searched for words. Then he spread his hands.

'Who can say? Look Dick, I wonder if you've understood what I'm telling you. Slade believes that with the right handling, the Rymers are big enough to get a single on the charts over there. Do you know what *that* could mean?'

'I can guess.'

He leaned forward, peering. 'I don't think you can, mate.'

'Poor boss-man doesn't understand anything,' Pipsqueak said, and giggled. Then she began to eat the sugar from the plastic bowl, shovelling it in with her teaspoon. The derelict had stopped drumming, and now looked at his spoons in perplexity; the rhythm had got beyond him.

Darcy smiled at me for the first time, and his voice became deliberately patient. 'Katrin's going to be a star. Slade *loves* her, and he loves Brian. He's comparing the group to Peter Paul and Mary.' He paused. 'There's no point in thinking about when we'll come back, mate. We may never come back.'

'Then I won't be going,' I said.

There was silence, inside the Hasty's din. As I returned his gaze, it seemed to me that his face grew more pinched. A twitching began in his cheek which wasn't the usual tic; there were at least three nerves jumping at once: a novel and oddly alarming phenomenon. His voice remained soft, but now it threatened me.

'And that stops Katrin going, you think. And that wrecks the group.'

'Katrin'll make her own decision. It's up to her.'

Burr had picked up the plastic salt-shaker, holding it delicately between finger and thumb, watching it as though it might detonate; suddenly, he became foul-mouthed. 'So she chooses between the group and your shitty little marriage. Well, she'll choose the Rymers,' he said.

I found myself staring at a feature high on the back wall; an illuminated box containing an animated toy band of 1940s vintage, powered by electricity. The bandleader in his tuxedo waved his baton; the musicians, with jerky little movements, played their instruments in a ghastly aquarium light, their smiles fixed and inane. With each tune on the jukebox, they'd strike up again, tonight and every night, above the roiling figures of the Hasty.

'You're afraid that Brady'll get into her pants,' Burr said. 'That's the trouble, isn't it? Better get used to it; that's what'll happen. You can't keep us all in a fucking box. Katrin and Brian are on their way. And the Rymers aren't yours, now, they're mine.'

The Hasty's din faded, as though the knob on some giant volume control had been turned down. Darcy's face, close to mine, was refined and exalted by the pure, ecstatic anger of obsession, making my poor concerns feeble; diminished. Beside him, Pipsqueak smiled delightedly, looking from one to the other of us. But Burr and I ceased to speak; we were empty.

I stood; I moved off between the booths towards the door, leaving him frowning after me, as he'd done in my series of dreams. Pipsqueak was eating the sugar again.

Darlinghurst Road was as crowded as usual; I was jostled by visitors from the suburbs whose faces searched daringly for vice. Prostitutes stood like sentinels in the doorways of closed boutiques, and the Duke of Darlinghurst Road passed me by, in his grey tent-coat and many waistcoats, trudging along the gutter; he glanced at me sharply, as though he saw my state.

I had looked back once, as I came, at the jumbled line

of terraces at the junction, one of which housed the Hasty.
The sherry bottle poured its green neon liquor, and the
terraces and all the other buildings of the Cross crowded
closer, as though to ingest me: private hotels, brothels,
chemists, strip-shows, real-estate agents, patisseries—most
of them housed in quaint Edwardian confections with cosy
bay windows and little first-floor balconies. They pressed
in and receded, distinct yet without perspective, and I
grasped my position.

This had been a place of refuge for Katrin; a surrogate
Europe in the utmost south of the world, where life had
forced her to stay. Why had I assumed she'd stay forever?
The lost north had always been waiting, and I'd scarcely
been married to her at all. She'd merely been a visitor in
my life, a refugee from that hemisphere to which talent
would now take her back: a hemisphere which was reality
for her, but only dream for me.

I ran up the stairs.

She and Brian were sitting at the table in the living-
room, a bottle of claret and some cheese and biscuits
between them. Their greetings and smiles were quiet,
almost meditative, as though offered to an invalid; they sat
in big-boned solemnity, and the sentences they spoke—the
sentences we all spoke—were like talk around a sickbed.
One imagines hope is gone at some earlier stage, in such a
process; but a small defiance of events has been nursed
unconsciously: a last little spark.

I sat down at the table, and Brian poured me out a glass
of claret, the clink of the bottle distinct; it was quiet in the
flat, with Jaan and old Vilde in bed. Brady wore his best
tweed jacket, but his hair hadn't been disciplined for the
IRC man's dinner; it was tangled as ever. Soon its Celtic
loops and spirals would be yearned over by larger hordes
of girls.

He passed me the glass. 'Get this into you, Dick.'

His voice had changed tonight: there was a new formality about him, as there had been about Burr; it belonged to

the future which Slade had delivered. But none of us wanted to begin.

'Brian didn't get on very well with Roy Slade,' Katrin said.

'No?'

'No,' Brady said. 'The Pommy bastard seems to think we're some sort of pop group. He thinks we're Peter Paul and Mary. You won't believe this: he wanted us to sing stuff like "Puff the Magic Dragon". I had to tell him if that's the sort of crap he wants, he's got the wrong group.'

'Darcy was very worried, at that stage,' Katrin said.

'Yair. Neatly wet himself. But you can't sell out what you do, and I bloody won't.'

'I think he respected you, in the end,' Katrin told him.

'Maybe. But you know what I think? When we get over there, he'll *still* try and turn us into Peter Paul and Mary.'

There was silence, while he took out the makings and began to roll a cigarette. Katrin watched me with an anxious smile that asked me to be reasonable.

'So you talked to Darcy.' Brady licked his cigarette paper.

'Yes.'

'And what did you decide?' He lit up, squinting at me sideways. Katrin had dropped her head, and looked at the table.

'I understand you'll be going indefinitely. In that case I won't be coming with you.'

'Richard.' Katrin had spoken with a sort of maternal reproof, but when I looked across, her head remained bent. I sensed her forlorn hope: when she raised her head again, all this would be solved.

Brady was contemplating me as he'd done on certain occasions in the past; with a mixture of contempt and bafflement. Head back, eyes half closed, he drew on his cigarette and released a slow stream of smoke. Then he turned to Katrin, speaking as though I weren't present.

'You can see how it is. He wants to stop us; Darcy was right. But we can't let that happen, can we, Kate?'

So he had a pet name for her.

'Please. Don't talk like this.' Her voice pleaded with him, but her head remained bent; she wouldn't look at either of us.

But I saw that he'd keyed himself up for this moment; there was no going back. Any emotion in Brady was surprising, and its intensity now almost checked my anger: he was white about the nostrils; he put the cigarette into an ashtray, and clenched his big fists on the table. His light eyes had always been hungry; now they stared at loss as though our positions were reversed.

'Katrin and I love each other,' he said, still without looking at me. 'We're meant to be together.'

Katrin raised her head, but her expression wasn't what I'd expected: she looked at him with sad prohibition, her mouth set.

'Brian—you'd better go home.'

When he began to speak, she said quickly: 'Please. You really must go.

He paused at the door and looked back at her, lower lip out-thrust. His expression now was one I hadn't seen since St Augustine's: the defiant boy's. He still ignored me; I'd become invisible, just as I feared.

'We leave for Melbourne at eight in the morning,' he told her. 'Darcy and me will bring the van around. You're still coming?'

'Of course.' She sat stiff-backed at the table, looking straight ahead, frowning as though from migraine.

When he went out, she turned and looked at me fear-lessly, still sitting erect, both fists clenched on the table as his had been. Her eyes filled with tears, but she didn't blink; she seemed unaware of them.

'I was fond of him,' she said. 'That was all.'

I didn't touch her, in bed that night; our bodies were turned to stone. When she slept, I lay awake.

For the moment, she'd chosen me; but only for the moment. Nothing she'd said to me before she slept had convinced me otherwise. Brady wasn't reliable; she'd said so once herself. There had been enough risk in her life,

nd Brady presented risk, unpredictability; this was the
eal reason she'd drawn back from the brink, I thought. I
vas reliable, and Brian wasn't.

She wouldn't go to Britain; but she was still going to
Melbourne for the concerts: they couldn't cancel them,
he'd said. In the morning, she'd be gone; she was gone
dready, and I listened to her breathing. Was I really to
elieve that he wouldn't be able to change her mind in the
ext three days—alone with her, five hundred miles away?

I studied her face in the dark to memorise it: the over-
mphatic lips and smooth Estonian cheekbones. I wasn't
ust losing Katrin, I was losing those memories that had
ow become my own; short Baltic summers; birch woods;
Dillingen and the Camp. I was losing the substance of my
ife, whose flavour was one with the heavy Estonian rye
read she'd never let the house be without.

I wanted to kill Brady, but I couldn't even hate him; it
vas futile, somehow; like hating a part of myself.

Paralysis had set in.

8

They were due back on Sunday.

Thursday and Friday passed without a call from Katrin;
nce I phoned her hotel, but she was out, and I left no
nessage.

On the Friday evening, old Vilde and I made dinner
ogether, moving about the kitchen-verandah while Jaan
vorked on his homework in the living-room.

'I have forgotten to buy the salt you asked me,' Vilde
aid.

He stood by the stove looking at me through his tinted
glasses with the vague, bewildered humbleness of the old;
ve'd aged a lot in the last year, although his thatch of
vhite hair was thick as ever. His striped shirts were still
dways clean, his trousers well-pressed, his shoes made
gleaming each day as though for business, and I admired him
or it. 'Very bad, to forget salt,' he said. 'Two things we
sed to say a house should never be without: salt, and bread.'

After dinner, when Jaan had been helped into bed, Vilde

and I sat in the living-room, drinking our evening vodkas.
He had a rug over his knees; he seemed to feel the cold
more, lately, even that of the mild Sydney autumn, which
had only just begun. His books lay on a small table at his
elbow; he now drew one of these from the pile, and passed
it across to me.

It proved to be a photograph album I'd not seen before,
and I found myself looking at old black-and-white pictures
of the Vilde family. Himself when young, handsome and
archaic-looking in a stiff, historic suit: a gentleman from
the time of Russia of the Czars, and the Austro-Hungarian
empire. His wife, in traditional dress. Their formally dressed
children, in a garden with larches and fir trees. And here
were pictures of friends: cheerful, big-boned Estonian faces
from a past that had once been happy, but which now was
stained with the terrible yellow of history. Nearly all of
them were lost, he said. His big finger pointed, trembling
slightly; this one had died in the war; that one had been
taken to Siberia.

He pointed again. 'Katrin,' he said, and looked at me
carefully, with age's deep enquiry.

She stood with her mother on a pathway in Tallinn, in
front of a clump of birches: eight years old, happy, wearing the national costume, with its full skirt, long-sleeved
blouse, little waistcoat and head-dress.

'She liked to wear her national dress,' Vilde said. 'Always a little vain, as all artists are. *Prosit*.' He raised his
glass and smiled with indulgent irony.

I felt briefly suspicious and resentful—how much did he
know? He'd been told of the possibility of a brief visit to
Britain by the group, but that was all; and I wondered now
if he'd guessed more.

He leaned forward. 'You will go to England with the
others? Or wait here?' The sudden question was uncanny.

'That'd depend on how long they went for. There's
nothing definite.'

'I could not come,' he said flatly, and wiped vodka
from his moustache.

'Wouldn't you like to see Europe again, *Vanaisa?*'

He shook his head. 'I am too old,' he said. 'And my Europe has gone. I would not like to see what is there now. Katrin is still in some ways a child; she imagines our old Europe is still there. She will have to stop being a child, soon. There is Jaan to think about; I cannot care for him as I did. And you should have children of your own.' He smiled at me briefly. 'Now I must go to bed.'

He pushed himself up from the armchair with both hands. 'God keep you.' He said this every night.

'Good night, *Vanaisa*.'

More of his certainties were gone than he thought; but there was no use in saying so.

On Saturday afternoon, no longer having the office to keep me from my thoughts, I went out walking, prowling the grey streets of Darlinghurst until I grew tired. At six o'clock, coming home through the Cross, I found myself passing the Catholic church in Kellet Street.

The same restlessness that had taken me in and out of the doors of shops, pubs and coffee lounges all afternoon led me in here.

Evening Mass was beginning; people shifted and coughed. I hadn't been to Mass for years, but I knelt in a pew and murmured the responses. A mechanism inside me would always do this, no matter what opinions I might hold, and it gave me an empty sort of comfort, like the rediscovery of a cherished habit. The Latin liturgy was soothing: an aged music of reassurance, confirming that even the terrible needn't mean despair; that the terrible could be dealt with. *In te Domine, speravi, non confundar in aeternum . . .*

The priest was in violet; violet cloths shrouded and entirely hid the statue of the Virgin and the figure on the Cross, making them like bodies in a morgue; the altar was stripped. We were well into Lent, and I hadn't even known it; an irrational sense of shame at this took me aback. The strangers around me were familiar, resembling those other Irish-made faces of every Sunday Mass of boyhood, at Sacred Heart in Newtown. The old man next to me had a stern expression and a cough, both of which grew irritating. I told myself I'd go, soon; but I lingered, still half embarrassed to leave before the end.

My attention wandered as it always had, inside the Latin; then it was briefly brought back by the sound of the Gospel in English. The priest in the pulpit was thin, nondescript and spectacled: a serious clerk. ' *"Walk whilst you have the light, that the darkness overtake you not; and he that walketh in darkness knoweth not whither he goeth . . . These things Jesus spoke, and He went away, and hid Himself from them."'*

Around the walls went the familiar, coloured bas-reliefs in their wooden frames: the Stations of the Cross, aesthetically primitive, resembling a comic strip. They marched as they'd marched through all the Sundays at Sacred Heart: a cartoon serial, its hero the man who'd consented to play the clown's role invented for Him, in the mock-royal robe and crown of thorns they'd forced on Him, bleeding and staggering between the ranks of malicious faces *(Jesus meets Veronica; Jesus falls a Third Time)*, arriving finally at the climax He had clearly brought upon Himself, in the sunset of Golgotha. This was the time of the Sorrowful Mysteries; the time of His imminent entombment. He had freed us, and soon it would be Easter: then He would rise, and joy would be born.

A line shuffled to Communion which I wasn't entitled to join; kneeling, I watched the faces come back down the aisle towards me, a transitory gleam of joy showing in all of them, a joy which was not quite fatuous, but which human beings can never sustain for long, and are perhaps not meant to. The old man who sat next to me was coming back too, his mouth munching frankly on the Host, large head bowed, bent frame encased in the pin-striped suit he plainly wore seldom; perhaps only here.

Christ inside him, he entered the pew and smiled at me, acknowledging the good fortune he thought we shared. Smiling back, I wondered why he'd ever annoyed me; I had an absurd desire to weep; a rush of tears; and I covered my face with my hands again, grateful for the pretence of prayer, staying that way until the final prayers

of the Mass: the ghetto appeals to Mary and to the orders
of angels, in which I joined.

' *"Hail, holy queen, mother of mercy; hail, our life, our
sweetness and our hope. To thee do we cry, poor banished
children of Eve; to thee do we send up our sighs, mourning and weeping in this valley of tears . . .*

' *". . . do thou, O Prince of the heavenly host, by the
power of God, cast Satan down to hell, and with him all
the other wicked spirits who wander through the world to
the ruin of souls."* '

The phone rang at nearly midnight, on its bamboo table by
the door. I was still awake, reading in Vilde's armchair,
and I picked up the receiver with my pulses accelerating; a
sensation that had been elicited by every call of the past
three days. I usually expected Katrin; but sometimes I
thought it might be Deirdre Dillon.

The operator's voice said: 'Melbourne calling, please
wait.'

Brady came on next.

'It's me. Brian.' He waited, as though I should confirm
receiving him; he didn't often talk on phones, and still
had a rural unease with them. They were things for
emergencies.

'Why I'm ringing is: I'm quitting the group,' he said. 'I
won't be coming back up to Sydney, so I thought I'd tell
you goodbye. Katrin'll fly back in the morning. I'm not
sure what Darcy'll do.'

'What's happened?'

'Hasn't enough happened? Do you want any more?'

'No. I suppose not.'

There was another silence, delicate and humming; interstate calls had the music of distance, then.

'So what will you do?'

'Go back on the road. Pick up what I can. I won't go
short of work now—neither will Katrin, if she wants it. I'd
rather sing what I want anyway. I never liked this fairy
stuff you and Darcy cooked up. He's ridden long enough
on my back. So have you.'

I said nothing.

'Darcy's looking for someone to blame, now his big London deal's all stuffed. You'd better watch out—I think it's going to be you.'

His voice held no real enmity, no concern: there was nothing personal in it at all; I might have been a stranger. It was the voice that had spoken to me in his smoking-spot by the cypress trees, in the St Augustine's lunch hour. *('Can't you see I'd rather go solo Pat?')*

'When'll I see you again?'

'Some time. Maybe never. It's you she loves. I got it all wrong.'

He'd gone, and I stared at the whirring receiver.

I was kept awake that night by a mixture of sadness and joy. They weren't as incongruous as they seemed; joy wasn't happiness, I'd learned that long ago.

I ended by taking a sleeping pill. When the knocking woke me, I realised it must have been going on for some time.

9

It seems at first to be at the bedroom door, and I sit up in the state of fuddled terror such deep-night knocking always generates.

It's still dark, and I switch on the bedside light. The small alarm clock shows five. The banging comes again, and now I realise it's at the front door of the flat, booming in the old, high-ceilinged landing.

When I open the door, I find Patrick Dillon.

I blink at him, relieved that it's no one more menacing. But he's sweating, and his forelock hangs over his right eye: a touch of disarray in Patrick, when he isn't drumming, and concern surges back in me.

'What's wrong?' I speak in a whisper. 'What's happened?'

'It's all right, Richard. Katrin's O K, if that's what you mean.'

His polite hissing, which smells of whisky, is only just audible. I have the impression he's drunk, but holding it well. 'She'll be here today—so will Darcy. I flew back last night.' He looks solemn. 'I'm sorry to wake you up.'

He attempts his wide smile, but it fades quickly, and his brow looks narrow and puzzled. From inside this mask, he appears to be asking for something to stop.

'I want you to come to the house at Palm Beach,' he says.

'Now?'

'The car's outside. Please, Dick. You have to come.'

The Barrenjoey Peninsula is different from the rest of Sydney. A long slender dragon basking in the Pacific to the north of the city, it basks also in the illusion of a different latitude and a different time-zone.

The latitude is the South Seas; and the time, for the Peninsula's cargo of beachside suburbs, is always holiday. Its temperatures are more equable than those of the city; in its humid warmth, bamboos, bananas and palms coexist with homely ironbarks and ghost gums. Houses are half-submerged in miniature jungles; orchids, gardenias and cannas blaze in its fortunate gardens: all the flowers of South East Asia, which suddenly seems as close as it is. Driving up the Peninsula, you are driving towards Asia.

On its inner side is the lake-like inlet of Pittwater, filled with safe yachts; on the ocean side are the big surf-beaches, tiny figures of board-riders fixed like dreams on the bottle-green prows of breakers, the sequences of red-gold sand running north in curve after curve: Newport; Avalon; Palm Beach. Tropical languour is dissolved in that foam, since the water contains a startling stream of cold: the Antarctic current that creeps up the east coast of the continent. Every bay has towering sandstone bluffs at each end, with faces like lions or gargoyles: stage-sets for disaster, where high shapes of spume rise like silent cries.

Patrick speeds us up the Barrenjoey Road in his red MG, driving into the sunrise. But now that he has me in the car, he can't or won't speak. He bites his lip, his eyes fixed on the road; he's certainly half-drunk, and is driving very fast; although there's little traffic at this hour on a Sunday, I'm concerned that he'll smash. But after one vain attempt to slow him down, I've given it up.

Now I try a question. 'What made you come back early?'

His mouth tightens; stubbornly, he doesn't answer or look at me.

He's plainly not to be reached, and I sit back. I've left a note for Katrin at the flat, telling her where I'll be. We swerve through easy suburbs of low brick buildings, where palm trees throw fingers of shadow across the road: a wishful California, pale with salt. When the day advances, the naked, sand-gold young will walk the warm bitumen here, surfboards balanced on their heads, looking for a last big wave before autumn ends. The MG's top is down; the tepid morning air is delicious.

Now we're on the Whale Beach Road, humming around towering cliff-tops past the hanging villas of the rich, the tacky beach houses of humbler decades left behind. Here where the dragon's body narrows at the neck, we're nearing Palma Beach on the tip of the Peninsula, and a huge, heart-lifting expanse of ocean has opened up below, dark blue and green, inviting us to fly. Clouds out there are lava-gold with dawn; ochre and cream headlands like memory recede to Sydney. There's a white half-moon.

Patrick decides to speak now, his face in profile. 'We're nearly there.'

His voice tries to reassure me, and I glimpse the beach's line of red sand. Beyond it, the tied island of Barrenjoey stretches out its hammerhead to the tropics, and Sydney finally ends. But all this disappears as the road drops down through a miniature forest of palms, the dark green fronds glinting like glass.

'I like it at the house. It's the best place to get away,' Patrick explains reasonably. 'You haven't been there, have you? I often meant—' He breaks off, compressing his lips with an expression of impatience; he sniffs and takes deep breaths, and I suspect that he's on something else besides whisky. His small double chin and the puffiness under his eyes make him look middle-aged; his young yellow hair flutters in the slipstream.

Now he takes a hand from the wheel, pulls out a handkerchief and blows his nose hard, wiping it for a long time. His eyes remain on the road. 'There's been an accident,' he tells me. 'Mother's dead.'

I'm now aware of nothing but the strong smell of humus out here: a compound odour of tropical decay, wafting into the car as we drive.

'She fell,' he declares. 'Deirdre fell and hit her head.'

'Who was with her?'

'No one. Only me.' He sniffs back hard and looks quickly at me, hazel eyes wide; the tragic heroine confounded. There's something indecent now about the quality and smartness of his sky-blue linen shirt. He's wearing one of his fighter pilot's scarves, loosely knotted; an orange one, today. 'It was an accident,' he repeats, and puts something into his mouth and chews.

Chewing, drawing uneven breaths, he pulls the car over to the edge of the road and switches off the engine. Then he puts his hand over his eyes, and sits quite still. The loud, monotonous calling of currawongs tears at the laden air, which is otherwise silent, and already growing warm. The time by my watch is seven-fifteen.

'Are we here?'

He nods, his hand still hiding his face.

'Is this where it happened?'

He shakes his head. Then, with sudden decision, he pulls out the ignition key, jumps from the car and runs across the road, reaching a white wooden gate. He opens it and disappears through, his yellow head quickly bobbing below the level of the road, disappearing.

I get out. The road's quite deserted, and a big cream bungalow above it on this side has its blinds drawn. Because of the downward slope of the land on the ocean side, the gate over there apparently leads to nothing: it frames sky, treetops, and a dark blue horizon of sea.

I cross the road and pass through, closing the gate behind me.

A long flight of steps, made from wooden railway-sleepers set into the earth, descended into a gulley. There was no sign of a house, or of Patrick.

I began to walk down, limping and jolting into a warm, muggy silence that enveloped me like sleep. The steps went into a tunnel; trees were its walls. To the right was a stand of giant bamboos some fifteen feet high; to the left, the smooth, leopard-like torsos of spotted gums, and the standards of more palm trees. The gulley's damp red floor was a tangle of morning glory, the electric-blue flowers flaring everywhere like lamps. The sea rumbled and sighed, out of sight. Mynahs and currawongs made their cries of empty concern.

The steps turned left past another palisade of bamboo, and now the house appeared, with a gabled roof of charcoal-grey tiles. Beyond was the sea and Barrenjoey Head again, its lighthouse visible through spindly Norfolk Island pines. I went on down, moving slowly.

Patrick's inheritance was a large L-shaped villa of sandstone and white-painted brick. I remembered being told that his father had used it only in the summer; they had kept it closed up in the winter. When I walked across the flagstones leading to the front door, there was still no sign of Pat. I called, but got no answer. Bees buzzed in the baroque pink trumpets of azaleas; young orange trees stood in blue ceramic tubs. Everything said wealth, and nothing moved.

The varnished front door was an odd one for so elegant a house; it had a porthole of clear glass at eye level, set in a nautical brass frame. I peeped through, and found myself looking down a hallway. At the far end, windows framed a perfectly-tended lawn; beyond this was the sea. A line of globular glass lamps hung from the ceiling; the wood-panelled walls had nautical decorations, like a seaside guest-house with pretensions: a barometer; framed prints of sailing ships. The door was locked, but I continued to peer at the view through the distant windows: the green lawn and open sweep of sea had the unreal perfection of a picture in a children's book.

I walked around to the southern side of the house. There was no sign of a lawn here; instead, the garden descended the hill in terraces, ending in a grove of gums and cypresses, through which the sea could be glimpsed in blue shards. Immediately below me was a long swimming-pool, from which came portentous washing sounds: Patrick was breast-stroking across it, his hair darkened by the water. His clothes and a white terry-towelling beach-robe were neatly laid on a redwood chair at the edge. Pop music was coming from somewhere, at low volume.

I walked down a short set of steps. 'You were quick,' I said. The normality of my voice surprised me.

He smiled at me from the middle of the bright blue pool, and pointed to a pair of swimming-trunks laid on another garden chair. 'Come in,' he said.

'No thanks. We'd better talk.' I took off my jacket and sat on one of the chairs, in the feathery shade of a casuarina.

He breast-stroked towards me, his face naked and happy. He seemed different; there was an ebullience I didn't understand; an unsound gaiety. He climbed out, dried himself briskly, and put on his rich terry-towelling robe; he was smiling the Alan Ladd smile, but his eyes wouldn't stay still. 'I used to love coming here, as a kid,' he said. 'It seemed the only place to come, today.' His voice trailed off and he looked down the garden, his smile fading as though he'd heard something; but there were only bird-calls. 'No one knows we're here,' he said.

He walked over to a redwood table on which sat his silver whisky-flask, a transistor radio which was the source of the music, and a paper bag. He held out the flask. 'Have a snort.'

'At this hour?'

'Please.' He took the chair beside me, gesturing insistently with the flask. 'You'll need a drink, Dick.' There was something wrong with his eyes; their variegated greens and yellows appeared to be dissolving, melting into each other.

He hadn't agreed to our having a coffee before we left, he'd been too anxious to go; so I was glad now of the whisky, and took two large swallows. Immediately, I began to feel hopeful; I decided he was lying, or fantasising on hash: she wasn't really dead.

He unscrewed the paper bag now, and took out two little cakes. One of these, which I saw was half eaten, he put into his mouth whole; then, cheek bulging, he held out the other. 'Have a cookie.'

I was hungry, but I studied it dubiously. It was an odd-looking cake, round and dun-coloured, with darker flakes. 'What is it?'

'A cookie. I bought it at a health-food store. Good for you, Dick. Roughage.'

It tasted inoffensive enough, coarse and cardboard-like. He watched me chew, his eyes certainly not normal.

'What are you on, Pat?' I'd finished the cake, and brushed away the crumbs.

'I'm just on cookies,' he said.

I jumped from the chair and stood over him. 'You stupid bastard,' I said. 'What was in that thing?'

He cowered as though I'd already hit him, and his face softened into totally childish lines. In a little voice, he said: 'It'll make things big or small; whatever you want.' Then he giggled.

I grabbed the front of the terry-towelling robe and drew my fist back; my outrage at my own stupidity produced a lust to bully him, and I shouted at him again to tell me what I'd eaten. I probably had only a few more minutes before I was lost, here in this beautiful garden.

'Just a few pieces of Darcy's magic mushrooms,' Patrick said. 'That's all.' He still had his arm up to ward off a blow, but his eyes had grown drowsy, the lids drooping. 'They won't hurt you, Dick,' he said. 'They're good magic, from the old Toadstool-god.'

I swore and let him go, and sank into my chair again. There was nothing to be done, and I asked him what the effects would be.

'Nothing bad,' he said. 'The mushrooms will change things, that's all.'

'Tell me what happened to Deirdre. Tell me the truth, this time.'

I was leaning back in the chair, staring at the glinting blue oblong. The Beatles were on the radio singing 'Ticket

to Ride,' their poignant, famous voices mingling with the
sea's distant sighing.

*'All I really wanted was Europe. I belong there, not here.
Would you believe how I love Greece? Something's in the
landscape that isn't here. The air's light, and the light's
magic. You should understand that, Dick. Darcy understands.'*

The swimming-pool was growing smaller: all that was
close to us grew distant; even Patrick's flask on the table. I
grew faintly nauseous, but wouldn't give in to it.

*'Deirdre started to get afraid of Darcy. She liked him at
first, but then she rejected him. Her soul was too small.
She could have come with me to Greece, but she wouldn't.
It would have been like living in a vision.'*

He was half turned to me, gripping the chair-arms, his
face thrust pleadingly towards me. But I watched the
swimming-pool, which had shrunk to a postage-stamp.

*'Deirdre understood, at first. She felt the action of the
god inside us. Have you ever felt the liquid of the moon go
into you?'* His voice went up and down, sometimes reasonable, sometimes cajoling. *'And then she turned into a
silly, frightened, bourgeois woman worrying about money.'*

'Why did you come back early?' My voice didn't seem
my own; it sounded inside my head. The nausea from
Darcy's little cake was growing.

He was silent; then he sighed. *'Brian's left us, did you
know? And now Katrin won't come to London either. Roy
Slade will never back us now: everything Darcy worked
for's ruined. But Darcy won't give up; he says we have to
form a new group. We need money to get to London, and
Deirdre could have helped us; she could have made us
free. I came back to talk to her about that. I wanted her to
marry me, did you know? Yes, you know that, Richard.
You know how I loved her.'*

The thick autumn sun which had recently been pleasant
now had a sickly glare: light in a photograph wrongly
developed.

'*We stayed up late talking, but she wouldn't listen. So I followed her.*'

'Followed her?'

'*I tried to reason with her, but she was violent. She smashed two of my records. They were King Olivers, irreplaceable.*'

Now we were both enclosed in a bright, amazing bubble. I wanted to cry out, but couldn't. I wasn't sure whether Patrick would hear me if I spoke, and at the same time I saw him clearly in the house at Point Piper, going from room to room after Deirdre. Clutching at her moss-green dressing-gown, her blanched hair trailing, she tried to get away from him. He embraced her; he fell to his knees and buried his face against her belly; but she pulled away, drawing the dressing-gown together, her white face cruel to him.

'*She ran down through the garden on to the beach— being silly. It was warm last night, and no one was there but us. She ran away from me, and I had to get her back to the house. She was making a scene.*'

Bright, merry specks began dancing in the air.

'*I tried to make her come back. Her dressing-gown was coming off, and there are houses there, neighbours. She seemed to be very light, just like a feather; she got away, and began to float. She really floated, Richard, right through the air. But she fell against a rock, and hit her head. It was an accident. An accident. They'll believe that, won't they?*'

'Where is she now?'

'*In bed. In bed. No one will come. Not until Monday; Fiona's away, and no one will call in. She's safe, in her room.*'

He was getting up from his chair, hugging himself in the terry-towelling robe as though it had grown cold. And it had. In our bubble, we were being chilled to the bone; the leaves of the gums and the fronds of the palms were all glinting with cold; the sun was cold.

'*I'm going up to my room, now. I have to sleep,*' he said.

He walked up the four sandstone steps that took him to the level of the house; but I followed him. We entered by a glass door at the back and passed through a clean-smelling kitchen, unused. He took no more notice of me now, shuffling on into the hall with the overhead lamps and turning into a pleasant bedroom with blue-patterned wallpaper. An old teddybear sat on a white chest of drawers.

He fell belly-down on the single bed, his face turned towards me in profile. But his eyes were open and glassy, and when I spoke his name he ignored me. There was nothing more to be done with him; I went back down the hall and out into the garden again.

I sat in the chair by the pool.

The effect of the mushroom was not so much to disorder thoughts as to disorder appearances, so that thoughts fled in panic. Trapped inside my bubble, sitting in the redwood chair, I found that nausea had gone; but the early morning light had changed to that of sunset. It came mustard-yellow and outrageous through the gums and palm trees on the hill that led to the road. The glow picked things out with a clarity that should have been delightful. Daisies by a border of stones leaped into life, each nodding and blazing white flower and each distinct shadow of each flower moving like marvellous music. A rubbery blue aloe at the top of the steps shone like a giant star, making me exclaim.

I saw them on the beach at Point Piper; saw them as though I were there; observed them with such distinctness that I made small noises, in my chair. There was nothing I could do to stop it.

The usual sandstone rocks at each end of the beach; not very clean sand. Deserted, at one o'clock in the morning. Lights of wealthy windows; lights on the water. They came hurrying towards me, Deirdre in front, he behind. He took her by the arm, pleading, meaning well, but alarming her; she struggled, her mouth an O. His hair had fallen down on his forehead; his face had grown red. She strained away from him, one arm foolishly reaching for freedom. She was flung; she flung herself, she flew.

Yes, it was an accident; her stepson stood helpless. She lay still among the stones of the beach, in her gaping, moss-coloured gown: a piece of Harbour flotsam.

'Why not here, among these pagan rocks?'

The rocks had always been waiting; these honey-colored slabs, these wave-sculptured barriers and entrances of ancient New South Wales. Why not here, in moonlight or in daytime glare? The glare had invited it, making city and Harbour excessive; too much to look at, all the high-rise buildings stacked like white plates. The mind found no relief here; no end or order; meaning and mercy fled.

I found that I was weeping, unable to stop. It had all been an accident; an accident.

The sunset glow continued among the trees; and then I realised that someone was looking at me, standing by the aloe at the top of the sandstone steps. It was Clive Broderick.

He stood quietly, just as he used to stand, his left hand thrust elegantly into the pocket of his navy-blue overcoat— which must have been oppressive, in the Sydney sun. His head was cocked, and his winter-blue eyes held a quizzing expectancy. He would always wait; he would wait through eternity.

But now I found that it was Darcy Burr, whose dark blue sports shirt had deceived me, and who stood looking down at me, severe and accusing.

'You're too late,' I said.

Whether I said it aloud or not I couldn't be sure. Burr began to speak, but his words made no sense, seeming to come from a funnel. His accusations were irrelevant; he'd become merely tedious, and I turned my head away.

Out above the ocean, the white half-moon persisted; the crone, Eurybia. The cold name shone briefly from the bottom of memory: a forgotten toy; something from my boyhood at Trent Street, with no more glamour.

And I knew now that it was all gone—like Harrigan Street and Broderick, and the district of Second-hand.